ONEIRO

JOHN S. GOLDENBERG

Copyright © 2008 John Stuart Goldenberg
All rights reserved.

ISBN: 1-4196-9383-2
ISBN-13: 9781419693830

Library of Congress Control Number: 2008902489

BOOK I

ANUMEN
ANUMINA
ANUMINOUS

FOR
ANN

WITH SINCERE THANKS:

DR. DORE GORMEZANO PHD
MR. MARK LYON
MR. MITCH MALOOF
MR. MARK OSOJNICKI (CAPTAIN)
MRS. JEAN SHUTTE,
DR. GRAHAM SOLOMONS PHD
MRS. A.M. ZENDER

*There are over
Fourteen-Hundred Greek Islands
Two Hundred and Thirty-Three islands
are Inhabited
Seventy-Nine Boast Inhabitants
Exceeding One Hundred Souls*

ANTÓNIO balanced the small blue envelope on a silver tray, soundlessly trekking one of the interminable pebble paths that intertwined the extravagant garden. Occasionally scattered were stone benches, fountains, clear water spilling into sparkling sands. Essentially, however, the garden was a shady, overgrown, riot of colors, flowers, huge palms and tropical plants. Nearly a rain forest. Totally unmanicured. More reminiscent of a Tahitian paradise than the Atlantic coast of Portugal.

The garden enclosed a massive fortified villa, a lush oasis perched on the jagged, windblown Costa de Lisboa. *O Mar dos Diabos.* The Devil's Sea. A fitting name. The ocean here is wild and riotous. Immense waves crash into incredible subterranean convolutions of stone, spewing the sea in explosive eruptions. Crackling geysers soar upward for meters. Crushing undertows flow beneath the waves. Whitecaps seethe into an endless blue horizon. An incessant gale blows. Treacherous and deadly. Majestic and astonishingly beautiful.

In striking counterpoint, the garden bloomed in quiet sun-warmed tranquility, secure within towering stone walls. Ancient. The Moors and the Berbers had found reclusion and protection here. Much history, power, and wealth have passed here.

ANTÓNIO found his employer comfortably stretched out on the grass by a shallow pond, fed by a tiny, splashing stream. Cool in the dappled shade, he was intently reading a book, the remains of lunch beside him. A half empty bottle of Vino Verde chilled in the pond.

"Sir, you have another communication from *the mountain*." He was alluding to an unknown site securely hidden within the Atlas Mountains in central Morocco. ANTÓNIO proffered one of the countless small blue envelopes received over the years from that obscure site high above North Africa. This envelope had been touched by many secret hands before reaching his master's.

"Thank you, ANTÓNIO." He tore open the envelope with undisguised pleasure. These elegant little blue envelopes always brought him work. Intriguing work and money. Sometimes danger. Often suffering and death. Never his own. He meticulously studied his orders.

Interesting...They want another face-to-face. This would call for a little theatrical games playing. He couldn't pin down who his patron really was these days. That venomous conclave held many friends and enemies. Any one would joyfully murder the other. Often, he simply received cryptic instructions and a number indicating the monetary amount being transferred to his bank. He hated leaving his garden, his villa, his family, his women and his pleasures. *Business was business*, however. And it paid for this little Eden of his.

He was already quite familiar with the problem assigned him. No less than three years had been invested in study and infiltration already. Several of his people had been involved from the start. He personally had stumbled upon the strange activities and the massive funding. Apparently his masters in the mountains were growing uneasy. Something had captured their interest.

He peered at the pond for a few moments, squinting into the sunlit ripples. A quizzical smile played across his dark features. This was going to be a formidable project, probably the summit of his strange career.

He withdrew to his study. He would remain sequestered there until his preparations were complete. No interruptions. Meals left at his door. Electronic countermeasures exterior and interior. White sound emitters. Secured phones and data communications.

His household was comfortable and happy, ignorant of his activities, in a well-removed wing of the villa. Two guards patrolled the grounds and exterior twenty-four hours. There had never been a problem. Few people knew he or his compound existed. He was painfully aware that they insisted upon hand delivery of their little blue envelopes to emphatically demonstrate their familiarity with and access to him. A tacit and menacing demonstration.

Three years of superlative intelligence equipped him with a commanding grasp of the situation and his tactical alternatives. Nonetheless, strenuous days and nights of plans and strategy, reports, phone calls, and technical evaluations were essential to his preparation. Ten days later, a highly secured courier was entrusted with the product of his labors: A thirty-four page, leather-bound report in ten copies. He was ready to travel thirty-six hours later, after a confirmed summons from his handler.

They came to an abrupt halt under the dramatically canopied, flower-strewn entrance of the Al Maha Grand Residence Hotel, Marrakech, Morocco.

It was 1100 sharp, as instructed, and as usual.

The doormen knew very well not to assist or interfere in any way. Two massive guards in anonymous fatigues descended from the cab. It was always the same matt-black, dust-covered, armored beast that seemed to ingest all light. It was truly ugly and clumsy. A vehicular, hexahedronal black hole semi-affectionately referred to as the "Black Box." Mockingly, he had always secretly thought of it as the "Toy Box."

They invariably used this monster for his secured transport, more to mask his curious eyes, and to deny him from unfriendly hands, than any concern for his well being. Although he suspected they did want him safe, for now anyhow. His belief was supported in part by the presence of two pursuit vehicles, 4×4s fore and aft of the Black Box itself.

He never knew exactly where he was taken. Didn't care. He knew the drill. He'd been through it many times. He stepped briskly to the rear of the vehicle as they silently opened massive double doors. They politely placed a step out to assist him as he wordlessly entered. They then stowed the step and smoothly locked the doors behind him.

He was well aware he was under surveillance, as he had been since departing Lisbon many hours before, so he was always discrete in his explorations of The Box. Then again, after considerable hours aboard, he was pretty familiar with its wonders. He'd picked up some information from the occasional boozy braggings of its owner, his current boss.

The only descriptive word for The Box's interior was "lush." No stooping to walk in *here*. Hardwood floors, rich Persian carpets, two expansive easy chairs, wet bar, and an efficient little galley, facing AV systems, communications and computers, external TV, a very advanced first-aid and medicinal inventory, gas masks, and fire suppressant systems, O^2 canisters, a small but deadly arsenal, individual passenger lighting and climate controls, and a compact, comfortable washroom.

The Black Box ran on six wheels, each with full power drive and turn capability (6×6+). Its heavy-duty tires were treaded for any weather or terrain (robustly shock absorbed), iso-foam charged, and could withstand a pretty respectable pounding by nearly any light to medium ordinance.

Buried somewhere amidst all this technology was a fourteen hundred horsepower, high-torque stable of supercharged diesel power. An array of batteries, huge water tanks and auxiliary fuel tanks extended the range of the Box to nearly 1800 kilometers. The recommended max speed was about 110 kilometers per hour, but he knew it could do far better in a push.

Inside this velvet-lined Black Box, he was silent, invisible, and damn near invincible. The drivers benefited equally from the security apparatus of The Box. They did require windows, however, and were totally segregated from the rear compartment. Even bullet-proofed they could be taken out, so the Box could be driven (albeit somewhat awkwardly) to a limited degree with the internal monitor and processor.

There were books, magazines, newspapers, foods of all kinds. There were even superb oil paintings mounted on richly wooded paneled walls, complimented by a gilded and frescoed ceiling. The paintings replaced windows, of which there were none. Nor were there any exits other than the two rear doors (fully paneled on the inside).

All of this was tastefully decorated to appear as innocuous as an elegant 17th century library belonging to someone wealthy—wealthy enough to enjoy a predilection for excessive luxury and excessive security. The Box was literally a land-going yacht.

He poured himself a generous scotch, buckled up, lit a cigar, picked up a newspaper, and leaned back in comfort to while away the ride. Not a bad way to travel really. He wondered how much this beastie really cost. How much it *weighed*. How much fuel it burned. *Must be one of a kind*, he mused, *or one of a very few*.

He often wondered who else rode in this vehicle. There must be some very special justifiers for an investment on this scale. *He certainly* wasn't the object of all this secure opulence. Such thoughts invariably gave him a little chill, so he concentrated on his newspaper and his scotch.

The ride took about an hour, over rough, mountainous terrain. Finally he felt the vehicle stopping, then turning into and down a long ramp, followed by turning and turning for what he had many times calculated to be at least six floors below. They backed up directly to the open doors of a large freight elevator that carried him down another four floors.

They escorted him through long sterile halls to a very small, unremarkable conference room. Furnishings consisted of two executive chairs facing each other over a small, round table, bearing two leather-bound reports, neatly stacked. Behind each chair was positioned a video camera, equipped with a lighting and sound-recording system.

One of the two chairs was already occupied.

The man himself! he thrilled. Apparently, someone was taking his report seriously. Nodding a silent salutation, he confidently settled himself in the opposite chair, smiling amiably, baring with a brief flash, a very expensive, gold canine tooth. Showtime.

Eyebrows slightly raised and without preamble, the interrogation started. Cameras rolling. Sound on.

"Is this true?" his interrogator asked, nodding at the pile of documents.

"It is true and far worse than we could imagine. They respect nothing. They create objects and plans of unspeakable evil. They are obscenity."

Frowning at the melodrama of the response, the interrogator continued, "Why have we not learned of them before?"

"They operate in total secrecy. They are well funded by many powerful interests. They operate from a secret, remote site unknown to the outside world, and their great wealth aids them in secreting themselves and their operations. Most of their activities are illegal, so the need for concealment is of the highest priority."

Again with the melodrama! "How long has this movement been active?"

"Decades."

"God help us."

"Yes, sir. God help us. They are growing constantly. They labor incessantly like the fanatics they are. Every day the threat grows greater. One day soon they will be unstoppable and their depravity will destroy us all. The end of civilization, and the world in ashes. They are going to kill us all. Not kill...worse than kill. We must stop them. We must eliminate them. We must..."

"Yes, yes," interrupted the interrogator "But what threat do they pose to *us*? To us *directly*? Present me with a *clear* and *present* danger scenario, a *succinct* evaluation." *Why does he play the buffoon?* He ground his teeth and calmly awaited the response.

"Indeed that is the real question isn't it?" He smiled "The answer is simply stated and fully documented. It is supported by the materials I have submitted to you and to the General Assembly."

"Respond *quickly* and *concisely*. This is being recorded, as you can clearly see. This interview will be presented to the General Assembly in closed meeting very soon. I want conclusions *only*. *No* details. No need for supporting information. *I* can read. *They* can read. In fact, I *have* already read your reports. Time is short. *Get on with it.*"

"As you wish, sir. Conclusions only...

They have a very clearly thought out plan of attack. It will be conducted as follows:

First, they will destroy our economy completely. Six months after their first engagement, our primary industries will be in ruins, totally supplanted. Six months after that, we will be facing poverty. In my best estimation, their first engagement will take place within a very few weeks.

Second, when our economy is in shambles, they will destroy our political institutions, our laws, and our leadership. The General Assembly and all the institutions surrounding it will be at an end. This will be initiated within four months of the initial surge, and it will be very easy at that point. We will be in chaos.

Third, they will destroy our culture. Our way of life, our civilization, our laws, our art, and history. All in ruins. This will be effortlessly conducted, nearly concurrent with step two. You have documentation in support of that assertion as well."

He sighed and drew a breath, flashing an obsequious smile, revealing a flash from his gold tooth.

"After that, sir, the game is effectively at an end in just a little less than one year. Our world will be living under a new regime. You and I, and probably everyone watching this tape, will be dead, forgotten, or in hiding if we're lucky."

Lips pursed, eyes half closed, the interrogator pushed on. "What do your suggest we do?" *Finally he was making some sense.*

"Since the submission of my report, we've been formulating detailed plans. We can mount an immediate invasion force. A coordinated assault by air and sea supporting a commando force of roughly 800. Deploying an airborne drop at about midnight, a strike team fully equipped with source-neutral, untraceable ordinance: automatic weapons (MP7A1s), high explosives (Cyclotol), and incendiaries (White Phosphorus), RPGs ..."

"... Spare me the details."

"Yes sir.

"We can clean out the entire site before dawn and we can be battle-ready for deployment within days."

"How many inhabit this Command Site of yours?"

"Probably as many as ten thousand."

"And you expect to take them out with 800 commandos?"

"They are virtually unarmed and poorly trained. The attack would be a total surprise. I can positively confirm that we can sterilize the entire site within a very few hours."

"I see. Define 'sterilize.'"

"No one left alive. Nothing left standing, not a wall, not a tunnel, not a piece of paper. Scorched earth."

"Extermination is the only option?"

"Our tactical assessment decisively indicates that a shock, surgical strike is the only action that will not require inordinate amounts of time. Any other method will attract attention. This implies a total extermination.

Their communications center will be taken out first using airborne incendiaries and gas, then a step-by-step assault through their entire facility, starting at their HQ. This provides an excellent ingress to all wings of the Center and cuts off any avenue of escape at the same time. One might almost think their Command Center was *designed* to be attacked." He smiled with satisfaction.

"Perhaps it was." Commented his interrogator dryly.

This drew a quizzical stare for a moment, then he resumed "When sterilization is complete, we will withdraw our forces by sea on four high-speed marine troop transports, made to look like an ordinary fishing fleet. Our air support will have long since returned to base and to whatever destiny you designate. The troop transports will be extensively mined with advanced High Explosive Limpets fixed at several key points on their hulls. These will be time activated upon launch. The task force will be at the bottom of the sea (around three thousand meters at that point) four hours after launch, without a trace. There will remain nothing that would indicate the prior activities of the site, nor our involvement in its destruction."

"You can destroy 800 highly trained commandos and four troop transports plus crews, at a stroke, with no reprisals whatsoever?"

"We can. We have. We're experts at this sort of thing. Please remember sir, we will be dealing almost exclusively with mercenaries and we will have a following support craft to mop up any survivors, and destroy any remaining debris."

The interrogator coldly regarded his subject for several long moments.

"It occurs to me that there may be things of great interest on this site. Yet I perceive the extreme difficulty in identifying such things in the midst of a massive 'sterilization.' Terrible waste."

Rashid remained respectfully silent.

"It's quite possible your conclusions could prove totally spurious. If so, you would be leading us into great folly. Your rashness presents a potentially grave danger to all concerned."

The interrogator watched his subject imperceptibly vacillate between feelings of outrage, insult, and real fear. All in all, excellent self-control. Better than he would have credited him with, particularly in the midst of his clownish performance.

"I'm going to suggest a different approach to the General Assembly. We must not be precipitous. I want you to insert additional operatives into this organization. I want far more on-site intelligence, totally reliable, totally unbiased. New operatives from *outside*. This will take time, but I think you will find we have more time than you've been led to believe. I want this belief of mine positively *dis-proven* and if I am in error, we will proceed with your proposed sterilization, summarily.

If my suspicions are *confirmed*, however, we will then act with patience and proceed very carefully. For the moment we will work under the assumption that my perception is accurate. I want your people to infiltrate as quickly as possible.

"Once well established, they will build a secret para-military organization within their ranks. Openly invisible. When complete, I want your operatives to build for them a defensive infrastructure, sophisticated, comprehensive, and deadly."

"Yes sir. That is consistent with their assigned tasks."

"I then want your operatives to build me a trigger." The interrogator looked at him piercingly.

"A trigger, sir?"

"A trigger when, once pulled, the serpent will turn on itself *and bite*."

"Expensive."

"This is your sole priority. Drop everything and proceed. Unless the General Assembly overrules me, you will actively operate under the assumption that your orders are fully sanctioned, and they will be in writing as quickly as possible.

"This is most definitely a Deep Black operation and will always remain so. However, I want you totally certain as to its support from the General Assembly, and its legitimacy. This is an official exercise initiated under the GA's discretionary powers, and at my direction. Clear?"

"Yes, sir. I appreciate it."

He knew only too well he would be waving in the wind, totally alone, at the first indication of trouble. *The big guys, the old bastards in every society on Earth, throughout history, never took the fall. Never pulled the trigger, or drove the knife home. Never smelled the blood. Never rolled in the dirt. Never watched their own life blood seep into the oily, cold mud.*

He would be the one tied to the post and hooded. He would be offered the last cigarette (Did they really do that anymore?). He wouldn't even hear the bullet, if he was lucky enough to be shot. Somehow he vaguely looked forward to death. He'd seen death. Been very near to it. Inflicted it many times. His own would be a sort of release. A final sigh. But far in the future he hoped.

"You will run an extremely detailed double check on your primary informant. But I want him kept safe. Ensure that. You will continue as I have outlined until advised otherwise and expense be damned."

"Understood, sir. I will keep you fully informed of plans and status at all times."

"Of course."

Without another word the interrogator arose and withdrew.

Whenever he worked at this facility there was never a handshake, never a simple "thank you," a lunch, a drink, a smile, hello, good-by, nothing. He departed as silently and mechanically and as suffocatingly alone, as he had come. He had the feeling that everyone, without exception, who called upon that icy summit, labored with speed and efficiency, leaving with all possible haste and discretion, seeking warmth and normalcy for hours to follow.

Back in The Black Box returning to his hotel, he was lost in thought. That bastard set me up! He read my report. He figured out what I would propose and then he took it apart by the numbers and made me look the fool. *Damn I like that man!* Fell right into step. Nice to work for someone with a brain.

Expense be damned. I like that too. A lot. He may be one son of a bitch. But I like his attitude. Money and death. Some of the deaths would be by his own hand. That was okay. It assured him a larger stake in all that money. This was going to be a very good year. The hardest part was finding the right people and getting them smoothly imbedded.

His current informant was toast if he had been misinformed. He had seen through that too. Just too damned eager to burn 'em down. *Intentional or not, that bastard was set to make a fool of me. Not a wise thing to do. Fat bastard. He had never understood his traitorous motivations. He was rich. He essentially had near autonomous power. Was he driven by altruism? Was he repelled by the activities of his colleges? Maybe he was insane. Whatever. President or not, his instructions notwithstanding, that SOB was going to die.*

After a time, he concluded the infiltration task was best suited to some high-priced sex and seduction skills. Kathryn. Yes Kathryn. He knew an expert to help identify her prey. She would connect with them, vet them, seduce them, convince them, and pay them...and then he would personally insert them. He was probably going to have to remove a few in-house boys to make room for Kathryn's ringers. And for a while at least, he was going to need the assistance of the President in getting their replacements imbedded.

Her targets would be two or three top guns, experts in their fields, but certainly not famous, or even well known. Good news. Lots of disciplines to choose from and lots of candidates to choose among. Mmm, actually not that wide a choice, come to think of it. No core disciplines. Strictly supporting fields. Otherwise too much brass on the selection committee. These boys of necessity were non-professionals and he certainly didn't want anyone to crack under examination. Have to maintain control. Have to be loners too. Straight. No tracks. No connections. Gilt-edged credentials without the glitter. Single, bright young post-docs, needing money and tenure somewhere, or some seasoned guys looking to kick back a little and make some money. Either way would work. Yes. He would dine with Kathryn tomorrow night in Paris. She was going to be a wealthy young lady. She would finish the job skillfully and fast, and then live rich and high. Bless her heart.

The inside paramilitaries were going to be the easiest part. They would comprise the "security force." He would handle that himself. He knew every major mercenary broker in the world. A few phone calls and then a subtle, steady flow of his fighters would be infiltrated and replace any existing forces, along with their new on-site commander.

He would recruit the commander himself. He knew any number of highly qualified and highly tarnished brass ready to jump at the job. He decided he would "blood" his new commander by assigning him the assassination of that fat bastard President when the time was right. No traces though. Didn't want to piss off his boss. He had a few other targets in mind as well. A few circles to close. He swirled his scotch. Smooth amber circles in his tumbler. He dreamt of circles. Full circles. Closed circles. Classical loops. Three-hundred, sixty degrees.

Full spin of the compass. What is the saying? Ah yes, "What goes around comes around." Great saying that. Great fun.

He poured himself a large scotch and luxuriated in smiling pleasure as he stretched out to daydream his way back to the hotel.

The next night he did dine with Kathryn. The Carré des Feuillants. An excellent très chic restaurant stylishly placed on rue de Castiglione between Rue de Rivoli and Rue St. Honoré. Kathryn shocked him.

"Please order for us both Rashid. No one knows fine French food like you.'

What the hell? She's coming across coquettish?

"With pleasure Kathryn." Smiling and balancing his attention between Kathryn, the waiter and the menu he ordered. "We'll start with Native marennes gillardeau oysters, caviar and seaweed tartare. For the main course we'll try the Truffled pierre duplantier poulard, spring vegetables in cocotte. And for desert Mango raviolis with passion fruits and coconut flan."

Clearly pleased with his choices the waiter smiled "Very good monsieur." And handed Rashid the Wine List.

They were comfortably seated in a quiet, discreetly decorated private room. They could speak freely without concern about eavesdroppers, or any other parties. Kathryn had no idea where they were going to dine. Rashid had booked under a different name. He would pay in cash. He had never been here before and would never return again.

"So what's the assignment?'

The real Kathryn had suddenly returned. Never any funny business with her. No fooling around, not even the most casual of flirtation. Work. Totally frosty professionalism. Well, she was the best he'd ever worked with.

Back at her apartment that night she went directly to work.

With impressive efficiency Kathryn located three top guns and took great care to seduce them, precondition them, and win their puppy-like devotion.

Meanwhile, he appointed his new Commander and commenced trickling his mercenaries onto the site.

He visited the President and prepared the way for his new agents. All warm smiles and firm handshakes. He even stayed around for a few days of relaxation.

During his relaxation, he personally attended to the sabotage of some climbing gear resulting in a two-hundred meter free fall to the beach below. He cut the throat of an alleged tourist in Algiers, and he permanently extended the dive of a researcher some fifty meters below the surface of the Aegean Sea. No questions. No suspicions. No connectivity. No disruption. With the exception of the climber, there were no bodies.

A few weeks later the ringers were in place, new troops arriving discretely all the time. The new Commander was assigned, on duty, and in absolutely unchallenged control. The fat slob of a President was still amongst the living, but that would be sorted out soon. Reports started coming in. Sure enough there was ample time for schemes and things and circles in the sand.

All was in readiness. His apparatus was well oiled and working perfectly. The trigger was cocked and locked.

Three years later

He was a leader, a scientist, a lawyer, a sailor, a fisherman, a consultant, a businessman, now wealthy beyond imagining and, simply put, a killer of quite some expertise. What in hell was he going to do now?

He thought about himself a few months ago. He had been a pretty innocent, carefree sort of fellow.

There he was in the middle of the crystal clear Aegean (at least he assumed it was the Aegean at the time—in point of fact he had no idea where the hell he was) in the midst of luxury he never dreamt of, or aspired to for that matter, having absolutely no idea why he had been called here. Pretty cool.

He fast forwarded his life as it brutally confronted him now:

"It's pronounced 'Ahab...*Ayeee-Haaab*.'"

"What?"

"I said 'Ahab,' the doomed captain of the Pequod. You pronounced it '*Aah-heeb*.'"

"Whatever-the-hell," said Professor Winchester irritably. "What do we do now?"

"Beats me." Phil murmured absently, running fingers through sandy hair, feeling very surreal, desolately perched on the margin of a cliff nearly four hundred meters above a blinding sea, booming and railing against an uneven margin of enormous, craggy rocks.

Who the hell was this man really, Phil wondered. He had learned to love him as a friend, even sort of a father. *Dr. Craig Webber had been an audacious genius, decades in advance of extant science. He had commanded profound powers in biology and cellular engineering, accomplishing marvels unheard of anywhere on Earth...yet a major part of mankind would have happily put him out of business—even killed him—were they cognizant of his work. In fact, they had. Phil supposed he was next.*

Dr. Webber *had been wealthy. Hell, he was damned rich! He was a scientist and a fine creative leader. Phil had visited upon him a legion of horrors utterly alien to his gentle world. Now he was gone and Phil was suddenly, wretchedly, alone. How futile! Everyone loses—good and bad alike. After all they'd been through, all they had accomplished, were about to accomplish, thrown off a cliff by some flathead that crawled out of the sand. His mind thundered at him in a wintry rage. There was going to be the devil's own hell to pay.*

Philip (Phil) Carr had a tendency, more of a talent really, to drift from topic to topic, relating thoughts and experiences with bonds that seemed tenuous at best to others. Sometimes these ethereal ribbons of logic formed relationships that were trivial, sometimes profound, but always accurate, fast, decisive, conclusive.

These subtle bits of mental legerdemain had served him well, mystifying and gratifying his employers and clients on many occasions. His talent often manifested itself by formulating stunning conclusions, discerning hidden strategies, identifying unforeseen opportunities, subtle patterns, plans within plans, and almost unbelievable syllogisms—insights seemingly entirely unrelated to the topic at hand.

On this occasion the result was insignificant. Captain Ahab indeed.

The first time Phil had met Dr. Webber, Phil was nearly lost in thought, trying to understand how hundreds of square meters (the Dr.'s immaculately manicured circular gravel driveway) could be perfectly smooth, not a tire-track, not a ripple, and most wonderingly, not a single weed, blade of grass, nothing.

Did he have an extraordinary gardener? Was there some treatment, or building method? Why couldn't he do this at his own humble town home in New York? And where did he find such smooth small stones—all of the same color and size?

His thoughts were interrupted as he noticed Dr. Webber waving an arm impatiently, clearly questioning why the hell this man was wandering about in killing heat, keeping him waiting, while he inspected of all damn things, his driveway. "Mr. Carr? Mr. Carr? Would you care to come in please?"

Strange, Phil thought, the first time I saw Doctor Craig Webber he was waving at me, and the last time I'll ever see him he is waving at me again. To where is he beckoning?

"Certainly," Phil said. "Sorry to keep you waiting, Doctor." Dr. Webber shook his hand at the door, warmly, Phil thought, despite their slightly awkward beginning.

Philip Carr was thirty-eight years old and liked it. Thirty-eight seemed a perfect age: plenty of money, youth, and a fair number of women, lots of options, and a long career to look forward to. Phil had thick sandy hair, closely cropped, and accented by a slight wid-ow's peak, emphasized by a very slightly receding hairline. He had been physically active all his life and enjoyed a well-built, healthy body. This, topped by an exceptionally symmetrical, precisely sculpted face and nearly transparent blue eyes, graced him with good looks that kept the ladies never far away. He wasn't married and had no such plans for years.

He had an impressive education: Juris Doctor Graduate from Georgetown University, specializing in International Law, Master of Laws (LLM) at Harvard, and pre-med at John's Hopkins. He had done quite well in pre-med, enjoyed the science very much, was warmly accepted, and nearly completed the entire course—but decided that medicine was not for him.

He frankly just didn't like the burden of intimacy and suffering it carried. The isolation of research was certainly not for him, nor the quietly disciplined leadership of teaching, so he continued to pursue his law career.

After graduation, his star began to rise. He was enthusiastically recruited by Barns, Levi and Richardson in Manhattan where they recognized his true skills, despite some rather gritty cross-orientation periods.

After a few weeks on the job, as a matter of familiarization as much as anything, Phil had been called in as a second-tier observer in the final briefing with a major investment firm. The principals lined a long conference table, while observers such as Phil lined the walls. Phil would describe the conference room as 'overly dramatically jazzy.' Huge abstract paintings looked down on trendy burlap carpeting and wonderfully uncomfortable furniture. All style, no utility.

A Senior Partner stood at the podium. "As most of you know, our client has been offered an exceptional opportunity to acquire exclusive license to a privately held oil and natural-gas initiative in the North Sea. Exclusivity will survive some twenty years. The investment could seriously tax, if not severely overextend, available resources. However, all parties, including Barns, Levi and Richardson, are convinced that, within four years, they would be not only 'out of the woods,' they would be impressively liquid. Our client and their investors would enjoy a considerably enhanced balance sheet.

We have confirmed that this undertaking is structured in such a manner it is consistent with their Charter.

We have painstakingly scoured and vetted the file. There are no encumbrances. All paperwork and licenses are in order. Seller financing is firmly approved in the form of various liens and notes. Hence, this meeting is in reality only a wrap-up prior to closing the financing and the investment itself."

To the mild irritation of first-tier participants, Philip raised his hand and interjected a few questions.

"What party would extract the oil?"

"Skorpen Undersea Technologies, Phil. They've been in this business forever."

"What's their ownership composition? In terms of financing, was there any relationship with the oil company? Were there any interlocking directorships? Why was *this* investment firm chosen for this venture?"

"Phil, most of that's in your *Prospectus*. Haven't you read it?"

"In fact I've reviewed it carefully. But a few points remain somewhat unclear in my opinion."

"In your opinion. Okay, Phil, lay it out for us. Quickly please."

"Thank you. SEC sanction?"

"Pending, with every indication that there will be no problems whatsoever. This may not actually be under their jurisdiction."

"How about the British, Norwegians, Belgians, Germans, EU? Client awareness? Who? Where did the initiative for this venture originate?"

"Well, Phil, we can't speak for the entire goddamned EU, but indications strongly, I repeat strongly, suggest that no objections are forthcoming from any quarter. As to initiation of the venture, that came directly from Skorpen."

"Fine. Can we discuss rate of North Sea current production? Projected production? Operating depths? Geology provider? Haven't North Sea operations already peaked? Assuming that about twenty-three billion barrels may remain for extraction, what would be the degree of difficulty?"

"Philip, we have the files right here. You have exactly fifteen minutes to review them while we break for some coffee."

After a few minutes, and to the not so mild irritation of all participants, Phil chuckled softly to himself.

The Partner turned in irritation from his coffee. "Care to include us in the fun Mr. Carr?"

"Certainly. Ever hear of a movie in the 50's called *The Tender Trap*?"

"Get to the point, Mr. Carr. *Now*."

"Okay. You are about to walk into a very devious, hostile takeover. And you will have absolutely no recourse to a remedy with which to prevent it." He described when, how, and why the takeover would work, as well as the motives in setting such a trap.

Phil convinced them to withdraw immediately and prescribed an appropriate corporate "poison pill" with which to inoculate them against further assault. It wasn't enough simply to walk away from the deal. However, within three hours, they had a consolidated plan of action and were sufficiently confident they were out of danger. Phil's astute questioning, reading, and understanding of the prospectus had saved the investors billions of Dollars, thousands of employees' jobs, and a huge firm in the balance.

All parties were embarrassed. Phil was most definitely a hero...soon to be legend... and there would be a few high level vacancies within twenty-four hours.

Phil had been sitting in boardrooms ever since. No litigator he. He found himself consulting to corporate heads, government agencies, military, even heads of small states. Nearly without exception, they all wanted two things. Was their project, product, or policy legal, domestically and internationally? If only marginally legal, how could they viably continue with the project?

How to achieve it within the labyrinth of government and competitor complexities with minimal risk and maximum reward. Where were the land mines and how could they avoid them?

He was far too valuable to engage in drafting contracts and doing research. Barns, Levi and Richardson provided such fodder. Phil was further unburdened by exclusive clients who needed coddling. This, in conjunction with his unusual skills, allowed him to deliver exceptional value, much faster than numberless and tiresome "milk-it-for-all-it's-worth," "by-the-numbers" legal and management consultancies, selling magical new snake-oil approaches to problem solving and nearly permanent, on-site contracts for problems Phil could clear up within weeks, if not days.

Phil's billable rate far more than offset the need for excessive billable hours. Follow-on work was even minimized. Barnes, Levi and Richardson did the "clean up" and stayed in the loop if need be. They called Phil HBRC (Hit, Bill, and Run Carr)—pronounced Hi-Barc.

Phil was becoming famous within a rather select sect. He traveled the world. Money was not a worry. In fact he had few if any worries.

Happily, he remained unassuming, avoiding the irascible arrogance colorfully paraded and worn like a consecrated cloak of wisdom and experience, by so many successful lawyers.

Phil Carr was a happy man, un-encumbered by any past trauma—or so he believed.

Nascent Preparations for Life

We hate some persons because we do not know them and we will not know them because we hate them.

Charles Colton

Phil had not always been so secure.

His father had been a highly successful lawyer in Washington, D.C., dealing mainly with environmental and regulatory matters. Phil always remembered him in dark grey suits, white shirts, and red ties with tiny white polka dots. He was very tall, gaunt, and distinguished looking. Phil always suspected at least part of his success was his intimidating appearance and resonant authoritative voice.

His mother, a petit handsome woman, taught world literature at Georgetown University. The three of them, along with his good looking, hard drinking, woman-chasing elder brother Michael, lived a comfortable life in an affluent tree-lined Georgetown neighborhood, just around the corner from the mansion, gardens and museum called Dumbarton Oaks.

Dumbarton Oaks continually fascinated the young Philip. Regardless of season, he haunted its park and gardens, kicking through piles of huge colorful leaves on fresh, clear autumn days, crunching through unblemished snow in winter and lying on its lush grass—peering up at enormous trees silhouetted against deep blue skies during spring and summer. It felt like his own little piece of the countryside, right in the middle of Washington, D.C.

Phil nearly worshipped his older brother. He followed Michael everywhere Michael would permit. One warm August evening, Phil had followed Michael and a promising young lady onto a tall, rickety, old pier at low tide. The sky was glowing with a romantic sunset. Seeking only the young lady's company, Philip's presence was a source of some irritation so Michael literally threw Phil off the pier into the cold, shallow water. Phil was uninjured, though surprised, embarrassed, and deeply hurt. Phil always gravitated back to Michael, so he forgave him immediately (didn't tell their folks). No real harm done, except Phil did suffer from nearly debilitating acrophobia thereafter.

To the surprise of everyone, Michael enrolled with a major in Middle Eastern Languages at Georgetown University. After successfully completing the majority of the courses, he abruptly entered a seminary in Maryland and, a few years later, he became an ordained a Priest—Father Michael. Imagine that!

Not long thereafter, Father Michael was sent to the Middle East on a mission of reconciliation. The Israelis were hammering parts of Lebanon, inciting militancy amongst Islamic factions, so it was thought that foreign Christians might lend a calming hand, particularly if they had the language skills.

Eighteen months later, Father Michael was dead. The murder site, motive, and perpetrators were unknown, always to remain so. All they knew was he had been found naked and filthy in a muddy ditch twenty-two kilometers south of Beirut. He had been brutally tortured (for their enjoyment only—Michael had no information to offer, or to withhold) and finally hung after weeks in captivity. That was all there was to know, and all that would ever be known. Phil had a deep, abiding love for his brother, and his death would become a lifelong source of fiercely malignant pain.

Much as one vexes a sore tooth with flexed jaw and probing tongue, Phil would have frequent fantasies about traveling to Beirut, seeking out the murderous bastards that killed his brother, reaping a fearsome, bloody vengeance.

His youthful mind felt the term *terrorist* conveyed too much dignity to these monsters and devoted hours at the library to translate *Murderous Cowardly Pig* into phonetic Arabic. The best he could come up with was *Khafa Qatala Khanzeer* or something like *Cowardly Killer Pigs*. He went so far as to write a letter to the White House suggesting that they use this term in lieu of *terrorist* outlining his rationale that this term (or the acronym: *KQK*'s [pronounced *Kaa-Koo-Kaa*'s]) would make them look foolish in the eyes of the world, render recruitment more difficult, and perhaps actually motivate some of them to appraise themselves and the repulsive atrocities in which they so lustfully indulged. From the White House, there was, predictably and understandably, no response.

Now they were a family of three. Phil was just entering high school.

During his seventeenth summer, Phil's parents, along with another couple, took a holiday to visit his mother's roots in Northern Ireland. Phil stayed with his Uncle Herb on the Chesapeake Bay. He was quite fond of his uncle. Herb reminded him of Mike in many ways. All-in-all he looked forward to a delightful two weeks exploring the diversely enthralling waters of the huge bay.

Phil was orphaned at sixteen.

While enjoying a lunch of local pub-grub on a sunny terrace just outside of Sligo in mid July, the pub, along with his parents and fourteen other souls were destroyed by a bomb. The bomber was never caught, his motivation never explained, and he never recanted the obscenity he perversely believed was somehow justified.

So Phil was alone.

He was frightened, bitter, and ached after revenge on person and persons unknown. All he really knew was the grief and horror visited on him was a direct result of a greedy, selfish grasping for power, exacerbated by (masquerading as) racial, political, or religious zealotry. His own hate rose in him from time to time so fiercely he could hardly breathe; he would literally gag on the bile that rose in his throat. Phil would become spasmodically nauseous. He painfully, violently vomited his acid hatred ... never successfully voiding the poisons so malevolently inculcated by his spectral *Kaa-Koo-Kaa*'s.

This, in conjunction with the frustration of not having a tangible target for his hatred, compelled him to lock away these feelings. He assumed the role of stoic objectivity respective to the odium surrounding him. Fortunately and regrettably, this served him well on his journey into adulthood and beyond.

Phil had the one remaining relative—his uncle Herbert—his father's brother. He was a big ruddy-faced, sunburned, bull of a man who made his living "on the sea" as he put it. Thick, steel-grey, close cropped hair, rugged regular features, and a powerful build lent a certain dignity to the man—which was sadly offset by a generous beer belly and perpetually red eyes. Uncle Herbert ("Call me 'Herb' boy—I work for a living!") sold the Georgetown house, the cars, the furniture, and all contents except those items personal or dear to Phil. He then settled their estate, cashed in on life insurances, did the tax thing, opened a trust account, threw Phil and his belongings into his rickety pick-up truck and headed for the Chesapeake Bay.

Herb lived in a crabbing shack just outside the picturesque village of St. Michaels, on an often rough, water-locked wash called the Miles River within the bay area itself. He lived hand-to-mouth fishing and crabbing from a sordid little beach adorned with smelly greenish-yellow nets, a rusting hulk of a boat (the "Sunrise"), seaweed, beer cans, and assorted litter. And of course, his silvery grey, peeling shack.

He fished and crabbed at many and various times, night and day, partly because he knew moon, fish, and tides, because he was drunk at many and various times. Tequila with a beer back was Herb's drink of choice although he was far from fussy ("Didja know Philly tha' tequila's th'only booze thaa's actually good foraye, and beer 'sis nearly as neu-neutritious as milk?").

The shack was surprisingly comfortable for Phil. He had his own tiny room with a view to the water through a cracked and cloudy windowpane, and even a drafty little private bathroom. There was a small frumpy living room with a grainy TV, a small kitchen (not exactly state-of-the-art, or state-of-the–health-department) and a cluttered, oil-blackened, lean-to carport, where Phil kept a motor scooter and Herb kept his pick-up limping along.

Life with his uncle had powerful effects on him. He learned to love the water, fishing, the winds, the weather, the tides, the moon, the banks, the sand bars, the channels, and the hundreds of ways the sea expressed itself. A Frenchman once wrote that, if there was anything magical on the planet Earth, it was water. Phil fully agreed and understood.

He saw sharks of all kinds and nearly every kind of creature the bay had to offer. He learned to love the seedy seafood joints along the shore, breaking crabs with wooden mallets on brown paper, crab flesh splattering everywhere amongst pools of stale beer on sticky wooden tables. He developed an abiding thirst for drink, which was seemingly tempered by his abhorrence of the excesses of his uncle.

Philip learned to be totally driven with a desire to succeed. No way would he find himself fishing from a broken-down shack, nor would people look down on him as they did while he lived with his uncle. He cared for his uncle very much and actually admired his unshackled, ram-shackled lifestyle. He had other things in mind for himself however.

Phil was pretty much an outsider at school. He wasn't native to the bay. His rough hands and permanent fishy scent, the manner of his home and family rendered him unfit for the gentry of St. Michaels, and Phil himself rejected the rougher elements that were invariably attracted to him. Aside from occasional moonlit liaisons with local girls, Phil was a contented loner.

Phil's singular associative abilities were already beginning to surface. His curious insights would manifest themselves in sudden conclusions, invariably leading to provocative observations, very much unexpected, and often unappreciated by his listeners. His flippancy got him into trouble more often than not, and his glibness would often find a mark in some humorless kid who would just as soon put a fist in his face as discuss things. As a result, Phil became an accomplished fighter—interestingly though, he found he felt better afterward if he lost the fight; winning was somehow burdensome—conveying a responsibility and a depressing sort of lingering guilt. Nonetheless, he continued wisecracking and generally winning fights. Honing both skills.

Uncle Herb was an impressively good seafood cook. His crab imperial was very special. Beyond that, however, it was strictly fried eggs, fried bread, and greasy bacon, so in self defense, Phil became a pretty fair cook himself. He learned to appreciate good cooking and would delight in fine food the rest of his life.

Herb was quietly pleased and even proud of Phil's academic achievement, as well as his enthusiastic embrace of the sea and its concomitant skills. Herb provided no supervision whatsoever and Phil needed none. All in all, except for Herb's incoherently drunken interludes, they lived very happily together.

Phil surprised everyone, including himself, at graduation. He graduated first in his class, was selected to be the valedictory speaker, had scholarship offers from several fine schools, and even had enough money in his own right to pay for a first class education. His valedictory address was not particularly well received, as it consisted mainly of observations about the future of the graduating class and the school itself. For a change, however, he didn't have to fight his way out of the gathering, and was soon thereafter savoring celebratory crabs and cold beer with his uncle.

There remained the greater part of his inheritance as yet unimbibed by his trustee uncle. So, with part time jobs, his own money, and hard-earned scholarships, Phil acquired a superb education and was immediately recruited into an excellent job as soon as he decided to enter the market.

He now found himself on an island unknown to him, with a Dr. Craig Webber of whom he had never heard, who had summoned him for reasons as yet unknown. This was really not so unusual in his business. In fact, Phil found this fun, interesting, and even exciting.

A First Class flight on Olympic to Athens. A short hop to an island called Lefkada. A beautiful drive to a small fishing port. Pickup by a very respectable looking motor yacht. A four hour sea voyage to a seemingly uninhabited island adorned only with a small jetty, graced with magnificent cliffs and great rugged natural beauty—picked up by a jeep which, after a rocky thirty-five minutes, bags whisked away, carried him to the intriguing driveway leading to this gigantic Edwardian mansion high atop the island.

The mansion was four stories high, at least 150 meters wide and 150 meters deep. From his perspective he could see that the rear of the mansion was terraced inward with succeeding levels. It was built like a fortress. Trimmed with imported white granite. Massive walls of flawless, albinic limestone. A circular portico outlined with six marble columns twelve meters high, accessed by concentric marble stairs. To the right and left of the drive were elegant, uncluttered formal gardens, accented with cascading marble fountains. Everything was of a Mediterranean motif.

In New York, a Senior Partner at the firm, Douglas Curtis, had called him into his huge, austere, oak-paneled and book-lined office. Curtis was vaguely familiar to Phil; they had worked together briefly, but mainly because he fit the classical mold. He was well groomed, rugged tan (sailing off Long Island Sound), with close cropped, steely hair, an impeccable pin-stripe blue suit, black wing tips, gold cuff links barely visible peeking out under immaculate French cuffs, and a watch worth more than most automobiles. Phil didn't resent the opulence, as it was merely the *uniform of the day*.

All his books were perfectly aligned and bound in exactly the same maroon leather with gold lettering. So perfect was everything, Phil realized the books were only window dressing and never opened. These tomes were not the stuff of paralegals, laboring away in lower floors, far removed. This office enjoyed a lofty view high above Manhattan. Huge, uncluttered, mahogany desk, maroon-leather, executive chair facing three maroon-leather, wing chairs, several brass lamps and little tables for note taking, and a prominent, mirrored, wet bar, Persian rugs and, of course, the *de rigeur,* Audubon prints mounted on textured, deep reddish-brown, washed walls above the oaken wainscot.

Central Park stretched off in the background, framed by a large window and frosty-green drapes, with zero personality. Not too shabby, either. Phil did find it of interest that the partner had placed his own executive, wing chair squarely in the middle of the large window, positioned inward toward his desk facing any visitors, spurning the diverting view. He had heard of this trick: On sunny days, the man's face would be unreadable in shadow, while his hair would glow from the ambient light—giving him an ethereal halo of sunlight—disconcerting to the uninitiated.

As Phil took it all in, he realized this was what he had trained for and was working toward. This gave him an inexplicably uneasy, even depressing feeling. He was aware he was starting to mentally drift again.

Curtis told Phil to delegate everything he had active and get to Greece. He didn't know what it was about and didn't care. All he really knew was there was interesting money involved and some impressively heavy hitters who had specifically requested Phil. "Pick up your tickets, travel advance, your itinerary, and the client dossier on your way out. Have fun. You could use some down time anyway. Keep me posted if you can. Have some fun if you can." Curtis gave him a firm handshake and a dismissive smile. "Have a good trip."

It turned out that the "client dossier" consisted of nothing more than a PR-quality photo of Dr. Craig Webber and a Work Order (retainer paid) to Barns, Levi and Richardson. Phil's services were specified. The billable rate discretely blackened out, which Phil found amusing and actually complimentary. All this had finally brought him face-to-face with Dr. Webber.

Dr. Webber was tall, slim, elegantly disheveled, with a deeply-lined, tanned face and a hearty chock of salt and pepper hair, favoring the salt. Expensive suede loafers, tan trousers topped by a beautiful blue blazer, covering a pristine-white button-down, no tie. Phil had the impression the Doctor might have "dressed up" for him.

After shaking Phil's hand, he ushered him into the cool entryway, which was more akin to a lobby, judging by its rather vast size, tall columns, gleaming marble floor, and austere furnishings. There was even a large, antique, unmanned, reception desk. "Do you live here?"

"Yes, I do." said the doctor "However, I spend most of my time at the 'U' where I have other quarters."

"The 'U'?"

"Yes, the University."

The Doctor insisted on walking behind Phil, which made navigation ungainly. But with terse instructions "left, right, straight" they crossed the reception area and finally arrived at the most sumptuous bar Phil had ever seen.

Everything was brownish, gold-streaked, highly-polished marble, the floor, the walls, columns, framing around the bar, and the bar itself. The ceiling consisted of a rounded, inset, somewhat abstract fresco portraying an azure Mediterranean sky intermediately draped with fluffy, nearly transparent clouds, dotted with tiny birds. He couldn't make out the light source. The bar was backed by opaque, greenish glass, supporting shelves made of the same material, holding all sorts of glasses, made of the opaque pale-green glass, dramatically silhouetted by backlighting accenting the colorful, uneven, festive mosaic of the bar-stock. Two large cocktail tables occupied the center of the room, which were predictably made of the same light-green glass. Each table was surrounded by eight large, brown-leather wing chairs. The effect was at once warm and coolly elegant. Phil could see himself happily drinking and talking in this room for hours on end.

A ruddy-faced barman, white shirted, no tie, black trousers, well-shined black loafers, generous belly, and equally generous smile approached. Raising his eyebrows in friendly interrogation, he was ready for drink instructions. Phil ordered a gin and tonic. Webber requested Ouzo.

A large carafe of gin, and a larger carafe of tonic, a bucket of ice, sliced lime, olives, and various snacks, a carafe of Ouzo, and a pitcher of water, stirs and glasses, all in the elegant light-green glassware, were quickly delivered. *I already like this place, no matter what*, Philip thought, as he mixed himself a tall cold drink.

Webber, sensing Phil's approval, said, "Lunch is not for awhile, so we can relax and get acquainted. There will be several people meeting us for lunch, and I would like you to be at least partially briefed. Okay?"

"Certainly. May I start?" Phil asked.

"Sure."

"Well, first, what island is this?"

"We call it 'The Island.'"

A shadow of wry smiles appeared on both men's faces.

"Okay, second question: What's the name of the University?"

"We call it 'The University.'"

Cheshire, catlike, mutual smiles were unrestrained this time.

"What is the objective of the University?"

"Academic stuff. Much the same as other universities."

"Why have you sent for me?"

"To answer your questions." Webber gave Philip a warm smile.

"Over to you, Doctor." Phil smiled.

"As you know, I am Dr. Craig Webber. I am an MD, a geneticist and a biochemist. I founded this Island, this University, and this project over twenty-five years ago. I have been working for many years on methods of improving human health and the human condition through the use of various sciences, with some success. Albeit we have greatly benefited from exploiting the wealth of scientific advances throughout the world in the ensuing years.

I inherited a considerable fortune from my father who was in plastic extrusions from its very early days; in fact, my family still generates considerable income from this industry. I used the vast majority of this fortune to establish this facility.

I then fostered a broad base of some twenty investors and contributors. These investors, along with me as Chairman, constitute our Board of Directors. We are in no position to offer tax benefits for contributions. Therefore, our benefactors are of necessity, very wealthy and very, very convinced of our worthiness. This is truly a billionaires-only club. They enjoy significant benefits from the products of our labors here on the Island. Should we ever elect to commercialize our products, they would stand to make a second huge fortune apiece. As Board members, they are well aware of, and strictly adhere to, our policy of absolute secrecy.

"Our operations here cost an *immense* amount of money. We have been exceptionally fortunate, as finances have never been an issue. Nor do we see this as a problem in the foreseeable future. We might consider becoming partly or wholly self-supporting. We have developed several products that would intrigue the outside world. This would assume we could accomplish marketing and distribution through a series of covering companies, totally masking our production, and even our existence.

This complex may seem large to you. It houses two bars, two dining complexes, extensive kitchens, an immense underground garage (with repair facility), luxury accommodations for up to thirty-two people, administrative offices for thirty people, an independent computer and communications center, five private pools, a gymnasium, two tennis courts, a putting green, a small library, three conference rooms, and a theatre seating up to fifty people, and an absolute state-of-the-art clinic, but this is only the tip of the iceberg.

Extending more than thirty floors below this bar, you will find classrooms, labs, conference rooms, dormitories, and private apartments, a full scale hospital, movie theaters, gyms and pools and gaming courts, restaurants and cafeterias, bars, even night clubs, shopping areas, warehouses, loading docks, a computer complex, power and climate control systems, and extensive security. We have a fleet of ATV's, boats, a private runway, and six business jets, a people mover, and we spare no expense to ensure the entire facility is bright, clean, modern, and an entirely pleasant place to live and work. We are constantly maintaining, expanding, and upgrading this complex. The Island itself is forty-three kilometers long and eight kilometers wide, almost completely surrounded by high cliffs...so there's lots of room for private roaming and, if you're athletic enough to get down there, some lovely beaches at the foot of much of the cliff line.

Our staff, faculty, students, and alumni, if you can call them that, amounts to some 6,000 souls, and growing (we will need to quadruple over the next eight years for reasons that will become clear). Ultimately, the complex will be some sixty stories deep. We are constantly expanding and have been operating for over twenty-five years. In all that time, not one staff or faculty member has requested to leave, although they are all fully aware that they may leave at any time with a *very* generous separation bonus in their pocket. Certainly, many students have departed to complete their education elsewhere, or on various assignments. Thus far, however, they have always returned.

Our people do take frequent business trips. They attend conferences and vacations on the mainland. Each professor holds tenure, a Professor Emeritus, or Chair at another university somewhere in the world, which they either already held, or we acquired for them—as a cover that allows them to attend conferences, freely interact with academic counterparts, and even be published, within reason.

No one feels caged in. The staff pretty much manages themselves. Beyond that, we would be best described as a scholastic community, led, but not managed, by our large cadre of professors and scientists.

In telling you all this, Mr. Carr, I'm not just trying to impress. I want you to know that this is a vast institution, replete with nearly unrestricted resources and a rich history. You need to understand this to accomplish your task in the next two days.

Until last month, we had only one real manager—a wonderful man—Mr. Alfred Wilcoxen. He died of a massive stroke last month, and we have been intensively searching for a successor since that time."

"I see." Phil said. "What are you attempting to accomplish with all this?"

"Not just yet, Mr. Carr. We first need to work on your relationship with the Island and the University."

"And what would that be, sir?"

"We want you to be our next manager. In this context, manager really implies a great deal more: President, CEO, COO, University Chancellor, that sort of thing. And we are prepared to make an exceptional offer."

Dr. Webber starting ticking off points on his fingers. "Money: You name a number remotely within reason, and you'll get it, tax free. Living conditions: A suite of apartments in this main building that would beggar the accommodations of many heads of state. Duties: Damned if I actually know in detail. No one specifically knows what Wilcoxen really did day-by-day. We do know he traveled the world managing the money, materials, and staff required. He kept outsiders from troubling us and governments at bay. Most importantly, he immersed himself in the projects we conduct. He related them, coordinated them and helped them evolve—not just keeping them on time and on target. He actually got involved in the science and helped determine the success of the result. You would have full access to his files and staff and pretty much decide what needs to be done."

"Doctor, I'm a lawyer …"

"And a damned good one, too, I'm told. We do need legal help from time to time, and there is a legal staff on site, which would come under your direct authority.

But you have a great deal more to bring to this project: Your international skills, the ability to analytically interrelate concepts and projects, people skills, scientific training and—perhaps most importantly—the talent to see through complex concepts and arrive at unexpectedly valid conclusions.

Added to this, and I hope this is not too personal, is your upbringing. We are convinced that has shaped you and your view of the world in such a manner that we believe you would enthusiastically support our work here.

Basically, you would be doing very much what you are doing today: Traveling the world, managing agreements, laws, governments, solving problems, and finding unique solutions.

The differences, he said, using his fingers to count again, "You would be doing this for a salary that dwarfs your present and future prospects. Your present career will make you wealthy. We'll make you rich. You would be working in a lifestyle you probably never dreamt of. I believe of greatest import, you would be doing this, not as a hit-and-run consultant, but for yourself and for a vision I believe you will wholeheartedly adopt as your own."

"Okay. This begins to sound interesting. Are we going to conduct an interview or whatever with your group next?"

"Mr. Carr, we spent a small fortune intensively searching for and exhaustively vetting someone exactly like you, in an extraordinarily short time. We found only one. You. Our board approved you for hire long before you boarded your aircraft for this meeting. We have already negotiated a generous payoff for Barns, Levi and Richardson if you choose to accept this position. We have specialists prepared to wrap up your affairs in New York and move or liquidate your belongings immediately if you wish.

I'm going to ask you to pour yourself another drink, review this non-disclosure agreement in the privacy of the bar." Webber then handed Philip a single sheet of paper and a small silver bell. "Ring the bartender when you are ready to join us for lunch. Please take your time." With that, Dr. Webber, hands in pockets, wandered away in a seemingly aimless, carefree manner out of the bar.

It took Phil less than five minutes to review and sign the non-disclosure agreement. After all, he had an active client/attorney relationship to respect and would therefore never dream of sharing anything learned during this visit. In fact, he was a little surprised at their naïveté in thinking a non-disclosure was necessary. Nonetheless, as briefly outlined in the agreement, they would pay him directly, as well as his firm, an impressive fee for devoting two days (this did deviate from the original Work Order) in reviewing operations on the Island, at the end of which time, Phil would decide whether to assume the position of CEO/COO and Chancellor of the University.

Should Phil elect not to take the job, he guaranteed never to reveal to any party any information revealed to him during his stay on the Island, even the existence of the Island itself, in perpetuity, under penalty of "appropriate remedy," whatever the hell that meant!

Tossing back the remainder of his second G&T, he rang for the barman. Non-Disclosure in hand, he followed the barman to lunch.

Dr. Webber, reading a paper in an alcove of plush-leather easy chairs just outside the dining room, greeted him. "That was fast!"

"I was a little concerned that there is not a clause absolving me of liability should withholding such knowledge constitute a tort of some fashion and, despite the fact that I was intrigued with parts of the wording, it doesn't take much thought to confirm an agreement reiterating, albeit slightly modifying, an extant contract in full force."

Dr. Webber frowned slightly trying to absorb Phil's comment. After the slightest moment, his frown cleared. "Point well taken, Phil. May I call you Phil? Please call me Craig."

Craig rose, pocketed the signed agreement, took Phil warmly by the arm and squired him into the dining room.

The dining room was possibly more elegant than the bar, with light, powder-green throughout, with matt-white accents on wainscoting, windows, ceiling highlights, and doors. Again, there was a recessed, round, frescoed ceiling with the same theme of sky, ethereal clouds and tiny birds. Some sort of light green backlit stone comprised the floor as well, with an exquisite inlay of black marble depicting a stylized sun.

Huge windows looked far out to sea and lent a wonderful golden light to the room itself. Kilometers out, the sun shone so brightly on the water it was blinding, even from such a distance. White French doors opened onto a large terrace covered with flowers and shrubs, tables, chairs, and umbrellas, as well as a generous rolling bar. The terraces' intricate stonework railing ended in a straight, 400-meter drop to the sea.

To the left, the terrace opened onto a lush formal garden, surrounding a swimming pool constructed of a black slate bottom, slate sides and stairs, and roughened slate edging. In the middle of the pool, a small waterfall trickled and babbled its return to the pool. Far below, he could hear the booming of the sea as it railed against cliff and rock and landing docks. *Breathtaking!*

Lunch was laid out in the cool interior at a large round table more than adequate to accommodate the fifteen diners for whom it was set.

There seemed to be a sort of cocktail party going on. A group of people dressed in business attire, lab coats, sports outfits, and casual clothes milled about in animated conversation, while white-coated waiters plied the room with wines and hors d'oeuvres.

Against a side wall was a buffet clearly intended as a starter course: there was smoked salmon, pates, grilled vegetables, cheeses, nuts, olives, cold shellfish, squid, octopus, salads, and crusty breads. The table sported several large, iced carafes of various wines, waters, and juices. Another table featured a variety of desserts and dessert wines and coffees and teas. The dining table was set only for the formal, main course.

Dr. Webber, noting Phil's interest in the setting, explained, "Normally, we just have a buffet lunch open from 1200 to 1430. We have a buffet breakfast from 0700 to 0930 and a buffet dinner from 1900 to 2130. We enjoy a formal meal only when we have guests such as you, or when we have the very occasional staff meetings. Only senior staff dines here, or has use of the bars, and we often go days without seeing many individuals. You may cook and eat in your quarters or have food catered in twenty-four hours a day.

We work hard here, but we work smart. We make time for relaxation, sports, entertainment, and good food. No 'burn outs' allowed here. As you will learn, we work under time pressure...but time in the broadest terms, expressed in a very long view, on very, very wide canvas."

When Phil and Dr. Webber had a glass of wine, Webber tapped on his glass, and the room became immediately quiet.

"I would like to introduce Mr. Philip Carr. As we all know, he will be with us today and tomorrow (and we hope a great deal longer) to review our operation and facility to assist him in deciding whether to join our society in the position of CEO/COO/Chancellor. I will ask each of you to introduce yourselves and your respective department when we are seated with our first course. So if you would serve yourselves and take a seat, we will get started." Phil was provided a small leather notebook and pen with which to take notes.

The group formed a reasonably orderly line at the buffet table and the sound of discretely clattering plates, serving utensils, and glasses (a sound which invariably provoked hunger pangs in Phil) soon commenced.

When all were seated, Dr. Webber said, "Let's go clockwise starting with Dr. Winchester on my left. Please introduce yourself and give us a brief description of your department. From this I assume Mr. Carr will determine his agenda for the next day and a half. Dr. Winchester, if you would please."

"I am Dr. Enoch Winchester—Applied Sciences. Good afternoon Mr. Carr. Please call me Dr. Winchester. I hate the name Enoch (laughter). I am charged with the disciplines of all forms of Mathematics, from arithmetic to algebra to geometry to numbers theory to the most advanced forms of calculus and trigonometry. We are responsible for physics, chemistry (except bio-chemistry), earth sciences, computer sciences, biology (except genetics), astronomy, and cosmology. We place a great deal of emphasis on Economics, Money and Banking, and International Finance. One of these days, our graduates will need to face the Landers and manage a variety of not insignificant assets. Of all the departments, we have the largest teaching cadre. This is our basic curriculum. However, it can be expanded very quickly to meet changing needs. Thank you."

Dr. Winchester was rather short, a bit pudgy with thinning grey hair and frameless glasses. Altogether, he presented a rather fatherly figure. Scottish. Definitely a Scotsman.

"I am Dr. Emily Johansen—Genetics. You *can* call me Emily (more laughter). Genetics in all its forms is our only occupation. We maintain a nominal teaching staff. However, research and application of the knowledge we have gained is far and away our priority. Toward this end, we have very few instructors and a very large staff of research geneticists. We consider it our task to watch for, and even provoke, Anomalous Numen."

Dr. Johansen had nearly copper-colored hair, perfect skin, and features and a figure that made Phil a little dizzy, although two gin & tonics and two white wines might figure into the equation as well. She spoke perfect English, but Phil thought he detected a hint of the stubby Icelandic in her speech.

"I am Dr. Sin Oua Siroa—Body Culture. You may call me Sin, or Sin Oua, or Siroa, or Doctor, your choice (again light laughter). I am charged with Sports & Physical Education, which is not too demanding a task. We do not engage in competitive sports. Instead, we concentrate on the body arts and good conditioning. Some of the mandatory courses our students seem to enjoy are self defense, weapons handling, and survival. The Island provides a superb environment for these studies. In accord with standing policy, though we're not too sure of the relevance, we are poised for ANUMINA should they arise. Thank you."

Dr. Siroa was a well built, good looking West Indian. He seemed serious and quite well qualified in his field and perhaps even in managing "Anomalous Numen," or ANUMEN's, or whatever they may be.

"My name is Dr. Simon Butler. I am the resident Cuisenaire. This means that I am in charge of all the various kitchens and of developing menus of all types. But more importantly, I am in charge of 'fusing' all major cuisines into a world hybrid— then documenting and teaching this cuisine to our chefs and students. I'm always open for a tasting, any opinions and any suggestions. My greatest hurdle is the acquisition of all types of arcane fresh ingredients. I hope that should Mr. Carr choose to lead us, he will find the time look into this matter.

I inherited from Dr. Johansen our food production facility—which is my overriding avocation and love. I would be most pleased to introduce you to its extraordinary capabilities.

Thank you."

Dr. Butler looked just as a good cook should: stout, jolly, and well fed. British. Midlands perhaps.

"I am Dr. Jackson Gear. I am an MD, and the primary duty of our staff is to look after the health of all our residents. We maintain The Nursery. For interested students, we will provide some pre-med training. However, if they wish to seriously pursue medicine, we send them to mainland universities. A tertiary duty is to constantly monitor for ANUMINA, although we feel it may be a bit early in the game."

There's that term again. What the hell is "Anomalous Numen"? Phil wondered, all the while maintaining a neutral expression.

"I am Dr. Anne Jones—Arts. We teach art in nearly all its many forms, paint, and sculpture, visual—you name it. We maintain a small cadre and more than fifty percent of students' time is devoted to developing a world class fusion, much as does our friend Mr. Butler in cuisine. In unexpected ways, this task is proving much easier than we envisioned and in expected ways, very difficult. We suspect, or perhaps remotely hope is a better term, that Anomalous Numen may manifest itself within the arts discipline. Thank you."

Dr. Jones sported a beautiful mane of chestnut hair, a gently attractive face and a slim provocative figure. Mr. Carr's appreciation of the arts was increasing. She looked like a California girl.

"I am Dr. William Gould—Music. We do with music what Dr. Jones does for the arts. There is little if anything I can add to Anne's eloquence. Therefore, I shall not try. Thank you."

Dr. Gould was a short, compact, long-haired fellow. Phil could imagine him on his podium beating the music stand with his wand and stamping out the rhythm with his foot for an intransigent orchestra. Very, very Austrian.

"I am Dr. Sun Kahn—Comparative Religions & Philosophy. First, we instruct on every major belief system on earth. Of necessity, we lack great depth and we do tend to concentrate on common elements between religions. However, when a student demonstrates a particular interest, we can arrange for special sessions.

I would emphasize, however, in the strongest terms, we do not encourage any student to embrace any given religion. Instead, we strive to instill in our students a posture of analytical detachment, much as an anthropologist studies tribal superstitions, or an archeologist researches ancient beliefs... always at arm's length...avoid going native.

Secondly, we attempt to reconcile philosophy with religion and what the Hellenic Greeks called 'ethos.' In many respects, this task is fairly straightforward. Again, it consists of identifying and matching common elements, and then contrasting discordances. Having identified the dissident concepts, the remaining work is to find a way of rationalizing them into a unified, logical code. We hope the result will contain meaning, maybe a certain elegance...perhaps even beauty.

This work assists us in the execution of our third and primary charge:

Much as a Duckbilled Platypus appears to be a creature designed by a committee, we toil to produce a hybrid system of belief and ethos that might prove potentially palatable to a world of opinionated, protectionist, murderous, bigoted, megalomaniacal yahoos.

We face a great challenge to produce something that may never be implemented, nor perhaps even be subject to an attempted implementation.

We have much frustrating, difficult, and probably thankless work to do."

Enough said, Phil thought. *What he was, where he came from was all unintelligible.*

"Dr. Shad Alexander—Government & Legal Systems. We instruct on all major forms of government. We do not teach law *per se*. The difficult task we face is to attempt to develop a generic, globally palatable form of government. Democracy is one obvious default. However, our studies indicate that this solution may not be easily generalized to all societies. We are trying to develop, maybe even invent, the perfectly generic system for all peoples and, thusly, perhaps find one key to human amity.

Such a system may lie somewhere between an iron-fisted dictatorship and blatant anarchy. Perhaps it resides somewhere outside these boundaries. Perhaps it lives within the heart of a more fully realized man himself. Anomalous Numen? Much work lies ahead.

Easier than governmental forms is hybridizing the non-bureaucratic law that underpins any governmental form. This is an easier task: reject the frivolous, the cruel, the dictatorial, the corrupt, and what is left is normally a core of common sense and ethics.

Are we qualified to make these judgments? Who knows? Who is?

We see our role here as simply providing a depth of background for our students. We perceive neither a substantive rationale, nor mechanism with which to disseminate, or in any manner impose our findings anywhere, including here. If we succeed, we will have produced a high-quality, well-researched and well-thought-out body of suggestions. If we're very lucky we may produce a totally nonpartisan, objective, truly non-subjective blueprint for an ideal egoless system of government."

An honest man in an appropriate role. Phil guessed Canadian.

"I am Dr. Judy McLean—Language, Culture & Literature. We are charged with selecting a global tongue. On what basis? Population numbers would imply Chinese or Spanish. Analysis might suggest Esperanto. Practicality should suggest English. Science might lend itself to German. Art could lead us to French or Italian. Once a direction is adopted, we are faced with the nearly mechanical task of translation, and computers are proving of great assistance. This is our task: to find or develop a *lingua franca* and finally dismantle the Tower of Babel."

A little severe. Most certainly capable. Definitely American, Phil thought, wryly.

"I am Dr. Eve Dunedin—Fear. No pun intended, but I believe this (mandatory) course is the most feared in the U. We were originally the Psychology Department. But in keeping with the evolutionary spirit of the University, we realized that our objective was not to produce psychologists or psychiatrists. Instead, in seeking potential realization, we perceived that psychosis, neurosis, phobia, inhibitions, insecurity, and feelings of inferiority, trauma, even physical modesty—in short: FEAR—might present the greatest barrier.

There are healthy fears and very unhealthy fears.

We teach our students the courage, or perhaps just the bloody-mindedness, to differentiate and face both in their journey. I fully believe that this is the most dramatic example of applied psychology and conditioning you will encounter. I am convinced that classical practitioners would seriously question our methods. At the same time, they could never compete with our results."

White lab coat, blond hair drawn back tightly into an almost girlish ponytail, no makeup, a severe yet lovely face—oozing self-competence. Somewhere from Scandinavia, Phil guessed.

"Dr. Sean Gray—Realization. I stand at the end of the production line, hands proffered, awaiting the first fruition of ANUMEN. Beyond that, I prepare and I watch and I watch and I watch."

Unruly steel-wool hair wandered all over his head. An equally unruly moustache with matching eyebrows framed his Einstein eyes. There was a very bright spark somewhere in that charming head.

"I am Dr. Robert Montgomery—History. This is a contiguous course of study, lasting four years, commencing at roughly 35,000 BC, up to the present. We give some attention to paleontology, however. In a very real sense, this course is a history of war: its causes, its effects, its art, and its horrors. In this manner, we dovetail with the general curriculum.

We absolutely do not overlook the *spikes* in mankind's development that are directly attributable to war. Advances in science, technology, even art and philosophy can be credited to wars over the ages. This is a lesson we dare not overlook, for if we eliminate war, we must find another *prod* to ensure our advancement as a species—to generate these spikes.

I am fully aware of the irony of this conundrum. The very purpose of this University is advancement of our species without war. I simply point out that history may indicate that the methods and tools we are developing here may not be entirely adequate human motivators in the longer perspective.

Thank you."

Interesting man, Phil thought. *Oxford. Only Oxford.*

Dr. Webber rose: "Thank you, ladies and gentlemen. I appreciate both your informative presentations and your forthrightness. I am sure you have given Mr. Carr a great deal of insight into our operations. We are all quite familiar with Mr. Carr's background and history (with our apologies for investigating you), which are most impressive. I suggest we commence with our main course and open the table for a general discussion."

With a gesture from Dr. Webber, four waiters descended with platters of steaming sea bass, drizzled with olive oil and spices and lemon, covered with shredded sautéed carrots and celery, accompanied by broad beans in a butter and sage sauce, tarragon rice, complimented by an ice cold Chablis.

Phil had doubts about the broad beans. Turning to Dr. Webber, he said, "This is Sea Bass isn't it?"

Dr. Webber, having just taken a bite, smiled a simple, "Mm-hmm."

Phil was familiar with Sea Bass. In the North Atlantic they grew up to six feet, sometimes seven feet, weighing hundreds of pounds. In these waters, nothing so large existed. His uncle's training clearly came back to him. In the sea surrounding Greece, these bass are called Lavraki, and never grow much over a meter. His fish was a steak, not a fillet, and must have come from a huge fish. It was totally fresh, without a single bone, no skin, yet grilled to perfection. Everything was delicious and Phil had soon cleaned his plate, ending his fish speculations. Light conversation continued to circulate around the table.

Phil noticed Webber watching him inspect his fish with some amusement and not a little appreciation, then Dr. Webber interjected, "Before we finish this excellent meal, perhaps we can prevail on Mr. Carr to share his initial thoughts with us?"

"Certainly, Doctor.

"First, I was impressed with the amount of information candidly conveyed, with great economy of words. You are clearly a unique group of academics (laughter).

You seem to have developed a most singular University. You are a University in the respect that you have schools addressing several disciplines. Yet in one aspect I would define you more as a College, in that all your studies, and all your research, and all your work appears to have a single objective. You have been intriguing me with the term 'Anomalous Numen' or 'ANUMEN,' or whatever, during your briefings, and I suspect this is closely related to your common objective. I will avoid the obvious trap of directly asking its meaning, trusting this will be made clear when appropriate.

I actually have very little remaining time here—what's left of this afternoon and tomorrow—and I should like to have an exit meeting with Dr. Webber tomorrow afternoon, which leaves in reality less than six hours in total.

Accordingly, I propose one-on-one interviews with the following department heads. Dr. Emily Johansen, Genetics, Dr. Sun Kahn, Comparative Religions & Philosophy, Dr. Shad Alexander, Government & Legal Systems, Dr. Eve Dunedin, Fear, Dr. Sean Gray, Realization.

The sequence of the interviews is not overly relevant in my opinion, so I would request interviews as you would like them scheduled at your convenience, or as you may deem appropriate. I certainly appreciate that no department has greater import than another, except perhaps Food Sciences, judging from this excellent lunch. I selected these because I feel I can gain a faster, broader insight on the Island from these specific disciplines in the time available.

If this is acceptable, I will await your schedule. I genuinely thank you for your hospitality and excellent briefings.

Meanwhile, I thank you again and call dibs on that strawberry tart on the dessert buffet (laughter and sliding of chairs)."

After dessert, the group separated to make arrangements.

A compact, well-attired, white-haired man approached Phil. "My name is Edward McKnight. I am assigned to look after your needs during your stay here." Phil heard a very cultured British accent. But he suspected that perhaps a little Cockney might surface given sufficient excitement.

The men shook hands. "My name is Phil Carr. Please call me Phil."

"As you wish, Phil, please call me Edward.

"May I to show you to your quarters? Perhaps you would like to freshen up? Your things have already been put away."

Edward led Phil into an elevator a short distance from the dining room, no floor numbers, and only two key activated buttons: Up and Down.

Approximately six meters beyond the elevator stood a pair of impressive oak doors. Edward said, "That will be your office during your visit, planned as your permanent offices should you elect to stay on.

"This is your private elevator, sir. It leads directly to the Presidential Suites."

Four stories up, the elevator opened silently onto a large, austere, circular, reception area, lined with six columns and accented with a large round Persian rug. The flooring consisted of warm beige granite, polished to a matt buff, as was all flooring throughout the suites. Walls throughout the complex were limestone with gray highlights on ceilings, doors, corners, windows, and closets. All ceilings were very high and of the same beige limestone, sculpted into graceful arches in every room and hallway. Paintings and statuary sparingly decorated all rooms. Curtains, shades, furniture, towels, bed clothing, and screens were all a powder blue. Persian rugs liberally decorated floors, and all lighting was discretely indirect. The entire effect was a soothingly elegant, artful environment.

The reception area opened onto three hallways. The first led to a sitting room, game room, bar, library, and washrooms. The second hallway led to a dining room, conference room, screening room, kitchen, pantry, a freight elevator, and washrooms. The third hallway led to a private office, dressing room, a series of closets, bedroom, sauna, whirlpool, an extravagant bathroom, and exercise room opening onto an outdoor pool built on a huge terrace that surrounded the entire complex. There was a small, generic, well-equipped lab, augmented by several telescopes, various computers, and a personal walk-in safe. The laboratory connected with a communications center, as well as some twenty-five monitors and a set of controls that would allow the user to instantly view any part of the entire facility. The lab provided a generous spiral staircase to the roof to facilitate astronomical exercises, as well as provide an enormous space for personal and group activities.

Phil noticed another small hallway leading off reception, ending in a closed door. He cast a quizzical glance at Edward.

"Those lead to my quarters, sir. I live in a separate area somewhat removed. However, I am immediately available twenty-four hours a day."

Phil quickly realized these apartments occupied the entire fourth floor of the mansion. "My god! Where does Dr. Webber live?"

Edward smiled politely, clearly expecting a question of this sort. "Dr. Webber has lived in the same suite of rooms for the last twenty-five years. They were constructed on the first floor at commencement of the project and I am sure that Dr. Webber is very comfortable. Dr. Webber and the Board believe it is absolutely imperative that the President of the Island and University provide an imposing image to staff, as well as any outside visitors. These apartments are part of that image. Other members of senior staff maintain apartments in the mansion, while some prefer quarters below, close to their labs and classrooms. We provide very high-quality guest quarters for visitors and an entirely separate facility for BOD Members, each having their own personally assigned suite of rooms."

"Not too bad," Phil breathed to himself. "Did Mr. Wilcoxen live here?"

"No sir. These apartments were expressly fitted for your use. Or whomever is the new President."

"I see."

Phil showered and changed into slacks, a polo shirt, and a sports coat. Shortly thereafter Edward appeared to escort him to his first appointment.

Getting to Know You

Edward led Phil through a maize of hallways, elevators, even a moving walkway some 300 meters long to the far side of the huge complex, some ten floors down. Hallways were brightly painted and well lit (without fluorescents). Plants, paintings, posters, and decorations were liberally sprinkled throughout the halls, eclectically representing an impressive body of styles. There were built-in display cases boasting figurines and pottery from the ancient Egyptians, pre-Colombians, Greeks, Romans, Hittites, American Indians, Assyrians, Africans, Persians...nearly every major ancient culture.

The greatest surprise was about a hundred meters into the underground part of the complex. Phil suddenly came upon a huge window looking far out to sea. At first, Phil assumed it was a skillful computer simulation until he realized the light from the sea was blinding and real. He looked at Edward who was smiling with pride.

"This is one of our many innovations. We have been able to perfect periscope technology, reflecting flawless, real-time images through shafts built into our walls, to the degree that these are actual windows looking outside, in every respect. One simply cannot detect any difference.

Sometimes you will feel like you are totally outdoors, with no walls, no floor, and no windows. Then again, you may be wandering along a desert scape and encounter a door balanced in seeming nothingness. Open the door and you may enter a classroom, an office, and a shop, whatever.

If we are looking onto a sunny, hot landscape we heat the glass, if a cold scene, we cool the glass. In other situations we can quickly switch over to IR and have a crystal clear view of a dark, nighttime scene. They can be adjusted to look directly at the sun, in which case we tint the light source, or appropriately position a scaled circular blackout spot and we can look at the heavens and magnify the light source. We can simulate a full solar or lunar eclipse at will. You will find a full set of controls for each window housed behind a hidden cabinet to the right of each window.

This is a great aid in maintaining a pleasant, non-claustrophobic underground environment. You will find hundreds upon hundreds of such windows down here in hallways, classrooms, and apartments. You will find a couple of such windows in the Presidential Suite."

Along the way Phil observed students in twos and threes walking, talking, and laughing in a very relaxed manner. They wore all sorts of styles and seemed normal in all respects... save one: Without exception they were all tall, slim, well built, clear skinned and, although not a very scientific observation, damned good looking.

They arrived at Dr. Johansen's lab, which had been cleared to allow a personal site review and private interview.

Although Phil had minimal experience with laboratories, especially genetic labs, he could tell this one was extraordinary. He estimated that it must be 4000 square meters—most machines were a completely unknown to him—and obviously highly advanced.

Central to the laboratory complex was an octagonal office, slightly elevated, with tinted glass angled outward with an unobstructed view of the entire laboratory. More than anything, it looked like a miniature Air Traffic Control tower. This was the office of Dr. Emily Johansen.

Staff had willingly agreed to both the content and sequencing of Phil's proposed agenda, so Emily was up first.

"Dr. Johansen ..."

"Please *do* call me Emily," she said and smiled.

"Okay Emily, I'm Phil.

Emily, let's clear things up from the start. I have some idea of genetics: RNA, DNA, Stem Cells, Recombinant DNA, amniotic fluids, and the lot. I believe in it. I see no reason why some mindless, soulless, clear little blob, aquiver at the bottom of a Petri dish can't be used to aid mankind. If one argues that use of this little drop of goo destroys a human with a soul as it were, then masturbation, not to mention any form of birth control, should be declared mortal sins.

I have some passing familiarity with eugenics—the aphotic facet of genetics—the shadowy side. At the same time, I appreciate that, as we improve technology, we simply expand our 'tool set.' However, if we improve mankind itself, the potential for exponential progress is formidable indeed. I suspect the potential for disaster may be equally formidable."

For Phil there was a satisfyingly pregnant pause as Emily was perhaps absorbing what Phil had just said.

"Well, Phil, you certainly don't beat around the bush, and you most certainly have some very clear, well thought-out opinions. The fact is, though, here at the U, we would never even passingly consider engaging in any form of eugenic selectivity."

"Well, don't I feel foolish?"

"Not in the least, Mr. Carr. I find your ideas interesting. I'm quite pleased you have a very open and informed mind and you've managed to immediately clear the air, so we can cut directly to the chase."

"You're very kind, Doctor. Suppose I keep quiet for awhile and let you brief me on your activities?"

"That would be fine. I will make this briefing completely non-technical. However, I would be pleased to present the detailed science in any area you find of interest."

"Thank you."

"First, we are now pursuing many wonderful ideas that assist us in our primary project, and much, much more, as soon as we have our arms around our current project. Dr. Webber would like to brief you personally on some of these areas.

Problem is, our 'current project' has been going on for some twenty-five years and is likely to continue for at least another ten to twenty more years, until it becomes self perpetuating, or if we are lucky enough to encounter a breakthrough in some form, as yet unknown.

Here's our take on the situation. Our vision, if you will." Emily was suddenly all business. "We hope we are moving away from the hate mentalities that have plagued mankind since the emergence of human civilization. Yet organizations like the Ku Klux Klan still flourish in the U.S. and their even more poisonous ilk in areas all over the world. Hate mongering is still a best seller. Although the pendulum exhibits a slight sway from time to time, race hatred seems to be a permanent burden to be borne by humankind. Apparently, it is endemic to our nature to self destruct.

If you walk down a street in nearly any city of the world (with some possible exceptions) and see a lovely girl of one race walking hand in hand with a man or woman of another race, you will find the tension surrounding them nearly palpable.

Almost as bad, the furtive glances from all quarters bestowed when it seemed circumspect. It's difficult to imagine the depth of regard such people must hold for each other to undergo the incessant race bigotry they endure. These people must be exceedingly brave, extremely unhappy within society, with eyes always on them, destined to always be differentiated and marginalized, often outcast by their own families, and yet *they represent the very future of mankind.*

Slowly, very slowly, too slowly, we are inter-breeding. We are gradually dissolving the tiny, nearly infinitesimal genetic differences that form the barriers between humans and that foster senseless hatred, war, and genocide. There is not a country on earth that has not suffered from this malignant malady in the past, present, and will suffer well into the future, I suspect. Disregard the pain and suffering and grief caused by race hatred, instead regard eliminating hatred as nothing less than a survival issue for the human race itself. Sooner or later our differences will recede, or they will kill us and our technology is racing much faster towards the kill than it is towards the save."

"As a species are we stagnating?" Phil asked. "Is that why the sense of urgency? Have we stopped evolving, and are we letting our differences overtake us?"

"All good questions, Phil," Emily said, "and none of them easily answered. First, we are not truly a hundred percent stagnating. Genetic drift, sexual selection, abhorrent conditions in many third world areas all contribute to micro-shifts in our amino acid make-up between generations. Second, the process simply takes too long to really measure, so we are forced to use the meager evidence available to surmise (albeit somewhat weakly) that the process is slowing to the degree that our differences may indeed overtake us. Undoubtedly we are accumulating recessive genetic baggage.

Ironically, the solution will ultimately invent itself. Many thousands of years in the future (should we be lucky enough to survive that long) we will in all likelihood have interbred to the degree we will realize the 'race of mankind'—the beginnings of truly modern man. One race: dark haired, light coco-skinned, with hazel eyes, tall, intelligent, good looking, fast, strong, healthy, disease resistant, and long lived—a true non-recessive human hybrid—probably benefiting from talents as yet unknown to mankind.

"I want to be *very* clearly at this point, this 'race of mankind' would absolutely not be the product of *selective* eugenics—quite the opposite in fact. It will be the product of a hundred percent blending, equally representing every human species extant on the planet.

We will *never* explore the 'aphotic facet' of genetics, as you put it. I would suppose your definition of the aphotic facet consists primarily of selective breeding programs, elimination of races deemed recessive, in a generally Third Reich style pogrom. Incidentally, I always found it interesting that the word pogrom traces its etymology to the Russian *pogramu...* *po* (to) *gramu* (destroy as a thundery tempest). That is not the science of genetics; it's the science of atrocity...exactly what we are attempting to wipe forever from the face of the earth.

From another perspective, eugenics has a very benign aspect. It is an attempt by society to simply manage the development of human heredity. In doing so, humans would enjoy a better quality of life, benefit from higher intelligence, better health, and all the attendant returns. Methods for achieving these returns range from limiting procreation, selective breeding, and genetic engineering.

Unfortunately, these methods include elements of genocide and sterilization. As it would require a nearly deistic wisdom to administer such programs without abuse, serious scientists have abandoned it, fearing that the dangers far outweigh the potential benefits. Although 'serious scientists' vigorously pursued eugenics in the not too distant past—and I'm not just referring to Germany, but all over the world including the UK, the US, Sweden, Russia, and more.

Even your Oliver Wendell Holmes' celebrated Supreme Court voted eight to one upholding the *sterilization* of a perfectly normal young lady who had been declared incorrigible and incompetent by her step parents, probably to avert the embarrassment of her rape and subsequent pregnancy by their nephew. Holmes wrote the *ab incunabulis* decision himself, '…Charlottesville [Virginia] can prevent those who are manifestly unfit from continuing their kind.'

Your aphotic side of eugenics shines its darkness everywhere evidently, Mr. Carr. It was only because of the excesses of the Third Reich that Germany got stuck with the bill.

Let's run down the major factors that divide humans and generate hatred: Race, Religion, Culture, Language, Politics, Fear, and Economics.

For all these factors, including economics, we are developing solutions we hope may mitigate these barriers and the horrors they engender, but here's the problem: Some humans love to hate. Some humans love to kill. Some humans love to destroy. Some humans don't give a damn about mankind's future. Some humans don't give a damn about anything.

Here's another problem: We don't have time for these pernicious factors to naturally dissipate. In fact, 'natural dissipation' may equate to extinction. Whatever, we are convinced we will not survive long enough. Despite all efforts to the contrary, we are taking the path to self-destruction. We cannot abandon ourselves to the luxury of simply waiting for this process to occur at the pace of normal evolution. We must perforce produce this hybrid human in a *hot house. And this University is that hot house.*"

Phil frowned deeply and murmured, "How?"

Emily smiled fondly, reached out, and almost affectionately bunny punched his shoulder. "I'll show you."

Halfway through the lab from her office they stopped at a row of approximately forty large, beige machines that looked very much like electron microscopes mounted on large boxes, mounted with remote control and robotic apparatus. It was integrated to a large, flat-screen monitor, processing unit, and keyboard. Along one side were a series of drawer-like mechanisms and a variety of glass tubes running in and out.

"This is what you could term an electron microscope, equipped with controls that allow us to manipulate extremely small particulate substances, essentially by using retrograde lasers acting as micro-tweezers. Are you familiar with the term 'blastiocyst,' Phil?"

He thought for a moment. "I believe it's a sort of a multi-celled organelle generated by the female shortly after conception?"

"Close enough and very good! That's one key to this entire project. We engage in tissue engineering, benefiting greatly from the work of Langer and Vacanti. Ever hear of the Vacanti mouse? Not important. You see, no one has the time to simply create an environment wherein we cross-breed every race on earth with every other race on earth. It wouldn't necessarily take thousands of years—but it would certainly take hundreds and hundreds. We want to achieve this much faster, using accelerators and materials such as MSC (mesenchymel stem cells), differentiating into chondrocytes, or osteoblasts (bone, cartilage, etc.), extra cellular matrices, including fibroblasts and such, although much of this work is targeted to supporting our lander BOD of course."

"Of course," Phil mouthed.

Noting Phil's gentle sarcasm with good humor, she continued in a more generic vein "And this is exactly what we are doing. First, we had to identify a totally representative population of breeders. Most people take it for granted that there are, or were, essentially six races of man.

"We realized immediately that this was a gross oversimplification, despite the fact that this would have been much easier. Instead..." with this, Emily brought up a display on one of the monitors—mounted a high lab chair and crossed her legs in a most distracting manner, "we identified races, not so much based on the classical delineation of the races of man, but on the contemporary races of man as they have evolved into the modern articulated races of today.

Here's where we are now." The monitor now displayed a simple list of races.

1. Nordic
2. Alpine
3. Mediterranean
4. African
5. Sahara
6. Melanesian
7. Central African Pigmies
8. Bushmen (Kalahari Dessert)
9. Australoids
10. Eastern Siberian
11. Eskimo (Inuit)
12. N. American Indian
13. Japanese
14. Korean
15. Chinese
16. Indonesian

17. Malay
18. Polynesian
19. Indonesian Man Indian (sub continent)
20. Middle Eastern

Emily turned away from the monitor and looked at Phil with a slight smile. "It boiled down to twenty representative groups or twenty breeders times two—male and female. Clearly this presents a geometric expansion of the task facing us, and using conventional methods, would involve centuries of work, which is unacceptable."

Re-crossing her legs, she said, "This brings us back to the blastiocyst. This wonderful little micro-organelle is allowing us to compress generations into years—and less—less all the time, in fact. We inhibit mitosis and subsequent cytokinesis at this point in favor of somewhat female oriented meiosis leading to binary fission. But I am going to skip the science.

If you decide to take the helm of our organization, we will have adequate time to review the actual processes. For now, I will simply state that, by splitting the blastiocyst six days after conception and inserting haploid spermazoa representing multiple races, we achieve non-recursive, non-biased temporal compression.

A zygote is produced through fertilization with a sperm. When the zygote divides upon itself sufficiently, what are called blastocoels result. Without intervention, in a normal environment, which we certainly do not support here, this organelle attaches to the uterus, which becomes the basis for the placenta. Within this body of cells is the basis for stem cells, incidentally. Among the unique developments here at the U, are some astonishing uses for such cells.

Later, things like the amniotic cavity develop and an embryo is soon on the way. Things are even more complicated from here. But I see no need to burden you with an inordinate amount of detail."

Phil clearly exhibited a look of relief.

"Of perhaps equal import, we can 'force' development of stem cells in a nutrient solution in a benign, slightly energized ambience, thereby allowing us to simulate fourteen-year generations in a matter of days. The primary element that slows the process is the time it takes for our own quality-control and monitoring process."

"You apply the term 'quality control' to human reproduction?"

"Any successful process, Mr. Carr, especially one as complex as this, requires extraordinarily redundant supervision. If you are offended by the 'QC' term, perhaps you would prefer something like...ah...'pre-natal perlustration'?"

A slightly rebuffed Phil simply responded with a lopsided grin, eyebrows raised.

"In any event," Emily continued, "as we have a geometrically expansive cross-breeding task, this still requires a great deal of time. Therefore, we are constantly developing methods to expedite and improve this process.

As we progress along this evolutionary path, we suspect—or hope—we will encounter an iterative generation that may exhibit unique abilities and maybe even assist in speeding the developmental process itself. This is what we refer to as Anomalous Numen, or 'ANUMEN.' *We* tend to slightly emphasize the middle syllable (ah-*new*-min). This concatenated acronym may appear to be unduly flamboyant," she said, changing the monitor to reveal a new display:

Anomalous & Numen
Anomalous—[*uh*-nom-*uh*-*luhs*] Deviating

from the common order
Numen—[noo-min] Divine power or spirit
ANUMEN—[*uh* -noo-min] Unexpected power
ANUMINA—[*uh*-noo-mi·na] Unex
pected Powers (Plural)
ANUMINOUS—[*uh*-noo-M*uh*-nuhs] The aeth
ereal quality of ANUMEN

However, the term was carefully coined to allow it to describe behaviors relevant, not only to science, but all disciplines."

"Clearly," Phil said, "you are somehow generating progeny as part of this process."

"Yes, of course."

"Are they aware of this?"

"They are taught every step of the process. They are fully cognizant of our motivations, and our future plans."

"Do they approve?"

"Yes, nearly without exception."

"And the exceptions?"

"They do whatever they want and go wherever they wish, with an impressive stipend in their pockets. Actually, they are content to stay here and find any avocation that interests them."

"What about security?"

"They were born here. They grew up here, and as *Islanders* they have an abiding affection, even loyalty if you will, to their roots. They will have been thoroughly de-briefed. Moreover, the single knowledge we withhold from them is the location of this Island, which is one reason we maintain an excellent island transport system—air and sea. Added to this, a description of this facility would stretch most Lander's credibility, compounded by the teller's total inability to locate the island, and I don't believe we face a problem. In fact, insofar as I know, no one has opted to leave. Even if we did, these are free people. That will never change here."

Landers? "One more question, Doctor. Dr. Butler mentioned inheriting some special technology from your department that he finds quite exciting. Can you give me some idea what he's referring to?"

"Phil, our kitchens serve the finest sea food, fruits, vegetables, wines, meat, and poultry in the world. This food is highly enriched in vitamins. It contains NO carcinogens. They convey immunity to disease, can be customized for special dietary needs, and require no special storage or preservatives."

Emily's eyes grew intense. Her face darkened and veins began to appear on neck and forehead. Nostrils nearly flaring, she warmed to her topic.

"It will NEVER make you fat. No food tastes better, or costs less to produce. We could feed the world practically using only our technology and the sea water surrounding us."

Phil found himself more and more exhilarated by her concepts and profoundly moved by her infectious passion.

Emily continued. "No plant or animal has died here by a human hand for years. There has been no suffering. No guilt. No terror. No pain. No hunger. No murder! We have freed mankind from the need to kill. We need no longer be predators. Perhaps we could even stop killing each other now.

We can even adjust food runs to cure many diseases, improve intelligence, eyesight, hearing, strength...we can extend life and improve the quality of life with this food. For god's sake, our bacteria can even produce a very non-pollutive form of gasoline from sea water!

In the same manner, we produce the finest furs in the world, leathers that would be the envy of any country. We make fabrics of all kinds that are non-allergenic, that last ten times longer than any other fabric, look better, feel better, and *are* better—and within a lower cost paradigm. I would be pleased to demonstrate when we have more time."

"Has this technology been generalized to human tissues by any chance?"

"Of course, Phil, with astounding success. That's pretty much the province of Dr. Webber and his team."

"This is beyond impressive, Doctor, but many of these developments have been talked about by scientists and science-fiction writers for many years."

"True. The differences are we actually started development and research literally decades before them. Thanks to Dr. Webber, we have had nearly unlimited funding, we have been totally unfettered by secular and non-secular interference, and we have had access to the finest minds and equipment in the world. They're just starting, while we have already achieved decades of real, tangible results."

"You know, Doctor, there's a whole hell of a lot of very powerful people out there who wouldn't find what you're doing a damn bit funny. In fact, in all likelihood, they would want you to take what you've found...and make you put it back."

"We are more than well aware that many Landers would be incensed, even driven to violence, were this facility to become known. Hence our emphasis on security."

"How much technological risk do you take?"
"It's the old R&R analysis."
"Risk and Rewards?"
"Yes. Something like that at any rate. The issue is to balance the risks inherent to fostering an incipient race of Homo sapiens versus the risk of NOT tampering.

We impost a minimum of three questions at the onset, and throughout any project: Can we do it with a reasonable expectation of success? If we do it, can we control it? Will it advance science and/or the human condition?

We have a cross-disciplinary panel activated at the onset of a major project, or ground-breaking technology. Membership is variable, based on the science, technology, and objective. However, any senior faculty member may attend if they choose. Normally, Dr. Webber and I determine the make-up of the panel. Despite the fact that staff meetings are relatively rare...these panels may have an active duration of several days and debate can be very lively."

What about cloning?"

Dr. Johansen bristled and her normally attractive face darkened perceptibly. "Mr. Carr, we're attempting to work our way *out* of stagnation here. If there is any technology that more pervasively promulgates stagnation than cloning, I surely don't know what it is!'

"Understood, Doctor. But what about regenerating an army of Einstein, Hawkings, Newton, Shakespeare, Pasteur, and so on?"

"Or perhaps an army of Alexander, Napoleon, Attila, Caesar, and so on?" Emily countered. "No, Mr. Carr, let the future breed its own prodigy. As for us, we're trying to improve on those models."

"How about factors such as recessive and dominant traits, doctor? Do you attempt to manage them? Do they make for uneven development?"

"The answers are no, we do not attempt to manage genotypes and, yes, they can yield somewhat uneven results. In fact, we sort of *steamroll* over such considerations. We have comprehensively demonstrated that the compression process itself produces iterations sufficient for the long term effects of such traits to be reliably negligible. I know it sounds like an oxymoron in this lab, but we absolutely let nature take its course, producing alleles and consequential phenotypes randomly."

"You know, there are those who would contend your work here runs contrary to nature...what you are doing is...unnatural?"

Emily's face darkened even more. "We humans are *products* of natural development. We are part of nature. We *are* nature. We are *incapable* of unnatural acts. Therefore, nothing humans can do, including what we do here, is or can be unnatural. Were I to take a stone in my hand and release it while standing on the planet Earth, and the stone were to travel upward instead of falling downward...*that* would be an unnatural act. One statement I would accept as applicable to our work is perhaps we are perhaps abrogating some of man's pristine taboos...but that in no way implies we, in any way, frustrate *God's* Laws.

We exist within the natural system, and we have neither avenue of escape, nor means to rise above it. To presume humans are somehow superior to nature and natural law is the greatest arrogance I can imagine. It is blasphemy in its purest form, in fact. As for the self serving, bigoted Bible thumpers that make such inane assertions, I can only quote

Dr. Martin Luther King. *'Nothing in all the world is more dangerous than sincere ignorance and conscientious stupidity.'"*

"Whew! I have much to think about and much to digest, Doctor. We have well overrun our allotted time...but I think it was well invested. I didn't fully understand your briefing. However, I do believe I have gained a workable insight into the direction of this Island and this University. It is late. I am exhausted. Can we schedule the second session with Dr. Kahn for 0900 tomorrow morning?"

"Certainly, Phil, I'll look after it. How 'bout something to drink?"

"Bless you!"

Shortly afterward they arrived at the terrace that fronted the dining room. After helping themselves at the rolling bar, they joined several other senior staff, already into their second round of drinks. Conversation, while very cordial, was a little guarded. Phil understood. This was quite normal. After all, they were with their potential new boss. So Phil finished his drink quickly, excused himself for the purpose of organizing his notes and his thoughts, promising to return at eight for dinner.

Looking Glass

The next morning Edward provided Phil with an interactive map and instructions to the complex. Phil enjoyed navigating himself throughout the maze. He suspected things were purposely convoluted to provide residents with the illusion that they were actually amongst the random sprawl of a city, instead of an underground complex. There were even squares, circles, tree-lined streets, shops, bars, coffee shops, and news stands. He had foregone the breakfast buffet in favor of a croissant and coffee in one of the local street cafes. It was surprisingly good and even more surprising when they presented him a bill. Luckily, they accepted US Dollars, Euros, and Greek Drachma. They weren't even adverse to a tip!

More and more, this place began to feel natural and comfortable. He even found areas where the ceiling was actually a huge periscope, and he enjoyed the light and the view of a beautiful, blue, sunny sky, punctuated by a few fluffy clouds and realized he was actually seeing the sky as it now appeared above the complex. He realized in awe that the hallway itself was fashioned in such a manner as to resemble buildings with a totally realistic margin at their 'roofs' to the 'sky' and actually cast a shadow over part of the 'street.' It must be beautiful at sunset!

He was even more surprised when he turned the corner. He was facing a small park with the same beautiful sky, flowers, trees, grass, well groomed shrubs, and students playing ball. He heard birds (though saw none). He heard katydids in trees. He smelled the flowers and felt a slight breeze. Most pleasingly, he felt the heat of the sun on his face and shoulders.

The park turned onto a broad boulevard lined with trees and colorful buildings with outdoor cafes, boutiques, restaurants, bars, and bookshops. Had he awoken to this scene unknowing where he actually was, he would have sworn he was in a beautiful European village.

Then he came upon the *'piece de résistance.'* He was suddenly 'Out of town-into the countryside.' He followed a trail into a small clearing. Surrounding him was the countryside of the island, rough rocks, scrub plants, dust, sand, a view down to the sea and an endless sky above. He felt the heat of the sun, felt warm breezes, smelled wild flowers, and heard birds, the sea, and insects calling. The Island's technology had apparently reached its zenith here. In the middle of the clearing was a rise of rock and sand upon which had been built a gazebo surrounded by plants and flowers. He sat in the gazebo for a few moments enjoying the shade and marveling at the absolute reality of the clearing.

Trekking on, he wandered block after block noting how styles and usage changed. He found apartments, dorms of sorts, and began to identify classrooms and labs and conference rooms. Never did an oppressive institutional style impose itself. He had to consult his map and push himself to move for his appointment with Dr. Kahn.

Nonetheless, he appeared at Dr. Kahn's office promptly at 0900. He found Dr. Kahn hunched over a computer working what appeared to be his mail.

Kahn looked up when Phil entered his office. "Good morning, Boss. If I may have one more moment to finish this mail... got to stay up and stay in step with the Landers," he said and smiled.

"I'm not your boss yet, Doctor. And who are the 'Landers'?"

"No. But I suspect you will be. You're too good a fit for all concerned. I personally hope you join us. As to the 'Landers,' that's our shorthand for mainlanders. If the term sounds a little patronizing...well it is, Mr. Carr."

"I'm called Phil, and you are…?"

"Please, call me Sun. I'm half Egyptian and half Korean, which renders me not only damn good looking, but remarkably brilliant, and some say ornery as hell.

I teach primarily religion and very little philosophy. We do a little Plato, Socrates, Aristotle, a little Seneca, a little Lysinco for laughs, some Hume, and Kant, and some Marx, some tastes of Epicurus, Locke, Sartre, Nietzsche, Spinoza, Russell, not to mention Dr. Sun Kahn, and so on...nothing very deep and pretty much confined to how they relate to religion or human development.

We are basically an ancillary function to the main objective of the U...and a function that may indeed never come to fruition or utility.

Most of my students love me. Of those that don't, most have unfortunate proclivities for some religion or another. Fortunately their flirtations are always brief."

Dr. Kahn had a very unusual accent, which was clipped and still somewhat melodic. It made him a pleasure to listen to and rendered his colorful language ("megalomaniacal yahoos") amusing and interesting.

"You're an atheist, Doctor?"

"Not even close. Although that would in no way prevent me from being a most excellent Professor of Religion."

"Of that, I have no doubt. Agnostic?"

"Nope. But we're getting ahead of ourselves. I assume you would like a briefing providing more detail about what we show and tell our students, as well as what, if anything, we develop?"

"Exactly, Sun."

"Coffee?"

"Thank you."

Sun called for coffee and then turned his attention to a large screen monitor and keyboard.

"Do we have much time?"

"Not really."

"Okay, I won't beat around the bush, or mince words. In fact, I will in all likelihood grossly overstate many concepts for the sake of speed and clarity. I am not going to brief you on the history, proofs, research, and analysis supporting our conclusions. I'm going to distill a nine-month course and twenty-five years of study into a very few minutes.

The best place to start is from a common point of agreement. Here is that point:

The absolute, single-most important object of this University is preservation of the human race. Failing that, all the sciences, art, ANUMINA, and whatnots mean nothing.

Anything that forwards that objective, we will call a 'Qualifier.' Anything that frustrates that objective we call a 'Disqualifier.' Qualifiers and Disqualifiers can be moving targets. Religion is an example of such a moving target. In the early history of man, religion (disregarding all its evils for the moment) provided a small list," he said, then proceeded to enumerate the items. He activated his monitor:

- A moral code and one basis for law (*e.g., The Ten Commandments*).
- A repository for knowledge and history (*e.g., St. Thomas Aquinas*).
- A repository for wealth and art (*e.g., The Vatican*).

- A counterbalance for the excesses of governments (*and vice versa*).
- One of the first building blocks of civilization, culture, and architecture, and to some degree science (*when it wasn't burning some poor bastard, labeling him a heretic and achieving just the opposite*).

"There's more. This will do for the time being. But the question is, now that we have all these things...is organized religion today a Qualifier or Disqualifier?

The answer is a resounding 'Disqualifier.'

The world's religions thoroughly understand this. And they don't like it worth a damn. They are well aware that they are living anachronisms. In their desperate attempts to regain relevancy—many have become anathema.

Religion has metamorphosed from a Qualifier to a Disqualifier, over the past millennia, and is getting worse...more dangerous, militant, and fundamental, greedy, paranoid, and power starved. They secretly concede that their solecism is foreordained.

I will explain. To continue to exist, control, grow, and acquire power, the world's religions find themselves forced to trap mankind in a kind of a time suspension—like a fly in amber. They must stop, or at least control, the development of mankind—or face an inevitable obsolescence. This was true a millennia ago in many respects, as well. Consider Galileo, Savonarola and Father Guido, as just a few examples. This renders organized religion as one of the greatest Disqualifiers skulking about on our planet today and to some extent, in all of human history.

Strong words, I know, but let me demonstrate.

At its best, today, religion is a sort of placebo. It really helps or cures very little, if anything—but it makes the vulnerable feel better about things. This is dangerously counter productive, as it syllogistically entraps us to overlook our true problems and to neglect the quest for the true nature of existence—instead of facing reality and trying to master it. One of Karl Marx's truer observations was that religion is indeed the opiate of the masses. Can you imagine a spiritual leader actually making the statement, 'Some things we just weren't meant to know or understand.'?

"But surely," Phil interjected, "there are spiritual elements of real value to people?"

"Such as?"

"Well, *prayer* for example. Isn't that a curative method for resolving personal issues?"

Dr. Kahn frowned. "*Prayer*? I believe in your context you're referring to the 'Sacrament of Confession,' which really is a salve for the remorseful psyche. And you're probably better off discussing this with a psychologist instead of a philosopher or theologian. From our perspective, as long as you are enticed to believe that repugnant acts may be repeated over and over—and as long as you confess in between such acts—everything's forgotten, you'll keep on engaging in antisocial behavior.

Real prayer, however, now that's another thing altogether!

Consider an omniscient, omnipotent deity, capable of creating a situation, say a ship sinking, and is therefore fully aware of all the consequences. Now, given that you have loved ones on that ship and you pray to that deity to save them, are you not in fact implying this god is basically irresponsible, or stupid? Or both?

Either he/she/it is so incompetent, or negligent, the sinking was unforeseen, which contradicts omniscience totally; or he/she/it was just so dumb, or just so bloody-minded malicious as to set up the sinking just for the hell-of-it, or from some mysterious godly higher reason, and the prayer is *de facto* stating that god was just mean—and please, please, correct his/hers/its *mistake*.

The basic concept of prayer renders monotheistic religion a fatuous delusion. When man prayed to a pantheon of gods and goddesses, they were simply shopping for help. When you pray to a the 'One God,' you deny its infallibility—its omnipotence, omniscience. You question its motives—rendering the deity a pompous sham.

Voltaire gave us a satirical book called *Candide*, wherein he poked fun at philosophers of his day who believed they lived in 'the best of all possible worlds.' An idea that would seem to discredit the idea of prayer. But he wasn't finished yet.

Voltaire promulgated a religion called Deism, and some neo-Deists believe that prayer is useless because the universe has been created in a state of perfection. So what's to pray for? Deists generally believe, first that the creator exists—evinced by creation (existence) itself. Second, they believe that the 'laws' of the creator manifest themselves in the working of the universal physical mechanism of the cosmos themselves. third, they believe that the creator, having set into motion this colossal clockwork, is not accessible to humankind—probably not even aware of humankind, and most certainly not accountable *to* humankind. So what's to pray for? Again, to make the vulnerable feel better.

Prayer is basically an affront to God.

"How about a *moral code* and the idea of *goodness*?" Phil asked.

"*Moral Code*? Please give man some credit.

"As for the idea of *Goodness*?...That's for cake mixes and Sunday school."

"Doctor, let me try some more concepts on you," Phil said.

"Sure."

"Are you at all moved by the incredible complexity, the beauty, the intricacy of the human mind, life, the universe?"

"You sound like some kind of neo-creationist for Chrissake. Intelligent Design? If you are even remotely familiar with the scientific method, and its limitations, you surely understand you cannot objectively observe a process from the *inside*. You perceive that your corpus is a wondrous achievement of the creator. That's because you *are* the corpus. You are in absolutely no position to judge your 'wonderosity,' because you are in and surrounded by creation, looking out—not looking in. You have no relative perspective...nothing to judge against.

"Do you believe, however," Phil said, "that there are people who, in good faith, believe in Creationism?"

"Phil, it's very difficult to objectively gauge another's dept of commitment ..."

"But do you believe that there are people who, in absolute good faith, believe unquestioningly in Creationism?"

"Look. The moon happens to be four hundred times closer to the earth than the sun. It, amazingly, happens that its image is four hundred times smaller from the earth. This extraordinary relationship makes a solar eclipse of the sun possible from the earth. Do you think that 'God' designed it this way so we could get a thrill? Study the corona? Go blind from time to time by staring at lingering cosmic rays still speeding our way during an eclipse? Live in fear of the gods? *A Connecticut Yankee in King Author's Court*? You really haven't the slightest capability to understand the intelligence or beauty of your design, or any other design in the universe, for that matter. You are *in and a part of* the universe.

"You are like a white mouse in a maze. The mouse will never know the maze, but it may wonder at its corridors."

"Doctor Kahn, do you believe that there are people who …"

"I understand the question, Phil. But I don't think you understand the issue. What *I* believe is irrelevant. What really matters is what people themselves believe and the effects their beliefs have on themselves and humanity.

But if you insist, my answer is, yes. I do believe there are people who absolutely believe in Creationism. I believe that these people are either insane, stupid, or unbelievably guileless, or simply hell-bent on a delusional refuge from a reality they cannot, or will not, face. Clear, Phil?"

"The evolution of human intellect over other creatures? A divine spark?"

"Intelligence is simply an adaptive survival mechanism, like long teeth, or sharp claws."

"You know things were pretty rough and rotten throughout Biblical times and beyond. So, if you convince some gullible fools they are immortal and may live forever in grace and joy, what do you suppose they might do? Naturally, they started committing suicide! Why did the church make suicide a mortal sin? Because they sold this idea too well. People starting killing themselves in favor of the promised paradisiacal afterlife. This could seriously cut into their market share, so *voila*! It's a *mortal sin*.

This same myth is employed by the worst terrorists, in reverse. They happily slaughter their own, stipulating, what the hell, we're just getting them up to their reward all the faster.

The fecklessness of your questions overwhelm me, Mr. Carr, and I suspect by intent! I think, in fact I'm sure, you're baiting me and some of my first-year students do it as well as you." Dr. Kahn accompanied this with his most ingratiating smile to take the edge off his contrived disgruntlement.

"Please defer your question about the illusion of equal rights and God-given rights to Dr. Alexander."

"Okay, Doctor, one last one...how about the purpose of everything?"

"Why are we put here? What's the purpose of life? Things like that, Phil? Nature of reality? *Allegory of the Cave*? Things like that?"

"Yeah. Things like that."

"Beats hell out of me, Phil. We're barely warming up on 'what and how' things work. We're eons from 'why' things work."

The origins of life. We are truly star-seed...the carbon-based organic molecules from dying super-nova. Transpermia? The first life appeared on Earth some five-hundred million years after formation of the planet, a heartbeat in cosmic terms. Damned fast in Earth scale too. Almost unbelievably fast. Perhaps life in the universe shares more than the heavy elements from dying stars? Perhaps we all share a common genesis? A colossal physical and mental cohesion, without limit, without end. Call it Cosmos if you like. 13.5 billion years is one hellofa long time to evolve into, or from a god, don't you think?

Funny, I always rejected the Transpermia idea as no more than a mental crap-out. Science couldn't quite work out how inanimate matter made the leap into living, moving, consuming, and reproducing matter on Earth. So we theorized it came from somewhere else in the universe. Doesn't explain a damn thing, but it allows us to evade the problem. I always felt the same way about water."

"Water?" Phil asked.

"Yes. Water. H^2O. They can't seem to define the forces that might have worked on Earth to generate such vast quantities of this interesting triangular bonding of hydrogen and oxygen. So, just as with Transpermia...they theorize that it fell from the skies...comets. Strangely, more and more these two theories make sense. Particularly if you view this as some sort of cosmic seeding process. And most in particular, if you view the universe as a single plasmic event."

"Sounds almost mystical."

"Don't think it's not. We have not developed, and may never develop, a unified field theory. Stephen Hawkings stated that if we achieved such a theory, we might 'understand the mind of God.' A brave sound indeed. But considering the source... could be. Or maybe string theory's the answer. Multi-verses. Maybe we're all just fiddling around."

Phil smiled at the small pun.

Dr. Kahn continued. "In the midst of all this wonderment, and far more, we are quite content to preach and pray and slaughter each other for a thousand bogus rationales, and a thousand loathed heterodoxy, greedily fondling our egos all the while. Meanwhile, I fool around trying to cobble together some sort of unified theory of religion so the masses can anoint themselves with goat's blood and dance around it."

"Doctor, I hope that one day you will discover the secret to mastering your meekness."

Kahn laughed appreciatively and not the least self-deprecatingly.

"In fact, you talk more like a scientist, a cosmologist, than a philosopher or theologian."

"Very true, Mr. Carr. Despite the apathetic pace of theologic thought and research, science hasn't been nearly so leaden. So in a very real sense, science, progressive theology, and philosophy grow closer all the time, whether organized religions sanction it, or not. Personally, I don't give a sprout's damn what the hell they think they can sanction."

Returning to his line of thought, Doctor Kahn continued. "The problem really started with monotheism and the eighteenth Dynasty Pharaoh Akhenaton (1350-1334 BC). Before (and after) there were plenty of resurrectionist gods to go around. The Egyptians, Assyrians, Romans, Greeks, Vikings, Persians, Babylonians, and many other civilizations benefited from this precept. People could pretty much pick and choose their gods based on the needs at hand like good crops, fertility, good health, fun on a Saturday night, whatever…so no one god became so powerful it could become totally despotic. True, there were Odin and Zeus and Amon and Osiris and their ilk. But even they weren't truly omnipotent. And they certainly never aspired to omniscience.

The gods and their attendant priests were compelled to become competitive. Gods existed to be worshipped and supported, thereby paid, and to serve their supplicants.

Politically, it took mankind many centuries to learn the relationship between rulers and the ruled and the democratic ethic, *dimokratia*. In fact, many are just now really becoming enlightened in this respect.

However, strangely enough, we somehow had a semi-democratic ideal in religion millennia ago. Gods were a product of the people's will and the people's needs. Then a bunch of monotheistic predators destroyed it.

Religion was always good business. Trouble is they got greedy. They wanted a monopoly. And, as with all monopolies, they ultimately disregarded the ideas and needs of the peoples they were allegedly serving. Goodbye theo-democratic ideals. I am well aware that 'theo-democratic' is my own term, unrecognized beyond this campus.

There were some benign, even gentle, haunts and bypaths on the journey to rigorous, inflexible monotheism...such as henotheism (the worship of a single deity that didn't require the destruction or denial of other gods), of course polytheism, and my personal favorite Kat henotheism (the graduation from god to god as the individuals needs and enlightenment evolved)."

With a slight tilt of his head, Dr. Kahn paused. "I trust you realize, Phil, that I am speaking in the broadest of generalities, for the sake of brevity, ennui, not to mention simplicity?"

"Don't think for a minute I don't appreciate it, Doctor."

With a knowing smile, Dr. Kahn continued. "At the time of Akhenaton, the god Amon Rae was becoming a source of concern...not Amon's fault...his priests were becoming too rich and powerful, to the point they started to challenge the Pharaoh. In fact, I personally suspect they may have been moving towards the precipice of monotheistic dogma themselves. This could be one explanation for Akhenaton's extraordinary theologistic leap. Mind you, this idea is entirely unsubstantiated."

Phil moued. "I don't think there is such a word as 'theologistic.'"

"Then we'll have to update the dictionary," Kahn said, smoothly unabashed.

The man does have an ego, Phil thought.

"Akhenaton's solution was to elevate a previously somewhat lesser deity (Aton—the god of the setting sun) to the 'One God.' In fact this was essence of heliolatry.

"Heliolatry?" frowned Phil.

"Sun worship. And on top of that, Aton would only communicate through Akhenaton and his lovely wife, Nefertiti. Then he moved all operations to a newly built city (Amarna), allowing him to easily ignore all other priests and gods, disenfranchise them, and terrorize the hell out of them by remote control.

Many have observed that the transition from Aton to Jesus Christ was very short. One easily metamorphosed into the other.

Did you know in Christ's time there were many messiahs preaching the same dogma? Son of God, born of a virgin, miracles and all that. Many were crucified. Yet they dwell now in obscurity. Marketing is everything.

Ultimately, Akhenaton brought down his own ruin and nearly of Egypt, itself. Luckily, monotheism was quickly stamped out. Unluckily, the seeds had been sown, and later came to fruition in the forms of Yahweh, Yahvé, Jehovah, Ahura Mazda, Elohim, Allah, Siva, God, Jesus of Nazareth, and so on...each the one true god, and a jealous god that must be worshiped and be served, more than serve.

There *was* some refreshing light from the East however. How much do you know about Buddhism, Shinto, Confucianism, and Hinduism? Shinto and Hinduism are beautiful, philosophical religions. And guess what? They're multi-theist! Buddhism and Confucianism are based on inner development. No one to worship, or be ruled by, or fight for, or die for, or kill for, or give your wealth to, or stoically persist in ignorance for. These ancient and sage religions are as healthy and dynamic today as they were millennia ago. Yet they haven't really made too much progress on their way West. I wonder why? Could it be they don't try to concentrate power and wealth?

Phil, am I bouncing around the map too much for you?"

"No, not at all, Sun. You're going fast, and that's good. I need a thumbnail sketch at double-time. You're doing great."

"Okay, so let's go a little further into the effects of monotheism. Multi-theism presented people with a whole pantheon of gods from which to choose. If one lets you down, try another. Stay loose, stay flexible, have fun...enjoy religion. If you want a child, there's one for fertility, good crops, love, good health, wealth, wisdom, necessity, debauchery, even war, whatever you want. These could be gods of fun and love...some liked to get laid by mortals on warm summer nights...some were even pranksters.

Plus there was a sense of sport, fun, even humor. 'My god can *whup* your god,' and so on.

All this was lost under monotheism, and something far darker took its place: Intolerance. When there were lots of fun, competing gods, it was rare to fight wars over religion. Certainly there were wars because peoples wanted other peoples land, or wealth, or they just didn't like them. But religion? Not really.

All the way back to pre-history there were wars of aggression, colonization, revolutions, independence and liberation, trade wars, dynastic succession, expansion, boarder disputes, wars to conquer, wars to stimulate business, disputes over economic and political systems, even wars based on kidnap, extortion, and assassination. There were wars where no one knew *what* the hell they were for. But religion? Not truly. Not until somewhat modern times.

Even the crusades were far more motivated by the acquisition of wealth and plunder, spices, and culture, and later bogus relics like the Holy Grail, the Sacred Spear, and so on, than true religious fervor. In these times, if you had one of these relics, you were required to build a church for it. Conversely, if you wanted to build a church, you needed a holy relic. All of this made for a booming business, built-in demand. And there was an endless supply. It could be a rag, a rusty piece of iron, a tooth, a piece of bone, or a nail. They favored these clap-trap souvenirs more than the thousands of bodies they ground into a gristly red paste to acquire them.

When the charismatic Pope Urban II called for a holy war to take back Jerusalem from the Turks, allegedly to assist the crumbling Byzantine Empire, he promised his recruits that, by engaging in this war, combatants would win an automatic entry to heaven, and for the purposes of the Crusade (Jihad?) it was alright to kill non-Christians (Infidels?). Sound familiar? You can almost imagine the Pope parading in robes through France and Italy, distaining his *camelauchum* and *mozzetta,* in favor of *jilbab* and *hadith.*

The resulting carnage, however, was *beyond* imagining.

Of course, today, we have Mullahs and Maumaus and Boombas and whatnot spewing the same idiotic poison and, if they push it far enough, I'm sure we'll have priests and ministers and Bible Thumpers and all manner of Evangelical shaman vomiting the same deadly crap. I suspect many already are.

Interestingly, this provoked the slaughter and plunder of tens of thousands of Jews across Europe. Not to mention the thirty million innocents (mainly Catholics and Protestants) ultimately killed in the Inquisition. The Spanish got a bum rap on that one by the way. The Spanish Inquisition? Hell no. The Church's Inquisition. All of Europe joined in the fun and profit. Many pious murderers grew wonderfully wealthy, while entire families were burned alive. God help you if you had a nice home, or a good business, or even a pretty face when the Inquisition Man came to town.

Our old friend Monotheism stipulates the 'One True God.' Any other gods are spurious and evil, as are the peoples who worship them.

Stamp out these gods. Raze their temples. Destroy their images. Exterminate their worshipers. And they did. With a passion. Under Gregory VII, there was a massive, passionate Crusade. A Passion of Jesus. After all, Jesus was crucified in Jerusalem. The streets ran red with blood.

Of course Islam retaliated. With a passion. Under Saladin, Salah ad-Din, Salahuddin Ayyubi, there was a massive, passionate Jihad. A Passion of Mohammad. After all, Mohammad ascended to heaven in Jerusalem. The streets ran red with blood.

In deference to Saladin, however (in reality a man to be admired), at the end of his siege, he relented and demonstrated mercy to the surviving Jews and Crusaders. He released them unharmed, in peace. Wonder weather the Crusaders would have demonstrated such generosity? Well they didn't.

One will never know for sure, but I am convinced that many did (and still do) kill for a real belief in their god, but certainly, most others masquerade in religious robes to disguise their own real unholy motives (and still do). Either way, monotheism paved the way for a legion of horrors to follow, and sucked the fun out of religion altogether, forever.

And in any event, their motives are irrelevant. Their overt actions and the effects are the same. Many would conclude that religion, used in such a manner, is like a cankerous tooth that must be uprooted so nothing can hang onto it, and nothing can hide under it, or rot behind it. I wouldn't have the remotest clue how to accomplish this without tooth extraction, other than to *vaccinate* the gums. As you may be aware, we are attempting to prepare such a vaccine here on the Island.

Tragically, however, humans have mandated monotheism into a one-way street. Man cannot now introduce a pantheon of new gods to mix and match to the needs of a troubled and essentially paganistic mankind. We're far too *sophisticated* and *advanced* to consider such a concept. Too many sanctimonious SOB's simply would not allow it. That ship has sailed. We're mired in monotheism like stink in a slaughter house."

Phil moued, "I don't think there is such a word as 'paganistic,' either."

Ignoring the remark, Dr. Kahn ordered more coffee and continued.

"Monotheism, by investing and concentrating the powers of one god into a church, geometrically advanced the cause and environment for organized religion. Simply stated, the new religions had to become even more highly organized to control the minds, actions, and wealth of millions of worshipers.

Let's review some attributes of organized religion. You may not agree with all of them, nor do all these attributes apply equally to all religions, but the number of them is nearly overwhelming. Please bear in mind that these are the attributes

that conclude that organized religion, monotheistic religion, is a *Disqualifier*." Dr. Kahn activated his presentation screen, and a list came into view.
- Intolerant
- Dogmatic
- Judgmental
- Domineering
- Chastising
- Self-Serving
- Acquisitive
- Ritualistic
- Political
- Sacrificial
- Warlike

"Now, if we seek documentary support of these assertions, we need only look as far as the Ten Commandments (there are actually a numbered seventeen) that dominate practically all religions in some form today. They date back in some form over 3,350 years and are first found in the *Egyptian Book of the Dead*, probably the oldest religious document in human history, and the basis for much to follow, including many elements of the Bible. Prior to production of the papyrus scrolls themselves, these writings were committed in pyramid text, or as inscriptions in the interiors of sarcophagi. Over 20,000 books in scroll form have been found, mostly in sarcophagi, or their tombs.

One of the most complex elements of the *Book of the Dead* is called the 'Negative Commandments'…more than forty or so 'sins,' each managed by a different god…and by responding in the negative to each sin, the soul of the newly dead moved on to the next step…weighing of the heart and so on...and finally to the afterworld if successful. Many of these Negative Commandments found their way into the Ten Commandments, in one form or another—however, they never fell into the trap of monotheism. In fact, a whole pantheon of gods participated in the Negative Commandments ordeals. These, interpreted in conjunction with the customized commandments, lead us to the early Jews and then Christians, who trace direct lineage to Egypt. In fact, in the case of the Christians, Isis, Osiris, and Horus serve as counterparts to Jesus of Nazareth and his lineage.

Bottom line? The *Book of the Dead* served as the basis of the Old Testament and the Koran, therefore, Judaism, Christians, and Mohammadism. Its primary difference? It was uncorrupted by monotheism.

There is an interesting little set of proscriptions called the Seven Noahide Laws. Much like the *Book of the Dead*, they primarily address things man should *not* engage in. Unlike the Ten Commandments, however, they are very straightforward and contain no monotheistic agenda. There's been a good deal of debate over the centuries whether these laws were given to Adam or to Noah, or to Noah from Adam. Whatever. They provoke some interesting debates as to whether man as a carnivore breaches a commandment. All in all they're pretty interesting. I can get you a copy if you like. Meantime, The Ten Commandments."

Dr. Kahn activated his viewer again:
The Ten (seventeen) Commandments (or Decalogue)
I. Then God spoke all these words:
II. I am the Lord your God, who brought you out of the land of Egypt, *out of the house of slavery*
III. You shall have no other gods before me.

IV. You shall not make for yourself *an idol*, whether in the form of anything that is in heaven above, or that is on the earth beneath, or that is in the water under the earth.

V. You shall not bow down to them or worship them for I the Lord your God am a jealous God, punishing children for the iniquity of parents, to the third and the fourth generation of those who reject me,

VI. But showing steadfast love to the thousandth generation of those who love me and keep my commandments.

VII. You shall not make wrongful use of the name of the Lord your God, for the Lord will not acquit anyone who misuses his name.

VIII. Remember the Sabbath day, and keep it holy.

IX. Six days you shall labor and do all your work.

X. But the seventh day is a Sabbath to the Lord your God you shall not do any work—you, your son or your daughter, *your male or female slave*, your livestock, or the alien resident in your towns.

XI. For in six days the Lord made heaven and earth, the sea, and all that is in them, but rested the seventh day therefore the Lord blessed the Sabbath day and consecrated it.

XII. Honor your father and your mother, so that your days may be long in the land that the Lord your God is giving you.

XIII. You shall not murder.

XIV. You shall not commit adultery.

XV. You shall not steal.

XVI. You shall not bear false witness against your neighbor.

XVII. You shall not covet your neighbor's house you shall not covet your neighbor's wife, or male or female slave, or ox, or donkey, or anything that belongs to your neighbor.

"You can see," Sun said, "that more than half of them are simply directed at enforcing the governing deity's power—long on monotheism and actually pretty short on advice for living a good life."

Phil gestured with his hand first at the screen and then in a general way. "I notice by your highlighting you seem to disapprove of the proscription against adultery."

Sun irreverently dismissed Phil's observation with a grimace. "Forced or ordained fidelity is no more than a bland form of benign slavery."

"I notice you highlight the irony that God freed the Jews from slavery in Egypt, so they could escape, only to own slaves themselves, with the apparent, or tacit sanction of God."

"Yes. For one thing, it's highly probable that the Jews were never slaves in Egypt, and I think it's a wonderful example of why the Bible is really no longer licit. It's pretty much an anachronism. It's like worshiping a third-century plow."

"What about your highlighting of the proscription against idols?"

"How exactly would you define the Crucifix, the Star of David, the Islamic Star and Crescent?

"So within the space of a few lines, we have a God who is self-admittedly ego-centric, insecure, and jealous, and a bigot, prejudiced to the degree that he acquiesces to the slavery of any poor *nebech* unlucky enough to be a *goyim*—a *goyim,* in fact, who happens to be one of his children, allegedly created by his own hand, in his own image, a product of his love.

Now, does that *sound* like the creator of the goddamned universe to you?!

"We—or I should say our students—have taken a cut at a redraft. We would never remotely have the temerity to call them the Commandments; instead, we call them the <u>Counsel of Ten</u>. Catchy title, don't your think? This time there really *are* only ten."

Again he activated the monitor.

Counsel of Ten

I   Humans are counseled that they alone are answerable for their moral codes & their laws
II   Humans are counseled to kill no thing, save to endure, or to righteously deliver others
III   Humans are counseled not to lie, steal, nor to honor wealth above the welfare of others
IV   Humans are counseled not to hate, nor to foment hate, angst, or animus within others
V   Humans are counseled not to persecute, save to survive, or to rightfully deliver others
VI   Humans are counseled not to willfully foster ignorance, nor to promulgate obtuseness
VII   Humans are counseled to cherish the fruition of existence and earth and the firmaments
VIII   Humans are counseled that no leader, or country, or dogma may absolve human warfare
IX   Humans are counseled to openly aspire to knowledge and quest the nature of creation
X   Humans are counseled to freely share knowledge, abstaining ascendancy, or dictum

"They take a little thinking. The prose is certainly a little grandiloquent—but this wording is florid by intent, to foster the need of interpretation and consideration. And humans just don't seem to take straight talk seriously."

"Is there a bottom line at the end of this, Sun?"

"You bet there is."

"Yesss, Doctor?"

"Something I mentioned earlier: Deism. Are you familiar with it?"

"Umm...I think so...something from revolutionary days in the American Colonies, I think."

"Excellent, Phil, though Deism goes back a deal further than the colonies. As I said earlier, we learned of it primarily through Voltaire and later through thinkers such as Thomas Paine. The elegance of Deism is it recognizes creation without all the baggage and the mumbo jumbo.

It accepts the creator—whether the creator gives a damn, or is even aware of what we do—who knows?

It rejects miracles, literature that claims to hold the word(s) of God, the holiness of the prophets, and Jesus as God's son. In fact, it rejects most elements of organized religion and has an interesting term for its purveyors—Priestcraft.

Priestcraft is a term which, I believe, can be easily generalized to all major religions.

But back to Deism. If we're looking for a common ground for all religions that does not offend or express a bias, we think Deism can be rigged for the part. A god with satellite prophets (Mohammad, Jesus, Buda...), all of which are paths to the same destination—which we are customizing for use by every human on earth—an enormous job. I believe you now have the answer to your previous questions as to whether I am an atheist, agnostic, or whatever."

"You're a Deist."

"Close." He smiled, then brought another image up on the screen.

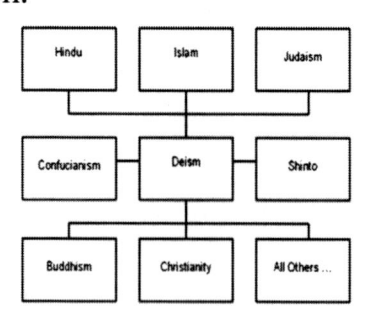

"In your own way, Doctor, you're bringing back multi-theism, as multi-deism!"

"Bingo, Phil! Our studies indicate that we might be able to attract as many as three billion, six-hundred million people if well executed.

"But here is the important part. We're not really trying to convert them. We're trying to *de-fang* them. Trying to coax them away from the darkness of their grandfather's ignorance and superstition and greed for control. We're not selling another damned-fool religion. We're selling peace. And it appears, unfortunately, that the only way to sell them peace is to sugar coat it is with another damned-fool religion.

"As we admit, there are many, many causes of war, man's own bloody-minded nature being one of the primary causes, and we can't attack all the causes at once. We happen to be working on one of the most pernicious—the cause called 'religion.' That's about enough for now. I think you get the picture. It really boils down into two simple areas (Sun brought up a graph on his monitor):

- Our studies suggest humans exist under an interesting paradox. The less danger we are in as individuals, the more danger we are in as a race. In early pre-history, humans could have easily been totally wiped out by animals, famine, disease, flood, volcanoes, or apocalyptic weather. These things still occur, but by-in-large the vast majority of us overcome them. Our current progress indicates that the primary threat to survival of the human species is humans themselves. Should we be lucky enough to survive, then comes cosmic danger. GRB's, huge comets, mountain-sized asteroids, our sun going nova or becoming a red giant, or a nearby

sun going super nova, mega volcanoes, and so forth. No surviving it.
- We must equip ourselves to face the cosmic extinction. Essentially colonize non-terran space. We humans have a lamentably short march of time with which to accomplish this. Yet, instead, we squander our time and resources on war, hatred, superstitions, and cynical, greedy charlatans masquerading as messiahs.

"Several disciplines have discovered incidents in the past that, were they to occur today, would kill so many contemporary humans, the death count would exceed the entire human population of say, 80,000 years ago. These incidents actually did occur in the realm of 80,000 years ago, or earlier. Yet mankind *did* survive them. These are empirically proven."

"What sort of incidents, Doctor?"

"Mmm. Mid to semi-major celestial events (comet or asteroid impacts), planet-scale volcanism (what they call "super volcanoes), extended or extraordinary or geographic extreme meteorology, and so forth."

"Can you give me an example of, say, a volcanic event that was race threatening?"

"Sure. Lake Toba in today's Sumatra erupted around 75,000 years ago. It covered the entire equatorial Earth's stratosphere with sulfuric acidic gasses for years. This profoundly cooled the Earth. And there was mass annihilation...across-species."

"So, how did we survive?"

"Beats hell outa me. Mankind's a pretty tough beastie, I guess. Or, what the hell, maybe something was looking out for us? Our objective here is not to sell mankind one more foolish religion as I said earlier, nor is it to tear down anything. We are simply trying to develop a moderating influence that may buy mankind some very, very valuable time, and maybe...maybe survive. Okay?"

"Cosmic death could make an incursion at any time."

"Correct. All the legions of hell could be crashing down upon us as we speak."

"So there's really nothing we can do presently to protect ourselves."

"Nothing. Not really."

"So we ...?"

"... so we move as fast as we possibly can. We try to develop a common sense of urgency."

Doctor Kahn paused, and Phil didn't say anything for a moment.

"Okay. Doctor," Phil said, finally. "I enjoyed it and I thank you. See you at lunch?"

"With pleasure, Phil. As Landers go...you'll do."

The Doctor unexpectedly turned on Phil, suddenly very serious, looking at him with an expression strangely akin to *sympathy*.

"Phil, do you believe that Jesus of Nazareth was unique?"

"Unique in what respect, Doctor?"

"Don't we *all* suffer and even die to some degree for the sins of our brethren? At least the best of us? To save them? A salvation of a quiet sort? Was he alone in this respect? I think not. I strongly suspect *you* will suffer exactly *that* in the future. And I believe, Mr. Carr...I believe your suffering will be *hell on wheels*." With a penetrating stare he closely regarded Phil for a time, until Phil began to feel rather uncomfortable.

Just as suddenly, he said, "I have an interactive map to Dr. Alexander's office for you, by the way. I think you would find it an interesting walk. However, I'm afraid you're running pretty late. I can call you a PM if you like."

"What's a 'PM'?"

"A People Mover. There are interactive guide transponders at every intersection and turnoff throughout the complex. The PM's allow you to stand, sit, or even lie down and let the PM take you to your destination quickly and efficiently. There are onboard sensors that detect pedestrians, other PM's, in fact any object on the route, so you can enjoy the scenery, read, work, eat, even sleep. The deeper and wider this complex grows, the more widespread the use of PM's. Ever read *Lost Horizon*?"

"Hilton's finest in my opinion." Phil said and smiled.

"Well, if you remember the Sub-Lama, or Assistant Dali, or whatever, he took sleep in very small increments, whenever the opportunity arose, thus saving time and conserving energy. We have hundreds of people doing the same on our PM's. Like to try one?"

"Sure."

Sun made a few quick strokes on his computer and then turned around. "Be here in two minutes. I took the liberty of alerting Dr. Alexander that you would arrive in 16.5 minutes."

In exactly two minutes, a very small vehicle stopped at Sun's office. It was a pleasingly sleek, soft blue ceramic looking sort of a three-wheeled chariot. A railing atop the front end was clearly intended for standing. Behind the tiny standing area was a fairly generous passenger seat with various controls on the right armrest.

Phil looked at Sun. "Pretty cool, doc. What's it run on?"

"Electricity I think...though I'm not really sure. It seems to draw power and navigation directly from the floor, or walls, or whatever."

Shaking his hand, Phil stepped aboard.

A throaty, gender-neutral voice quietly inquired, "Ready to depart?"

"Yes."

"Please take hold of the hand rail or be seated. Should you elect to be seated, please fasten your seat belt as well."

Philip decided to stand and take hold of the railing, but (though there were few people in the area) he quickly felt self conscious—like a triumphant general parading on his gilded chariot into ancient Rome—so he chose to be seated, and the PM noiselessly continued its journey to Dr. Alexander's department.

The Prudence of Jurists

The law of God is a law of change, and...when the Churches set themselves against change as such, they are setting themselves against the law of God.

George Bernard Shaw

The PM's seat was very comfortable, much like the wing chairs found in gentlemen's clubs, except for sleek styling and materials that perfectly blended with the PM itself. Its assembly was skillful to the degree that it had the appearance of a singly-cast unit. His attention was first drawn to the armrest controls, slightly recessed into the side of the right armrest. Some sort of communications apparatus assisted with a visual display monitor and what appeared to be a miniaturized, very flat PC. He could detect tuning apparatus for the same monitor. For the moment the monitor only showed "Mr. Carr to Dr. Alexander" and some sort of coordinates. There was a tiny liquid dispenser, with small drop-down cups. And perhaps most interesting was a selector for "Mode of Motivation," so he pushed it. Immediately the monitor displayed four choices:

- Standard Mode (with an "*" blinking beside it)
- Bicycle Mode
- Hand & Arm-Drive
- Bicycle & Hand & Arm-Drive

Clearly, this vehicle could be used for exercise as well as transport. The basic power of the PM seemed to be electric, although he made a note to ask about this. He noted recessed pedals for feet on either side of the standing area, as well as hand pumps at each end of the handrail. The feature he missed was a steering mechanism. Apparently, the PM reserved this function for itself and Phil assumed that, should there be some loss of power or function, either to the PM or its guidance acuities, the vehicle or vehicles would simply stop. Then he realized that the Arm-Drive handles would double for steering.

Phil was traveling through the most remarkable periscope yet, down a small windy road between two massive peaks toward the sea. Sea *en face*, beach down below, azure sky above, he seemed to be alone, so he unselfconsciously activated the "Recline" indicator regarding the beautiful clear sky and quickly found he was so comfortable he was convinced he could indeed cat nap *à la Lost Horizon*.

Back in sitting position, he watched as the narrow road wound down closer to the sea, surrounded on both sides by mountainous outcroppings culminating in huge cliff faces. The almost needlessly excessive winding of the road and its swift descent would render it very difficult to see from above, or from the water, or even the land for that matter. Phil perceived this as a tactical advantage not altogether unintentional. At the same time, he failed to see its necessity.

Prismic technology seemed to have an unending capacity to surprise.

Phil felt a cool ocean breeze, laced with the rich scents of seaweed and salt, with flinty sand blowing up the small canyon between the cliffs. The wind was rising and the temperature dropping. Suddenly, he was on the beach. Pristine white, blinding, richly textured cliffs to one side and a dazzling aquamarine sea to the other, wind whipping through his hair, it literally took his breath away.

Then came a sharp right turn, into the surf and under the water! Cool, surrealistic and so clear. Here, he appreciated the power of prisms to the right, to the left, above and below. The effect was complete. He was underwater! Above, he saw the sparkling sea in reverse, below the surface. He never tired of the view when he snorkeled and it was never more hypnotic than this. He could see for dozens of meters in all directions.

Suddenly, his PM had become an undersea sled and Phil chuckled inwardly as he found himself actually holding his breath. Good grief! Think of what they could do for marine exploration and research. He envisioned huge labs constantly monitoring particularly interesting reef and seabed areas with no more risk or inconvenience than commuting to an office. What a tourist industry.

How about an underwater museum with visitors strolling around, in and out, and over the Titanic, the Great Barrier Reef, volcanic vents two miles down? As far as he knew, there had to be a physical link between the periscope and the viewing area. If that link were unnecessary, or could be broken, he could see these things in orbit, on the moon...a new era of space exploration. The uses were endless.

As his vision became more acclimated he saw, just beyond total clarity, a wall! The wall was built on bedrock, rising some twenty meters to the surface of the sea itself. A sort of artificial reef spanned the limits of his vision, it was crudely constructed by piling large even blocks from a wide base to a peak some twenty-five centimeters below the surface. It was quite obviously contemporary. There were no significant growths, nor had the sea worn away its crisp lines. Phil knew he was seeing real-time periscopic images. What he was seeing existed. It was real. It must consist of hundreds of thousands of blocks. But why?

Before he could consider this further, he rose from the sea as quickly as he had entered it and quietly stopped in front of Dr. Alexander's office door.

Upon entering, Phil found a fairly routine reception area. A pretty young lady at the reception desk, lots of chairs and coffee tables covered with magazines and tasteful décor all round. He felt back at home.

"Hello, I'm Philip Carr to see Dr. Alexander—and very late I'm afraid."

"Hello, please go in. Dr. Alexander is waiting for you."

A real lawyer's office! Books everywhere, paneling, green lamps, lovely view to the sea, and a huge desk with several visitor's chairs, made Phil feel really at home.

Dr. Alexander stood, extended a hand and gave Phil a firm handshake and a genuine smile. "Welcome, Mr. Carr. I imagine this is the most familiar surrounding you have encountered yet."

"That much is certain, Dr. Alexander. I'm terribly sorry to be so late."

"Clearly, you're coming from Dr. Kahn, so you should count yourself lucky to be here before lunch. Besides, most people are late around here, and it's refreshing to hear someone apologize. How did it go with Dr. Kahn, if you don't mind me asking?"

"Excellent. Very interesting. I think I'm starting to understand what they are trying to achieve."

"Good news indeed. Coffee?"

"No thanks."

"I didn't ask about Dr. Kahn out of mundane curiosity. You see, we take the approach that law grows out of the ethos and philosophy of society, culture, or religion if you like. This places us squarely in the chase position in the production line after Kahn. So, whatever Kahn's people come up with, we pretty much try to bolt on. We will take their *ethos* and express it in terms consistent with an interpretable, enforceable legal framework."

"I understand, Shad."

"Do you agree with our approach?"

"I really don't see another approach. On what can a legal framework be based, if not a system of pragmatic ethos?"

"Exactly. I believe you would agree, along with the briefing yesterday, we fully understand each other?"

"Essentially, yes. But you did make one statement yesterday about democracy not necessarily being the ideal form of government?"

"Well, to be honest, I don't see democracy's track record as that much better than other forms. Democracy has most certainly suffered its share of abuses and inequities...even despots. Hell, the old Soviet Union and the Third Reich masqueraded in democratic garb...elections and what not.

However, I really stated that it might not be the *ideal* form of government for *all* societies. Quite different than saying it was not *the* ideal form. There are four main issues at work here. First, Legal Systems; second, Economic Systems; third, Government Systems; and fourth, Human Rights. The first three can be mixed and matched, pretty freely and in a very pragmatic manner.

You could have a democratic communist who employees the Napoleonic Code, a parliamentary socialist, a capitalistic monarchy and so on. The first three types are really not worth fighting wars over, despite the behaviors exhibited by some countries. They are neither malevolent nor benign. They constitute simply a pragmatic means of managing peoples and economies and critical services within a common geography.

If you ask me, the U.S. and the U.K., and to a far smaller extent the EU are as domineering and dogmatic as the old USSR was in spreading Communism, in their pervasive attempts to promulgate Democracy worldwide. Someone should tell them the Cold War is over. They won! They behave as though they actually *miss* the Cold War. Maybe they do. Perhaps it was the most efficient method for maintaining a state of widespread anxiety, without actually pulling a weapon? Keep those defense revenues coming in? Keep people hating each other and loving their gaily-colored bit a cloth they call "flags"? This may be a graphic example (not to mention an elegant guise) of how world leaders attempt to spread their power and control, not their beneficence. Not remotely close to beneficence.

How the hell can one autonomous country believe they have the right to determine, or even influence, the governmental structure of another autonomous country? They *don't* have that right. But they *do* have the moral responsibility to ensure that no peoples anywhere on Earth are abused and robbed of their rights.

Here's a very frivolous Platonic allegory: One man sees that another man is drowning. Assuming he has the physical prowess of doing so...the man has an obligation to attempt to save the other man's life. Can we call that a given, Phil?"

"Yes. Certainly."

"Okay, now we take the same two men. This time the other man is not drowning. In fact, he is in no difficulty whatsoever. He is swimming just fine and enjoying the Back Stroke. This time, the first man jumps in the water and starts pulling him about, nearly drowning him, because he is not using the Dog Paddle. Ridiculous. No?"

"Quite ridiculous. Yes."

"So, Phil, we substitute 'drowning' with 'death or Suffering' and 'save' with 'human Rights.' We substitute 'back Stroke' with, say...'Communism,' and 'dog Paddle' with, say...'Democracy.' Pretty silly, eh?"

"Damned silly."

"So...the real issue is the fourth issue of Human rights. Who cares what the form of government is, or the economic system, or even the legal matrix in some respects, as long as fundamental human rights are rigorously respected. The right to freedom, life, even-handed, non-corrupt recourse to the courts, speech, and an open, non-biased forum for thought and opinions. These are things worth fighting for.

Instead of spreading democracy, Marxism, fascism, socialism, or some such hoodoo throughout the world, we should be spreading human rights and stop confusing those poor bastards we're allegedly trying to aid."

Dr. Alexander stopped for a breath and a sip of water, then continued.

"Human rights and democracy are not necessarily linked by the way. Case in point, remember the Bill of Rights had to be appended (or amended if you will) to the Constitution before American democracy truly recognized basic human rights. The Constitution was ratified on September 17, 1787. The Bill of Rights was not appended until December 15, 1791. So, we marched along for over four years in the absence of guarantees about our rights of free speech, bearing arms, freedom of assembly, protection from search and seizure, freedom of religion, and many more.

By the same token, communism, monarchies, and such don't necessarily, or sometimes even remotely, preclude human rights.

Logic would suggest then that we might be well advised to sever the connection between a governmental form and the cardinal issue of rudimentary human rights."

"Doctor, surely you recognize that there are forms of government much more susceptible to abuse?"

"No, Phil. I do not. Not conclusively. Every governmental form is subject to monstrous abuse or capable of great benevolence. Checks and balances found in Democracy and Parliamentary systems mitigate the potential for misuse to a degree. But no matter what the system, it is always incumbent on those who lead to assure that the misuse of power does not occur. The tyranny of the minority, the cowardly extortionists concealed in the guise of a legitimate movement, the blind fealty to societal and political dictates—these will not go away of their own volition, and all depends on the checkered proclivities of man himself."

"Can you give me some examples of this type of behavior?"

"Certainly. *The tyranny of the minority*: consider recent demands in the US and the UK for separate washrooms; that is, infidels too dirty to share space with Allah's chosen.

Cowardly extortionists concealed in the guise of a legitimate movement: the brown shirted bullies and thugs heralding the third Reich is an excellent example.

Blind fealty to political dictates: can't even ask a fellow employee out for a cup of coffee anymore…male or female, for fear of everything and everyone.

I believe the cold reality comes down to this: sooner or later every human must take some share of responsibility for the form and activities of their government, *and of their leaders*.

The eternally helpless victim is a myth, and the pathetic result is always and forever the same. The overall suffering would have been far less had the people simply removed their leader by whatever means and costs necessary, than the suffering undergone during the agonized wait for the despot's ultimate downfall.

Here is a case in point: millions of Americans are horrified to this day by the use of nuclear weapons against Japan. But many say, perhaps rightly so, that those bombs ultimately *saved* lives. In real point of fact, conventional warfare prior to the nuclear attack was already killing roughly two-hundred thousand non-combatants a month throughout Asia.

A single firestorm bombing mission over Tokyo killed over 80,000, the majority by suffocation, a hellish way to perish. One million civilians had already died. The nuclear attacks on Hiroshima and Nagasaki killed a combined 150,000, not factoring in after-effects, marking the end to any further conventional or non-conventional combat.

The numbers alone unequivocally supports the 'saved lives' conclusion. It's pure arithmetic. The bomb *saved* Japanese lives. The bomb *saved* American lives. The bomb *saved* Asian lives. Any other interpretation is nothing more than self-delusion, and overly-emotional pandering. And even that could have been averted had their leaders been more courageous and less self-serving.

History invariably belongs to the victor. In this case, however, history very faithfully records that it was the Japanese civil and military leadership (as well as a couple of *gongyè hézuòshè* translators) that cold-bloodedly brought atomic bombs down upon themselves and their country simply to feed their pertinacious egos, their code of honor: *Bushido*.

This was further compounded by the mistaken belief that the Russians were working with them (in the context, or pretext, of neutrality), representing their interests with the Allies.

It turns out that the Russians were already holding hands with the Chinese. Whatever.

Japan suffered Hirohito. Uganda suffered Idi Amin. Germany, Hitler. Italy, Mussolini. Chile, Allende. Russia, Stalin. Iraq, Hussein. China, Mao. Argentina, Peron. Rome, Caligula. Haiti, Papa Doc. France, Napoleon. Mongolia, Tamerlane. Macedonia, Alexander. Cambodia, Pol Pot. The list is nauseating, endless, and bloody, extending far back into prehistory."

"Sobering words, Doctor."

After a moment, Phil picked up the conversation. "Okay, Shad. What about 'the evils of communism'?"

"I think you're baiting me, Phil. You may as well discuss the evil of a can opener. It is no more than a tool. Neither good, nor evil. Communism is an economic tool. We both well know that Karl Marx developed the most gentle and naïve economic and philosophic system in human history. So forthright and credulous was it, in fact, that it was easily subdued and made into something monstrously murderous, by cunning and exploitive bastards like Stalin and Mao. Untold millions died.

It was not *communism* that was evil. Nor did communism fail *per se*. It was the communist leaders who were evil, mismanaged it, and provoked its ultimate downfall. These sons of bitches could have as conveniently masqueraded as *democratists*, fascists, socialists, royalists, or witch doctors, for that matter. The system was not the problem. As always, people were the problem, the paranoid bastards that grasped for power. Communism only provided an easy foothold from which to access totalitarian control over a populace that was only seeking a few of the basics in life...maybe even a little human dignity...a reasonably fair share. That sort of thing.

Those intransigent communists who hang on in today's world are right, and you know they are right, when they refer to the 'evils of *capitalism.*' Capitalism *is* exploitive, it *is* capable of great abuse, and it *does* lead to a profound and inequitable gap between the 'haves' and the 'have nots.'

The primary reason capitalism succeeds where communism does not, is because capitalism is very capable of defending itself. It concentrates power as much as it spreads it. And it appeals to the basic human instincts of survival and acquisition. Calling a spade a spade...greed. Capitalism exploits these facets of human nature to create an environment of competition and progress. To an impressive degree it can sometimes generate efficiencies. So, all-in-all, capitalism is not the stuff of Boy Scouts, but it *may be* the stuff of survival."

"That was interesting, Shad. I must give it some thought. You know, being trained in the law is not the same as being trained in, or even familiar with, government, economics, or ethos."

"Too true, Phil. That disappointing reality is one of the basic factors alienating lawyers from those they are charged to serve. It makes for some appallingly poor politicians all too often."

"One more question," Phil said. "Are you familiar with Dr. Kahn's First Exhortation? Do you agree with it?"

Dr. Alexander smiled broadly, and by way of answer, swiveled his chair 180° and pulled open a window curtain looking into a large lecture hall attached to his office. Above the lectern was a large nicely lettered banner:

Humans Alone are Accountable for their Ethos, Moral Codes, and Laws

"We do have staff meetings from time to time, Mr. Carr," Shad said and smiled.

"Then I would correctly surmise you are developing a sort of Deistic derivative legal system?"

"Here's our current work inventory," Doctor Alexander said, in response.

- Accusatorial/Inquisitorial Systems
- Adversarial Systems
- Buddhist Law
- Canon/Catholic Law
- Civil Law Systems
- Common Law Systems
- Customary Laws
- Gypsy Law
- Indigenous/Folk Legal Systems/Native American Law
- Islamic Law
- Napoleonic Code
- Soviet System

"We start with the code of Hammurabi and Justinian's codex *De Justin. Cod. Confirmando.*

His smile gone, Dr. Alexander sighed. "Big job. We're working on it and attending on Dr. Kahn. For us, the differentiators between law and government are becoming increasingly fuzzy. We're kidding ourselves if we don't admit we're trying to re-invent society itself.

This is one hell of an enormous task. I don't know if we have the time, materials, or credentials to accomplish it. But the worst part is, I question whether anyone will ultimately give a damn. On a more hopeful note, perhaps what we're doing will be superfluous because it is eclipsed by other developments here on the Island."

Phil looked around "You've got everything you need?"

"Meaning?"

"Meaning, do you need anything?"

"No. Not really. Thank you. You know, Phil...as we discussed...we develop laws based first on nature and then how those laws evolve into philosophy and ethos."

"Yes?"

"Well, this is not just a process we use for grinding out juristic dictates. It's a law unto itself. We cannot just dream up laws here. They must first have evolved."

"Yes. I assume this works out well for you?"

"Sure. We do fool around with what we call proto-laws from time to time."

"Like what?" Phil felt a much firmer footing in the law department. Welcome comfort after intense science and wide ranging philosophies.

"One law is: *Eat what you kill* This has been under review around here off and on for some time. We do think the proto-law has been vetted. It has passed all our criteria so far. It lacks only proto-history. Is that really indispensable? We think it might have great long-term potential. But it is very controversial."

"That's it? That's the law? Clean your plate?"

"Yes, that's exactly it. But what happens if you kill another human?"

Phil just sat, stunned, staring at the Doctor, searching for a response.

"Anthropophagy?"

"Yes."

"Doctor I believe you are serious. I know you are aware of the nature of your statement. I would add three observations about your proto-law. First, you're too damned late. If this law were a 'holy of holies' from say 40,000 years ago, it might be imbedded in the human psyche by now. It might be a functional element in group ethos. Second, by attempting to introduce it now, you appear to be sanctioning cannibalism. And Third, there have been cannibals and headhunters for centuries, and their ways appear to remain fairly savage. How do you justify something of this nature?"

"Very easily, Phil. It renders murder and war abhorrent. Were it inherent in human culture centuries ago, it would most probably be accepted practice today. However, with our upbringing, most humans today simply couldn't *stomach* it."

"I can see that, Doctor. Very clever, really. Might even work. I actually agree. But what would you do if people actually began to consume one another?"

"Fine by me, Phil. And another good question is if humans ever did engage in such activity."

"I thought that was a given."

"Not at all. There is minimal evidence in the form of cooking pots and very rare faeces uncovered in the American Southwest. There is some evidence that this was a Christian practice at times. Syrian Crusaders more than a thousand years ago. Consummation of the flesh and blood of Christ rituals that are still figuratively practiced now. Insofar as South American Indians and South Pacific Islanders, they reveal all the telltale evidence of legend to keep foreign competitors at bay.

Most genuine incidents are connected with survival itself, such as plane crashes, ships sinking, pioneering gone awry, apocalyptic pestilence and famine, China and ancient Egypt, that sort of thing, and invariably accompanied by intense contrition. What remains after that are the exceedingly rare sociopaths who engage in such activities for God knows what sick reasons. So, we're dealing with fairly untrod country here. Such a proto-law would be anathema throughout the world."

Phil chuckled. He thought about this at some length. *Protein is protein. If you kill something, it should not be for sport, or hatred, or war, or profit. It should be for survival. Either protection or food. Hmm.*

"Try to sell the idea to the world at this point and they'll show how cannibalism really feels. They'll have you for breakfast. I couldn't support this new proto-law. Very interesting though. As you said in your briefing, you're providing depth and background for your students. This one's a cutie."

Doctor Alexander wryly regarded Phil for a time without comment.

Phil reopened the briefing himself. "Dr. Kahn suggested I ask you about equality under the law."

Lost in thought, the Doctor said, "Right. Okay, take a look to the wall on your left. That's a quote from George Bernard Shaw. We believe it is as true, and as insoluble today as it was in Shaw's time. You will certainly find nothing new or original in it, other than perhaps its eloquence. What you may find new and original are our innovations in certain areas. If not solutions, they at least lessen the impact of legal inconsistency. I fear that would be for another day however."

The law is equal before all of us but we are not equal under the law.
Virtually there is one law for the rich and another for the poor,
one law for the cunning and another for the simple,
one law for the forceful and another for the feeble,
one law for the ignorant and another for the learned,
one law for the brave and another for the timid,
and within the family limits one law for the parent and no law at all for the child.

"Perhaps the only real tangible gains since Shaw's era are embodied in children's legislation. Their rights are being recognized to an encouraging degree. The question is how they may be enforced. Yet this is not really a question of the law *per se.*

An almost uniquely American inequity in the law is the inequity between states' laws (as in say...Texas v. New York, or California v. Alabama, etc.).

We're all aware of the dramatic, historical debate between federal and states' rights when framing the American Constitution. The 'Great Debate' and the 'Great Compromise' that followed had some relevance to the self-serving de-centralists of the time ('The Great This' and 'The Great That' always make things seem wiser and more profound, even cut-rate magicians for that matter). Using European monarchies as a totally specious analogy, they preached against the evils of too strong a centralized power, totally disregarding the Executive, Judicial, and Legislative Triumvirate already foreseen and in place. But they won States' Rights, at least in part. If not 'in part' we would have sadly been born as thirteen countries.

Americans salute the same flag, they are bound by a common amalgam of federal laws, they carry the same passports, fight in the same wars, they pretty much pony up with the same taxes, most try to speak a common language...and they allegedly enjoy the same rights.

Yet an act that may incur a few years in prison in one state may demand the death penalty in another, and there are literally hundreds of such examples. Hell, sometimes you can serve hard time in one state for an act that's not even a deemed a misdemeanor in another...won't even warrant a warning ticket. The illusion of equal rights for all Americans has been totally frustrated by the self-serving precept of States' Rights, as if things weren't complicated and stupid enough.

"The U.S. Department of State will sometimes exert near Herculean efforts to save a citizen from death in some foreign land, where laws are diverse, even perverse. Who stands up for some poor bastard in Mississippi? The Supreme Court? I refer you back to Mr. Shaw."

"You seem to know quite a bit about American law, Shad."

"I should. I practiced law in D.C. for fourteen years and taught at GW for some time as well. I've done a fair amount with the Justice Department and I know my way around the Federal Triangle."

"So, Shad, what's to be done about all this deplorably bent justice, in the U.S. and worldwide?"

"Beats hell out of me. Nonetheless, the first step in solving a problem is to recognize it. Along these lines, I find the more fundamental question is whether men indeed *are* created equal, and if the law can deal with social anomalies. This *is* my job. We already know men are not pragmatically equal under the law...are they equal in any way at all? Here's what Aldous Huxley (opposite wall) had to say about this:"

That all men are equal is a proposition which, at ordinary times, no sane individual has ever given his assent.

"Evolution did *not* (nor did God, if you like) create men equally intelligent, strong, fast, brave, heroic, wealthy, moral, handsome, talented, tall, svelte, desirable, likable, healthy, creative, or equal in a thousand other ways.

Our upbringing and our racial, cultural, and economic heritages further exacerbate these inequalities.

So now we *rightly* conclude that neither in the eyes of God, nor execution of the law, nor geography, nor society are we truly equals...so why are we pretending?

The answer is quite simple," Dr. Alexander said, answering his own question, "We have no other choice. That simple reality generates an unbelievable amount of disillusionment, misdirection, and near-Chauvinistic adherence to principles having no basis whatsoever in reality.

Are there other choices? What factor would balance the equation in a totally non-biased manner? Would it render all men unquestionably equal? What would it look like? Add a few grams of due diligence to counter-balance a few grams of bigotry? What? How would it work? Who in hell would have the wisdom to administer it? Is this discussion totally theoretical? Yes. Does it have any practical application at all? No, afraid not. We must look elsewhere than legal mechanisms. Justice and equity must reside in our viscera, the very stuff we are made of."

Dr. Alexander stood and stretched and walked about.

"So what have we learned? Well, we know that equality should at least extend to human rights. Without question. That's quantifiable and generally doable. The rest is for another day I suspect."

"Tell me, Shad, is your staff part of the Island's legal department?"

"Absolutely. We *are* the legal department. This gives us a nice balance between, teaching, theory, and practical application. We couldn't work nearly as well without that element.

I am Chief Legal Council. You are my primary client and, unless you so stipulate to the contrary, I am your personal legal council. That is assuming you accept the position, of course."

"Well, if I come aboard, I'm going to need some real hand holding to fully understand the legal matrix of the Island and the University."

"With pleasure, Phil. I hope we get the chance to work together."

"As do I, Shad. Thanks for some excellent insights. One truly final question and then I will leave you in peace."

"Yes?"

"What the hell are you, Dr. Alexander? Marxist? Royalist? Parliamentarian? Democratist? Feudalist? Non-secular Republicist? Papist? Socialist? Holy See? Caliphate? Tribalist...what?"

There was a very significant pause.

"Good question, Phil. As do so many others here on the Island, I believe the answer lies in our genes. I believe that when we have sufficiently evolved, we will no longer need, nor want witch doctors and snake-oil merchants running about in blue pin stripes, or ridiculous holy robes.

I truly hope a Perfect Anarchy awaits us in our distant future. When we're ready. The problem with lawmakers is that's pretty much all they're any good for...making laws... always making laws. How many goddamned laws does mankind need? The ancient Jews had 613, and many thought that restrictive and excessive. We have thousands and thousands. Thank God there's politics to keep them entertained, or our lives would be a living hell!"

"I understand. Okay Councilor. Can you help me get to Dr. Dunedin's office?"

"My receptionist has an interactive map for you, but it's a pretty good hike to her department, and you are running *really* late. I suggested she call you a PM."

"Great. Thanks, Shad...see you at lunch?"

As they slowly rose and grasped hands, Shad said, 'Wouldn't miss it."

Belly of the Beast

Let the fear of danger be a spur to prevent it he that fears not, gives advantage to the danger.

Francis Quarles

Phil was already getting quite fond of the PM's. They were fast, comfortable, efficient, and one never got lost. He was beginning to appreciate how much clutter was removed from his day through the use of these simple, friendly little machines. The only disturbing by-product of their use that he could see was that he was not learning how to find his way about. Aside from Dr. Johansen's office, he had no idea where the hell he had been or was going. This could be disquietingly dangerous under certain conditions. Having given that problem its due consideration, Phil leaned back to enjoy the ride.

After a short stretch of beach, he turned inland up another winding trail, into a broad, brightly lit, tree-lined boulevard. Shops, restaurants, apartments—and students filled the streets. Hundreds, maybe thousands of them! He had finally reached the heart of the University and it felt good. He was on campus! Until now, things were unsettlingly quiet and surreal. But here there were pedestrians and PM's, parked and active and people everywhere. Laughter, pretty girls, crowds, shoppers, diners, and bustle filled the scene with life. This was normalcy. This was a university town. This was fun. Phil was sorely tempted to stop at a sidewalk café for a quick aperitif. Then he decided instead to invite Dr. Dunedin to join him. Surely their briefing could take place over a mid-morning drink on a sidewalk, in the sunshine, on such a beautiful day.

Soon, the PM came smoothly to a stop in front of Dr. Dunedin's offices. He was immediately ushered into her office by what appeared to be a student.

"Good morning, Doctor Dunedin. Sorry I'm late."

"Considering your agenda this morning, I'm impressed you made it at all. Please, call me Eve."

"I'm Phil. Eve, ah, is there anything in your briefing that requires use of your offices, or facilities?"

"Not a thing. Why?"

"Well, considering the proximity of lunch and the proximity of the beautiful boulevard outside your office, I thought I might invite you for an aperitif at one of the sidewalk cafés. We could hold the briefing there."

"Find idea. I'd love to."

Within five minutes, they were comfortably seated on a sunny sidewalk, in the mottled, shifting shade provided by huge elm trees, around a small French café table with two stemmed glasses of sherry.

Phil smiled at Eve. "So, tell me what you do for a living, Doctor."

"Alright, Phil. How familiar are you with psychology, and specifically phobia?"

"Passably."

"Well then, I'll give you a quick little history from right here at the University. We first began with a classical psych curriculum...starting with Freud, Racial Memory, the Behaviorists, the Russians, Psycho-testing and Statistics, the Oral Stage, Oedipus/Electra Complexes, Retentive/Expulsive, Abnormal Psychology, Psychosexual Development, and so on. We tried some psychometric testing with mixed results in terms of interpretability.

Then some very bright staff, mainly Dr. Webber, observed that aside from some basics, we were trying to teach people who don't get colds—about colds—possibly a waste of some very valuable time and resource. This became evident several years ago and, at the time, we started searching for something of real value and relevance to a community of students who should be exceptionally well adjusted—yet would be forced to deal with a world populated by psychotics, neurotics, sociopaths, megalomaniacs, deviates, perverts, cowards, heroes, homicidal killers, suicidal killers, thieves, as well as perfectly normal decent people."

"Well, doctor, wouldn't that lead one to believe classical training was more important than ever?"

"Intuitively, yes. However our people will not be going out into the world to treat it. They are neither physicians nor missionaries. They will be going out to 'vaccinate' it. You don't teach antibodies about the immune system, the circulatory system, or the lymphatic system, or viral and bacterial bodies. You just let them go. They can deal with nearly anything. They act independently and without hesitation. They are *fearless*. I know I am employing anthropomorphism in describing a microscopic, single-celled organelle as *fearless*. But the analogy is apt. We are building antibodies here at the U, and they *will* be sufficiently fearless as well. We are making an inoculation of them, so that they may infuse the human race."

After a brief and awkward pause, Phil said, "That's a remarkable statement. I think I'll have another sherry. How about you?"

"Sure, thank you."

After the drinks arrived, Phil haltingly continued "Okay... okay. So how do you *vaccinate* our students against fear?"

Eve smiled inwardly. She wondered if Phil realized he had said *our* students. "Easiest thing in the world," she said. "And you used the exact term when you said *vaccinate*. When you vaccinate a living being against a certain disease, you simply introduce a small amount of antigen, or antigens into its body, and let its body produce monoclonal or polyclonal antibodies automatically."

"Please give my memory a boost, Eve...monoclonal and polyclonal?"

"Monoclonal antibodies are derived from a single antigen, while polyclonal antibodies are a product of a variety of antigens. In other words, they provide a broader range of protection."

"I suspect you're oversimplifying."

"Certainly. But this is essentially the concept. The question is whether we can produce poly, or if necessary in certain cases, mono, psycho-antigens, and whether the human mind can in turn produce poly-psycho-antibodies and mono-psycho-antibodies (PPA's and MPA's)."

"Can this be done?"

"In a certain sense, yes. And we can produce them of sufficient efficacy to actually immunize our students against fear."

"What does it really mean to immunize against fear?"

"Excellent question. Were we to render our students literally fearless, they would enjoy very rich lives, full of happiness and even joy. They would try anything, appreciate nearly everything, without inhibition. They would behave rather stupidly and probably be fairly short lived. Fear is a fundamental necessity of life. Consider the 'fight or flight' instinct in all animals. Can you imagine the ridiculous scenario of an aroused Sea Bass willfully engaging a Great White Shark in a fight to the death—and a very short fight at that?

"No. We must have fear. But we must learn how to use it, manage it, and indeed in some human cases, totally overcome it. There are unhealthy fears, of no practical value. These are phobias. There are fears that restrict the limits of our happiness and enjoyment. These are inhibitions. There are fears of pain, loss, dying, failure, falling, and suffocation, and so on. These are healthy, normal fears. There are fears of things like public speaking, poor sexual performance, rejection, and unrequitement. These are common, non-debilitating fears, needing only fear management conditioning.

"We needed a polyvalent fear manager that engages immediately, addresses nearly every type of known fear, as well as hitherto unknown fears."

"So how do you introduce these antigens?"

"This is really oversimplifying it, but it's a five step process.

"Each student has a tutor/councilor that monitors their health and progress throughout the course. Should the student need psycho-counseling, the tutors are on hand to provide it. We present a standard fear curriculum. However, we dynamically adapt it to provide a personal journey for every student, every step of the way. The student and councilor meet at least once a week. Their session is carefully monitored by three to five instructors. They, along with the councilor, constitute the student's guidance committee. This committee determines if training should be adjusted, escalated, retarded, repeated, or stalled for a time. They say the greatest mercy is to just stop for awhile. We are not above mercy in the right circumstance.

"In the first Step, we teach them about the nature and uses of fear, and the disuses of fear. We teach them how to 'wrap' emotions into a packet to be discarded, or for later service—fear being our primary interest. These packets serve as the basis for antibodies at a more advanced stage. Learning to *wrap* is a process requiring three to four weeks, of two-hour sessions, five days a week.

In Step Two we practice."

"Practice?"

"We scare the living hell out of them. We terrify them, and we keep on doing it until we are convinced they are variolated with the broadest arsenal of extremely powerful Poly-Psycho-Antibodies—or as we call them PPA's. We hope this long and *very* unpleasant process may one day trigger ANUMEN. We suspect trial by ordeal is the fastest, most effective method for provoking dormant ANUMINA, if indeed it exists."

"Can you give me some idea how you 'scare the living hell' out of these people?"

"Sure. I'll just rattle off a few examples if that's all right? Please bear in mind that we are trying to variolate against inhibition, phobia, neurosis, even psychosis, as they manifest themselves through fear. Therefore, these exercises run the gamut from ludicrous to obscene, to nearly deadly."

"I understand...I think."

"We make them speak in public with and without notice, on topics of which they may or may not be familiar. We force them to undress before the class and exhibit their genitalia. They are required to engage in sex with males, females, and combinations thereof. We require they engage in many forms of sex in front of their working group. We throw them off the cliffs surrounding the Island into the sea. We submerge them in water until they pass out. We put them in shark cages off the coast and provoke feeding frenzies. We desert them in the dark for hours and hours on end. We electrically inflict non-injurious, albeit intense, pain repeatedly and without notice. We dump them into pits filled with reptiles. We tie them up and sink them in mud and quicksand until they are fully submerged. We force them to relieve themselves in front of others. They are required to run hazard and survival courses. We drop them by parachute from planes. We submit them to what we term 'Hell Week,' where for twenty-four hours a day, for seven days they may be attacked and frightened in any number of ways without notice of any kind—and we're not talking about panty-raids and 'Boo!' here. It may require several instructors to administer Hell Week, so each student undergoes it serially, and no one knows when their turn comes up.

"During Hell Week, and other times, we are not above the use of drugs. Of particular usefulness are the drugs known as the "Date Rape Drugs" GHB (gamma hydroxybutyric acid), Rohypnol (flunitrazepam) and Ketamine (ketamine hydrochloride).

"These drugs can be administered orally in food or drink. They are mostly tasteless and colorless, although GHB can be slightly salty, which is great to sneak into a Margarita! Dependent on dosage, the student may awaken in a nightmare situation, having no idea how or why they got there. Lesser dosages are even more effective. The subject does not pass out. Instead, they have no ability to control themselves or their surroundings. You can imagine what we can do with that.

"We have limited our uses of GHB and Rohypnol, because the subject retains no memory of the experience. This *may* be counter to our objective. We're still studying this aspect. Perhaps we are providing unconscious conditioning. We're just not totally sure, so we tend to favor Ketamine. Using

Ketamine the subject loses time sense, they may experience mild hallucinations, self-identity is weakened, sensory distortion may occur, certainly the subject loses control, loss of some feeling at extremities, out-of-body experiences are not unusual, and things take on a sort of dream-like quality.

"This is the ideal state with which to administer fear. It is quite effective, and the subject retains a relatively vivid memory of the experience. When this is complimented by some counseling and wrapping exercises, the result is quite effective. The students can make strides in a few days that otherwise might entail weeks.

From time to time we use LSD, STP, and Ecstasy, all to great effect, if we are convinced the subject can withstand it. Please bear in mind, the more they can withstand, the more they suffer, and the more they gain. Of course, we use selected drugs that induce fear and paranoia, sometimes even psychosis, as well."

"Of course." Phil echoed.

Ignoring Phil's sarcasm, Eve continued. "We force them to take part as actors in plays where we know they will make fools of themselves. They must climb cliffs and swim until they are near drowning. They run until they drop, walk until they pass out from heat exhaustion. We force them to self mutilate and we force them to mutilate another person. Mutilate in this context consists of a twenty centimeter or so razor cuts, which are allowed to bleed for a bit, then immediately looked after. We bury them alive."

"Bury them alive?" Phil looked at her in disbelief.

She stared back mutely for a moment, then returned to her subject. "We force them to engage in bare-knuckle street fighting until they or their opponent can no longer fight. We give them a secret word and torture them until they give it up. If they give it up too easily we either give them another, or just keep on torturing them...pretending we are convinced they revealed a phony word to us.

We do all these things, and much, much more, mercilessly, coldly, clinically, and sadistically, over and over and over until the subject responds in such a manner as to convincingly demonstrate active PPA's to our satisfaction.

No commando training, no POW, no terrorist hostage has ever gone through anything more stressful than this (short of execution itself)—and this is only Step Two."

Phil flagged a passing waiter …

"I'll have a Scotch, please.' He looked back at Eve. 'That's the *damnedest* thing I ever heard. What percentage of people drop out?"

"No one drops out, Mr. Carr. Ever."

"We're nearly out of time, Eve." Phil said curtly. "Can you give me thumbnails of Steps Three, Four, and Five?"

"Step Three involves a high degree of customization, or specificity. In this case, we are attempting to produce Mono-Psychotic-Antibodies, or MPA's. We hook the student up to a variety of monitors: eye-blink, iris diaphragm activity, galvanic skin response, heartbeat, muscle tension, brain activity, saliva production, breathing, and so on. We then project about 625 holographic images before the subject at a rate of one every ten seconds.

These images are very graphic and very realistic representations of known phobias, and a few we concocted ourselves. When feasible and useful, we augment the image with sound, smell, movement, temperature, or dialogue. Obviously, this requires us to present the image for more than ten seconds. The presentation is divided into six sessions to avoid fatigue and wandering interest. Incidentally, if we do detect wandering interest, we unhook them and slap the hell out them. We record the subject's response to these images and can very effectively detect if the subject suffers from any of these phobias."

"But, surely, anyone would respond to these graphic images?"

"Yes, indeed. Therefore, we rely on the subject's reactions relative to other images."

"I understand. That makes sense."

"You can guess the next part I imagine."

"Yeah, I'll bet I can!"

"Yes, well, we relentlessly submit them to phobia conditioning over and over, as in Step Two, until whatever phobia the subject harbors are ruthlessly purged, wrapped, or managed. In other words demonstrably active MPA's."

Phil sighed. "I can't wait to hear about Step Four."

"Step Four will surprise you. It is nearly a lesson in philosophy. Have you ever heard the term "*weltschmerz*"?"

"Can't say that I have. *Sounds German. Weltschmerz.* Let's see...*welt*, world. *Schmerz*, pain. Worldpain?"

"Both right. It is German. And it does literally translate to Worldpain. In fact it was the German existential philosopher Martin Heidegger who applied this term to philosophy. We apply it to the human psyche.

At one time *Weltschmerz* was the province of poets. Weltschmerz describes a sort of a deep fugue state that can consume a person when they are traumatically disillusioned by a keener reality. The world, as opposed to their concept of the world. Worldpain can be horrendous when this reality comes crashing down on you. Unlike you and me and our staff here, our students are not encumbered by very much emotional baggage. We've been kicked around in the real world a good deal. We are already pretty much disillusioned. A *Weltschmerz* for you and me can be acutely painful, modifying our perception, even our love and reverence for life.

For our students who have been reared here in *Shangri-La*, it can be utterly devastating, and the cognitive dissonance we unleash on our students is truly a monster...claws like a Bengal Tiger, fangs like a Cobra, icy dispassion of a Great White Shark. It demands all their strength, training, and courage not to be ripped to shreds and poisoned for life. Executed properly, this is the most pernicious and strengthening element of the Ordeal."

"So how do you *Weltschmerz* our students?"

There's that "our" again! She thought.

"Well, this is a fairly straightforward process. It requires a little analysis and customization, but computers assist greatly. We submit each student to a lengthy multiple-choice test about the world—around 400 questions. There is no subtlety involved. We simply want them to choose the answer to each question best describing their understanding of the world. When we have matriculated their responses, the computer formulates a video, a very realistic video, which proves them totally absurd. We throw in a fair amount of drama and pathos to add power and provoke an emotional response. We find it particularly effective if the subject has been feckless enough to have a special girlfriend or boyfriend. In these cases, we show their partner in exceptionally compromising and debasing activities with someone else, sometimes many someone elses—and repeatedly. In this specific case, we show no mercy whatsoever."

"So, essentially, doctor, you teach them that everything they know, everything they believe, everything they value is false, unworthy and vulgar."

"Well put, Phil. We teach them that everything they ever loved or valued is common and base. But that element requires far more in-depth explanation than we have time for today."

"Sounds almost like Zen." Phil said, then he quoted from memory:

On the day of his enlightenment, in front of the lecture hall, Tokusan burned to ashes his commentaries on the sutras. He said: 'However abstruse the teachings are, in comparison with this enlightenment they are like a single hair to the great sky. However profound the complicated knowledge of the world, compared to this enlightenment it is like one drop of water to the great ocean' Then he left the monastery.

- The Gateless Gate

Eyebrows raised, Eve asked, "You really do have a capacity to see through things don't you?"

Phil was silent. *Where the hell did that come from?* He wondered.

"So how about Step Five?"

"Final exams. Nothing could be easier. All we require from the student is to test the mettle of their 'wrappings.'"

"What does that mean?"

"We simply engage them in a very brief retrial of certain elements of their previous fear training. We try to frighten them. Believe me, by this time they don't frighten easily."

"Is this a pass/fail situation?"

"Yes. They must exhibit no-flinch responses more than 95% of the test items."

"How many test items?"

"Roughly 125."

"Jesus! Had many failures?"

"Believe it or not, less than 1%."

"Impressive. What do you do with the failures?"

"Keep at them until they pass. After they pass, we give them a tent, supplies, and set them out by themselves somewhere remote on the Island for three days. After their fear training, they have a lot to think about. And school's out. Do you have any further questions?"

"More than you could possibly imagine, Eve."

"Okay. I suggest we mate a couple of PM's and handle your questions on the way to lunch."

"'Mate' PM's?"

"When two or more people want to talk while riding PM's, they can be magnetically coupled together and people may discuss things as though they were on a single vehicle. One vehicle is 'slaved' and the other assumes control."

"Let's get going."

Once the PM's arrived and were coupled, they had roughly ten minutes until they arrived at lunch. They were sitting side by side on two vehicles. Considering the quiet and smoothness of the ride, it was like sitting together on a couch. Suddenly, Eve brought the PM's to a halt.

"Phil, if you don't mind, I would like to preface your questions with a couple of thoughts. I know you're upset by what you've heard, and if you regard this as a lawyer, or a University Chancellor, or just an ordinary person, you're going to have understandably serious misgivings. To understand what we are doing and why we are doing it, you must bear in mind we are trying to develop an advanced, composite genus of homo-sapiens.

This involves more than simple genetic blending and a hybrid education. We are compelled to develop a creature capable of facing a planet of potentially unbelievable hostility. Their strengths must come from their genes, their minds, and their viscera. Otherwise they will perish and we will fail.

We are not sadistic monsters. We abhor what we are forced to do. Believe me in this. We have no choice. In a very real sense, in this course, we are training their viscera for survival itself. Another perhaps more prosaic aspect of this is both the Island and the University provide a very pleasant ambience. Perhaps too pleasant. Perhaps too idyllic. I don't know of a more effective regimen for hammering into our students how deadly serious all this really is.

If you buy into the objectives of the U, it is far easier to buy into the Fear Curriculum. So that's the first issue you personally need to resolve, if you haven't already. 'Do I subscribe to the desideratum of the University?' If the answer is 'yes,' the rest pretty much falls into line."

"Good points, well made and well taken, doctor. I'll certainly try to keep them in mind. Ready for questions now?"

Eve reinitiated the PM's "Shoot."

"The first thing that occurred to me was, aside from the use of certain drugs, your Fear Ordeal doesn't really take much advantage of technology. It would seem to me with all the breakthroughs in areas such as corneal input, computer assisted learning, special effects, electronic muscularity and pain induction and so forth, your job would be a lot easier if technology was more aggressively exploited. Why is that?"

"Our studies have indicated that it would be easier. Yes. More effective? No. Certainly we could use mechanisms to stress our students, faster and easier. However, we are convinced, with certain exceptions, it is the physical presence of a human tormentor that has a far more profound effect on the student. We do use machines for selected tasks, particularly when we're seeking a high level of dispassion."

"That makes sense. Is what you are doing legal, in your opinion?"

"Yes. We have already cleared it with our legal staff."

"Is it ethical?"

"Absolutely. It's not only ethical, it is mandatory, as I previously explained."

"Do you have any sort of release forms from the students?"

"We wait until the students have achieved their majority. We then get a blanket release."

"So, fear training starts only at eighteen years of age?"

"Correct."

"Are students aware of this training during their early years at the U?"

"It looms in their minds. It's almost fear training itself knowing this awaits them."

"So they live in fear of Fear Training?"

"Most certainly. One of the very, very few infractions subject to disciplinary action is for a student undergoing the Fear Ordeal to describe anything about the course, things of the smallest detail, to a younger student."

"What is the penalty for doing so?"

"The student who shares this information has to re-take the previous three months. The student who listens will have to suffer an additional three months as well, when they undergo the Fear Ordeal."

"If everyone fears the course, why don't they all drop out, or just refuse to undergo the course?"

"Pride, peer pressure, curiosity, the desire to achieve something and to improve themselves, the desire to graduate, a general, albeit inaccurate, feeling that they don't really have a choice, a basic belief that it's for their real benefit, and the suspicion (however misguided) that it's the only means of remaining on the Island. The fact is they could refuse the course, drop out of the course, even drop out of the University, and we would still have a place for them here on the Island. You can't assign normal Lander values to these kids, or to tenets of the Island University."

"Aren't there any lingering after effects—even breakdowns?"

"That's what the counselors are for. They ensure that the course is paced and placed in such a manner that the student can handle it. To date, we have experienced no lingering mental impairment as a result of the course. I use words such as merciless, ruthless, relentless, and sadistic. But do not misunderstand. We administer this course with the greatest clinical care and empathy."

"Are people injured? Has anyone died?"

"No one has ever been remotely close to death. Cuts, abrasions, sprains, bruises, burns, infections, bites, finger nails scratched off, temporary hearing loss, partial loss of digits, hair loss, short term breathing impairment, fleeting sexual dysfunction, fungal septicity, one shark bite, a wealth of concussions, and a plethora of broken bones. Yes. But never anything serious or permanent. These are really tough kids."

"Do they hate you after this process?"

"First, their counselor is never involved in the exercises. Second, the instructors who do administer the training are masked at all times. This adds to the fear element and avoids any possible reprisals at a later time, although I am convinced the course is administered in a sufficiently clinical manner the students never take their abuse personally. The students know this is not done for kicks on a slow Saturday night. They know it is an integral element in their survival training. There is minimal if any residual resentment."

"What is the total elapse time of the course?"

"That is a considerable variable based primarily on the needs and capabilities of the student. I would say it is nine months to a year on average."

"Who fares better, males or females?"

"Good question. Males tend to resist the process and take longer to learn. They are, however, calmer students once they have *engaged*. All in all, though, I believe the females get more out of it in the long run. They seem to really develop during the process. Students are not graded. So it's difficult to quantify actual results by gender. The only grading system we employ is a pass/fail final exam. In terms of failure, which are few (non-existent, if you factor in the re-try period), there is roughly a 50:50 split between male and female."

"If I accept the position here at the U, would I, or should I undergo whole or part of the training?"

"Every member of staff here has undergone the course. I would recommend it highly."

"Does it actually work?"

"Better than you could imagine. Believe me."

"What are students like at the end of training?"

"Relieved. Proud. Stronger. Braver. Wiser. Sadder. Older. A little resentful as I said. Disillusioned, but happier for it, I think. And the most interesting response to me, most students (and no staff thus far) seem to develop a sort of mystical private place in their psyche they keep to themselves alone. You can tell when they are there. On a PM, walking, or just sitting alone, tiny wrinkles form around their eyes and they glaze, their breathing is almost undetectable, and it takes a few seconds to gain their attention. It's not ANUMEN, but maybe it's a start.

"Ah. Here we are. I imagine lunch has already been served. Any last comments or questions, Phil?"

"Many. But I'll ask only one final question for now. You are the Department Head. You innovated, designed, continue to develop, and administer this course?"

"Yes."

"Your students suffer a good deal during this course, for good or ill. The question is do *you* suffer? Do you feel their pain? Do you feel remorse? Do you live with guilt, Eve?"

There was a short, full pause.

"What the hell do you think, Mr. Carr?"

"I see. This was an extraordinary briefing. I thank you, and I need some time to think. If I join the U, I *will* take your course. What say we have lunch now?"

Launch Lunch

The entire staff was already seated, and most had finished eating when Phil and Eve entered the dining room. As the staff dawdled over coffee and wine, no one seemed to note their tardiness or, if they did, they showed no concern.

Phil smiled all round (attempting to conceal that he was a little shaken) and prepared a plate for himself following Eve. He ate quietly and quickly, keeping almost broodingly to himself. His luncheon partners respected his quietude and seemed to understand his mood.

When he was nearly finished with lunch, Phil opened the discussion. " My apologies to Dr. Gray. My agenda was clearly overambitious. I was lucky to fit in as much as I did. For the time being, Dr. Gray, I will rely on my notes from your preliminary briefing if that's alright?"

"Certainly, Mr. Carr. In fact I really don't have much of significance to add to that briefing. No problem."

"Thank you, doctor, and I thank everyone for their time and interest. In particular, I am grateful for the exceptional reviews conducted with doctors Johansen, Kahn, Alexander, and Dunedin. I am awed by the formidable scientific and academic achievements I have seen. I am quite sure I would find advancements of equal import in your other departments. This is indeed a singular and unrivaled institution.

"Dr. Webber, if possible, I would very much appreciate some of your time after lunch."

"No problem, Phil. I've set aside the entire afternoon. We have you scheduled for an 1830 boat."

"Thank you, doctor. Thank you all. And this time I would like the blueberry tart."

Door Number One

The best way to predict the future is to invent it.

Alan Kay

This was the first time Phil had been in Dr. Webber's office. It was obviously long used and loved. Photos everywhere displayed family, politicians, celebrities, colleagues, students, pets, homes, boats, the Island at many stages of development, and many unfathomable pictures that appeared to be taken using electron mitography.

His window overlooked the beautiful back terrace, swimming pool, and the sea far removed. Phil could not tell if he was seeing the real thing or a periscopic image. Where there were not pictures or windows, there were books of all sizes and description, well worn, well used. All this framed an exquisite antique desk and conference table surrounded by green leather chairs.

The office was actually a suite. It connected to a room of equal size with a settee and three easy chairs, a coffee table, a wall sized wet bar, and other walls boasting several very fine paintings. Phil noticed some were signed 'Webber.'

Dr. Webber ushered Phil into the sitting room and, without asking, placed a glass of cognac in his hand. Webber took one as well and sat down.

"You paint, Craig?"

"When I get the chance, which is damn seldom."

Dr. Webber—eyebrows raised—opened with a pleasant interrogation. "Well, Phil, how 'bout it?"

"What you are doing here scares the hell out of me and I think what you're doing here is unique on Earth—even unique in human history. I want to be part of it. I want the job, Craig. Who wouldn't?" Phil smiled. "I can name my salary. I can walk to work, and the food's great."

"I'm pleased more than you know, Phil. Congratulations and a warm welcome aboard!" They tipped glasses.

"So, what about the money, Phil?"

Phil handed him a small neatly folded piece of paper. Webber unfolded it, mounted his reading glasses and read it. "You could command a good deal more than this, you know."

After a short pause, Phil said, "Maybe we should discuss this again after a few months. But that's fine for now. I am curious about is the meaning of money on this Island?"

"Good question. We use money much as any other society, as a means of expressing a unit of energy. We provide money to all citizens of the Island, and if they make an additional contribution, we increase their allowance. This allows them to acquire luxuries, as well as mobility whenever in the outside world. Under no circumstance is any citizen provided a sub-standard lifestyle. So, money is more or less is for fun and trips to the mainland. Should any citizen elect to relocate to the mainland, they would be well provided for. *You* would be rich."

"In that case, I would elect to discuss this again at some indeterminate time in the future. However, I would appreciate an 'enlistment premium.'" I personally already have a fair amount of money."

"We are aware of that."

"Ah, yes, uh, but there is major purchase I may want to acquire in the near future."

"I see. No problem. Here is a *pro forma* contract," Dr. Webber said, handing Phil a folded document. "I would ask you to review it and make any modifications you'd care to, including your signing bonus. We'll review it in a few days."

"Okay."

"Do you want to return to the mainland tonight and get your affairs in order?"

"Yes, I'd like to very much. I think I'll need about five days at a minimum. You said you had people on site in New York who could help?"

"We sure do. Two or three experts."

"In that case, I can probably get it done in four days, tops."

"That'll be fine, Phil. So, we've already got the money, the contract, and the move covered. We're doing really well! But you still look like a man who has things to talk about."

"Indeed I do."

"Now?"

"Yes, if that's okay. Do you have the time?"

"Sure. Can you give me a quick rundown? I may need to bring in some staff to assist."

"Understood. I would like to discuss security, organization, and how you see my role in a little more detail."

"Agreed. Let's start with the easy one: How I see your role. The answer is I don't. You tell me your role once you've been on site awhile, and I'll tell you if I have any problems with it. I really see only titles and results. You are CEO, COO, and Chancellor of the University. You manage us. You keep us out of trouble. You drive and coordinate us. You keep us on track and enrich our vision and direction. You are our face and conduit to the outside world. You're the boss."

"Does that equate to 'fall guy' should something go rum?"

"It sure does. So keep us straight! I personally guarantee the authority, backing, and resources to do so. You have my word.

In terms of organization, everyone reports to you, except me and my secretary. You report to me. The BOD is not exactly an emeritus body. Neither are they actively in charge.

I have little if any respect for chain of command by the way, so don't be surprised if you find me working directly with your people, with or without your knowledge. I would never undermine you, or go behind your back. But neither will I encumber work with protocols. I don't have the time, the patience, or the inclination. I'm referring to the science of this facility, not its management, or policies. The best approach in my opinion is that we work closely together and communicate very extensively. I imagine you'll be off-island quite a bit anyway.

Okay?"

"We're on the same page, doctor."

"Excellent. That covers role and organization. By the way, you will find extensive org charts among Al Wilcoxen's files. They may be of some use to you. If nothing else, they provide a full inventory of skills, staff, and departments.

"Now, let's move on to the more complex topic of security. I'm going to call in a Mr. Stephen Ryerson. He is our Director of Security, but he's one hell of a lot more than a night watchman. He's Ex-Special Forces, Ex-NSA, and an Ex-Presidential Advisor. He views this as his last job.

He's a small arms and hand-to-hand combat expert having served in Viet Nam, the Gulf, and god knows how many covert activities. He has reported directly to the White House on occasion. I do not know what his final military rank was. I don't really care. He's an expert in surveillance and heavy weapons, with some experience in armored and airborne assault vehicles. When he doesn't know something—he knows where to hire those who do.

He's damned expensive and not the sweetest, kindest of people. In fact, he and his group enthusiastically assist in our Fear Training as it pertains to survival, hazardous course exercises, small arms, and hand to hand training. He often conducts torture and interrogation exercises personally. This is a welcome relief to many staff members, but not, unfortunately, to our students.

I would never have any idea where to find such a person. Personally, he makes my skin crawl. I think of him as a sort of a high-paid killer spook and he's certainly out of place around here. But we need him, and I'll explain why, if you haven't already figured it out. I suspect you have since you listed security as one of your first discussion items.

He was recruited by one of our Board members in the defense industry who guarantees that his loyalty and discretion are absolutely irrefutable. I don't like him, but I do trust him. I think you'll feel the same. Then again, we have no real choice. You won't believe the arsenal he commands right here on the Island...larger and more deadly than many small countries. Ready to meet him?"

"I...I suppose so."

"I know how you feel." Craig pushed a button on an end table. "Please send in Mr. Ryerson."

Stephen Ryerson looked exactly as advertised—early sixties, close-crewed gray hair, darkly tanned, with a deeply-lined face. He was good looking in fact. He was tall, around two meters, very slim, and very fit. His cool grey eyes were framed by a perfectly even face—a face that seemed to inspire trust. Ryerson was neatly dressed in khaki trousers, brown loafers, and a maroon polo shirt. The only jewelry he sported was an expensive-looking gun-metal watch.

After a firm dry handshake and pouring himself a glass of cognac, he took a seat.

"Steve, Mr. Carr here is our new CEO/COO. He is Chancellor of the University. You will be reporting to him. We have every confidence in Mr. Carr and he has access to all information regarding your Department. Clear?"

"Yes sir, quite clear. Congratulations and welcome aboard, Mr. Carr."

"Thank you. Call me Phil. Steve, we have plenty of time if you do, and I would like a pretty thorough rundown on security."

"Certainly." Ryerson pulled a small radio from his belt and pressed a button. After a tiny squeak of static, he said, "Marion, please bring an easel and our current defensive schematics to Dr. Webber's office. Thank you."

Within a few moments, an attractive, middle-aged lady entered bearing the requested objects and set them up in the middle of the room. Phil assumed she was Marion. She had a large wave of chestnut hair, dark brown eyes, nice face, and well fitted slacks and blouse. Phil had met many like her before. They were invariably efficient and pleasant. But their best feature was always an excellent, wry and mischievously flirty sense of humor. They always made waiting rooms much more bearable. Marion handed Ryerson a pointer with a smile and left the room.

He stood beside the chart and commenced the briefing without preamble.

"We conduct two types of security here on the Island. First is Internal Security. This is far and away the easiest. It ensures little more than the halls and all areas are regularly patrolled and surveyed twenty-four hours a day, backed up by rapid response teams.

"This is a very, very unusual university town. We have effectively no vandalism or graffiti, no fights, no drugs or drunkenness, no car accidents, no theft, rape, assault, murder, missing persons, or vagrants, even very few accidents or emergency health problems. Security is a dream. Our greatest danger is complacency. Rigorous enforcement of procedures and strict staff supervision are the remedy.

In terms of assets," he said, flipping a chart page, "we have

- CCTV monitors Throughout
- Periscopes 90% Coverage
- Motion detectors all Key Points
- Dogs and Guards on all Beaches
- Each department has Independent Securities
- Guards at Every Entrance—Unseen
- All Guards Double in Manning Security Installations and act as Field Commanders in Martial Training Exercises
- Electronic Scans at Every Entrance— Unseen
- Hidden Electrified Barriers Surrounding the Island on the Cliffs at a Level of 30 Meters

Suffice it to say, at least for the present, internal security is not a concern. I don't believe there is a safer place on the planet.

External Security. As with Internal Security, we are under no current threat. We are in Level Green prevention mode and hopefully we will stay that way. We are aware, should our existence become known, we would in all likelihood attract unwanted attention and even aggression from diverse factions. Fundamentalist religions, political movements, governments, terrorists, military and paramilitary crackpots of every description. Many of them well organized, well trained, well equipped and very dangerous. All more than willing to mount all out assaults on the Island for the flimsiest of reasons.

As a consequence we have systematically built a defense infra-structure unparalleled in any non-governmental context."

Ryerson turned to the chart, flipped to the next page, and pointed to the perimeter of the Island. "Our first line of defense is an artificial reef that surrounds the entire island at a distance of some fifty meters."

Phil interjected, "I saw that through a periscope tunnel on the way to meet Dr. Alexander. It must have cost a fortune."

"On the contrary, Phil, it cost nearly nothing and solved a difficult problem at the same time. As we expand the U underground, a byproduct is thousands and thousands of limestone blocks. Since we are trying to disguise the Island as an innocuous luxury resort known as Halios Geron Resorts, we would be hard pressed indeed to explain thousands of stone blocks piled on the Island, or on the sea bed in our proximity.

However, as an underwater reef, they are unobtrusive, cost nothing, and provide a very effective first line defense from a marine assault. Reefs are not common, but neither are they unheard of in these waters. Normally, such reefs are not coral based. Instead, they are similar to ours based either on ruins, or geologic or vulcanized 'blooms.' There are a few openings in the 'reef' allowing access to our passenger and cargo jetties. These jetties are marked Halios Geron Resorts and they are mined. We can destroy any or all of them within five minutes, as well as those gaps in the reef."

Pointing to each item in turn, Ryerson said, "Our runway, hanger, maintenance buildings, and even the roof of this mansion are marked Halios Geron Resorts.

At the highest elevation on the Island, Proteus Point, about five kilometers from here, is a radar installation disguised as a communications and satellite television cluster—in fact, that is indeed part of its function. From this installation, we can detect anything approaching by sea or air. Any underwater intruders would be caught by sensors at gaps in the reef and other underwater sensors.

In terms of ordinance, starting at the reefs, are 824, R12, heat-seeking torpedoes every one-hundred meters, imbedded in the cliffs at a depth of five meters. These torpedoes are pre-loaded and can be calibrated, activated, and doors-open from ten different locations around the island, within minutes. Sonar sensors surround the island. Maintaining these installations is one of our major tasks.

Hidden within the cliffs surrounding the island, at a height of one-hundred meters are one-hundred, forty camouflaged installations equipped with 20mm M61 Vulcan electrically activated and enfired Gatling Guns, along with 35mm cannons and air-to-ground missiles.

Hidden on the surface are eighty mortar installation and eighty surface-to-air rocket repositories. Most of these can be manned in less than ten minutes. Proteus Point is manned twenty-four hours a day."

Ryerson turned to another page. "We have an underground armory with 8,000 M4A1 carbines, 1,000 45 caliber automatic hand guns, 500 9mm Micro Uzi fully automatic hand-held machine guns, 200 35mm grenade launchers, two million rounds of ammunition—all types, 10,000 camouflage combat boots, 10,000 camouflage sweat suits, 10,000 flack vests, 10,000 camouflage helmets, 10,000 black battle packs (ammo belt, canteen, pack and first-aid kit), 9,000 field radios, 1,000 communications concentrators, 50,000 C-ration packs, and 10,000 conventional and night vision binoculars.

Two-hundred feet below the surface is a hardened 40,000 m3 steel & flint re-enforced concrete bunker, eight feet thick, equipped with its own water and sewage, air purification, power, communications and library, field hospital, and food for eighteen months, actually unlimited now, benefiting from our production-line food technology. Periscope technology is used here to great advantage. Not only does it provide fully concealed 360° surveillance, it lights and makes the bunker very cheery and non-claustrophobic.

Hidden in our hangar we have two Apache Attack Helicopters equipped with air-to-ground and air-to-air rockets, 35 mm cannon and two door-mounted 35 cal machine guns.

All staff, students, and faculty are required to qualify on all light ordinances. That pretty much sums it up."

"Holy shit!" Phil breathed.

"Quite so." Craig agreed.

"I hope to hell we never have to use this stuff, Steve."

"As do I, Phil. But we should recognize the necessity and take some comfort in the protection it provides."

"Agreed. Thank you very much, Steve. When the time is appropriate, I would like to review these facilities in person."

"With pleasure, sir."

"Thanks again."

Ryerson collected the easel, turned and left the office. Phil had an uncomfortable moment when he thought Ryerson was going to salute.

"Well, there you have it, Phil. What do you think?"

"What the hell did all this cost?"

"Believe it or not, the majority of this equipment was totally free: surplus, and things that fell through the cracks from our defense industry Board Members. All of this ordinance is new from the crate. However, much of this material is considered nearly or already obsolete, or was never even commissioned for use. Yet these items are perfectly serviceable and wonderfully effective. Our board has done us a good turn indeed in this respect."

"Are you ready, or should I say prepared, to give me the composition of the Board?"

"Let's save that for when you return from New York. There is a Board meeting a couple of weeks after you get back. So I can brief you on the Board and then introduce you personally. Okay?"

"Sounds good. Is Ryerson responsible for the installation of the security matrix?"

"Yes."

"Does he report the project as complete?"

"Yes. He stipulates everything is Ready-For-Use and is now only in maintenance and recurrent training mode."

"No further development needed *whatsoever*?"

"None."

"Not in *any* area?"

"No."

"How many people are on his staff?"

"Something in the neighborhood of two-hundred, I think."

"Landers?"

"Unfortunately, nearly all are from off Island. We simply aren't producing people suited to this type of work here."

"Understandable. Military or security trained?"

"Primarily military I believe. Many were recruited and even trained to some degree by Ryerson."

"How much does Ryerson actually know about what goes on here on the Island?"

"Well, he's fairly familiar with the Fear Course. He knows we are doing some in-depth research into genetics. But beyond that, he shouldn't know too much. Although I cannot really say I have detailed knowledge of his familiarity. If he were interested, we wouldn't hold anything back…particularly from our Director of Security."

"It's conceivable he could know a great deal then?"

"I suppose so. Uh. Yes. Absolutely. What are you driving at, Phil?"

"In terms of what I think of Ryerson's operation…I did have in mind suggesting a major overhaul of Island security based simply on what I'd observed. Nothing of this magnitude, mind you, but I am perhaps certainly surprised, if not a bit overwhelmed. And two out of five is a start I guess."

"Two out of five?"

"Yes, Doctor. Two out of five. *One.* Internal security, as Ryerson stated, very straightforward, almost sophomoric. *Two.* External security. Lots of drama. Lots of sizzle! Trouble with most of that firepower is it can shoot in any direction."

Webber was growing confused and a little frustrated.

"We must now address the three other critical areas, Craig. Personal security. People such as you, key staffers, people in sensitive positions, people who know everything. They require protection from assassination and perhaps even more dangerous, abduction. I should think that thirty or forty well trained, highly-discreet bodyguards will suffice as a start."

"Mr. Carr, I wish you knew how abhorrent that idea is to me."

"I as well, doctor. Welcome to the world."

"Do you suppose we could draw from people on site? I really hate to bring in more Landers than absolutely necessary."

"You mean like me?" Phil said and smiled.

Webber chuckled lightly in a semi-embarrassed manner. "Present company excepted Phil, and no offense intended. But what makes you think you're a Lander?"

Phil frowned, somewhat taken aback. "None taken. Perhaps when I return from New York, I can meet with your Human Resource Director and we can work out something."

"That would be appreciated."

"The fourth area of security you're going to like even less."

"Yes?"

"Industrial espionage. In just a day and a half, I've been briefed on products and processes here worth potentially billions. I assume for the sake of anonymity you do not currently hold patents on these items?"

"By and large that is true."

"Then we are in urgent need of protection. International patents, via shadow companies as a start. And we must ensure Islanders do not take any unauthorized materials off Island."

"But, Phil, are you seriously suggesting that we search every person before they leave the Island?"

"You're damn right I am. We can mitigate the impact of this by requiring all luggage be checked twenty-four hours prior to departure and only minimal carry on permitted—books, purses, things like that. For all the good that will do."

"Meaning?" Webber was growing just a little irritated.

"Meaning your wealth is tied up in intellectual property. Any damn fool can send an email, a file, codify an innocuous looking report, pass messages over Internet Sites, or use any number of digital means for smuggling your secrets to the Landers. Hell, they could even float a message in a bottle. This could apply to communications with terrorists, lunatic fringe groups, fundamentalists, evangelists, militant lifers, and the like."

"Well, then, there's not one damn thing we can do about *that*."

"Actually there is. We can intercept all inbound and outbound traffic and delay it momentarily while we submit it to a series of automated tests to detect hostile transmissions. This would occur fast enough that users would not detect the delay. This is all satellite chatter anyhow, so miniscule delays, even garbling, are to be expected to some degree. I have long acquaintance with a world-class expert in this field, who can be absolutely trusted. I don't want anyone from the inside working on this, or even aware of it."

"Okay, Phil."

"We can carefully monitor any communications not routed through the Proteus Point cluster concentrators. I'll bring this fellow and all the requisite equipment with me from New York. I'll need a bank in New York by the way, and access to some cash."

"I'll see to it. What's the fifth area?"

"Insurrection. We are facing a tight-knit group of Landers who have exclusive charge over an arsenal capable of taking total control of this Island within a matter of minutes. Ryerson is just the boy who knows how to skillfully engineer such a takeover. Developing an effective covert protection against this is going to be tricky indeed. I need to give this some thought and, sooner or later, we're going to have to tackle Mr. Ryerson's 'gang of 200'. Our own individual security and background checks, possibly a total replacement. One feasible intermediate step could be to immediately outsource to a major security firm. We'll see."

"Why hasn't Ryerson brought any of this up?"

"That's the question, doctor. I see one of four possible reasons: One, Mr. Ryerson is stupid and incompetent. I don't think so. Two, Mr. Ryerson is basically a military man, and such concerns might not occur to him. That is nearly impossible. Three, Mr. Ryerson didn't see these aspects of security as relevant. This is even less realistic. Or four, Mr. Ryerson does not feel compelled to secure us in these respects.

"Sadly, number four appears to be the only credible diagnosis. If that diagnosis is indeed correct. Then Ryerson is brilliant. He assembles what appears to be an invincible arsenal, with deadly gaps. I wonder why?"

"Good question Phil. Why?"

"He must have his own agenda. Economic, political, philosophical, religious, who the hell knows. Or he's working for someone."

"What shall we do?"

"Plug the holes. Shut down all inbound and outbound communications and travel for an indefinite and supposedly brief period. Dream up some excuse, technical, terrorist threats, whatever. Any exceptions to be cleared only by you or me. Watch like a hawk. Find someone you can absolutely trust to very discreetly keep tabs on Mr. Ryerson.

"When I return from New York, I will send Mr. Ryerson to Moscow, Johannesburg, and Santiago to review and negotiate some new opportunities for Kalashnikova Modernized—AKM AK47 assault rifles, and various armored assault vehicles. We can stretch that into two or three weeks. Ryerson will bitterly resent the idea of bringing in Kalashnikovs, so he'll burn some serious daylight qualifying them, or from his perspective, disqualifying them.

When he returns from this little goose chase, we will either have cleared him, or I will then discharge and perhaps pay off

Mr. Ryerson for cause of incompetence, negligence, or something even darker, as soon as I find a qualified replacement. It sickens me to say this, but in our position we shouldn't ignore the potential necessity of eliminating him altogether."

"Philip!"

"I know, I know. Imprisonment here on the Island is an alternative, as well, but a terribly awkward one. This all depends on the degree of culpability we uncover. Maybe we can really just fire the son-of-a-bitch. I hope so. Christ! Maybe we can even keep him on. But this may be an extremely dangerous game."

"Jesus Christ, Phil. What are we into here?"

"Craig, we are into just the kind of world you are attempting to heal from a millennia of wounds. I think you should get in touch with your Board contact and have Ryerson double and triple checked. Can you call your secretary in please?"

Webber's secretary, a motherly-looking lady incongruously named Jackie, entered and sat down, pen and pad in hand. With an expectant smile she indicated she was ready.

"Jackie, we need a deep background check on Stephen Ryerson. We need to know everything possible about his background, his family, his known associates, periods in his life unaccounted for, women, gambling, drugs, debts, bank accounts, criminal records, credit reports, all assets and liabilities, sexual deviations, susceptibility to extortion and any physiological profiles and tests available.

I would like to have a complete copy of his 201 File, as well as FBI, NSA, and CIA Records. I would like to have a fresh set of prints and a DNA sample. But I'm going to bring in a young lady who can look after that. Dr. Webber's Board member will assist in all this, and we would like you to boil all this down into a coherent, succinct request.

I would like you to contact Mr. Howard Doyle in Chicago. He's an investigator with Doyle and Philips; they're in the book. Tell him we want a "full court press" on Ryerson and give Howard any information he asks for that you are able to provide. Brief him on what we are already trying to find out and assure him that we have no objection to duplication of intelligence. In fact, we would like to have confirmation from his end. So everything we request from the Board Member, we should request from Mr. Doyle. Clear?"

"Yes indeed, Mr. Carr."

"Tell him we have little time, but lots of money, and we need shoes on sidewalks all over the country, *now*. At the same time, I would prefer that your Board Member is totally ignorant about the researches of Mr. Doyle."

Both Webber and Jackie indicated their agreement with a nod of the head.

"Craig, are your technical people capable of discreetly monitoring Ryerson's communications? Landline phones at his office and quarters? Faxes? Mobile phones and that cute little radio he carries around?"

"I'll look into it."

Jackie was noting all parts of the conversation, to Phil's relief.

"Dr. Webber, Jackie, I strongly insist these matters remain only between you and me and, to an absolute minimal degree, your Board member, for now. Try to make it sound like a routine update and audit of our security files."

"Do you suspect we are now in any immediate danger?"

"Beats me, doctor. But I am sending immediately for a Miss Rachael Stone, who will be your research assistant on a special short-term project you are currently completing as a favor to a colleague at the University of Michigan.

Ms. Stone is smart, pretty, and very efficient. Keep her near you at all times. Please instruct her to get a set of latent finger prints and a DNA sample from Ryerson, obviously, without his knowledge."

"We already have his prints on file here, Phil."

"I want a new, independently acquired set. The prints we have on file may be corrupted. I would like to have the help of your Travel Department to get Rachael Stone here as quickly as possible. She will bring her own equipment. Please have your boys help her in this respect as well. She'll be flying in from New York, so I suppose your travel experts there can easily assist. I'll look after her payment when I return.

I know you must be wondering why I wish to leave at such a critical time. There is a very good reason for this. I want everything to look perfectly normal, as much as possible. So it's reasonable for me to leave and look after affairs in New York. I hope you understand."

"Sounds reasonable," Webber said.

"Let us make no mistakes here. We may already be in deep trouble."

"Phil, is it possible that we are overreacting here?"

"I really don't know Craig. I certainly hope so. But we would be negligent as all hell if we don't move fast to get our facts straight and plug all holes. Most of these actions we would have taken anyway, so we're not wasting much resource."

"Agreed. And Phil…"

"Yes?"

"… good to have you aboard."

New York, New York

Following a short and somewhat wheedling call to Rachael Stone in New York—copious promises of generous bonuses, immunity from any liability, first class accommodations, easy and interesting work—Phil had secured her agreement to delegate, or subcontract, her current assignments and come to the Island. She would be contacted by Webber's people in New York. All she had to do was pack her bag, package her equipment for transport, and grab her passport. The boys would handle everything else. After the call, Phil looked around with interest, the scent of fresh paint having caught his attention. This was the first time he had entered his new office.

Soon he was in his new apartment, pleased to find that Edward had already laid out fresh clothes, and then completed his packing. Edward had even prepared a generous Gin & Tonic and a light snack. Then Phil was into the jeep and off to the Halios Geron Jetty.

He made the 1830 boat with minutes to spare.

It was the same motor yacht that had brought him to the Island two days before. Phil noted five or six students clustered in the Yacht's bar and for or five workmen huddled on the fan tail playing cards and smoking. *So much for my moratorium on travel,* Phil thought. However, this was probably too fast for Webber to react. He hoped this would be the last transport of any kind.

Luxuriating in a huge, leather swivel chair in the ship's salon, his second Gin & Tonic in hand, Phil thought about the last two days. Two days!? It seemed more like a week, and a long week at that. He suddenly realized he was exhausted. He was nervous and excited. Hell, he was scared! Yet he was ready for this. The first thing to do was stamp out the dangerous elements and then take on the business. Afterwards, take on the science and get the job done. He wouldn't miss the law firm, or New York, or anyone, or anything in New York compared to this. He had finally found some direction in his life... and it felt wonderful.

Energized and up, he toyed with the idea of buying a decent live-aboard fishing boat and convincing Uncle Herbert to work the Aegean, as a partner with him, for a couple of years. It would be interesting for Herb (might even slow him down on the booze a bit—add a few years to his life), provide some familiar company for Phil from time to time, and give him a sort of an "bolt hole" back up in potentially difficult circumstances. Someone he could trust. He filed that away as an idea with merit and went promptly to sleep—not to awaken until they docked at Lefkada.

He could see nothing of the night drive to the airport, so he slept, and then slept through to Athens. He then slept halfway to New York, spending the remainder of the journey eating, drinking, watching a silly and thankfully forgettable movie, and making fairly trivial modifications to his *pro forma* contract.

Manhattan was awakening to a lovely clear rose and blue dawn and Phil enjoyed his cab ride home. After a brief lie down, shower and shave, breakfast (it felt like he had been gone for weeks—yet there was still fresh eatable food in the fridge), and forty-five minutes or so of TV news, Phil called Douglas Curtis at the law firm.

"Hi Doug. Phil Carr here. I'm back in New York."

"But not for long I hear. You've already cleared post with us. We've received the settlement payment from Webber's people. Your final check, as well as the few contents of your desk, will be delivered by courier to your home this morning. We'll have your final settlement in a couple of weeks. We stopped at Knickerbockers' Lounge last night and had a *great* going away party for you—even had a big banner, 'Goodbye Good-luck Hi-BARK.' We drafted the damnedest, most glowing letter of recommendation I've ever read. That will be delivered this morning as well. Everything's done my friend. If you ever want to come back, you're seriously welcome, in a heartbeat. Best of luck Phil. We'll miss you. Really."

"Thanks, Doug. I'll look you up next time I'm in New York. Bye."

Phil had never heard Curtis as friendly, relaxed, and personable. Maybe he wasn't just a fancy, empty suit after all.

Phil called a couple of special lady friends and set up a farewell dinner for the next night and the second young lady for the night after that. He made a lunch date with his accountant and scheduled a breakfast meeting with his real estate broker.

He then set to work sorting his belongings into three categories: Move. Sell or Goodwill. Throw away. The "move" pile boiled down to a single box of pictures, documents, and keepsakes. This was going to be easier than he thought.

Around 1100 the doorbell rang and Phil was facing Dr. Webber's three moving experts, Chris, Al, and Harvey. Informally well dressed, relaxed, friendly, professional, and ready to take over. They presented Phil with a Power of Attorney that extended to his home, his car, any belongings he left, and any open bank accounts. Harvey was a Notary Public. They would file his change of address. Non-secure mail and phone calls were funneled through a "blind" in Athens. His phone would be cut off on Friday, newspapers and magazines stopped, and his insurance policies canceled when appropriate. A provider in Athens was ensuring his address was maintained and directly accessible from the Island. In other words, they would generally ensure that he smoothly and transparently slipped out of town.

They further provided him with a pre-signed and acknowledged Rescission of the Power of Attorney for his counter signature, when he deemed it appropriate.

They assured him that Rachael Stone was safely on her way to the Island, her equipment safely packed away and shipped at the same time. This was almost too efficient. Phil had hoped to have a few minutes to brief Rachael prior to her departure. However, he could rely on Dr. Webber to suitably familiarize Rachael on the situation and her mandate. After that, Phil had every faith that Rachael would quickly have matters well in hand.

At noon, Phil invited the three to lunch at his favorite nearby restaurant.

Over a couple of bottles of crisp iced Chablis and cold lobster with grapefruit and mayonnaise followed by a *baba au rhum*, they discussed prices for his townhouse, his car, and those belongings they felt warranted sale. Except for the belongings, they came to an immediate agreement. Phil wanted the goods to go to Goodwill. However, the three were welcome to take anything they fancied for themselves. Some of the stuff was really fine quality. The three would take Phil's place at the breakfast meeting with the real estate broker, so Phil was left with only the meeting with his accountant. This he decided to defer. He felt that, after a few weeks on the Island, final settlement with his law firm, and the sale of his townhouse, he would be far more knowledgeable about his needs and his options. So he called the accountant and cancelled.

This imparted a delightfully carefree feeling. Aside from a couple of quick phone calls, he had two-plus well earned days off, with nothing to do but enjoy New York in the early fall. What a deal! Endless clear blue skies, leaves just turning color, invigorating fall air graced Manhattan with a fresh, colorful cleanness unique to New York in the autumn. He would do some museums, maybe a matinee or two, and hit all of his favorite restaurants and bars for breakfast, lunch, and dinner.

He first called his uncle.

"Hi, Uncle Herb. It's Phil."

"Philly! Where the hell are Ya?"

"I'm in New York."

"You okay?"

"Everything's fine. How're you doin'?"

"Fishing's great...women'r better and I'm feeling fine."

"Good. Good. Look, Herb, I've taken a job in Greece."

"Great. Congratulations. Athens?"

"No. Not in Athens. On an island, but I'll be pretty much all over the world, and Greece will only be a base. There are lots of islands in the area."

"You know your way around over there?"

"Yes, I know Greece pretty well. I like it. I particularly like the food and the sea there. The area I'm thinking of is the Aegean Sea."

"Not the Med? The what ...?"

"...the *Aegean*. The weather's great there and so is the fishing. So I had an idea I thought I'd run by you. A sort of a business deal, you and me. Have some fun at the same time."

"What's up, Philly?"

"Okay, here's what I had in mind. I've got a pile of extra cash right now so I thought I would buy a fishing boat. A really good one. Twenty or thirty meters, live aboard, fully equipped, freezers, power winches and cranes, electronics, radar, sonar, radios, satellite TV and radio, even air conditioned...the whole bit, first class...and a slip on one of the islands with security, shore power and water, attached to a nice little fishing village."

"Want me to run if for you?"

"Yeah. You'd captain the boat, we'd work out the profits, and have some fun for a couple-a-two-three years...longer if we like."

"Open-ended?"

"Yeah. Howssat sound?"

"Well, I've pretty much settled in St. Michaels, Phil."

"What the hell did you forget in St. Michaels that you need to go back there for?"

"I've got one hellofa girl friend at the St. Michael's Inn..."

"They got women in Greece too. Damn good looking ones!"

"Yeah. I'm sure they do. But this one is kinda special if you know what I mean."

"Okay. Well, think about it. If you wanna do it we should bring you over in about two months, pick out a boat, an island, a town, and a slip. I know how to get all the permits and everything, so don't worry about that. Meanwhile, why don't you get a passport, and try to find your Master Mariner's License?"

"You're really serious about this, Phil?"

"Yeah. I really want to do it. I hope you will too. Give it some thought and let me know. Bring your lady friend with you if you like (*That'll slow him down a bit!*). I'll get hold of you in a couple of days and let you know how to contact me. Bye, Uncle Herb. Take care."

Herb had reacted much better than Phil had expected. Phil didn't know about Herb's girlfriend, but doubted it was all that serious. He was sure he wouldn't bring her to Greece. So maybe it would work out. Who knew?

Next he called Charlie Stein. Charlie was a top gun in communications and computers.

"Hello, Charlie. Phil Carr here. How are you?"

"Doing great, Phil, how about you?"

"I need your help, Charlie. I need you to pack a bag and catch a plane with me Thursday evening. Bring your passport."

"Where're we going?"

"Actually, I'd prefer not to tell you until we're near to boarding the aircraft. There's some real security involved here and we are badly in need of your talents. I think you'll be gone three to six weeks, tops. I'll pay top dollar and a bonus that'll curl your toes. Everything first class, everything on the up and up, and right up your alley. In fact, I imagine you will find the work pretty simple and straightforward."

"What kind of work?"

"Essentially capture, stall, and interrogate all types of messages, with a fairly sophisticated AI processor to detect anomalies within the text of messages, reports, Internet Sites...stuff like that. We need to install some high-quality and very fast radio detection, and triangulation apparatus. You should buy all the hardware, right down to coax cable, here in New York before we go. I'll take care of the shipping and I'll front you as much cash as you need. We have our own generators, so we can do 110, 220, 230...whatever. This is very similar to the work you did for us in Brazil—only secure this time!

"You on board, Charlie?"

"This is really gonna cost you, Phil."

"I figured that. No problem."

"Aside from money for equipment, can I have an advance up front?"

"Will fifty thousand U.S. do?"

"That'll do just fine. I'll need the specs on the existing installation."

"I requested they send you that by email as soon as I have your thumbs up. How much do you think for the hardware?"

"Mmm, without seeing the specs, I'd say at least Nine hundred and fifty grand, maybe more. And really, seeing the specs won't change much, if anything."

"Why don't you stop by my place at around five o'clock this afternoon, and I'll have say...a million in cash. Can you have all the hardware in hand by Thursday afternoon at say 1400? I need to get it packed and shipped on the same flight."

"Sure. No problem."

"So we're a 'go,' Charlie?"

"Yeah."

"Great. And Charlie, this is just between us. Not a word to anyone. Say you're going on vacation should anyone ask. We're even going to need a Non-disclosure. Okay?"

"You got it, boss."

"Fine, I'll see you this afternoon at 1700. Bye Charlie."

He then called the Island.

"Jackie? Phil here. Everything's a 'go,' here. Please send that email to Charlie Stein we put together. Thanks, Jackie. See you soon."

Now he was off to the New York Museum of Natural History, just off Central Park, his favorite museum in New York. Afterwards, the bank. After that, dinner at his regular deli and, after that, drinks at the bar haunted by his associates from the firm. And finally...sleep.

He enjoyed the museum as much as ever, particularly the planetarium, except he never saw so many children running, laughing, screaming, doing everything except looking at the exhibits. So he made his visit a good deal shorter than he originally planned.

Then he went to the bank, leaving with a cute black plastic envelope *cum* toy attaché case, fat with ten-thousand hundred dollar bills, drawn on an account authorized by Webber, and then home again, just in time for Charlie's ring at the door.

They exchanged warm handshakes and friendly smiles. Phil and Charlie had worked together a good deal over the years, never anything fishy, but not without a certain amount of jeopardy from time to time. Through it all, they had developed respect and a genuine trust in each other.

"Hi, Charlie. Here's the money," Phil said handing him the case. "Not to sound too paranoid, but I think we should keep contact at a minimum here in New York."

"Gotcha, Phil. I'm outa here."

"Dress nice, we're flying First Class."

"Not to worry. I'll be pretty as a picture."

"On site, you'll be masquerading as a para-legal acting as my liaison to Barns, Levi and Richardson, helping clear up some active files while I get acclimated to my new job. Cover story has it that this is being done as a personal favor to a Dr. Craig Webber—a VIP client of the firm. So buy some smart casual clothing, get a hair cut, and find an attaché case somewhere. I'll cover the costs."

"Damn, Phil! What am I, James Bond?"

"That reminds me, get some cards made in your name, no title, Barns, Levi and Richardson, Suite 10553, 4431 Avenue of the Americas, NY, NY. Look up the telephone number, zip code, and web address. Make up a credible electronic address that you can reroute to your own. See you Thursday at 1400. Bye, Charlie."

"Yeah, see you Thursday, Phil." Charlie left sporting a slightly quizzical, slightly comical expression.

Half an hour later, Phil was using napkin after napkin managing the butter and mustard on his hot pastrami on rye, a huge pickle, potato salad, all knocked back with an icy beer, followed by a ridiculously tall slice of cheese cake. The meal, for all it's common fare was ambrosia!

Tomorrow, the best char-broiled, medium rare cheeseburger in the world at P.J. Clarke's on Third Avenue! he thought. Four days were not enough. He still wanted to do the Oyster Bar, Mexican, Chinese, Clam Chowder on the waterfront, the best New York Strip steak and baked potato on the east coast at Morton's. Eggs Benedict at the Excelsior Hotel on Central Park, frozen Vodka at Petrosiam's with all the trimmings, the best Italian food outside of Milan, and two or three fabulous hot dogs with mustard, sour kraut, and hot peppers with a cream soda—not to mention his two dinner dates with the lovely ladies.

There was a Wednesday matinee on Broadway he wanted to see, as well as a couple of good movies, and of course the Met.

Then he had to hit the bookshops, some clothing stores suitable for the Island's climate, and a pharmacy. Clearly, he was going to have to be very efficient and selective.

Over drinks that night with former colleagues, he found he was already an outsider. Everyone was a little spooked by his abrupt and mysterious departure to parts unknown, and he was no longer involved in either their cases or their office politics. So despite the fact he was suddenly a figure of romance and mystery, links had been broken and things were awkward. There was some fun and jokes about his going away party *in absentia*. Then Phil bought a round of drinks, afterwards excusing himself early with the excuse of packing and made a swift getaway, to the mild relief of everyone, including himself.

The next morning broke sunny and clear—just what he wanted. Before leaving for breakfast to have Eggs Benedict, he called Craig Webber to confirm that Rachael had arrived and had been properly briefed.

"Yes, Phil, she's here and quite nice. I approve. Rachael is already on the job. I don't see her often but she's always around in her lab coat and somehow manages to look busy with 'research,' so she has attracted no untoward interest.

I shut down communications and travel. That did raise a hell of a lot of questions and some real ire. I said we had detected some unwelcome queries from parties we definitely wished to avoid, and I would allow no potential for leaks, or communications of any kind. End of discussion.

Logistically we can stay shut down nearly indefinitely. But practically, this can't go on for long. When are we going to see your wonder boy?"

"I'll bring him with me. His cover is my liaison with Barns, Levi and Richardson as we close down and transfer some important active files. Okay?"

"Sounds fine, Phil."

"How's Mr. Ryerson taking all of this?"

"Interestingly, I dodged one phone call from him and, since then, I haven't heard a word. Good news if you ask me. I wasn't looking forward to lying to him or dodging him. I'm thinking of locking myself up in my lab with Rachael until you get back."

"Damn good idea. I'm not going to rush back. I'm going to take the full four days. I don't think we want to convey any sense of urgency at this point."

"Agreed. Enjoy New York."

"I will. Craig, can Jackie put me through to Mr. Wilcoxen's ex-secretary? See you soon."

"Hello, this is Maryanne Parker."

"Hello, Maryanne, this is Philip Carr."

"It's nice to meet you, Mr. Carr, if only by telephone."

"Nice to meet you too, Maryanne. Tell me, did Mr. Wilcoxen have meetings with Mr. Ryerson, the Director of Security?"

"Not really, or at least not regularly, although they did meet a couple of times near the end, if you know what I mean?"

"Yes I do. I don't suppose you have the dates of those meetings?"

"Can you hold a moment, please?" A few moments later, Maryanne came back on the line. "Yes, I have it here in Mr. Wilcoxen's calendar. They met on Wednesday the 12th of July and then again on Friday the 21st."

"And not before that?"

"Not that I am aware of Mr. Carr."

"Thank you very much. Can you pass me to Dr. Gear, please? Thank you."

"Dr. Gear, Phil Carr here. How are you?"

"I'm fine, Mr. Carr. What can I do for you?"

"When Alfred Wilcoxen died in July...was there an autopsy?"

For a moment, there was a pause.

"Where are you calling from, Mr. Carr?"

"From my home in New York."

"If you can arrange to provide me the phone number of, say a phone booth close to you, I will call you back within five minutes."

"Very well, doctor, I'll call you back as soon as I have the number. What number shall I call you on?"

"Wait one moment, please, and I'll get it for you."

Ten minutes later the phone rang at a booth a couple of blocks from Phil's home.

"Sorry for all the cloak and dagger, Phil. But we need a clear line and I had a few visitors in the office. So, what is it you need?"

"Do you act as coroner on the Island?"

"Yes."

"Is Mr. Wilcoxen interred on the Island?"

"Yes."

"Was he cremated?"

"No."

"Did you perform an autopsy?"

"Only to the extent that I confirmed Mr. Wilcoxen's cause of death."

"I see. Massive stroke. Correct?"

"Correct. Considering his weight and health habits, not a great surprise."

"Could you exhume the remains and conduct an extensive autopsy?"

"I am not a forensic pathologist, Mr. Carr."

"My question stands."

"I suppose if I cobbled some staff together and did some boning up, I could perform such an autopsy, or I could call in an expert. I know a top man in Athens."

"No. This must be kept strictly confidential, on and off Island. When can you proceed?"

"As early as tomorrow, I suppose. What am I looking for specifically, Phil?"

"Murder."

"How?"

"I don't have a clue. However, judging from the circumstances, I would surmise some sort of poison was involved. But I don't want to bias your analysis in any way."

"How shall I communicate the results to you?"

"When you have the results, contact Jackie, and she'll provide you with a secure Fax number. Thank you, doctor."

Phil made his next call.

"Hi, Howard, one quick question. Can you provide a highly qualified forensic pathologist?"

"You mean to do some work on that island of yours?"

"Yes. Sort of on 'hot standby.'"

"Please hold on a second, Phil." After about three minutes, Howard came back on the line. "Phil, I can have a top gun ready to roll with six hours' notice. Need a private jet, and from there it'll get expensive."

"Worse than that, Howard. I'll probably want to move the body to another island, close by, off site, so your man would need to bring his own equipment as well."

"We can't use your lab facilities?"

"Howard, if I have to go off-site, I certainly don't want any locals knowing I've brought someone in. I'll need a couple of boys to move the body too."

"Well, we can do it, Phil. This is certainly a first for us, and I thought we'd damned near done it all. When will you know if you need this?"

"It all depends on an autopsy report that will be submitted by a Dr. Gear. Based on the quality and nature of his report, we can decide whether we need to bring in some outside talent."

"I see. Okay. We'll hang tough. I'm probably going to have to pay some sort of retainer to our pathologist. Is that alright?"

"No problem. Thanks, Howard. I'll keep you posted."

Phil took a cab for brunch.

He had a beautiful view of the park, the Eggs Benedict were perfect, the Hollandaise sauce was the exact balance between sweet and savory with a touch of lemon, smooth as silk, just the right consistency. He washed it down with an excellent chilled Bandol Rosé, and for that moment, Phil was more than content.

At home again, he called and Italian restaurant for reservations that evening. Then he napped, showered, changed clothes for his date, and kicked back with his TV.

As the old joke goes, Phil was in bed by 1030, and home by 0330, an end to a perfect evening.

Late the next morning, Phil shaved and dressed while watching the news. Same old stuff. Fundamentalist fascist-bent, Nazis-flavored vermin, vomiting poison on brainless, chanting fanatics and apparatchiks.

Didn't they ever grow sick or at least weary of the same hateful idiocy unendingly day after day? Everything worthy and decent flows from peace. Blood and bile and death and pestilence flow from hatred and war. Is it so damned hard to make the choice? Do they really believe that God, or Yahweh, or Allah, or whatever mumbo-jumbo, really wants a living hell on Earth for humanity? Phil wondered.

Why did they hate him and his society? Why did they even care? He didn't hate them. Although he was getting close these days, he certainly didn't care about them. He wished he'd never even heard of them, or ever would again. He could only assume they hated him out of fear of losing their tyrannical domination over their idiot followers in favor of western blue jeans, cheeseburgers, Rock 'n Roll, movie stars, freedom, and a love of life...not death...not hate, or murder, or death.

Return to the desert, herd goats, ride camels, abuse your women, flash your sabers, live in tents, murder your neighbors over a goat-skin bag of water. Just as beauty and grace do exist, so it is with evil and foulness. Go away and go to hell.

Hydrogen and lunacy, the two most abundant commodities in mankind's hellish, self fashioned little purgatory.

He froze. A sudden inward flash. A distant rumbling of thunderous shame.

Phil fled his home in self-disgust and revulsion from his own bile. *Christ! Was he becoming as twisted as they? Venereal disease of the fucking mind?*

With relief, he entered into the bright, crisp, clean, autumn sunshine. He flagged a taxi intent on the best bagel and cream cheese in Manhattan, when in one of his perverse insights, he asked the driver, 'If we were to just drive around aimlessly for awhile, would you be able to tell if someone were following us?"

"You serious?"

"Deadly serious."

After a few moments, the driver hedged an answer. "Yes. I suppose I could. It would take a little time and a little luck. To be honest, I don't need any problems, so it wouldn't be cheap."

"How long? How much?"

"Probably an hour, giving the impression we were actually going somewhere, or they would get suspicious, *if they exist*. It would cost two-hundred, fifty bucks."

"Here's three-hundred. Go."

They pulled out and soon it was clear to Phil the driver was no dummy. First he headed for traffic, in the direction of the East River. This would force whomever to keep fairly close. Then he headed toward the Manhattan Bridge onto a parkway unfamiliar to Phil. This provided a credible route and a few long stretches to spot or confirm a tail. Not bad.

Thirty-five minutes later, the driver cheerily reported, "Yes sir. We are indeed being followed. First time in my career."

"Mine too," said Phil, wryly, as he pulled out a pad and pen. "I don't want to turn around. Can you describe the car? Make, model, year, color, license number?"

"It's a brand new Mercedes-Benz. E-Class. Dark grey. New York License number EK 1420."

"What's your name?"

"Joseph."

"You're good, Joseph."

"Now, can you find a large office building near here? I want to walk in, kill a few minutes while you wait conspicuously out front, then I'll come out, get in your cab, and we'll go back downtown to the 5th Avenue Café. Okay?"

"You got it."

An hour later, after his dream breakfast at the 5th Avenue Café, Phil found a phone booth and used a credit card to call Howard Doyle in Chicago. "Hi, Howard. Phil Carr here again. Did you get a call from Jackie?"

"Sure did, Phil. You want quite a bit, but we're on it. Gonna hafta pull some long strings 'ol buddy. This'll be fairly dear."

"Fine. Please keep me posted if anything interesting crops up. Meanwhile, can you get me details on a new Mercedes-Benz E-Class with New York plates EK 1420?"

"Sure. I'll have it within the hour. How do I reach you?"

"I'll call you. Do you have any boys in New York City right now?"

"We always do, Phil."

"You have the address of my home in Manhattan. Can your people see if my phone is tapped, if there are any listening devices or anything else nasty on the premises?"

"No problem, Phil. It'll take a few hours. What kinda shit are you into?"

"I wish I knew, Howard. I've got a lot of pieces to put together. I'll leave a key under the mat. I don't want to be there when they come. Can they dress like workmen, or cleaners, or whatever? I would appreciate it if they replace the key under the mat when they go."

"Can do. I've got an interim invoice coming your way by-the-by."

"Understood. Send it to Jackie, please. Talk to you in about six hours."

"Bye."

Some vacation, Phil thought.

He made it to his Broadway matinee. It was disappointing, silly, and forgettable. This cooled him off to the two movies he was thinking of. So he went in search of vodka and caviar he knew would not let him down. It didn't.

Back to a phone booth and credit card. "Well, Howard, any luck?"

"I've got a bit. None of it good. Let's start with the car. It was stolen in Boston a week ago from—get this—a car rental company! Pretty smart. No tracks at all."

"What about the previous renters?"

"A nice Japanese family hired the car at JFK two weeks ago and turned it in at a downtown garage for Avis in Boston. They didn't turn it in at Logan, or it would have been more difficult to steal. The car was standing by for another one-way rental or a ferry back to JFK."

"If nothing else, Howard, the timing clears them of any connection. Two weeks ago I didn't know one damn thing about this mess."

"Secondly, your house. Clean."

"Well, that's good news."

"I 'spose it is good news. But we might have learned something about them from their bugs and taps.

"And thirdly, and this one is interesting, Stephen Ryerson is beginning to shape up as a composite."

"What the hell is a *composite*?"

"Well, based on the chronology, a skillful, nearly carbon copy repetition of certain file information from a variety of legitimate sources, and most importantly, the total impossibility to back track data found in these various files, it looks like Ryerson was phonyed into existence from a collection of other records. They cobbled him together from a collection of real files about real people. Fairly skillful. Certainly expensive, and deadly serious. You don't ding around with records at the Army/FBI/CIA/NSA, unless you have something heavy on deck. We should have a clearer picture in a couple of days. Meanwhile, steer clear of this SOB. In my opinion, he's dirty and dangerous."

"Howard I was followed today by the Mercedes you checked out. Can you put a good man on me? I'm in town until Thursday night."

"Phil, wait one hour and then go home. As soon as you get there, we'll attach men twenty-four hours a day, and you'll never see them. Keep going out. Don't change your habits. Don't make them suspicious. Don't reveal in any way you know you're being followed. Don't look behind you. Don't use shop windows as rearview mirrors. Don't try to lose them. Don't do anything clever. Are you expecting any callers at home?"

"Only Charlie Stein on Thursday afternoon. You know him. I've got some relocation experts that will drop by about the same time. You wouldn't know them."

"Yeah. If these relocation experts show up, put on a baseball cap as you let them in the door to confirm it's them. You got a baseball cap?"

"Yeah. Mets I think."

"Fine. Let me know if you expect anyone else. If you let anyone friendly into your home, wear the baseball cap. If they're unknown or unfriendly, no cap, and our boys will know what to do. We've got you covered, Phil. Don't worry."

"Howard, did you receive a Fax from Jackie, something about autopsy results?"

"I sure as hell did, Phil. We had to bring out some talent to interpret it, but we now know how this guy Wilcoxen bought it."

"How? How'd he *buy* it?"

"Well, it looks pretty slick, actually. First, Wilcoxen was administered a drug known as Rohypnol mixed with a fair quantity of scotch. There was remaining evidence of both in his systems because he died before he could eliminate them in a number of classical ways. Basically, there were still trace amounts in his stomach that embalming did not totally destroy. The effect of the Rohypnol was to render Wilcoxen senseless and defenseless.

Next, he was administered a massive concentrate of female hormones known as Sympathomemetics. The point of delivery was into a vein in the area of the anus, by syringe. These things are normally given to women suffering from various sorts of female complaints, and certainly not into anal veins. We assumed the anus was selected as the injection site to avoid detection. It seems a hefty overdose can cause a serious stroke, or heart attack, or God knows what, in sufficiently susceptible males or females.

In Wilcoxen's case, he was susceptible as all hell, and it killed him within minutes by provoking a massive intracerebral Hypertensive hemorrhage, or stroke. This was detected by a broad range of tests on brain tissue. Excellent pathology and a damned sophisticated murder. Think Ryerson is our killer?"

"I'm absolutely sure of it. Wilcoxen started meeting with him for the very first time just before his death. Wilcoxen must have been on to him and was naïve enough to confront him or show his hand in some way, poor bastard. Howard, I really owe you. Thanks."

"Take care, Phil, and *be careful*. Bye."

Minutes later at home, Phil enjoyed the convenience of using his own phone.

"Craig? Phil here. Don't talk. I got some things to report and I'll make it fast.

First, it looks like Ryerson may be a complete ringer. This is being confirmed. But he may not actually exist *per se*. Our guy in Chicago says that he was artificially created from a collection of legitimate files.

Second, someone is following me here in New York. Whoever it is, is a professional, and I suspect dangerous. That's all for now. I'll keep you posted. Be careful, Craig. Stay the hell away from Ryerson. Bye."

Phil then called his "second girl" and cancelled their date for that evening, citing an urgent, fictional, late-night teleconference with clients in the Far East. He didn't feel like a date, and he saw no reason to involve an innocent girl in his troubles.

He spent the evening at home with some light pasta, half a bottle of Scotch, and an excellent bottle of California Red.

Over breakfast the next morning, what was left? A little shopping. Screw the movies. He wanted a steak. So much for Wednesday's itinerary.

Thursday was going to be pretty short. Breakfast at home. The Met. Some hotdogs. Finish packing and meet Charlie at 1400. So much for Thursday.

He had a plan.

He grabbed a cab.

Shopping was more work than he remembered. Walking from store to store, wind howling through breaks in the buildings. Sorting through rack after rack. Double checking sizes. Working to understand the various styles. And what he hated the most was trying on the clothes to see how they looked and if they fit. So shopping was mostly standing around on a cold tile floor, in socks and underwear, fighting with packaging, pins, and hangars, buttons and zippers, curtain barely closed, knees and elbows knocking into everything while he stood under a closed circuit TV (He hoped it was closed circuit!), much too near a cheap mirror to see how the damned things looked anyway!

Then standing in queues, going through payment rituals, removing those insulting little plastic security knobs, and hauling bulky, over-engineered bags around—that was shopping.

Did women really enjoy this? he wondered.

Twenty minutes later, he had a double, extra-dry martini "up with a twist" then an open-faced crab sandwich with a glass of cool Chablis and another martini. He followed that with chocolate mousse. Another martini. Then home for a nap, and to hell with the pharmacy and the bookstore.

He was up at 1830, watched a little TV, carefully avoiding any news, while he showered and changed, then he was off by taxi to his favorite steak house downtown. In case his ex-date should happen upon him, he had a cover story prepared...something about a dinner break between teleconferencing sessions.

He was shown to a nice table on the ornate brass and marble ground floor near the bar. He liked this area since it was difficult to tell if he were alone, waiting for someone, or perhaps his partner was just making the rounds in the crowded bar. He started with another martini. He then ordered cold vegetables in oil, a medium-rare New York cut with a huge baked potato, accompanied by onion rings and green beans, and a bottle of slightly chilled, light red Fleurie. He finished with a ridiculously large slice of carrot cake and a Cappuccino. His shopping afternoon was completely forgotten.

After settling the bill and collecting his coat, he strolled around Manhattan up to Broadway, breathing in the cool evening air and actually spotting one or two stars between the buildings, despite the ambient light. He suspected it would be a while before he saw New York again, so he enjoyed the city all the more.

Home to a dreamless sleep.

He awakened Thursday morning a little late with a slight headache. He always drank too much when he was out and about in New York. The Island would add years to his life—if something or someone else didn't shorten it prematurely and permanently for him.

After a coffee with milk, some yogurt, and a buttered English muffin, his fridge was nearing empty. He had some beer left, which he was sure Charlie and the movers would take care of.

The Met was the same as he remembered it. And no kids... no crowds! He assumed the children would invade later in the day. He took his time and strolled his favorite areas. He had forgotten how peaceful the museum could be in the morning. Footfalls echoing, warm sunshine from skylights, and enormous slanting windows looking out on the parkland. The Temple of Dendur had been lovingly transplanted stone-by-stone from Upper Nubia, surrounded by its own moat in its vast private chamber, his favorite.

Three hours later, Phil found himself with two fully loaded hot dogs in the bright sunshine outside the museum. Balancing his dogs with his cream soda, he found his way to a bench and ticked off another stop in his farewell, nostalgic, culinary tour of New York with great enjoyment. The only place the hot dogs were better was O'Hare Airport in Chicago. He'd have to try them again, sometime soon.

He was home at 1400. Charlie was waiting at the door with two suitcases and three large crates.

"Hi, Charlie. Come on in. I'll help you with this stuff. Get everything you need?"

"Yeah, and more. I've got some nifty surprises for you. I'll show you when we get wherever we're going and do the unpacking."

"Charlie, I trust there's nothing packed away in all this that would piss off customs?"

"Good grief! Hell no, Phil! I still don't even know where we were going for that matter."

"Sorry, Charlie. Just checking."

"Understood. Here's your change by the way. I held back fifty G's as we agreed. Okay?"

"Spot on, Charlie."

Charlie handed Phil a handful of bills and receipts.

"I bought some real pretty clothes and a briefcase. You'll find the receipts in the same pile."

"Beer, Charlie?"

"Sure. And maybe then you'll tell me where the hell we're going?"

"Sure. Why not?

We're going to a University on a Greek island in the Aegean Sea."

"What's the name of the island?"

Phil grinned, despite himself. "It's called The Island."

"Uh, okay. What's the name of the university?"

Phil deadpanned, "It's called The University."

"Look, Phil, if you don't want to tell me…"

"I'm telling you nothing but the truth, Charlie. You'll get used to the names, or perhaps I should say the no-names. They're doing some pretty arcane work at the University, a lot of it could be sensitive politically—and some of it's worth money. So we are looking seriously into security. You're a key element. We have to monitor and restrict all types of inbound and outbound communications: Landlines, wireless, analog, and digital.

"We're lucky because all authorized communications on the Island are concentrated through a single cluster. I hope you have equipment to detect and triangulate on any unauthorized traffic?"

"You bet, Phil."

"There may be some bad guys on site right now, so we can't dawdle. We have a flight from JFK at 2100. There'll be some guys along soon to pick up our goods and our bags. Try not to carry anything on board other than your briefcase. Did you get some business cards?"

"Yeah."

"Okay, Charlie, I think we're ready."

A few minutes later the bell rang and Phil found Chris, Al, and Harvey smiling at his door. Phil stepped out on the landing and casually donned his New York Mets cap. "Come on in, guys. We're ready for you."

After distributing some more beers, Phil watched the movers open and re-pack every box and every bag. They added packing, tape, address labels, steel ribbon, and weighed everything. They even had Lot Labels, Bills of Lading, Custom's Declarations, and Security Labels. Phil was intrigued that they boxed the luggage as well, then he realized that all of this would travel together that way, and they would never be bothered by carrying suitcases about. He was sorry he had bothered to pack at all. These guys did a much better job.

Three hours later, Harvey gave Phil their trip itinerary, tickets, and receipts.

"A limo will call for you guys in about half an hour. The next time you'll see all this stuff is in your lodgings at the Island. We'll clear up everything else as fast as possible, Phil. It shouldn't be any problem at all. Have a great trip."

"Thanks, guys, you're the best."

An hour and a half later, Charlie and Phil were relaxing in the Olympic Airways First Class Lounge, boarding passes and drinks in hand.

Nine and a half hours later, they were wandering wearily through Athens International Airport.

Eight and a half hours after that, they were fast asleep in their respective quarters on the Island.

Breakfast Broken

I wasn't looking for a job when I got this one.

US Army (Draft Era)

After a late wake up and a fast cup of coffee Phil figured it must be about 0830 in Chicago, so he was on the phone immediately to Howard Doyle.

"Hi, Howard. Phil here. I'm back in Greece. Anything up?"

There was a brief pause. Phil could hear Howard rummaging through papers. "Phil are you calling from a secured line?"

"Secure as I can get from my end, anyway, for the time being. I'm using a mobile phone and a phone Card I bought last night at Athens Airport. How 'bout your end?"

"Clean. So let's get started. Well, Phil, you're boy's a ringer alright. Thanks to your lady Rachael, we used his photo and an image of his prints, and we know who he is. It was ridiculously easy. We don't really need his genetic material, but when we get it we'll double check if we can. Looks to me like whoever fobbed this crud off on you thought you guys were either stupidly gullible or naïvely trusting."

"A little of both, I suppose, Howard."

"Well whatever, I think your Island is now a plague ship."

"So who is this guy?"

"His name indeed is Robert Ryerson. That's nearly his only facet that's not a fabrication. He's a Canadian who's been doing a lot of work here in the U.S. and out of Bahrain for about the last ten years. This man is bad news. Got one hellofa resume: Assassin, Mercenary, Terrorist Instructor. Our investigations indicate he has no less than twenty-three notches on his gun, I'd guess twenty-four with that poor bastard Wilcoxen, and probably many, many more. He really *is* an expert in small and heavy arms, hand-to-hand combat, and the whole spectrum of ground and airborn assault vehicles. Rachael tells me this SOB has got a whole troop working under him on your site. There is no doubt in my mind that these guys are dirty too. You got a problem. Were I you, I'd get the hell out of there. Get out of Dodge right now."

"I can't do that, Howard."

"Okay, then get this boy out of town."

"For once, I'm actually ahead of you. I've set him up on a junket to Moscow, Johannesburg, and Santiago, leaving tomorrow."

"Great! I've got just the guy in Moscow. He can meet Ryerson and help him along on his way."

"What are you talking about ,Howard?"

"You know damn well what I'm talking about. Ryerson is raw effluent that happens to wear shoes. Net gain for the world when he's lost. He won't let you fire him. He won't let you lock him up. Right now, he runs the Island and he's gonna come after you very soon.

You got three choices, Philip. You run. You die. Or you act now. So do I have a Work Order?"

"Christ, Howard! You guys really do this kind of stuff?"

"Not in the DUS, Phil. And we never do it ourselves. We farm it out to the best multinational contractor in the world. Many governments, including the U.S., use them. We resort to it only in life or death scenarios and even then, only when the situation is sufficiently virulent that running away or shutting down is not a viable option. They have fused planning, discretion, caution, and skill into an art form. There is none better on the planet."

"DUS?"

"Domestic U.S." Howard said, a little impatiently. "So do I have a Work Order?"

"Any chance this'll come back to haunt us?"

"Are you kidding, Phil...in Moscow...a total disappearance at that? No traces. No witnesses. Nothing. Just gone. *Philip, do I have a Work Order? This will be a complex job with lots of planning needed. So we have very little time. Work Order?"*

There was a long pause on Phil's end of the phone, while he kept Howard waiting.

Phil had vivid memories of those times in his life when he faced a threshold, a frontier, a parting, a watershed in his life. He thought of the deaths of his family. The first time he got in a seriously violent fight in St. Michaels. Helming into his first major storm at sea. Bringing in his first really large shark. The sudden, almost violent surfacing of that peculiar insight he seemed to possess. Accepting the job at the Island. At all these times and many more, he realized he was acutely unaware of what lay on the other side of the nebulous border he was about to invade. It was not necessarily a matter of fear or danger, it was simply that the consequences were totally unknown.

This was most assuredly *not* one of these times. On one side of the frontier lay Philip's innocence. On the other lay blood and regret and guilt that would haunt him to the end. He was not contemplating Shakespeare's 'Undiscovered Country.' No. He was contemplating Shakespeare's *"First Murderer. Where's thy conscience now? ..."* Knowingly, deliberate, well conceived, cold blooded murder and the onus was totally his own. *"I go, and it is done. The bell invites me. Hear it not... for it is a knell that summons thee to heaven or to hell."*

"Yes, Howard, you have a Work Order."

"In a week or so, we should talk about the two hundred beauties still on your site. My best suggestion is we pull out the stops and bring in guys from firms all over the country. This would give you time to do your own recruitment and training and flush the excrement off your Island. But getting rid of these creeps is going to have to be slow and delicate surgery. A lot will depend on your new head of security. If you find the right man, it could be a smooth exercise. We can help you with that if you like."

"I'm sure we would appreciate your help." Phil sighed. "You know, Howard, I thought one benefit of this job would be cutting down on the booze."

Howard chuckled. "If I were you, Phil, I wouldn't even think about quitting drinking for at least six months."

"I'll send you Ryerson's travel itinerary. It includes the name of a fictitious arms dealer who wants to demo late model AK47's and various assault vehicles. All the details are in the file. Do you need anything else?"

"Not a thing, Phil. We already have his photo and his dossier. But tell me, what the hell were you going to do with this joker when he got to Moscow and you had no arms dealer?"

"My plan was to tell him there was a delay and to stand by. Our original intent was only to get him out of town for a few days until we could sort things out. I had no idea he was quite so dangerous."

"I understand, Phil. Don't worry, our plans will be much more concrete."

"Howard, this joker was foisted off on the University by a very, very high-level Board Member who's apparently a big noise in the defense industry. Whoever this guy is...he gave our Chairman every assurance Ryerson was one-hundred percent reliable. Is it possible he was unaware he was recommending a ringer? What does this say about this Board Member?"

"It says he's dirty or stupid, or both. Or, most likely, he trusted the wrong man and he's a little naïve. Who ever slipped this SOB into your operation thought *you* guys were stupid as well. Thanks to you, you're not. Who is this Board guy?"

"Don't know. I'll let you know when I find out."

"Do that. I'll keep you posted as things move along. Take care of yourself."

Phil took Howard's advice and invaded his new apartment's bar for the first time. He poured himself a very large brandy and then inspected the house phone, finding a button for Edward's number.

I've got to face down Ryerson. That SOB's going to fight me every step. If he buys off on the arms dealer story he's going to resent the hell out of it. If he doesn't buy off...if he smells a rat...if he senses a trap...he's going to be really dangerous. He could come after me right now just like Wilcoxen.

"Yes, sir?"

"Edward?"

"Yes, Phil."

"Do I have a secretary?"

"Why, yes sir." Edward said, smiling. "We made a temporary assignment until you find someone you feel might be more suitable."

"Okay, please contact her and have her bring Mr. Ryerson's upcoming travel itinerary, including the contacts and schedule of meetings, to my apartment. have her Fax a copy to

Howard Doyle in Chicago. Jackie has the number. Then have her contact Ryerson and tell him to meet me in my apartment in thirty minutes."

"I'll look after it immediately, sir. Would you care for something to eat?"

"Thanks. Maybe in an hour or so on my terrace, a charbroiled Sea Bass, couple of cold bottles of Retsina, and something for dessert. Please have Charlie Stein join me."

"Charlie Stein, sir?"

"The guy that came back with me from New York. He's in one of the guest suites."

"Ah. Indeed. I'll take care of it."

"Oh, and Edward, I ah...I need a gun, a 32 caliber Beretta if you can locate one, but any automatic will do, with a full clip. I need that immediately if you can."

"Yes, sir. Would you care to have a Tazer as well?"

"Good idea. Thanks, Edward. Would you bring a coffee service for two and some pastries please? Are you familiar with those large paste board containers bakeries use to box their pastries?"

"Yes I am, Phil."

"Can you bring the pastries in one of these boxes?"

"I'm sure I can."

"Please do. Thanks, Edward."

Ten minutes later, Edward brought Phil a tiny rechargeable SG95a 950,000 volt Tazer, an S&W 9mm Model 39 automatic, a box of shells, two clips, and a cleaning kit, as well as Ryerson's itinerary. "Apparently the Island does not inventory the Beretta, Phil."

"This is fine, Edward. Thank you. Will you be here when Mr. Ryerson reports for our meeting?"

"Yes, I will, sir."

"Then please show him into the conference room when he arrives, and I want audio-visual records of the entire meeting, all cameras on Ryerson."

"Yes, sir."

Phil loaded and pocketed the pistol, slipped the Tazer in a pocket of his sports coat, and stowed everything else in a sideboard except the itinerary.

Damnit! he thought. *I've got to get all this Mickey-Mouse cloak and dagger crap over with and start getting to work. That SOB Ryerson scares me. The real truth is I can't wait until that bastard is "toes up" somewhere in Russia. But then we'll still have this mysterious Board Member to deal with, the "wild bunch" right here on the Island, and God knows who or what else.*

He began to wonder whether he had erred in taking this job. Bit late now.

Phil poured himself another brandy—there was a very cold feeling in the pit of his stomach—his hands were trembling—he went to the conference room to prepare.

Moments later, Edward appeared in the conference room with a coffee pot, cream, sugar, silverware, cups and saucers, napkins, all on a large silver tray, along with a pastel blue pastry box bearing the name "Islander Bakeries" in highly-stylized dark-blue letters, with phone and E-coordinates, as well as five addresses within the Island complex.

"This is perfect, Edward. Please just leave everything on the tray on the table. One last thing. Would you bring in a pair of scissors and a hard copy of the Security Department's organization charts?"

A few moments later, Edward entered the conference room, scissors and file in hand with an intrigued look on his face. *I think I'll enjoy working for Mr. Carr,* Edward thought.

"Thanks, Edward. We're all set. Please show Mr. Ryerson directly in when he arrives, and please announce him. By the way, a Mr. Bill Kelly will be coming in at 1600, and I want a full AV of that meeting as well."

Phil piled the pastries on a saucer and placed one pastry on a plate in front of himself, a particularly sugary, crumbly one, along with a napkin. He then used the scissors to cut a rectangular hole in one side of the pastry box sufficiently large to comfortably accommodate his hand and the pistol. He checked the pistol, ensuring a proper load, switched the safety to off, and placed it in the box— hand hole facing him— gun facing Ryerson' chair. He then placed the napkin over the box covering the hole. When he had irregularly stacked the paper files in front of him—all was in readiness, and he still had ten minutes left. These he invested in wandering back to the bar for another brandy.

If he tries to do me, I wonder how? I doubt he would use a gun or a knife. A dart? Poison? Hi-tech? Certainly he's got something better, or at least different than he used on Wilcoxen.

I have no doubt he could take me apart with his bare hands. He could then just throw me off the terrace. Shit! What am I into? He's going to be mad as hell. He's going to suspect I've got his number. He might even feel a little scared and trapped. The people he works for probably react very badly to failure. The odds are getting better that he may do something rash. Wish I'd brought Rachael in—but it's too damned late now. Jesus!

"Mr. Ryerson sir." Edward announced with a smile.

Phil had a sheet of paper in one hand and a half eaten pastry in the other—mouth full—crumbs on chin. He dropped the paper and the pastry, and grabbed his napkin. Wiping his chin and hands in feigned disarray; he then carelessly threw the napkin on his side of the pastry box and extended his hand.

"Hi Stephen. Good to see you again. Have a seat. Coffee? Pastry? Help yourself."

"Thanks, Phil. Good to see you too."

Ryerson took the chair across from Phil and helped himself to coffee. Phil casually reclined in his chair, legs crossed and forearms on the table.

"You missed all the excitement, Phil."

"Excitement?"

"Yes. Dr. Webber cut off all communications and travel. I assumed you knew about it."

"Yes. In fact, Dr. Webber discussed it with me in New York, prior to implementing the ban."

"You approved?"

"Sure. For a limited period, why not? Apparently some of our people in the U.K. ran across what they believed to be some unwelcome interest. Almost looked suspiciously like they knew about the Island. Right? Webber's folks should have some sort of confirmation, yes or no, in a day or so. I reckon it'll turn up nothing. But better to err on the side of caution, eh?"

"Yeah, I suppose so. I do believe I should have been consulted, however."

Phil frowned slightly and hesitated a few moments, as if confused.

"Point well taken, Steve. I was pretty caught up in New York, so I assumed Webber was working with you. *Mia culpa*. Craig is not too strictly wed to chain of command as I'm sure you are aware, so between Craig and I, you fell through the cracks. I didn't even think to ask Craig about it. Sorry. It is his island though and he's the boss. When I get just a little more settled in, you and I and Craig should get together and review things."

"That would be fine. Meanwhile, can you give me some details on this U.K. thing?"

"I would if I could, Stephen. I haven't got a thing. I'll see what Webber has when he finds some time for me. He's on some kind of special project with the University of Michigan and is locked up for a few days."

Silence ensued as Ryerson lowered his head and tilted his eyes piercingly at Phil. It made Phil feel like a small boy lying to his mother about stealing cookies.

"Mmm I see. So how was New York?"

"Great! Got everything done I needed to and still had time to enjoy autumn in the city. So I'm a little embarrassed to report, aside from some business, I had a wonderful time. I think I put on half a kilo."

"Good. What can I do for you, Phil?"

"Right. I've got an old college buddy, actually more of a lifelong friend, really, named Anatov Alyosha. Anatov has amassed an extraordinary fortune in the arms business. He does business all over the world, yet I would surmise only an extremely small handful of people know who the hell he is. Or even that he exists. Everything is done through a labyrinth of front companies and blinds. Everything's on the up and up, mind you—truly gilt edged. He just likes to keep a very low profile. Considering the nature of his business, not a bad idea.

Anyhow, Anatov contacted me in New York. He knows many of my clients are Heads of State for medium to small countries. He was unaware I'd left Barns, Levi and Richardson, but I explained we might still have some common interests. Based on that, he extended an extraordinary offer for the latest upgraded AK47s and a variety of assault vehicles. All new, state of the art, prices that will never be seen again. I suspect Anatov may be getting out of the business. A wise move in these times.

Anyhow I've committed you to a short junket to Moscow, Johannesburg, and Santiago to evaluate the equipment and the deal.

Here's your itinerary," Phil said, handing Ryerson those that he had received. "You'll find everything there. Flights, hotels, contacts, and agenda. I think you'll find that Anatov's people will give you real VIP treatment. I imagine you'll enjoy it."

He handed Ryerson the few sheets of paper with a smile, taking another powdery bite from his pastry, as Ryerson read the itinerary.

As he chewed, he said, "Well Steve?" *Here it comes!*

"AK47s?"

"Mmm Hmm."

"With all due respect, sir...*Are you bleeding crazy?*"

Phil stared at him for a moment. His expression a blend of surprise and chagrin at being address in such a manner.

"The AK47 happens to be the longest and most widely used weapons in human history. I'm sure you are aware of that."

"We have a full compliment of M4 carbines!"

"A lot of people would contend that the M4 is no more than an M16 re-hashed. And our compliment needs expanding within twelve months. I see no reason to invest something of such importance in the hands of a single vendor. We must have flexibility, a portfolio of vendors, options, and your people would no doubt appreciate the opportunity to expand their qualifications and expertise. Let's take a little longer view here. Shall we?

In terms of the assault vehicles, I know nothing about them, but Anatov tells me they're unique in the industry. I don't even know where they're made, or what they do. I do know we have no such vehicles and that may be a chink in our armor.

I want you to familiarize yourself with this ordinance, qualify it, and even close the deal, coordinating closely with me, of course."

"For Chrissake! We're getting our hardware virtually *free* right now!"

"Not relevant. Reliability, flexibility, security. That's relevant, Mr. Ryerson. Nothing else. Understood?"

"Things are moving very fast around here suddenly, *Mr. Carr*. Almost out of control."

"Things will continue to move fast, *Mr. Ryerson*, probably even faster, but I think you'll find we're *very* much in control. I suggest you try to keep up."

If he makes a move it'll be soon...

Phil took his napkin and wiped his chin again. Then he placed the napkin on the box and casually slid his hand under the napkin and into the box, gripping the gun.

Ryerson quietly sipped his coffee and boldly, almost disdainfully, stared at Phil. The moments stretched out. *Was Ryerson casting glances at the box!?*

Phil could feel small drops of cool sweat trickling down from his arm pits and could practically feel the heat of Ryerson' hatred radiating out at him. Looking at Ryerson, he realized even his face had several scars. It looked like he had tried to have them removed—and skillfully too. *If his face looked like that, what about the rest of his body? God this SOB must have seen some shit.* Phil's shirt was now sticking to his back. He could feel the cool, uncomfortable wetness down to his belt line. *Glad I'm wearing a coat.*

Phil's left hand was obscured by the napkin and the pastry box, and he quietly tapped his right hand on the table, feigning impatience, actually to cover the shakes that seemed to be cropping up.

Ryerson gave him a hard, unflinching stare. Ryerson' right hand dropped very slowly, very deliberately, and very smoothly to his lap under the table. Discrete, but no attempt to hide it. *Shit! This was it.*

He had to act quickly.

"Who's your number two Ryerson?"

Ryerson frowned. "I beg your pardon?"

"I asked who your number two man is."

"Bill Kelly. Good man." *Ryerson was caught off guard.*

"How is your department organized?"

"What do you mean?"

"How is your department organized? Civilian or Military? I have your org charts here but they are very unclear."

"I don't see…"

"… not a difficult question, Ryerson. Listen up. How is your department organized? Do you have shifts, and managers and supervisors and guards…or do you have companies, platoons, squads…heroic commanders, brave squad leaders, strack little footy soldiers and so on?"

"Look you son of a…"

"Do your guys salute? Do they carry arms at all times? Do they wear uniforms? Spit-shine, brass and polish…do you play at inspections and parades…maybe a little 'Dropsy-Soapy' in the showers…hmm?"

"Look! You goddamned feather merchant…" *Both hands above the table now!*

"I want Bill Kelly to report to me at 1600 today, in this conference room. Arrange it. Whether you attend the meeting or not is up to you. I don't give a flying fuck either way."

He sees it! He sees I was baiting him, and he sees the danger of losing it now.

Phil felt the wetness of his palm as he slightly loosened his grip on the pistol and forced his other hand flat on the table to hide the shaking.

"Do you have any questions, Stephen?"

"No…I don't believe I do."

"Do we understand each other?"

"Yes. Absolutely. Couldn't be more clear."

Phil watched Ryerson' jaw muscles working.

"I want *daily* written status reports by Fax while you're gone."

"Understood."

He wordlessly exited the room.

Phil pushed back his chair and tried to control his trembling hands.

Whew! I think we actually made it to first base. Think I'll get another very small brandy.

Je T'adore—Shut the Door

Any sufficiently advanced technology is indistinguishable from magic.

Arthur C. Clarke

Phil took his brandy onto the terrace and made the full 360° rectangular walk around his complex to calm down and clear his head. Needless to say, he could be in real danger now. Ryerson might be planning how to take him out right now—and Kelly was possibly assisting.

Phil feared he might have overplayed his hand. But, at the same time, he was pretty sure he'd be facing this scenario in any event. It was only a question of timing. At least he had the initiative of sorts, for now.

Ryerson had the firepower, the expertise, and his two hundred boys. Yet if he were to overtly seize the Island and take out people like Phil and Craig, he would probably defeat his mandate and bring down the wrath of his handlers and masters. So it seemed to Phil that Ryerson, and he for that matter, had little choice but to play out their remorseless little charade—at least he hoped so. At the end of the day, though, he had to face the fact he and Craig and probably many others were facing death at Ryerson's hands were he to stand idle.

Ryerson was scheduled for a 0930 boat. But he needed to get Ryerson out on a plane, instead, and positively confirm he had gone. You can always turn a boat around, kill the skipper, jump ship...lots of ways to reappear on the Island unexpectedly from a boat, especially if you control Island perimeter security. Such surprises were not an option at this point. The same applied to the Athens to Moscow flight. He had to confirm that Ryerson was onboard and had really departed on both flights. Howard would let him know if he no-showed in Moscow. But who could he find to watchdog him from this end? The seven-hour interval between Athens and Moscow could be deadly if Ryerson skipped the plane. He felt very isolated. Now that Ryerson had had time to consider things, he could always change his mind and make a move unexpectedly.

Charlie appeared right on time, well dressed, well pressed, clean, shaved, coiffed, even wearing cologne, attaché case in hand. He was actually a good looking fellow when he looked after himself.

Looking at Charlie appraisingly, Phil said, "Damn Charlie! You clean up good!"

"Thanks Phil. Is this penthouse really yours? You live here?"

"Well, I've lived here very little so far...but yes, these are my quarters."

"How are your accommodations Charlie?"

"Great. But I've *got* to have a tour of *this* place!"

"Well, I could use a little refresher course on this place myself, and it's still a few minutes before lunch. So let's walk around a bit."

Starting in the reception area, Phil somewhat sheepishly showed Charlie through the sitting room, game room, bar, library, dining room, conference room, screening room, kitchen, pantry, office, bed and dressing room, sauna, whirlpool, exercise room, pool, lab, and communications center.

As they sat down to lunch, Charlie said, "My God! Trump doesn't live like this in Manhattan!"

"We're not in Manhattan, Charlie. Have some sea bass."

Phil poured the wine and they both ate hungrily.

"This is really excellent...but what the hell kind of wine is that?"

"It's called Retsina. Retsina's a good white wine aged in barrels treated with pine resin, made only in Greece. They've been making it for over three-thousand years. Do you like it?"

"It grows on you, I guess."

"Well, some say it's either an acquired taste, or it tastes like turpentine. I find it very refreshing in hot weather with food. They make a rosé which has a softer tenor and is harder to find."

After dessert and coffee, Charlie opened the dialog. "I'm ready to start work Phil. Can someone take me to your cluster?"

"Ah, things have changed a bit. I want you to wait a day or so before you start. Why don't you rest up from your trip, just relax and enjoy the facility?"

"It's your dime, Phil. I'll lie around the pool and drink your booze with pleasure."

"Okay. By the way, you said you had some surprises?"

"Yes. I'll be installing the first surprise as soon as I start—a very advanced SDF array."

"SDF array?"

"Signal Direction Finders. They operate continuously, twenty-four hours a day. They are triple redundant so there is never a "blind spot" for even a second. They are solar and wind powered with a back-up, continuous charging battery, so they are virtually carefree. They phone home feature should anyone attempt to tamper with them. They are very small. Very hard to spot. They mount on a rotating base with a sort of metal wind sock that protects and camouflages the equipment, particularly the wind generator. They generate a signature so faint it is detectable only by the most sensitive equipment, so sensitive in fact the equipment does not exist outside scientific applications. Never before in field use, until now. They are capable of detecting signals of equal spectrum.

To give you some idea of their sensitivity, the SETI project has been using this technology for some years at sites like the Arecibo Radio Telescope in Puerto Rico. One of their experts once stated that the aggregate energy of all the incoming radio signals they had captured and analyzed over the years was roughly equivalent to the energy produced by a single snowflake landing on earth."

"That's hard to imagine, Charlie. We can still track signals of that faintness?"

"The SDF detectors engage a GPS transponder and forward a high-speed, compressed, encrypted message burst within far less than one second of any transmission emanating other than from the cluster concentrator. This message contains the exact location of the transmission to within a few centimeters, and the actual text of the message up to the time of alert—whether it is interpretable or not—and they continue to capture and re-transmit the text afterward until termination of the message. They are targeted up to ninety degrees above the horizon, with a hundred-eighty-degree sweep, so they can be placed nearly anywhere. I can install an option that instantly activates a scrambler upon unauthorized detection. Pretty cool huh?"

"Does this apply to inbound transmissions?"

"Only insofar as it activates the scrambler feature. When we detect an inbound bandit not addressed to Proteus Point we can scramble the message, but we cannot pinpoint the source of an incoming."

"Suppose I were to take my transmitter to a position right next to the Proteus Point Cluster.?"

Charlie smiled.

"The SDF doesn't sanction bandits based on source coordinates. Position relative to the concentrator is not the least bit relevant. The other software and hardware I will be installing places, among other things, an imbedded Time/Date/Approved stamp in every outbound message. Without my stamp-of-approval, it is an unauthorized transmission, and the SDF reads that."

"And what about, say...a legitimate mobile phone transmission generated from another part of the Island?"

"We will be requiring all mobile phones used as their primary address to be the Proteus Point Cluster, which in turn, will connect the user and relay the message, once interrogated, to the messages' secondary address. We will issue cards to all authorized mobile phones and PCs. All legitimate mobiles are routed through the concentrator anyway."

"So, I know within a second or less the exact location and text of an unauthorized signal, and I can block the outward signal by scrambling it if I wish. Any way you can tell me the depth?"

"Depth?"

"Yes. This complex may exceed sixty stories underground. If a signal emanates from underground, I need to know how deep. Otherwise, I would waste a great deal of time going from floor to floor trying to triangulate its source."

"And you think they can transmit from way down there?"

"I don't know. You're the expert. But I need to cover all bases."

"I see. We do have a solution for that...though it's not totally precise. Here's how it works. You preset an assumed power of a normal transmission based on the hardware you know is probably in use, and the requisite range. You express this assumed power in a unit of measurement called a jansky, notated as 'Jy,' which expresses the flux density of a given signal. You load the floor-by-floor diminishment of Jy strength, based on actual measurements. The SDF then measures the janskys of a signal it encounters and reports not only the location, but the depth of a bandit.

"Interestingly, janskys are normally used to measure *inbound* transmissions from galactic sources. We will now use it for *outbound* measurements and detection. This I think is totally new."

"That *is* pretty cool, Charlie. Just what we need. If the rest of your goodies compare with this, we should be in great shape." Phil thought for a moment. "Say, Charlie. You know Athens?"

"Never been there. Always wanted to go."

"How about I put you on a private jet and fly you there tonight? We'll put you up in the best hotel, everything First Class for two or three days"

"What's the catch Phil?"

"I need you to go the Athens airport tomorrow morning around 1030 and watch a guy get on a plane for Moscow. Watch him get on. Watch the doors close. Watch the blocks off. Watch the wheels up. All the while ensuring he doesn't get off that plane. Report back and then have a ball for a couple of days. I'll give you a picture of the man, the flight number, and that's all you need."

"Any risk?"

"None whatsoever. This guy doesn't know you from Adam. We'll put you on a jet tonight under cover of night and total security."

"Jesus, what kind of shit are you into?"

"Would you like to go to Athens?"

"Okay. What the hell. Sounds fun."

"Be ready at 1930 sharp. We'll send someone around for you. I will have all the arrangements by then."

Charlie went off happily to pack a bag and Phil got on the phone.

"Jackie? Can you get me a flight to Athens airport at 2000? Not for me, it's for Charlie Stein our new communications genius. This needs to be totally secret. The aircraft should be fueled and prepped *now* to avoid attracting attention at night, and only the pilots and one tower controller should be aware of the flight. They should know nothing of their passenger. I want them to board the aircraft first, do their preflight, close their door and not open it again until the passenger has deplaned in Athens, and they should file their flight plans at the last possible moment. Their passenger should carry the passenger manifest onboard. Clear?"

"I can arrange it, Phil."

"Can you get Charlie a suite in the best hotel in Athens and arrange the same flight for Stephen Ryerson at 0930 tomorrow morning to connect with his Olympic flight to Moscow."

"Sure."

"Who do I speak to for a regional weather forecast?"

"That would be John Alemanno, Operations Manager. Shall I get him on the line?"

"No, Jackie, thanks, I just need his extension. I'll call back if Craig's available to meet. I need to speak to Rachael."

"They're both here and waiting to speak to you too. John's extension is 3275."

"Great. I'll call back in about three minutes."

He went back to the house phone.

"Edward?"

"Yes, Phil."

"Would you please contact a John Alemanno in Operations on extension 3275? I need a regional weather forecast for the next twenty-four hours all the way to Lefkada. I'm particularly interested in any storm fronts coming though, even if they're not directly in line of flight between here and Lefkada."

"I'll get back to you, Phil."

"Thanks."

He made his next call.

"Hi, Jackie. Me again. Can I see Craig and Rachael at 1645?"

There was a brief hold. "They'll be waiting for you in Craig's office."

"Good. See you in a few minutes."

Edward came on the house phone.

"Yes, Edward?"

"John tells me there's a pretty strong front coming out of the Southwest. It's not headed directly for Lefkada, but the weather may get rough nonetheless."

"Perfect. Thanks, Edward."

Phil called Jackie again.

"Jackie?"

"Yes, Phil."

"Please have the travel office contact Stephen Ryerson and tell him he has been rescheduled for a 0930 flight to Athens tomorrow morning. As a result of some incoming weather he cannot travel by sea. They should assure him he will connect with an earlier flight to Moscow."

"No problem, Phil."

"Thanks."

Promptly at 1600 Bill Kelly arrived at Phil's conference room...*alone.*

Now here's a dead giveaway. Kelly's dirty. Ryerson trusts him to meet with me unsupervised. Surely Ryerson would be aware that he's tipping his hand. I wonder what he's trying to tell me. Or is this just a good 'ol "spit in the eye"?

"Bill Kelly? I'm Philip Carr. Glad to meet you."

"Glad to meet you, Mr. Carr."

Kelly was solidly built, a little on the short side, which gave him the impression of being even more sturdy. He had short, red hair, a fair complexion and almost translucent blue eyes above grimly thin, humorless lips. Phil didn't think he and Kelly were destined to share a future as close buddies.

"The sun's over the yardarm, Mr. Kelly. I think I'll have a drink. Care to join?"

"Sure. Thank you."

"What'll you have?"

"Whatever you're having is fine."

"Okay."

Phil picked up the phone and keyed a direct dial.

"Edward, please bring in a bottle of Jack Daniels and two glasses. Thanks."

"Where do you come from, Bill? May I call you Bill? Call me Phil by the way."

"Please do call me Bill, sir. I come originally from Shannon, Ireland, but I grew up in Seattle, Washington."

"You a military man? I haven't seen your file yet."

"I was a Navy SEAL for several years, and I have spent a good many years as a military advisor in South America, the Middle East, the Far East, and the Philippines."

"Impressive."

Edward entered the room with a drink tray and a large bowl of potato chips. The two men mixed their own drinks. Phil noted that Kelly poured himself a very weak drink—just enough whiskey to color the water, in fact. *Here was a man who worried about keeping his wits about him.*

"Bill, you may know that Steve Ryerson is off on a business trip for the next couple of weeks or so. Since security seems to have 'hotten'd up' a bit in the last few days, I thought we should meet each other in case we need to do some work together."

"I understand, sir."

"I've been reviewing our security apparatus with Mr. Ryerson. It's very formidable. Do you agree?"

"I certainly do, sir. I've never seen anything quite like it."

"So, how would you evaluate our current readiness status?"

"I would say we are fully ready. We can certainly take on nearly any conventional threat."

"In your opinion have we overlooked anything?"

"No, sir."

"Any other actions that we should consider taking?"

"No, sir."

"Internal or external?"

"Both are totally comprehensive, sir."

"I see. Thank you for your assessment, Mr. Kelly. By the way, I may need to see you again at 1600 tomorrow. Please keep that time slot open for me."

"I certainly will."

"Thank you, Bill. That will be all."

After Bill left, Phil got back on the phone. "Edward, will you please ask Rachael Stone to join me in my conference room? She's presently with Dr. Webber."

Five minutes later, Rachael Stone entered the room. She had rich auburn hair, a lovely sculpted face graced with extraordinary green eyes. She was not tall at all, but she had a very provocative figure. All in all she was not someone you would suspect could kick your ass without thinking twice. She was pretty good with a gun. She was no detective, no top gun, spy, or anything else very arcane. She was simply a very professional bodyguard and pretty tough considering her size. Basically, in her company, you'd be kept safe. The main reason she was respected as one of the best was her total diligence. Like a bulldog, always alert, never letting go.

"Hi, Phil! Thought I'd never see you. You been busy or just hiding out?"

"Busy, Rachael. I wish I could hide out." Phil smiled. 'Damn it's good to see you, Rachael. I truly appreciate you disrupting your schedule to help us out."

They shook hands and roughly hugged at the same time.

"Damn, Philip! Are these really your digs?"

"Umm hmm." Phil replied absently, as he carefully wrapped Kelly's glass.

"I'm impressed. Coming up in the world I see. I need a tour of this fortress. I can't tell whether you've landed in the honey pot or the shit pot. From what I've been hearing I would guess both."

"You've got it. Why don't we have dinner up here and I'll give you the nickel walking tour at the same time?"

"Sure. Whatsitake to get a good steak around here?"

"I'll look after it. Do you mind if it's a rather late dinner? We've got a flight to see off tonight."

"No problem. What flight?"

"I want to make sure that Charlie Stein gets off to Athens on a private flight I've arranged. I'd like you to help ensure that the flight is unobserved and unmolested. Come fully loaded, and it's dark out there.

"Meanwhile, we need to put together another file on a Mr. Bill Kelly for Howard in Chicago *tout de suite*. I assume that Bill Kelly is an alias. There are prints on that glass. We served some nice greasy chips just to make sure they come out well. We'll get a photo right now. Think Howard can respond by 1530 CET tomorrow?"

"He delivered fast on the Ryerson file. I'll need his personnel file, even if it is mostly BS."

"Okay, take the glass and do what you do, and we'll get Kelly's file at Craig's office. That'll have a photograph of him as well. We're late for Craig by the way. Let's go."

Phil dialed the house phone.

"Edward, would you retrieve the Ryerson and Kelly DVD from today and take it down to Dr. Webber's office please?"

Dr. Craig Webber rose from his desk immediately upon the entry of Rachael and Phil. He took Phil's hand in his two hands shaking it with a warmth that belied his pleasure at seeing him. Clearly the doctor had been nervous, perhaps even frightened and alone during his absence. Phil felt a tug of guilt thinking of the fun he had in New York while the doctor sweated things out nearly alone here.

"Let's go into the other room and be comfortable."

As they entered the sitting room, Dr. Webber headed for the bar to mix drinks, while Rachael excused herself to make a call to Howard Doyle and send him Kelly's file.

"What can I get for you, Phil?"

"Scotch rocks would be great. I need a big one."

"Why? What's been going on?"

At that moment, Edward entered, DVD in hand.

"I'll show you Craig."

While he inserted the DVD and turned on the various units, Phil said, "You already know Ryerson is as dirty as they get. I assume Kelly is as well...not to mention the two-hundred buckaroos reporting to them. We could find ourselves in some very deep shit unless we finesse our way through this with great care."

"Who followed you in New York?"

"I have no idea. My best guess is someone who works for Ryerson."

"Any other troubles?"

"No. I had my place checked out for taps and bugs. It was clean. I got a couple of guys to watch over me and Stein until we left for Athens. Nothing came up."

"So Ryerson is off to Moscow?"

"I hope so. We're shipping Stein out tonight to confirm that he boards the Moscow flight from Athens, and we've cancelled his boat using the guise of bad weather in favor of a flight at 0930 tomorrow morning. We will make damn sure he's on that flight. We'd never be sure he actually left if he departed by boat."

"I see. Good thinking. And your arms dealers in Moscow. Is that arranged?"

"Yes. All set."

Craig peered at Phil for a few moments. "And the business deal. Are their prices and technology really that interesting?"

"Well, I suppose based on..."

At that moment Rachael entered the sitting room.

Phil looked up. "Ah. We can start the DVD now."

Craig continued to stare at Phil as he started the DVD. A few minutes later, the show was over.

Craig stood and went to the bar making another drink. Then he turned and stood directly in front of Phil. 'Well I'm damned."

Craig thought for a moment. "The camera was positioned behind you Phil. I guess that's so we could observe Ryerson and Kelly more closely. What was in the blue pastry box, Phil?"

"A Smith and Wesson 9 millimeter automatic pistol... aimed directly at Ryerson's heart."

"You've got more balls than I do. What was Ryerson going for under the table?"

"I honestly don't know. Definitely there was something. If I were to hazard a guess, I would say some kind of dart, or pique, or maybe some type of fleshette. Quiet. Poisonous. Probably deadly. What do you think Rachael?"

"I'm out of my depth here. Fact is I don't know whose depth this is. But I would tend to agree he was going for some kind of a thrower. He would have done you right under the table and you probably would have never known what hit you, nor anyone else for that matter."

"Okay. Why did he stop?"

"He saw that I was baiting him," Phil said, "into something that would ruin whomever's plan he was charged with. And I think it scared hell out of him. Whoever his masters are...he doesn't want to piss them off."

Craig sat down heavily and gave Phil a piercing stare. "Phil, I think a lot of Rachael. Can we discuss *anything* in her presence?"

Phil glanced at Rachael.

She cleared her throat. "Anything I learn or hear on this job...stays here. You have my word on that."

"Alright. Phil, I think this 'arms merchant' is so much bullshit. What's going to really happen in Moscow?"

Phil looked at Craig intently. "There were never any arms. I don't know anyone named Anatov Alyosha. We're going to take Ryerson out. We have the best people on this. Moscow's the perfect venue. Things like this happen daily there. There is absolutely no risk, nor loss, nor alternative, nor interest by the Russian authorities. Ryerson is a serial, professional assassin. If we don't kill him. He *will* kill us. That's a fact."

"We can't just throw him off the Island? Fire him. Tell him to simply get the hell out?"

"Craig, he's got more than two-hundred goons on this island, and he's ready and willing to kill us. I am quite sure he's acting under orders. So there's no dissuading him. You are suggesting suicide to take any other action. Don't think I want this. I can't stand the idea, but I can't think of another way. Not only your life, but your life's work is at stake here as well. You know I'm right, Craig."

Webber stood and walked over to his paintings. "Shit! Shit! Shit! Is this the end of it?"

"Well...given that we have a reasonable interval before there is suspicion as to Ryerson's whereabouts, and we can take some positive action to neutralize his goons...Maybe."

"Keep me the hell out of this from now on. You asked if you were the fall guy. Well you sure as bloody hell are. Don't fail. Don't fall. Just get rid of this horrible infection we somehow contracted."

"Fair enough, Craig. I'd like to keep Rachael onsite for an extended period if it can be arranged." He looked at Rachael.

She nodded consent.

"I'll handle everything from here, Craig. Rachael and I will bust ass to keep you safe. But you should be aware of one last thing."

"Yes?"

"We're practically convinced that your Board Member is up to his neck in this. I understand his second report on Ryerson reaffirmed that he was clean as the original investigation concluded. We're going to have to talk when the dust settles a bit. Okay?"

Silence.

"Okay Craig?"

"Yes godamnit! What would have happened, Phil, if you *hadn't* come on board?" There was accusation and bitter resentment in his voice.

"Probably nothing, Craig...not until the time came for them to kill you, your staff, and students, destroy the Island, and steal all the good work you have done. I can't even begin to conceive of the body count. Ryerson murdered Wilcoxen, and I think you damn well knew it, or strongly suspected it."

After a few moments, Webber seemed to collapse into himself. With a gray face and a shaky voice, he acquiesced. "I know you're right. My apologies. These are dark waters for me. I feel like dousing the whole damned Island in disinfectant, myself included. I'll work with you on the Board Member whenever you like and I'll give you every cooperation. *Anything* to purge the foulness from this Island."

Webber released a long, shuddering sigh. "So...why don't we just sit down, have another drink, and just be pleasant for a few moments?" he almost whispered.

Rachael and Phil smiled thoughtfully at each other and went to the bar.

At around 1930, Rachael silently appeared in night camouflage, carrying a high powered sniper rifle equipped with a night-vision scope and a small radio, atop the hangar. This afforded her an unobstructed 360° view of the area and a bird's eye view of activities around the aircraft, which was being quietly rolled out now.

"How's it looking, Rachael?"

"All clear, Phil. Not a thing out there for at least four hundred meters in any direction."

Two uniformed pilots boarded the aircraft from the hanger. A few moments after that, another figure boarded the aircraft, closed and dogged the door, engines revved, preflight checks, power reverse swerve onto the runway approach, full power, and swiftly launched into the darkness.

Half an hour later, Rachael and Phil were dining poolside on his terrace, taking in the coolness of the evening, a thousand stars sprayed across the sky, a lustrous silvered moon glowing bright, and the thunder of the sea far below.

"This may be the best steak I've ever eaten!" Rachael raved. 'Where do you get your beef from?"

"Believe it or not, we grow it right here on the Island."

"That hardly seems possible. I haven't seen cattle anywhere."

"We grew that potato, the vegetables, and the salad, even this excellent Cabernet Sauvignon we're drinking and, when the time comes for a superb fruit dessert, every ingredient will have come from this Island. We import no food or drink, whatsoever, or fuels, or most medicines for that matter, except flour, grain, coffee, tea, chocolate, hardware, appliances, and a few other staples. Many students insisted we import lander fashions as well, and it was a harmless indulgence we were pleased to provide. Predictably, however, our shopping centers now carry every kind of lander style, fad, gimcrack, and knick-knacks. In fact, we import less and less from off-island all the time, notwithstanding amusement and style items. One day we may consider exporting."

"How's that possible?"

"Essentially, we train biologicals to manipulate substances at the molecular level. For example bio-fuel is basically seawater biomass, micro-manipulated so that hydrogen and oxygen are bonded. The energy for such bonding is the problem. Our scientists use the energy potential at the sub-molecular level. This incites the bonding process, without additional expenditure. When you've been here a bit longer I'll show you more in detail."

"Phil, I try not to ask too many questions from my clients. But there is a great deal more going on here than meets the eye."

"That much is certain."

"And you're in charge of it all?"

"Yes. I report to Dr. Webber. I am CEO, COO, Chancellor, and Craig is Chairman of the Board."

"Look. Dr. Webber gave me the most cursory of briefings when I came. Basically, he said I should keep him alive because bad guys had invaded the campus and, frankly, I am intrigued about what the devil really goes on here. Why all the secrecy if this is just a University? What the hell do you guys actually do here? And why do you have a whole troop of Neanderthals freely running about ready to kill you?"

Phil and Rachael regarded each other for some time. In the soft glow of moon and candlelight they should have been enjoying the reverie of the evening.

"Frankly, we both need more information in that regard," Phil said. "I'll work with you on that. Ready for dessert?" he asked, as he poured more wine and pushed a small button for Edward.

"Sure, dessert is fine. So when do I get the tour of these palatial digs?"

After dessert, coffee and cognac, Phil gave her the tour; and Platonically kissed her good night at Phil's elevator "See you in the morning?"

"Yes. Why don't you come up for breakfast around 0930? We should get a call from Charlie Stein just afterwards."

"See you in the morning, Phil."

Ryerson had given some serious thought to his situation. He hadn't been caught off-guard like that in years.

You can kill people. But you can't just kill them at will. Just because they piss you off, dammit. That's stupid and dangerous. It achieves nothing. He should have refused the assassination of Wilcoxen. He should have found a rationale out of it and made it stick. Killing Wilcoxen triggered this whole mess. Alarms were blaring everywhere in his mind.

That bastard Carr. Carr wouldn't have been here if Wilcoxen were alive.

He would have to be an idiot not to admit, at least to himself, that he'd been marked. Had someone dropped a dime on him? He thought not. There was no logical who or why to this idea. And if someone actually did so, they would know the inescapable danger involved.

Perhaps that son of a bitch Carr had simply figured it out and fingered him without help. He suspected that Carr was a bit of a player. Maybe a bad ass. What was in that damn blue pastry box in his office? Who would have walked out alive if he'd have called him on it?

Wilcoxen was dead and now he was facing Carr. Things certainly weren't looking up. Well shit happens.

He considered long and hard whether to brief his boss on this, and finally concluded that it might backfire. His boss might reveal him as Wilcoxen's killer to the big boys as an expedient fall-guy to simplify the situation. Good-bye Ryerson.

Or, simply by reporting it to his boss, he would make himself appear incompetent, perhaps fearful, and somehow unable to handle the situation. A cry for help? This was definitely not the time for that.

On the other hand, they would get pretty edgy if he failed to report something so important. This, however, he could easily explain away by responding that he was involved in normal planning activities, playing along with the game, and everything was exactly as it looked on the surface. Nothing really to report.

Tricky situation. That bastard Carr. Should he have Carr checked out? Hell no. That was just stupid. The University would have brought all its assets to bear on ensuring who and what he was since he was born. Besides, they probably already knew him well when they recruited him. Forget that.

Conclusions: Go to Moscow. Have some fun. Report to no one. Christ! Why not go ahead and buy some AK's? What the hell did he care? Maybe he'd take out that SOB Carr when and if ever feasible. Brief Kelly to keep his damned mouth shut, and put the fear of God in him should he screw up in any way.

He packed his bag and readied for the flight.

A lovely morning broke with light mist on the sea and a blinding sun, but not too hot yet with a cool breeze from the east. Rachael and Phil breakfasted on his terrace, with coffee, juice, fresh pastries (despite the memory they recalled to Phil), and the best sausages either one had ever tasted.

"Rachael, I'm sorry to play things so close to the vest right now. You know? If you took over as Director of Security here, there wouldn't be one damn thing about this place you wouldn't know."

"Mmm, that could be interesting for awhile. Are you serious?"

"Could be. Interesting work, money no problem, a little excitement, and a very pleasant ambience."

"Let's talk when the time is right, Phil, if you're still interested."

"Deal."

Edward entered the terrace carrying Phil's mobile phone.

"Mr. Stein on the line from Athens for you Phil."

"Thanks."

"Charlie? How goes it in Athens?"

"Your boy's on the flight. I guarantee it."

"Great! Thanks, Charlie. Have a ball in Athens."

Into the Borscht

Death is nothing to us, since when we are, death has not come, and when death has come, we are not.

Epicurus

Ryerson checked into a suite at the Baltschug Kempinski Hotel just outside the Kremlin, and slept well into the next morning.

Over room service breakfast the phone rang.

"Mr. Ryerson, my name is Ivan Borishevski. I work for Anatov Alyosha. Welcome to Moskva, Mr. Ryerson."

"Thank you."

"Do you know Moskva, Mr. Ryerson?"

"Yes. I've been here many times—during and after the CCCP."

"Excellent. I was going to offer you a tour of our city, but instead we can move along to even more pleasant things, perhaps. Mr. Alyosha will join us tomorrow evening. In the meantime, I propose we send a car for you, to take you to a most excellent village called Sergiev Posad, about 70 kilometers to northwest of Moskva. This is one of the more picturesque villages in Russia, with some very famous architecture and monasteries. In fact, the Trinity-St. Sergius Monastery is located there. We thought you might enjoy a brief walkabout there and a good Russian lunch.

Mr. Alyosha has a wonderful dacha there that was one of the hunting lodges of Catherine the Great, Dacha St. Sergius. Anatov would like you to be his guest there during your stay. The dacha boasts a vast underground complex where we qualify and demonstrate our various products. I think you will find it most useful and interesting.

Does this sound satisfactory Mr. Ryerson?"

"It sounds fine."

"Excellent. In that case I suggest you dress comfortably, a little warmly, and a car will call for you in half an hour in front of your hotel if that is alright?"

"Fine."

"The car is a black Mercedes limousine, and you will recognize it by a blue crest on the side with stylized "AA" in the middle. Please don't bother re-packing or checking out of your hotel. That will all be looked after for you."

"Okay."

"We'll see you soon, Mr. Ryerson. I look forward to meeting you in person."

"As do I. Goodbye."

Ryerson looked forward to a little pampering, some relaxation, and some good food in a royal hunting lodge, maybe some women, and he wanted to get his hands on the latest AK47. He had no choice but to play out the game as Carr had engineered it. He might as well calm down and enjoy it. Besides, to do otherwise would mean his instant execution. So he eagerly finished breakfast, changed clothes, and descended to the lobby. As promised, he found a large black Mercedes limousine waiting in front of the hotel. As he approached the car, the driver dismounted and opened a rear door for him.

"Good morning, Mr. Ryerson. I am Viktor. We will be driving you about seventy kilometers today to a classical Russian village called Sergiev Posad. You will find all sorts of drinking materials in the cold box, and there are reading materials in the cupboard to its right.

We have a beautiful day, so please enjoy the ride and let me know if you need anything."

"Thank you, Viktor."

They smoothly pulled out into traffic and after finding their way to the Tverskaya were heading north out of Moscow. Ryerson soon lost his bearings, but he did see some of the anti-tank barriers constructed to block the German tanks during WWII. Looking like huge black children's Jacks, they provided a familiar reference. He found them a fitting relic of the war.

The road to Sergiev Posad runs through huge birch forests and rolling hills, a little bleak this time of year, as well as past groups of country homes, or dachas. Dachas aren't the sole province of the wealthy. Ryerson remembered the bizarre stories about the goings on at Joe Stalin's humble dacha. Many Russian families own one, and they run the gamut from nothing more than primitive weekend shacks, to luxurious millionaire retreats. With the advent of the new Russian moneyed class, the modern dacha had come into its own.

Icy vodka in hand, Ryerson reclined and enjoyed the ride.

About an hour later, the limousine pulled to a stop in front of what appeared to be a country inn. And indeed it was. The driver opened his door and ushered him into the warm interior of the Inn's bar, empty at this time of day.

Seated before an open fire, Ryerson spotted a man who must be Ivan Borishevski. Borishevski rose and extended his hand as Ryerson approached.

"Mr. Ryerson! It's a pleasure to meet you. I am Ivan. Please have a seat."

For lack of a better term, Ivan was "lumpy" looking. He had a ruddy, pock-marked face, a large nose that had clearly been broken a few times, and teeth that badly needed straightening. His neck was somehow not symmetrical and his shoulders were actually uneven. All this was emphasized by poor posture, frogish legs, and gnarly knuckles. He was powerfully built and had the habit of habitually squinting his eyes, as he laced his fingers.

Ryerson thought he was the last man he would hire as a sales representative. But as an arms dealer he seemed strangely appropriate, especially considering the repellent bastards that probably comprised the lion's share of his market base.

"It's a pleasure to meet you, Ivan. It was a lovely drive up here. I'm looking forward to seeing more."

At that moment a pretty waitress brought glasses, a frosted bottle of vodka, a bowel of cucumbers mixed with onions and sour cream, tiny crackers, caviar, and some unidentifiable nuts mixed with dried fruits.

"I thought we would have lunch here and then have a look around the village. Then I have arranged a functional introduction to the Kalashnikova. As I told you on the phone, Mr. Alyosha maintains a very large armory and arms-testing area deep under his dacha where you can exercise the equipment as much as you like without disturbing neighbors. Such a thing would not be possible in Moskva, so this facility is most useful to us."

"I understand. Will we be evaluating more than just the AK47 here?"

"No. I will accompany you to Johannesburg on Mr. Alyosha's private jet. There we will see some ground-assault vehicles, and later in Santiago, we have two or three airborne assault vehicles for your inspection.

"Mr. Ryerson, I notice you seem a little uneasy discussing these things in a public bar. I assure you that any sales we conduct are with the full knowledge and legal sanction of the

Russian government, as well as major governments around the world. I should point out," Ivan said and smiled, "that Mr. Alyosha owns this Inn."

"I am pleased to hear that. I was given this assurance before my departure. On the other hand, we as buyers require discretion in all such dealings."

"I fully understand, Mr. Ryerson, and I suggest you pursue that with Mr. Alyosha when he arrives tomorrow. We have had similar business relations many, many times in the past, and I can attest to our complete confidentiality and ability to mask the end user."

"Good."

"And finally, Mr. Ryerson, after some time on our range, we would like to offer you dinner in the dacha. I have taken the liberty of inviting a few lovely guests to join us?"

"Sounds great, Ivan."

"Perhaps we should proceed to our private dining room for lunch now."

Cold Borscht with sour cream, beet and onion salad, boiled beef with spiced cabbage and boiled potatoes. A lingenberry torte was accompanied by a sweet red wine and the ubiquitous bottle of vodka. Ryerson knew he was indeed in Russia. Not that it wasn't good, it was distinctive.

Two hours later, they arrived at the dacha. It resembled a huge sort of a two-story A-frame with ornate dark wood carvings covering the outside. Inside, it was stunning. They had apparently relinquished Imperial Russia in favor of Malibu modern. It was complete with a state-of-the-art kitchen, lighting, sound system, baths, and security. Furnishings came all in shades of sandy beige, floor coverings, furniture, and even the art works. It made a nice contrast with the ornate exterior and the bleak, late, Russian autumn.

They showed Ryerson to his bedroom. They had laid out toiletries, fatigues, and boots, explaining that the fatigues were for the range and that his belongings would arrive in about an hour. Ryerson quickly changed and went downstairs.

"This afternoon you'll be firing the Kalashnikova Modernized—AKM AK47 assault rifle, 7.62x39 mm Caliber, Gas operated, rotating bolt with 2 lugs, 870 mm length overall, 415 mm Barrel length, 3.14 kg empty weight, magazine capacity thirty rounds, cyclic fire rate of 600 rpm and a maximum effective killing range of around 400 meters. The killing range is extended a little farther with a sniper scope if you're good enough.

"This is one rugged piece of hardware. Any weather, any terrain, the roughest handling, it takes it all and more. It hardly jams (unlike the M16). It is reasonably accurate (unlike the M16). And it is easy to use, requiring very little training.

"But let's go down and give it a workout."

Ryerson followed Ivan to the rear of the dacha, through a heavy, locked door, through another, and finally down a poorly lit spiral staircase hewn from ancient stones, down and down. After a few moments, they came to a landing and another heavy locked door. Upon entering the door, they found themselves in an enormous long room with a curved brick ceiling, tile floors, and a great deal of arc lighting. At their end of the room was a neatly piled little bunker of sandbags and at the far end of the room (about thirty meters) were a variety of well lit targets, ranging from black paste board silhouettes, to classical bulls-eyes, to several prop windows which currently stood vacant and unused.

In the little bunker rested an AK47 and a generous supply of banana clips. Ryerson was amused to see next to the AK47 a silver tray bearing a bottle of vodka, two glasses, an ashtray, matches, and cigars. He could practically smell the Cubans, Nicaraguans, Salvadorians, Africans, and Mid-Easterners who had blown cigar smoke through here.

"Mr. Ryerson do I need to check you out on this weapon, or are you familiar with it?"

"I've fired dozens, Ivan."

"Okay. Good. Let's get started."

Ryerson stepped into the bunker and took up the '47, inserted a clip, cocked the weapon, switched off the safety and kneeled against the bunker, steadying the gun atop the bags. As Ryerson snuggled his face into the stock preparing to aim and fire...Ivan quietly walked up to Ryerson on his left, withdrew a .22 caliber pistol and very slowly squeezed off a shot just at the base of his skull. No blood was spilled except a small stain on one of the sand bags. The entire mini-bunker had been piled atop a large gray waterproof canvas.

Ryerson experienced the wonder of entering into an entirely new and alien, though unbelievably short-lived reality.

For the fleetest of nanoseconds, Ryerson's universe consisted solely of an intense nova of blinding, soundless, overwhelming white light and an unbelievable, searing pain. Such an explosion of pain seemed beyond reason, beyond reality. The flash of light dimmed to nonexistence like a lightening flash from a distant horizon. The pain ended instantaneously. Then nothing. Not even blackness.

The three men then wrapped Ryerson up in the canvas and carefully bore him upstairs and outside to their waiting van. After loading him into the van, they drove through the forest for about two kilometers down a logging road to a deserted spot where a hole one meter, by two meters, by four meters deep had already been neatly excavated by a machine used on the logging sites. They called it a "Ditch Witch" and were very amused by the name.

They lowered Ryerson down the hole, opened the canvas and covered him with ten liters of uncut, concentrated Hydrochloric Acid, which would serve to render the body literally unidentifiable and almost totally break it down. After waiting for well over two hours, smoking and drinking from a flask of vodka, intermittently shifting in concert with the light breeze to avoid toxic fumes rising from the hole, a nearly invisible, deadly will o' the wisp, they covered the remains with a thick layer of a white powder consisting mainly of Calcium Oxide and trace amounts of other Oxides, Magnesium, Aluminum, and Iron, a mixture commonly referred to as quicklime (CaO). This would aid in masking odors generated as a result of any remaining decomposition. Although at a depth of four meters, this was hardly a major consideration (especially taking into account twenty-five kilos of deer droppings they were going to mix into the final layer of soil).

This they covered it with another canvas. They covered everything with local stones, sand mixed with a moistened viscous clay, to a thickness of one meter. Within a relatively short time, this would form a concrete hard, air-tight barrier.

They refilled the hole and artfully covered the mound with local stones to look natural, even planting a small indigenous fir amongst the stones. They covered the entire site with sandy topsoil, dead leaves, and then pine needles. They removed all tracks back to the logging road.

Their landscaping was complete and flawless. Ryerson would never be discovered and, if discovered, never identified. As they drove away, snow was already accumulating its long winter blanket. When the snow finally melted, months from now, an army of forensic experts would never suspect this site concealed murder.

They returned to the dacha and loaded the van with their sand bags, the targets, the weapon and ammunition, as well as the remainder of their food, flash lights, clothes, pails, and gloves. They cleaned the house, rubbed it down for finger prints, removed the toilette kit they had loaned Ryerson and rubbed down his room as well.

They double checked everything, locked the house, and drove away under a glowing sky as the cold white wintry sun rose. They didn't own the dacha and had no idea who did. They did know the owner used it only for holidays, if then, and was presently under surveillance by other members of their team. They were therefore safe from discovery. They had used this dacha for this same purpose numerous times in the past.

They didn't know their victim. They had no idea who had ordered this assassination. They didn't care. They did know they were at least seven layers removed from their actual client. Their excessive pains were expended as much in their client's interest as their own protection. The result was a thoroughly reliable, professional job. They each maintained rundown, cold-water flats in the worst parts of Moscow. They were each employed as manual laborers by the same shell company and when not "on the job" they each enjoyed luxury villas in surrounding countries. They paid meager taxes. They had friends and family. Each would stand up to a reasonably close scrutiny. None had ever been apprehended for any reason. They weren't top guns, nor super assassins, or spooks of any description. They never employed hi-tech, arcane killing technology...too easily traced...and not the least bit necessary. Often they carried guns, but only for self protection. The murder itself was frequently more effective and less risky when simple tools, ropes, hands, and garrotes were used. They were careful, well trained, well disciplined, and highly skilled and experienced...workmen.

"Ivan" had called Ryerson's hotel room from a pay phone at a nearby post office.

The Mercedes limousine had been stolen and was now resting in twenty-three meters of water at the bottom of Lake Pleshcheevo, about sixty-five kilometers north of Sergiev Posad.

The "Coat of Arms" was simply a cheap magnetic appliqué. It had been removed, burned, and all carbonized remains buried.

The only traces of Ryerson/Ryerson in Russia were his effects in his hotel room, his check-in form, and his entry papers into Russia.

During his last day in Russia, and on earth for that matter, not one person had seen him who was not in the employ of the assassins, except a room service waiter and the hotel's desk clerk when Ryerson had walked out to his death.

A man roughly the appearance of Ryerson appeared at the Kempinski Hotel around midnight the next day. He went to Ryerson's room, dawned surgical gloves, neatly packed his bag and his passport and, with key in hand, proceeded to the front desk to check out. All charges were paid in cash, and the man walked out uneventfully into the dark Moscow morning. If anyone were to investigate, Ryerson's last seen whereabouts would be misreported by a factor of at least thirty-six hours.

That morning, Ryerson's belongings, including all cash monies, were taken deep into the woods, burned along with about two tons of trash and wood cuttings. No trace remaining.

Russian Immigration would eventually determine Ryerson had never left Russia, at least not officially. Their last record would be Ryerson's check out and phony forwarding address. They, in turn, would notify the police, who in turn, would notify the FSB (the new KGB) who would place him on their Watch List—and then after a few months, would forget about him altogether.

Back on the Island, Rachael took Ryerson's belongings, crated them, and had them interred in hardened concrete on one of the Island's active construction foundations.

She planted a cover story to the effect Ryerson had taken a job as a mercenary somewhere in South America, added a letter of resignation to his personnel file, shredded all copies of his trip itinerary and tickets, burned the video of his interview with Carr, cut a final settlement paycheck, and cancelled all credit cards in his name.

Ryerson no longer existed, and not one person on God's earth gave a tinker's damn.

Offers Accepted

Change is the constant, the signal for rebirth, the egg of the Phoenix.

Christina Baldwin

Phil awoke to the ringing of his mobile phone.
"Yes?"
"Phil this is Howard. One-hundred percent success on the Russian project. All is done without a single hitch. Not a thing to worry about."
"Thank you, Howard."
"Now, about this Bill Kelly guy. His real name is Vincent Harvey. He is nothing more than a thug. He's a professional killer and that's all he has ever been. God knows how many notches he has in his belt. Clearly Ryerson had some serious wet work in mind."
"Howard, you've really come through. I am in your debt."
"You damn sure are, Phil. Wait until you get my bill!"
"It will be settled with pleasure and then some. Bye, Howard."
Phil had breakfast with Rachael again. He briefed her on Ryerson and Kelly.
"What are you going to do about Kelly?"
"Well, I think I can pay him off, throw him out, and give him every assurance he will be shot on sight if he ever sets foot on this Island again. All my instincts tell me he was just a paid workman and has no connection with, or knowledge of, the puppet masters."

"What if he asks about Ryerson?"

"None of his damned business."

"If he refuses the offer?"

"Then we'll just have to figure out a way to safely take him out."

"Jesus, Phil! You're really getting hardened to this stuff."

"On the contrary. It's the most bizarre thing I've ever been involved with. I get a little dizzy just thinking about it. In fact, to be honest, I don't think about it if I can. But there's no choice. I'm fighting for my life and many others as well, whatever the cost. I will not let a bunch of two-bit murderous hoods destroy what has been achieved here.

I haven't told you this, but I believe the developments on the Island have a true, long-term importance. This is a cause, aside from survival itself, that is well worthy of fighting for, even killing to protect, if there's no alternative."

"I hope that's enough for you, Phil. I've known others who just couldn't deal with it. Please be careful. I think the world and all of you. I have every faith in your judgment and integrity. But I've got to tell you, you're pushing me right to my limit. Sooner or later, and it's *got* to be sooner, you must open up. I'm getting into this up to my neck, and I don't even know what I'm getting into. *You* wouldn't put up with this. You can bet I won't either."

"Okay. You are absolutely right. How's this? I will sort out Kelly at 1600 this afternoon. If I am successful, you will assume the position of Director of Security for as long as you care to hold it. Your first task is to hire three of the best damn bodyguards in the business, present company excepted, of course, to look after your personal safety, mine, and Craig's at all times. Your second task is to recruit your number two. Your third task will be to attrition out every clinker in the "wild bunch" and hire people you can trust. All during this process I will see there is not one element on this Island you are not fully aware of.

Of course, normal Island security must be maintained, and you'll have a good deal of familiarization work to do as well. Should be fun.

Money? Give me a number. Duration? Let's play this by ear, your ear. You can bail at any time. Duties? Well, you know your job. You may need to get up to speed on some of the hardware, but that's all. How does that sound?"

"It sounds just fine, Phil. I would like a personal overview from you as an immediate part of my familiarization."

"You got it."

"You've got a deal then." Rachael said and smiled.

"Great. Let's finish breakfast. Then I would like you to brief Craig on everything we discussed, including Kelly. Dr. Gear (he's in charge of the medical staff) has contacted me and insists that I give him a couple of hours, so that's where I'll be. After I finish that and my 1600 with Kelly, I'll contact you. Then I'll brief you on my meeting with Kelly and give you a full briefing on the Island and the University."

"Okay."

They finished breakfast on a much more relaxed footing and then left on their separate pursuits.

On his way out, Phil stopped. "Edward, can you arrange the conference room exactly as we did for Ryerson? Everything from coffee to pastries and audio visual. This time it's for Kelly at 1600. I'll be up at 1530 to prepare. Thanks, Edward."

Womb—Dome

There is...nothing to suggest that mothering cannot be shared by several people.

H. R. Schaffer

The PM commute to Dr. Gear's office was disappointingly short. Each PM trip had been different so far and exceptionally enjoyable. This was no exception. Ironically enough, this trip took him through Greece. The architecture and the periscopes combined to create a Greek village, wooden sidewalks, and intense white stucco buildings silhouetted against an infinite cloudless blue sky, with the rugged, dry landscape of the Island as a backdrop. It was even hot and dry, and Phil could see and hear the ocean booming on the horizon far away and far below. As he neared the Doctor's office, he passed a couple of very authentic looking restaurants. There was even smoke emanating from their roofs and the enticing scent of a Greek BBQ. Maybe he could con the good doctor into lunch?

He dismounted his PM and entered the clinic. With a jolt, he found himself in an ultra-modern, well lit, air-conditioned clinic and was quickly shown into the doctor's office. Dr. Gear stood when Phil entered. "Welcome to our clinic, Phil, and congratulations on taking the helm. We've been looking for you at meals and in the bar, but you've been quite the phantom."

"Sorry, Doc. It's been a very hectic few days. I trust things will slow down soon. I'm planning a staff party so we can all get better acquainted. I hope to have it next week. I want to thank you very much for your help in the Wilcoxen matter. I know it was out of your line and probably very unpleasant for you."

"Glad I could help. Sorry we missed the forensics the first go around."

"No need for that, Doctor. This sort of thing would be totally unexpected on the Island and it was very skillfully done."

"I certainly agree there. Is there some sort of professional assassin working here on the Island?"

"At the time there probably was. The trail is cold now and it's probably best if we just let it be. But we'll be vigilant in the future. Lessons learned and all that."

"You don't think we should contact the authorities?"

"What authorities, Doc? *We* are the authorities and we're doing the best we can. So what can I do for you today?"

Dr. Gear peered at Phil for a moment, and then he seemed to rouse himself. "Well for you I would normally make a 'house call,' but we're all a little rushed just now, so I thought it would be better to get you in for some quick work."

"Quick work?"

"Here on the Island, it is the holy of holies that new entrants be given a comprehensive physical—particularly as that may relate to communicable diseases. We're actually in a very small, closed system here. So we are particularly sensitive about such things. Therefore, with your kind permission, we will give you a quick overall physical and take some samples. I promise it won't take long."

"Proceed, doctor."

Half an hour later Phil had been thoroughly poked and prodded, pained and drained.

"You're in excellent health, Mr. Carr. As soon as we get some lab results, you'll have our seal of approval."

"Great. This actually went a little faster than I expected. I had planned to invite you to lunch at one of those intriguing Greek restaurants near here."

"I accept with pleasure. You're right though, it is a bit early."

"In the meantime, perhaps you can give me a briefing on the students, from a health and physical standpoint?"

"With pleasure. Let's see. Mmm, our students are without exception, specimens of humankind without equal. They really don't get sick. They are stronger, faster, smarter, and more intuitive than any other group on Earth. They are emotionally more stable than any group I have ever encountered. They have no interest in vices, that is, habits contrary to their physical and emotional health. They have a very active sex drive. Their appetite for food is unparalleled. They eat rapaciously. This is explained by their inordinate amount of musculature and miniscule body-fat, as well as their exceptional metabolism. This is one element in their immunity to illnesses as well as their extraordinary healing powers... not to mention that they are physically and mentally active nearly twenty hours a day. Sometimes when they get really hungry it's almost frightening. They become totally fixated on sustenance. It was very difficult to fully explain their food idiosyncrasy until about fifteen months ago. A student was killed while climbing one our cliff faces. Frankly, I found the whole affair somewhat suspicious. His rope snapped. Things like that simply don't happen here. The death of a student is nearly unheard of, so we conducted an autopsy and, in fact, a dissection as well."

"Okay."

"Have you ever heard of the 'enteric nervous system'?"

"Mmm, yes, in passing. Something about neuron bundles in the mid gut?"

"Close. Enteric nerves are probably a genetic inheritance dating back beyond the dinosaurs. Medical science discovered the enteric layer about a hundred years ago and have pretty much ignored it since. It's located in the upper digestive tract, consisting, in humans, of a network layer of some hundred billion cells. Science is beginning to strongly suspect that in a very real sense, this represents a literal second brain, where actual decision making may occur; reactions are taken before the mind is aware of them and actions initiated via the spinal chord. And we're not just talking about knee jerk reactions here, we're speaking of true complex analysis and decision making, that the main-brain may actually steal credit for…labeling it a gut reaction if you like, or intuition…or perhaps call it the *subconscious itself*. This 'second brain' knows when, how much, what, and how important it is to ingest food …"

"This is truly fascinating, Doc, but …"

"…during our autopsy of the dead student, we discovered the student's enteric layer to be more than twice the mass of a normal human…more than two-hundred billion cells."

"My God, Doctor, what the hell does that mean?"

"Well for one thing, it may explain their proclivities for food. But I think a great deal more may be inferred. For one thing, they may possess an intelligence that we cannot know, or quantify, or test, or even understand. Our IQ scores have always seemed highly questionable. Inordinately and unreliably favoring what we consider to be the low side in view of their skills and acuity.

I can assure you these scores would be considered far from low in a normal environment. In fact, they would be considered extraordinary. Not here, however.

The enteric system could be one explanation why we are unable to adequately test them. They may posses an intelligence we don't even know about. One more thing. We have used scanners to look at later and later generations of students, and the enteric layer continues to expand dramatically. It's almost frightening.

On another topic altogether, perhaps you might want to invest a little time looking over one the most fascinating places on the Island?"

"You interest me, doctor. What would that be?"

"Our nursery."

"Your nursery?"

"Yes. One of the prime mandates of this Island is to produce babies. As you know, those babies are well and truly parentless. We make up for that by providing them with *many* loving parents. And we provide it in a unique environment, to say the least, shortly before they are weaned and until the child itself decides it's time to move along, as long or short as they like. Care to see?"

"Certainly."

Phil followed Dr. Gear through the clinic and down a fairly lengthy passageway. At the end of the corridor, they paused before a large laboratory door, which allowed air to exit but not enter. They pushed through.

They entered a mammoth chamber. Phil would later remember it as a titanic womb-like structure, not a ninety-degree angle to be seen anywhere, floor to ceiling. It was at least twenty thousand squared meters, and the ceiling was about thirty-five meters above them.

Phil was nearly knocked off his feet.

The air was rich and warm and filled with a hundred scents. Cinnamon, chocolate, honeysuckle, vanilla, orange blossom, lemon and lime, garlic, barbeque, bread, doughnuts, apple pie, vegetable soup, pot roast, turkey, roses, pepper, mint, and many, many more. The scents came in waves, somehow clearly delineated, lasting but a few minutes and very intense. The womb must have an exceptional ventilation system—tens of thousands of cubic meters of air moved within minutes—concurrently maintaining humidity and temperature and rotating the many scents—without an appreciable breeze—impressive!

Of equal intensity, but not volume, were sounds. There were a dozen bird calls, surf, wind, brooks, animal howls and growls, cars, boats, rockets, fighter jets, dozens of types of music, a crackling fire, laughter, speech, cow bells, church bells, thunder, rain, singing, and more.

And there were images covering the convex walls and curved ceiling, swirling and changing, huge two- and three-dimensional images, many synchronized with the sound. There was sunrise, sunset, the sea a dozen ways, every type of animal and fish, dinosaurs, forests, fields and streams, lakes, mountains, deserts, huge cities, balloons, rockets, kites, aircraft, the sun, butterflies, the moon and all the planets, huge nebula, novae, comets, storms and blue skies, flowers, lightening, clouds, rain, wind, clowns, a hundred different colors and designs, cartoon figures, dolls, toys, and dozens of examples of architecture and clothing styles...some stationary images... some animated.

Phil had no idea how long he stood there taking it all in. When his eyes adjusted he started to perceive the actual nursery below. There was a sort of a floor made of a soft warm rubbery or foamy substance. The floor was molded into a thousand different contiguous forms and colors which comprised toys of the sort that could be cuddled, grabbed, pulled, hit, chewed upon, sucked upon, played with, and even slept upon. Between this amalgam of shapes were shallow pools of warm and cool water. Some pools were filled with food and drink. Some pools were simply empty for comfortable sleeping.

Every few minutes or so, it 'rained.' At first he didn't even notice the rain. He saw it before he really felt it. Looking across the womb, he noticed something between a mist and a drizzle gently descending from somewhere above, covering and rinsing the total area of the womb. After a bit, Phil did find that he could 'stand out of the rain' in the entry area where he had started. He tasted the moisture on his lips. It was a warmish-tepid, very light saline solution laced with just a hint of a soft lanolin-like substance. After a few tastes, he realized they were using these cleansing showers in much the same way they used sound, shape, light, and scents. To expand the sensory acuity of the infants, they were using taste. Each shower, aside from the mild, barely-detectable salinity and lanolin, they added subtle tastes of orange, lemon, cinnamon, clove, cherry, blends, other unidentifiable flavors, as well as a few savories. The shower needed no draining. However, the pools of water and food and drink that were drained prior to each washing, were quickly refilled. Without asking, Phil *knew* there were a variety of nutrients and immune boosters (glucasan sprang to mind) enriching the mixture. He could practically taste them when he concentrated. These were some kind of special kids!

In the midst of this cacophony of sound, scent, form, light, shapes, and liquid were the children...hundreds and hundreds of them. They slept, fed, drank, played, passed waste, crawled, walked, ran, rolled, or just laid there taking it all in. None wore clothing of any kind. They laughed, cooed, screeched, but amazingly, almost none cried.

There were loners, couples, groups, every sort of grouping, and Phil could make out a certain social order in their interactions. He would be briefed later that the children developed teams, leaders, and a sort of daisy-chain organization they used for games and strange migratory movements throughout the womb. There was clearly a loose social order, but even the Island's best psychologists after months of study were unable to clinically describe it. This was one of the growing mysteries of the Island's gifted bounty.

Discretely, a very few naked nannies, male and female, moved amongst the children, playing with them, holding and petting them, cleaning them, talking and laughing with them and clearly examining them for any health problems at the same time.

The only nannies that were not constantly engaged were seated around a large pond area. The pond indentation was of the same rubbery substance as the rest of the womb's soft base and was molded to a maximum depth Phil guessed as a little more than a meter. The pool's gently sloping beach was non-slip, and the children easily ran, walked and crawled along its banks. The pool itself was rather large, about ninety square meters, with little islands dotting the calm surface...and there were children! Running, crawling, sleeping and, most of all, swimming, dozens of them, underwater nearly without exception, and very skillfully at that. They were fast, agile, and decidedly having fun. Phil had a suspicion that the kids could hold their breath quite well and perhaps for an impressive length of time. The pond was somehow softly lit from below, clearly illuminating the children above and below the surface. The nannies never took their eyes off them and the lighting was clearly a great assist.

Phil was amazed, uplifted, nauseated, frightened, depressed, horrified, dizzy, and even slightly amused. He had to sit down, or he was going to fall down.

Dr. Gear gently took Phil by the arm and led him out of the chamber to his office and placed a large cognac in his trembling hand.

"You took that pretty well, Mr. Carr."

"*Pretty well?*"

"Damn right. I've seen men twice your size fall down in a dead faint the first time they faced the nursery."

"May I ask why the hell you didn't warn me?"

"Well, we tried that at first. Turns out we can't describe it adequately, so we just let people walk in and pass out. The floor's as soft as a baby's bum anyway. And, in a way, I think it's good for you. Sort of a psychological kick in the pants."

"For God's sake, it ought to be part of the Fear Curriculum!"

Looking over his glasses, Dr. Gear regarded Phil curiously for a few moments before he quietly responded. "What makes you think it's not, Phil?"

"So tell me, doc. Why? What does all this do for, or to, those kids?"

"Well, let's see. They suffer none of the frustrations and phobia and hang-ups of babies. They aren't tightly cocooned in fabrics until they can't move. They aren't strapped into chairs and cars. They aren't imprisoned in bassinets, cribs, perambulators, or any other device of torture. They don't spend their young lives too hot or too cold. They live on their own schedule. They live without frustration. They are independent. They eat when they want, drink when they want, void themselves when they want, sleep when they want, and play when they want. They are given more love by more people than any Lander baby ever dreamt of. They know how to interact with other humans better than any child ever built. Aggression, frustration, inhibition are concepts unknown to them.

They are a hundred percent healthy. They are a hundred percent happy. They are a hundred percent neurosis free. Anal retentive or expulsive bullshit, no pun intended, is unknown. They are never, never abused physically or verbally nor are they ever subject to neglect. They are guarded and watched and supervised constantly and unobtrusively. They benefit from the richest ambience humans can devise. Sexual and personal hang-ups play no part in their lives.

The adoring, benign tyranny of the mother and father figures play no part here. Oedipus and Electra are unknown. These children are free of preconceptions, bigotry, bitterness, the entire range of beliefs that humankind has hobbled itself with. They have no baggage to suffer. They are simply the happiest and healthiest children on earth. And when they grow up...get outa the way! Next question."

"Can I go back in?"

"Honestly, Phil, we recommend that the first-time viewer give it a day or so before they try it again. You really don't know how this may have affected you."

"How long do the kids live in there?"

"They stay as long as they wish. They walk out when they're ready."

"What about diseases? Special dietetic requirements? Unique needs?"

"I'll answer your questions in the order you asked.

Diseases. They get them all the time. The biological make-up of complex organisms often allows them, even compels them to selectively matriculate germs and even viral forms as they are needed by the organism to develop its immune system. Such biologicals pass like clouds through the womb and all the kids are immunized perfectly. It's the adult care providers we have to worry about.

Diet. They crawl around and find what they need.

Unique needs. Between other kids and the nannies they get what they need."

"You guys aren't just being lazy are you?"

Dr. Gear chuckled lightly "Do you have any idea how much research and thought and work and money went into that titanic womb?"

"Okay, okay. Just pulling your chain, Doctor. Lunch?" Phil said and smiled.

"You bet!"

Lunch consisted of Ouzo with ice and water on the side, cold beans in their own sauce, bar-b-queued lamb chops perfectly spiced and nearly paper thin, with a Greek salad on the side with some fried potatoes, served up with an iced cold Retsina Rose. Dessert was a white cake with cream and copious fruits. Phil was himself again.

"Where do these kids go from the womb Dr. Gear?"

"Right into school. And they really kick ass. There's quite literally nothing we tell them they aren't capable of, can't do, shouldn't do. The results are astounding."

"Sounds to me like you impart in them a certain courage, a sort of boldness about achievement. What they are capable of. Not to be timid. Not to be unduly humble, or insecure."

"Well put Phil."

"May I come back tomorrow afternoon, say around 1600, and bring someone?"

"Bring someone?"

"Our new Director of Security."

"Oh? What happened to Steve Ryerson?"

"He had an exceptional opportunity and permanently relocated to the mainland."

"You may certainly bring our new Director tomorrow. I'll make sure I'm available to carry him out afterwards."

"*Her*, Doctor."

"Oh. In that case there'll be no problem."

"Are you serious?"

"Couldn't be more serious. Women walk in there, they don't blink an eye and they have few if any questions afterward. That's one reason I have so much faith in it."

"Doctor, I thank you for your time. I hope you can attend our reception next week. You'll let me know about the physical? And I'll see you tomorrow at 1600."

It was nearly 1500, so Phil headed back to his apartment to prepare for his 1600 meeting with Kelly.

Kelly Green

Endless money forms the sinews of war.

Cicero

When he returned to his apartment, Phil decided to lie down for half an hour. He didn't know if it was the womb, the Retsina, or both, but something had drained him. He fell into a deep sleep for twenty-five minutes and awoke totally refreshed.

Upon entering the conference room, he found Edward had been his usual efficient self. Coffee service, pastries, blue box, and scissors were just as he needed them. Phil brought his pistol and Tazer, so all was in readiness very quickly.

Precisely at 1600, Edward showed Mr. Kelly into the conference room. Phil was sporting his powdered sugar chin, napkin, and pastry regalia.

"Sit down. Coffee?"

"No thank you."

"As you wish."

Phil immediately wiped his chin, threw the napkin on the box and inserted his left hand. With his right hand he withdrew a brown, letter-sized envelope from his coat. The envelope bore no address, but it was tightly packed with something. He threw it on the table with a slap.

"Do you know what's in that envelope, Mr. *Harvey*?"

Harvey/Kelly appreciably blanched, in fact turned a little greenish.

"No. No I do not, Mr. Carr."

"This envelope contains your last month's salary and a dismissal payment of USD fifty-thousand—all in cash. I suggest you take that envelope, pack your belongings, and catch a flight to Athens. I have scheduled you out in half an hour. Security guards are waiting to escort you outside this door. If you contrive to miss that flight, or ever re-appear on this Island, you will be shot on site and thrown into the sea. Are we clear?"

There was a pause.

"May I ask about Mr. Ryerson?"

"The affairs of Mr. *Ryerson* are none of your goddamned business."

Harvey picked up the envelope, pocketed it, turned, and left the conference room without a word."

"Rachael? I've finished with Harvey. Please see that he departs on the 1700 flight as scheduled. Your guards already have him. Please come up to my conference room afterwards. I'll brief you and we'll discuss your introduction to the Island. See you soon."

Rachael appeared around 1730.

"Mr. Harvey departed as scheduled on the 1700. How'd it go with you two?"

"Fast and easy. He rolled over without a word. I think we can forget about him...no problem, I hope."

"Excellent."

"Here's your contract by the way," Phil said, handing here a small stack of papers. "You can terminate whenever you wish. The money's as you stipulated. Please look it over and let me know if you have any problems. Do you need a move from New York?"

"Not right now. Can I do it later?"

"Sure. How 'bout something to drink?"

"G&T?"

"Certainly." Phil pushed a phone button. "Edward, may we have a bottle of gin, tonic, ice, and three glasses in the conference room, please?"

Edward brought everything in immediately.

"Edward, Rachael is our new Director of Security."

"Good news and congratulations, Ms. Stone."

"Please, Edward, call me Rachael."

"Edward, I ordered three glasses because I thought you should join us for a drink. I think we all deserve one. We've worked our way through the first phase of cleaning out quite a mess."

"With pleasure, Phil." Edward made the drinks. "Cheers!"

Edward finished his drink quickly. "Will you be dining in tonight, Phil?"

"No thank you, Edward. I think I should dine with the staff tonight. Rachael, I'd like you to join us, and I will introduce you, if you don't mind."

"Certainly not. I look forward to it."

Edward excused himself and Rachael started the discussion.

"I've found a number two. His name is Ted Richards. He's a good man. I've worked with him for years. He has no family, and he's willing to make a permanent move. Would you like to see his CV?"

"He's your guy, Rachael. Your call."

"Okay, I think I can have him on site within two weeks. I'm working through the HR Director."

"Good. How about the 'wild bunch'?"

"Howard is ready to send temporary or even permanent replacements, and he guarantees they'll be clean. This leaves only the problem of getting rid of the bad boys on site. My idea is to check out three or four a week and attrition them piecemeal."

Phil frowned. "So let's see, at a maximum rate of four per week, it'll take close to a year to fully clean house?"

"That sounds about right. Assuming that some of these boys don't figure it out and leave early of their own volition."

"So you're thinking about a pretty low-key approach? No big bang, just a slow leak?"

"Yes. I would assume the last thing you want is to unleash a small army of dissident mercenaries ready to sell any information they can about this operation. My belief is only one or two of these beauties acting alone wouldn't have the credibility to sell their mama a Girl Scout Cookie. But as a group, they might actually present a risk. So we slowly push them out in such a way that they may not even be aware that their ranks are being dissipated."

"Won't this raise a red flag with their real bosses?"

"I don't think the big bosses would ever get involved at this level. It's Ryerson that presents the problem. We'll be alert for queries from any questionable sources, and we may be able to fend them off with business trips, vacations, and illnesses for awhile. Sooner or later, though, the red flag will be raised."

"Red flags wave both ways. Especially here. This takes a little patience. But I see the wisdom. It reduces the risk of a full-scale insurrection. I would like a progressive status report reflecting the current balance—the number of bad guys attritioned, number of bad guys remaining, who was eliminated, when, and some indication of how dirty they really were. Incidentally, just a phony name is cause for severance. Well done. Go for it. Are you going to let the good boys know who the bad boys are?"

"Yes. We've worked out a rationale that lets the new ones know that the old ones are being attritioned out and who exactly they are. The new ones will be sworn to secrecy. But we're not briefing them about *why* the turn over. It's all very hush hush. We're already getting reports from Howard. We're moving along. So, how about my briefing, boss?"

"I'm going to provide your briefing in a few steps. The first is dinner tonight. I want you to meet the senior staff, and they will quite happily fill you in on what they do. The second step will be over lunch tomorrow; we'll discuss what you've been told and I'll fill in the gaps. The third step is you and I will take a little trip starting at 1500 tomorrow. We'll board what they call a PM (People Mover), and we'll take a tour of the highlights of this facility, or as much as I am familiar with them. We'll then visit a most unusual site at 1600. After that, we'll play it by ear. Okay?"

"Okay by me."

"Let's take a break. I want to get cleaned up. Suppose you meet me back here at around 1930 and we'll go down together for drinks and dinner."

"Sure. Is there a dress code?"

"Not really. I would suggest smart casual."

"No problem. See you then."

Phil used the time available to try out his pool and take a quick sauna, followed by a whirlpool. He arose from the water *à la September Morn*, a new man, dripping wet, ready to face the evening.

Wine and Circes

Rachael appeared promptly at 1930 looking stylish and rather provocative in dark pants and a white blouse under an open satin shell in a light maroon.

Moments later, they entered the dining room, retrieved a couple of glasses of wine, and proceeded to the terrace where they joined about thirty faculty members already over cocktails.

When they entered, spontaneous applause broke out by way of welcoming and congratulating Phil. Smiling, Phil raised his glass.

"Thank you very much. I am really pleased and honored to join your company. I'll make every effort to help you make this incredible endeavor even more of a success."

Glasses were raised in agreement.

"I would like to introduce you to Ms. Rachael Stone. Rachael is our new Director of Security, and I imagine she will be working closely with all of you. During this brief period before dinner, I would be most grateful if you would take this opportunity to introduce yourselves and perhaps give her a brief idea of the activities of your departments. Thank you."

With that, the group broke into smaller groups and Rachael was immediately in the midst of several staffers.

Phil went directly to Dr. Webber.

"Good news about Rachael, Phil. Well done. How goes everything else?"

"Well, Ryerson and Kelly have departed the Island. Rachael has located a promising number two, and we have a solid plan for weeding out the rest of the bad guys. I think we're on our way out of the woods, Craig."

"That is a great relief indeed. Thank you. How long before we can truly say this is behind us?"

"Nearly a year. We decided on a rather plodding strategy, to diminish the risk of insurrection and mitigate the possibility of leaks motivated by reprisal or greed."

"I think I understand. When do you want to discuss the Board Member?"

"I'm not sure we need to jump in with both feet yet. I think a discreet, low profile is called for here. If you could provide a name, coordinates, and just a bit of background, we'll make some very, very quiet inquiries. Let's see who we're dealing with and then talk."

Dr. Webber sighed with relief.

"Thank you, Phil. I'll have Jackie bring you the file tomorrow. Meantime, is your contract OK?"

"Signed and delivered to Jackie."

"Fine. We do need to prepare for a Board Meeting in a couple of weeks. Let's get together next Wednesday with our financial people and start preparing."

"We don't need more prep time than that?"

Craig smiled. "Our board is not exactly a collection of control freaks and they're certainly not micro-managers. Board Meetings normally last around half an hour. We run some numbers, bring up anything of interest or overriding import, and get to the bar ASAP. A lot of these guys like to use Board Meetings as an excuse to discuss and do business with other members they don't normally see, or want to be seen with. These are all very solid citizens. But they're no boy scouts either. In this meeting, I envisaged I would introduce you, run the numbers and then give you the floor to broach the subject of self-sufficiency—if you like."

"Sounds great. I'll have a presentation for your review next Wednesday. I'll keep it very high level, just the start of a Risk and Rewards and Market Analysis. Ten minutes max with time to spare for Q&A and discussion."

"That's perfect, Phil."

"And I suppose I should be prepared for a resounding, 'Hell No!'?"

"You bet. And you may hear my voice amongst them. Hell, you may hear *your own* voice amongst them! The mandate of this outfit is not to make a profit. A profit wouldn't hurt. But in some respects this might be seen as a sort of 'spit in the eye' by some Board Members, sort of like telling them they are no longer needed. Self sufficiency is anathema if it endangers our work and anonymity in any way. But you well know that already."

"No. I understand. Might it be premature to bring this up to the Board?"

Dr. Webber frowned, paused for a moment without saying anything, and then got another drink. "Yes. Dig up something else to talk about. Maybe there's something interesting happening in one of the departments?"

"I'll dig around and have something for you on Wednesday."

"Great. Let's eat!"

On that queue, everyone moved into the dining room.

Phil found himself next to Anne Jones, the head of the Art Department over dinner, and had the feeling that the seating had been engineered. If anything, she was more attractive than the first time they met. Phil had the feeling that she spent a good deal of time on the sea. Her hair was bleaching out somewhat, and her tawny tan was growing deeper.

"Phil, would you have any time available tomorrow morning?"

"In fact I would. What's up?"

"Mmm...something interesting I think. Something I'd like to show you."

"Fine. Suppose I stop by your office at around 0930?"

"Would 1000 be possible? I have a class at 0830."

"No problem. I'll be there at 1000."

After dinner, Rachael accompanied Phil back to his apartment. They had a couple of brandies on the terrace, enjoying the stars and the sea.

"That's quite a group of people, Phil. Most impressive. And I like to think I'm not impressed easily. I couldn't believe how open and friendly they are. They seem to hold back nothing. They really want to show what they have created. There were a few questions about my predecessor."

"Did they buy the party line about a job in Africa?"

"Seemed to. At least it stopped the questions."

"Good. They *are* an imposing bunch. I feel as if I have barely scratched the surface of their capabilities. In fact, that is true. I've really only had a couple of days to review their operation, and I'm awed. I want to see much more."

"As do I. By the way, do you mind if I skate lunch tomorrow? I have a few invites for departmental tours with lunch thrown in."

"I don't mind at all. I'm pleased you're working in so well.

"Incidentally, tomorrow Jackie's sending up the file on the Board Member we're all so interested in. I would like you to pass it along to Howard after you look at it. And I would like him to run the most discreet, lowest profile and the most secret check he can provide. Tell him to take his time on this one. Discretion and thoroughness are more important than speed. Okay?"

"You got it. I think I'll pack it in for the night. Early meeting tomorrow."

"Me too. Is one of your appointments tomorrow with Dr. Gear? No? Okay. I think we can dispense with the tour at 1500. Are you still up for the 1600 visit?"

"Sure. I'll be here at 1530. Good night."

A Peek in the Closet

The Art Department had been recently relocated to the deepest, newest part of the complex. After descending more than twenty floors, there still remained a fairly significant journey to the far side of the complex. The intervening area was still under construction, so Phil found himself traversing a remarkable corridor that had been lined, walls and ceiling, with colossal periscopes for hundreds of meters. His senses told him he was speeding (The PM's could really move under certain circumstances.) over the surface of the Island—with balmy wind in his hair under a mild sun. This time of the morning there were literally no other travelers. He found it all very peaceful.

As always on the Island, he arrived at his destination much too quickly.

"Good morning, Anne. How are you?"

"Fine, Phil. Care for some juice?"

"Sure. Thank you."

They sat down at a large table in the department's large, complex reception area.

"I would offer you more than juice. However, I think that is not advisable just now. I would like to invite you for lunch. We have quite a good Blind Restaurant and Sightless Lounge down here."

"Blind? Sightless? Hardly terms one expects to hear in an Art Department."

"True. We have paintings and sculptures done by blind Landers, and we have many fine works done by our own students in total darkness. The restaurant and bar are part of our Touch Gallery."

"Okay. I'll bite. What in hell is a Touch Gallery? Sounds like some places I used to see on 42nd Street in New York before they cleaned it up."

"Happily, our Touch Gallery is nothing of the sort." Anne said, smiling. "Here in the Art Department, and throughout the University for that matter, we look at art in the broadest of terms. If you've analyzed the nature of art, you've found, among other things, art attempts to portray, or interpret, or imitate existence and, in doing so, provides us a greater insight into nature and in the best cases, life.

To accomplish this, there must be a communications media, some sort of connection to the human psyche—the brain. This connection is achieved via the senses. For the ear and the mind we have music, poetry, literature, and the theater arts. For the tongue we have the culinary arts, wines, and alcohols. For the nose we have both the culinary arts and the broad spectrum of scents and perfumes. For the eye we have painting, sculpture, architecture, fashion, and landscape and many, many other art forms. For the final sense, touch, man has developed very little if anything that might be construed as art *per se*. We therefore have developed an experimental 'touch' art form."

With a skeptical look Phil asked "What is it conceptually?"

"Well, the first thing we did was break down touch itself into its various phylum and sub-phyla. Feelings such as solidity, sharpness, dullness, softness, hardness...then temperature, including cold, hot, frozen, steamy, the conditions and states of matter...then textures like metallics, fabrics, stones, woods, plastics, flesh, fur, scales and so on...then liquids, including acidic, basic, and oily...then combinations thereof. Think of the feel of pasta floating in tepid water as a simple example."

"Sound's a little like head art that missed its calling back in the 60's."

Anne smiled despite herself.

"After we had broken touch into its component elements, we had the basic tools with which to create art—much as a painter blends pigments to produce texture, hybrid colors, and beauty. We now had the tools to blend touches. We created Touch Panels for solids or Touch Tanks for liquids that convey meaning, maybe beauty, maybe even emotions."

"I've never heard of anything like this, Anne."

"Neither had I, Phil."

"How does it work?"

"Pretty simple, really. The gallery is broken down into three primary areas. The Panel Hall A., the Tank Hall B., and the Blind Art Hall C. The panel and tank halls are maintained in total darkness, and there's no sound, no smell, no tastes, and a totally neutral temperature. The visitor enters the hall's anti-chamber and spends a few moments acclimating to sensory deprivation, then proceeds into the hall itself, which is narrow enough for the visitor to touch both sides of the hall at the same time. In Hall A. the visitor experiences panels.

Upon exiting Hall A. the visitor does a U turn into Hall B. where the same experience is repeated, only with tanks. Between tanks, we provide a rinse mechanism preventing unwanted mixing between tanks and to refresh the epidermal pallet. At the end of Hall B. the visitor is given a towel to dry hands and then enters Hall C., which is only partially lit to view and touch blind art. At the end of this, we have the Restaurant and Lounge along the same motif as Hall C."

"This is interesting. So did your experiment work?"

"I would call it an eighty-five percent success. We're still working on it. I hope to approach a hundred percent in the near future for a few reasons. We have another gallery of conventional art by our students, and I think it is more than worth a visit or two. We have some *very* talented students here."

"So I take it we're here this morning to review these two galleries?"

"No. Not at all."

"Pardon?"

"I asked you here this morning to review only one piece. It occupies a private room here in the art complex, and only two other people aside from myself and the artist have ever seen it.

Would you care to step this way please?"

Phil followed Anne through a series of corridors that ended in an unused part of the facility. Anne unlocked a door to a room at the end of the hallway.

"Please step in, Phil. I'll turn on the light."

Phil entered the room in darkness. Anne turned on the light and left the room, closing the door behind her. The room was roughly three meters by three meters with no furniture, bare floor, and stark white walls. There was nothing in the room except a painting hanging on the far wall.

As Phil glanced at the painting, he judged it as a very well done abstract that somehow portrayed a close up of a single human eye—although the pigmentation had nothing remotely akin to human coloration. The shapes were interesting as well. The painting was actually a series of shapes that somehow formed a composite representation of a human eye. In fact each shape was the product of many smaller shapes, and the smaller shapes were built of smaller shapes that, in turn, were composites of smaller shapes it derived from other smaller shapes, in which even smaller shapes were imbedded, and there were still smaller ones, and smaller ones after that, and smaller ones and smaller ones and smaller... *good God!*

Those goddamn shapes went on forever, and somehow they were changing color, and somehow they seemed to even move just at the periphery of his vision. The shapes were so basic. They were fundamental. They were like clay, or blood, or semen, or sweat, or mucus, or like inhaling his own breath. Something deep within him responded to them and resonated with an abrasive wail. He could practically feel and taste them! There was something revoltingly *intimate* about them—invasively familiar...The painting wasn't *unearthly*. It was too Goddamned *earthy! This fucking thing is alive!* He moaned. *It never ends! It knows me!*

He started to blink, and his eyes burned. He realized that sweat was pouring down his face and into his eyes. His breathing was shallow and very fast. He was smothering in the heat. He became nauseous and dizzy and his heart was pounding. His hands started to tremble and his knees were weak. He felt his hands clenching and unclenching. His mouth was open and he was actually drooling! He lurched backwards and looked away from the painting for a merciful instant as he comically staggered backwards and sat down very hard on the cold, sterile concrete floor.

He stared at the painting again. He lost track of time. He felt tears streaming down his face and he was softly whining. Suddenly, he was thrown forward and violently vomited between his legs. He attempted to get away from his mess, and quickly realized he had wet himself. He closed his eyes but couldn't block that pernicious, poisonous, obscene swirl of form and colors. It was as though his eyes were still open. Please. Please! Get out! He was now in the fetal position. *God! "Help! For God's sake help!"* He sobbed.

Anne rushed into the room and literally dragged Phil out. She had a dilute brandy at the ready as well as a sedative. She forced both into Phil. She assisted him to his feet and half carried him to another room. In the room was a medical cot and a shower. Anne lay Phil down on the cot and quickly undressed him, tenderly raising shoulders and hips to slip off his clothes. She brought him to his feet and held him under a warm to tepid shower for what seemed hours to Phil. She calmed him, rubbed his neck and back and shoulders and slowly fed him a large full strength brandy, while she talked to him and calmed him.

"It's okay. Try to relax. Put it out of your mind. You're fine. I'll take care of you. You're out of there now"...and so on.

Slowly she ran the shower up to hot and then down to cool. She helped him out of the shower, wrapped a towel around him and escorted him to the next room, which contained a Jacuzzi at the ready, bubbling away. Once he was installed and relaxed in the Jacuzzi, drink in hand, she brought in a cold, wet towel and placed it on his forehead. She brought in a neatly folded set of clothes. Shirt, coat, trousers, socks, underwear, belt, and shoes, toothbrush, toothpaste and even cologne. By way of explanation, she said, "I took the liberty of calling Edward. He took away your other clothes and brought you a clean outfit. Whenever you feel up to it, you can dry off and get dressed. Don't hurry. I'll be waiting for you."

About half an hour later, Phil appeared, stone faced in Anne's office. He sank down, still a little shaky and realized his ass hurt. He peered at Anne for a long time. She peered back, unabashed.

"How long was I in that room?"

"I'd say about forty minutes."

"You set me up!"

"Yes. Yes I did Phil. Can you imagine what it was like for *me* when I discovered that painting for the first time, completely alone, completely *unassisted*? I thought I was going to die."

"So you felt compelled to share? So did I. I feel like you know me extremely well now, doctor. I feel like I know you better as well. For one thing, I know you've got one hellofa bizarre sense of humor."

"I didn't do this for kicks, Phil, or for laughs. I needed you to experience the first tangible example of ANUMEN. And I needed you to experience it personally, unexpected, and without forewarning. When I crawled away from that painting the first time, I had that room built, as well as the shower and Jacuzzi. I keep the only key to the painting room."

"What else has that student done?"

"Good question. He wandered in one day. He's not an art student, but anyone is free to come in anytime and work. He knocked out that painting in about six hours, put a cloth over it, and has not been back. I discovered it afterwards, damn near killed myself, and have been wondering what the hell to do with it ever since."

"Who are the other two people that have seen this work?"

"Both are senior staffers here in the department."

"How do they describe it?"

"'A work of inestimable genius and unspeakable depth.' It damn near killed them as well."

"You know, Anne, I've seen the nursery womb. I've seen bio-technology beyond imagination. I've been overcome by a loony tune professor of philosophy and religion. A professor of law has turned a lot of my beliefs upside-down. I've been horrified by a briefing on Fear Training. I've been playing footsy with real life and death games, and now *this*. This goddamn Island overwhelms my mind and my senses. I'm exhausted, and it's only been two bloody weeks."

Phil was shocked to feel a tiny tear forming just in the corner of his left eye. He blinked, clamped his jaw, set his lips, and tried to ignore it with determined dignity.

Anne rose and walked over to him.

"Why don't we get you a proper drink and some lunch?"

With that, she leaned down and tenderly took Phil's face in both hands and kissed him softly.

After a moment, she straightened and smiled "I'm starved. How about you?"

"Sure. Let's go to lunch."

As they walked, Phil thought of something. "Anne you've been through Fear Training haven't you?"

"Yes, I have."

"Did it help you when you faced that painting?"

"It probably saved my life."

"I better think about signing up."

"Have you been in contact with the Music Department? Do they report anything like this?"

"I haven't spoken to them. Perhaps we should. I have heard some strange rumblings from the Language Department though."

"Language?"

"Yes, that seemed odd to me too. Then I heard that someone believes the students may have innovated some sort of natural language, which they all seem to have mastered."

"What is a *natural* language?"

"I have no idea. Maybe it's what a chimpanzee speaks."

"Things are moving fast, and accelerating faster and faster all the time, I think."

"I think you're right," Anne agreed.

They dropped into easy chairs in the lounge. When the waiter came, Phil said, "Large scotch straight up with a twist, and don't stray too far."

Anne said, "a white wine, please."

When the drinks arrived, Anne raised her glass and her eyebrows. "To friends and forgiveness?"

Phil slowly but warmly smiled. "To friends and forgiveness...and a burden shared."

"Thanks, Phil."

Phil looked around in the semi-darkness, looked at the art, the décor, Anne's provocatively crossed legs, and the unusual bar. "What's with the bar?"

"That's blind art. It's very soothing to sit at that bar with a cold drink and simply run your hands over it."

"I must try it sometime."

They had one more quick drink and went into the Restaurant.

After a carafe of Chablis, pork fillets in port wine and sage sauce, sautéed stewed potatoes with plums and beets, snow peas with bean sprouts, and iced cream, Phil thought, not bad. He was very slowly starting to feel like himself again.

"Well, Anne, I've got to run. I credit you with one of the most unusual mornings and lunches of my life. One last question, rather personal."

"Yes?"

"Have you faced that painting again?"

"No."

"Has anyone gone back for a second viewing?"

"No."

"May I?"

"Phil, you're welcome back anytime, and I'll pull you out again. I really wish you'd find the time to visit our Touch Gallery and Conventional Gallery as well."

"I'll take you up on that. How about Saturday morning around 1000?"

"No classes on Saturday, so that's a perfect time. The restaurant and lounge are closed on Saturdays, so I'll stock up on extra brandy."

"Sounds good. By the way, I think I'll visit the Music and Language Departments tomorrow. I'll ring you up afterwards and give you a briefing if something interesting comes out of it."

"Thanks, Phil. See you at dinner?"

"Sure."

On his way back to his apartment, Phil used the PM's com system for the first time. He called his office.

"Hello?

This is Phil Carr.

What's your name?

Hi, Cindy.

I understand you're my secretary.

I'll try to get down there and meet you as soon as I can.

Would you please set me up meetings tomorrow with the heads of the Music Department and the Language Department at 1000 and 1400 respectively?

Thanks, I'll come down tomorrow and we'll introduce ourselves. Bye."

Phil arrived back at his apartment with a little time to spare before Rachael was due to arrive. Edward was waiting for him.

"Are you alright, sir?"

"Yes, Edward, I'm fine now. Thank you."

"May I ask what on Earth happened to you?"

"Later. Please let me know when Rachael arrives. Thanks."

Phil went to his bedroom and lay down. He was out before he knew it. When Rachael arrived, Edward explained that Phil been through some sort of trauma and was lying down for just a bit. Would Rachael mind having a drink and waiting for ten more minutes?"

"No. Thanks very much, Edward."

"Is anyone waiting for you?"

"Not that I know of really. I'm not sure what venue was intended."

"I see. I'll call Dr. Gear and let him know you'll be a little late. On second thought, why don't I just cancel? Would you like to wait?"

"No. But please keep me posted."

"Certainly. I'll call Dr. Gear and I'll call you when he wakens."

"Edward, do you have any idea what happened to him?"

"None, Rachael. I have no idea. He was in the Art Department needing a change of clothes. That is all I know at present."

Phil didn't waken. He slept through until 0700 the next morning. He took a swim, soaked in the sauna, exercised, ate a substantial breakfast poolside, and was ready to face the Island again.

Face the Music and Rants

Those who dance are thought mad by those who do not hear the music.

Anon

Dr. William Gould looked across his desk at his new Chancellor. "It's good to see you down here, Phil. We don't get many visits from Top Management as you might imagine. Is there anything special I can do for you?"

"Two things, Bill. I would like to see your department. It sounds fascinating. I understand you have most major instruments from around the world."

"Not just today's world, either. We have antiques that go back centuries, and we have some experimental instruments, totally new designs, acoustics, and in electronics (although we tend to avoid electronic and digitized instruments)."

The two toured the department for well over an hour. They toured three auditoriums, a studio, dozens of practice rooms, and an instrument storage area that took nearly forty-five minutes to cover thoroughly.

"You have students who can play these instruments?"

"Phil, we have students who can play *all* these instruments, and well too, along with voice training."

"Impressive. I wonder, do your students exhibit any unusual talents?"

"Well, we certainly have our share of prodigy. Some have shown extraordinary skills. But you have to remember with music, unless you are composing, or improvising, you are basically interpreting someone else's creation. In a certain sense, that can be very restrictive, so creative genius may be more easily found elsewhere. If it's ANUMINOUS you're looking for, I think insofar as music goes, that would be found in Music Theory & Composition."

"Well?"

"Well we do have some students who are composing. But if you want the truth, I can't make heads or tails of it. In terms of degree, I'm not referring to, for example, how the world first reacted to the works of Igor Stravinsky and his works such as *Pétrouchka,* or *The Rite of Spring.* No. I'm talking about sounds that seem totally random. Noise versus music and totally incomprehensible. I don't think it's ANUMEN. I honestly don't know what the hell it is. My best guess is it may be the first step in an evolutionary process. I hope so. It's gorilla-ugly right now."

Phil smiled at the allusion. "Do you ever have recitals of this stuff?"

"From time to time. We'll make sure you're invited to the next one."

"Thank you, doctor, and thank you for your time."

Happy Talk

Language can only deal meaningfully with a special, restricted segment of reality. The rest and it is presumably the much larger part is silence.

George Steiner

Dr. Judy McLean stood as Phil entered her office and extended her hand. "Coffee?"

"Sure, thanks."

"By the way, I missed dinner and drinks the other night, so, please let me say "Congratulations and welcome aboard.""

"Thank you, Judy. I'm planning a little cocktail get together next week. I hope you can attend. I am pleased to be aboard. This is a most interesting place."

"I agree. There are so many exciting things going on I want to be involved in everything...of course that's not possible... so it's a little frustrating. Languages are my life, but the study of language pales a bit compared to what goes on in some of the other departments right now.

I had understood you were making the rounds of the various departments. I'm afraid you may find Language a little drab by contrast. All I can show you are some language labs, our immersion center, classrooms, and a pretty extensive computer complex."

"Actually, Judy, I came for two reasons. The first was to get acquainted as you indicated. The second's a little tougher."

"The second?"

"Yes. I heard you might have encountered a manifestation of ANUMEN. Is that true?"

"Oh damn! I had hoped this was going to stay within the department until we could analyze it further."

"Meaning?"

"Meaning we haven't even qualified it as a language, much less a *bona fide* ANUMEN occurrence. It could be a style, a fad, the product of a particularly gifted student who concocted his own language and then decided to disseminate it amongst the students himself. Hell, it could be a joke. All we really know for the present is it seems to have extemporaneously manifested itself."

"Meaning?"

"Meaning an apparently hitherto unknown language spontaneously erupted in the lab about a week ago. When I say 'spontaneously erupted,' I mean the language itself (if it is indeed a real language) suddenly appeared without traceable development or discernable etymology. Secondly, we could not locate the source of the language, meaning the student or students who might have developed or introduced it cannot be found. Thirdly, all students, starting with generation nine hundred and seventy-six, including remarkably young ones, seemed to apprehend the language at roughly the same time, immediately, without instruction."

"How young?"

"Less than one year. Actually, less than six months in some cases. Interestingly, this language does not rely on a hard palate."

"Jesus!"

"Please, Mr. Carr. We cannot afford to get excited. We need time to work this out…if we can."

"What does this language sound like?"

"That's perhaps the most disturbing part. It sounds like nothing I ever heard out of a human mouth, and I've heard every living language on earth."

Phil served himself another cup of coffee and thought for a few moments.

"Doctor, is it true humans may have thoughts or concepts that, if there are not words to express them, are lost? Is it true that, if we don't have a word to depend a thought from, we cannot retain that thought?"

"I suppose that is true. Yes. Some sort of mnemonic is normally required."

"Would such a limitation impose sufficient stress *cum* frustration to provoke ANUMEN capacity?"

"An excellent question, Mr. Carr. You've raised a line of investigation we will definitely pursue."

"Another element that occurs to me is, if this is truly a new language, born full bloom, then it must actually have a basic visceral genesis. There's no other local repository for something spontaneously generated at the same moment within a given population."

"Say again, please, Phil?"

"I mean these kids must be speaking a genetically imbedded, genetically resident language."

There was a short pause as Judy thought about what Phil had said.

"You're a very quick learn, Mr. Carr. That's an extraordinary idea."

"Can I hear this language?"

With that, Dr. McLean swiveled in her chair and activated a tape recorder on her credenza. "We recorded this in one of the student lounges."

Phil heard a series of drawn out whines, clicks, bass growls, and hissing. Forced to describe it, he would have to say it was like listening to a conversation between a whale, a dolphin, a Cobra, and a puma. He felt a tingling down his spine.

"That was phenomenal, doctor."

"I fully agree."

"How long before you make some sense out of all this?"

"I don't have one damned clue...days, weeks, years, never."

"Have you tried discussing this with the students?"

"Yes. They are most open about it. They find nothing unusual in it. They simply state they have no idea where the language came from, or how they learned it."

"Do they prefer it to other languages?"

"Most definitely; it's all they speak when they are alone."

"Can they translate from their language to say...English?"

"The students state they can convey the general meaning in some cases, but not a translation *per se*."

"Is it a written language as well?"

"They say no. And they've really tried to reduce it to writing. It defied phonetic notation. They are now actively experimenting with ideography interpretations, cuneiform, hieroglyphs, runes, curiology, script, symbolical notation, symbology, cuneal, or whatever might work. It may even take *them* a great deal of time. And if they succeed, I'm not sure what utility it will provide. Perhaps our computers can work out something. I don't know."

"They cannot develop an interpretable dictionary then?"

"No."

"What do you suggest I do?"

"With respect to what, Phil?"

"I am obligated to report this to the Board of Directors. Do you have any objection?"

"No, not really I suppose. I suppose you're right. This will be all over faculty and administration within a couple of days in any event so there's no way to keep this within the department. Circulation of this news would attract a great deal of interest, and we can use all the brains we can draw upon to crack this. Would you like me to prepare a presentation for you?"

"I would appreciate it greatly."

"I'll have it for your review in two days."

"That would be fine."

Phil frowned for a moment.

"Dr. McLean, you opened our discussion by telling me how *drab* things were in the Language Department. Shall I infer from this statement you hadn't intended to brief me on this development?"

"You're quite right, Phil. However, I had no intention of withholding this information. I simply wanted a more complete set of facts before I introduced the subject."

"I see. Well, doctor, please proceed with your presentation and let me know if anything new develops. Thank you."

"Thank you, Mr. Carr."

Phil went directly back to his new office. "Hi, Cindy. Philip Carr. Sorry to be so long in getting here. Would you please get Anne Jones in the Art Department on the line please? Thanks."

Phil left his reception room and entered his office for his first real look around. His office was very modern, with a glass desk, matching glass conference table, cocktail table, and visitor's tables, topped off with a huge, glass, wall-sized bar, all slightly green tinted. All the chairs and couches were in identical dark maroon as were leather mats on all the glass furniture. The walls were gray with white highlights and an elegant gray rug. One bright window behind him (Phil had to smile...maybe they knew the halo trick?) looked out on the huge booming surf onto a pure white beach. Based on relative positioning, it was clearly a periscope. Looking around, he found an attached sitting room, a bathroom, a small bedroom, and a AV room. Just then the phone rang.

"Hi, Anne."

"Hi, Phil, we missed you at dinner last night."

"Sorry, a few things came up. I'll be there tonight. Will you?"

"Sure."

"Anne, as we discussed, I met with the Music and Language Departments today."

"Yes."

"There may be something coming out of Music, but not for a good while, I think. Language however is phenomenal. They do indeed have a new language in common usage among the students, like nothing I've ever imagined. I'm convinced it's ANUMEN. Dr. McLean is playing it a little more conservatively. Anyway, I'll give you a full briefing over drinks this evening."

"Great. Are we still on for 1000 Saturday morning?"

Phil felt a thrill of fear and excitement run down his spine "You bet."

"Okay. I'll finalize some small modifications."

"See you soon, Anne."

As soon as he hung up, Cindy knocked once and entered Phil's office with a sizable stack of papers. "This is your mail and various papers for your review and/or approval. Would you care for some coffee?"

"Thank you. I think I'll need it." *Paperwork was part of the job Dr. Webber didn't mention!* Three hours later he was ready for a shower and a drink.

"Evening, Edward. How are you?"

"I'm fine, Phil. How are *you*?"

"Much better. I'm going to take a shower and have dinner downstairs. How are your Martinis?"

"Stirred over ice, dusty dry, up with a twist and an olive and one or two drops of Scotch for tang. But I'll let you be the judge, sir."

A Sea, Island, Village, Harbor, Slip, Boat, A Home

"Hello, Uncle Herb? This is Phil."

"How the hell are you boy?"

"I'm okay I guess. Been very busy. The job's not at all what I expected, by a long shot.

"How can it not be what you expected? You're the boss aren't you?"

"Well, Uncle Herb, there are bosses and then there are bosses."

"Where are you?"

"I'm in Greece. It's beautiful here. You'd like it. Have you given my offer any thought?"

"Well, let's see. I've given that girl in St. Michaels the gate. I have my Master Mariner's Ticket. I have a brand new passport and a valid Driver's License. I'm ready to lock up my 'Villa by the Sea,' and 'Fly away to the Islands.'"

"You actually sound excited."

"I am, Philly. Let's get this show on the road."

"Great news. I'll send you a prepaid ticket on Olympic to Athens out of Washington, and then on to an island called Lefkada. Can you leave tomorrow out of Dulles?"

"No problem."

"You'll be flying over Athens into the airport of Preveza on the mainland, which is actually in the Ionian Sea. You should take a taxi to the Armonia Hotel in a small village called Nidri, on Lefkada. Nidri is on the island, about half an hour via tunnel to the island. Everything is all set at the hotel. Have them find a car for you and I'll be along soon. Take the time to get acquainted with the island, the villages, and ports. I don't think you'll find a boat there, but I've got a line on a good prospect in the port of Piraeus, and I'll bring the specs with me. I'm going to Fax all this to the First Class Lounge at Dulles, so don't bother writing it down. You can pick it up after you check in. I'd show up at about 1500."

"First Class?"

"Yeah. So act and dress nice. You need any money?"

"No. I'm fine."

"Okay. I'll be along in a few days. Have some fun. Get to know the island. If you don't like it, there's lots more to choose from."

"Where are you located, Phil?"

"Aw, I move around a lot. Still trying to figure out the best base site."

"Is everything alright, Philly? You into anything you're not happy about?"

"Things are one hellofa lot more difficult than I expected. But I think I'm getting things under control. I'm definitely happy I took the job."

"Good. See you soon, boy."

"Seeya, Uncle Herb."

Promotions and Premonitions

Cindy entered Phil's office with another stack of papers, much to his dismay. He was going to have to figure out a way to offload this damned paperwork. *Cindy?*

"Cindy would you please ring up Dr. Sean Gray and see if he can meet at 1400?

Two minutes later, Cindy re-entered. "Dr. Gray confirms your 1400, sir."

"Thank you. Say, uh, Cindy...do you look at these papers before you bring them in?"

"Is anything wrong, sir?"

"No. No. Nothing at all. What I mean is, do you understand these papers? Would you know how to action them perhaps?"

"Well I would guess I know how to handle about ninety percent of them. They are pretty routine, and I've been in executive administration for nearly five years. The other ten percent either need your personal approval and signature, or some sort of decision, or policy call."

"I see. And what is your title?"

"Executive Secretary."

"So, if it were to say 'Manager Executive Affairs,' then you could handle the ninety percent?"

"Why yes, I'm most certain I could."

"And how about your other duties?"

Cindy couldn't help but smile. "You are my duties, Mr. Carr, and at least thus far you don't seem to require very much."

"That probably won't change too much, Cindy. So would you be interested in the job?"

"Indeed I would!"

"Good. Cut the papers, salary, and terms, and I'll sign them. Then we'll cook up some procedures. Okay?"

"Yes, sir."

"By the way, would you please put out some sort of invitation to all senior staff and directors, and of course to Dr. Webber, for a cocktail reception I will be hosting at 1900 next Thursday on the terrace."

"Certainly."

"Invite yourself, as well, and I'll introduce you in your new position."

"Thank you, Mr. Carr."

"Please, call me Phil."

Dr. Gray arrived at 1400 on the nose. Everyone kept referring to the chronic tardiness of people on the Island, so Phil had to assume these people were on their best behavior.

"Hello, Sean. Good to see you."

"Likewise, Phil. We haven't seen much of you since you first visited the Island."

"I know. It's been a little crazy. But I hope things settle down soon."

"Coffee, Sean?"

"No thanks, I just finished lunch."

"Sean, I remember from your presentation my first day here, you said something about standing at the end of the production line waiting for the appearance of the ANUMINA."

"That's essentially correct. I administer tests, run samplings of various abilities, interview students for any unusual perspectives or abilities, and I work with the various departments looking for anything anomalous."

"And?"

"And I've found some fairly impressive advances in native intelligence, some unusual skills, and a surprising consistency of attitude."

"Consistency of attitude?"

"Yes. Almost without exception, these students are very well adjusted, happy, confident, humorous, uninhibited, and impressively open minded."

"They have no individuality?"

"On the contrary, they all have very vivid, pronounced, and diverse personalities."

"How about measurable results? IQ for example."

"They're range from about sixty-five to eighty-five points above average quotient, maximum so far is 286."

"That's all genius isn't it?"

"It sure is, and far beyond, and this applies to the entire population...a sort of Flynn effect with afterburners lit."

"Flynn effect?"

"The Flynn effect is a widespread, fairly plodding increase in IQ scores, particularly at the lower end. Nothing exponential, but steadily upward. These findings are under dispute, however.

What is not under dispute is the incredibly advanced intelligence emerging from our students. Problem is, we aren't at all sure that standard intelligence testing is really applicable to this population. In fact, they could be far more intelligent. They exhibit wonderful health, excellent healing properties, and well above-average physical proficiency. And well... although it doesn't sound very scientific, they're really good looking. They have very even, symmetrical features, beautiful bodies, intriguing greenish-gray eyes, flawless skin, well formed chiseled features, and aside from eyebrows and scalp, almost no body hair whatsoever. Males do not shave their faces. Females do not shave legs or underarms."

"How are their social skills?"

"You've hit upon what may be a true anomaly. There are no fights, no bullies, no jealousy, and no abuse of drugs or alcohol. Tobacco does not exist. They eat ravenously. Yet they do not overeat. They certainly don't suffer from Anorexia Nervosa, Bulimia Nervosa, Compulsive Overeating, or Binge Eating Disorder.

They do not steal, lie, or cheat. Essentially they have no need for such motivation. They do not develop cliques to the exclusion of others. They genuinely like each other and most are not even remotely monogamous."

"You mean they are promiscuous."

"Mmm. Promiscuity is a negative Lander's word. It connotes a lack of self-respect and respect in general that just doesn't apply here. We would never use terms like slut, or tart, or libertine or philanderer, adulterer, cuckold, or whatever."

"Bisexual, heterosexual, homosexual?"

"I suppose heterosexual applies the best."

"At what age do they become sexually active?"

"Oh, I suppose generally from twelve to eighteen, give or take. As far as we can see, there is no pressure on them. They develop at their own rate. Certainly we don't raise any barriers to the healthy release of their hormones."

"I understand part of the Fear Ordeal involves overcoming any sexual inhibitions."

"True. And the majority skate through this aspect of the training. If there are any remaining inhibitions, Fear Training eliminates it. Once through the gauntlet, they evidence love, favorites, best friends, and so on. But never does this appear to imply specifically fixated sexual or bonding tension. Nor does it seem to foster what we call the 'Chattel Compulsion.'"

"By that you mean that mutual affection does not mandate exclusivity, or the illusion of ownership in these people?"

"Yes. Well put. They've done away with suspicion, jealousy, and all the baggage of insecurities and serfdom that constitute the burdens of monogamy. We perceive the Chattel Compulsion as a fairly trivial socio-psychological phenomenon, an archaic leftover from a brutal past, but one that creates an inordinate amount of grief, disruption, and even violence in the outside world."

"What about the family group, Doctor?"

"Obsolete. The womb and then the *Island* constitute the family group."

"So I ask the question, again. Bisexual, homosexual, heterosexual? What?"

"You're referring to student sexual preferences?"

"Yes."

"I'd have to say all of the above."

"Do you suppose this is the result of some sort of genetic imperative?"

"Interpreting your question, I would see it as suggesting that if sexual orientation is genetically driven, then the individual really has no choice, and we should therefore indulge them for whatever sexual propensities they may harbor? And if they are acting on choice, then they are misbehaving in some way?"

"Mmm, Doctor, you seem to find my question as judgmental."

"You're damned right I do, Phil."

"Well then, do you find anything wrong with a given orientation?"

"I'll tell you what I do find wrong. I despise anyone who purports to take it upon themselves to dictate the beliefs and actions of others."

"Your point's well taken, Doctor. I agree. Let's move on. I trust there is never any such interplay between faculty and students?"

"None. Absolutely never. This is the most carefully assessed and hand-picked faculty in the world. Not only are their academic credentials the finest available, they are subjected to the closest psychological screening. Aside from the ethics involved, they are aware that any unforeseen progeny would be genetic pollution of the worse sort."

"Who does all this screening? The Security Department?"

"No. This type of qualification is exclusively the province of Human Resources in cooperation with your offices. I recommend that you meet their Director for a better briefing than I am qualified to provide. Their entire backgrounds are painstakingly investigated. They are not allowed spouses, children, or even pets."

"Sean, I don't think I was investigated in this manner."

"I imagine you were, Phil. Probably more thoroughly if anything."

"What about birth control?"

"Selective dietary additives."

"Venereal Diseases?"

"None. Constant monitoring. Although they actually appear to have an innate immunity."

"You said that spouses, children, and even pets were prohibited. Why?"

"Basically security. Family members are very difficult to control and are therefore a significant security risk."

"Sounds like the staff and faculty must be pretty lonely."

"Not really, Phil. Staff and faculty embrace pretty much the same mores as the students."

"You're saying they freely interact?"

"That's exactly correct."

"To be honest, Sean, I've been briefed in-depth by most departments and I still don't fully understand how these kids have developed to such an advanced stage."

"It *is* difficult to grasp fully and I'm not at all sure anyone really does completely understand. Perhaps I can help with a short summary of what we know thus far.

First, through the biology involved, they have compressed many generations into a relatively short period. They go through a two-cycle process. They first *compress* through the use of blasticyst, then they *release* to advance to maturity after simulation of multiple generations. Then they compress again and release again, *repeat* and *repeat*, endlessly. I would surmise by now, the latest generation is probably genetically advanced by about 800,000 to 850,000 years. Not much really, but perhaps an edge. In fact, our best archeologists don't have much of a handle on how mankind may have been measurably different in intelligence, capability, and nature 200,000 years ago.

This was Homo sapient sapiens—our same race. They may have been really primitive and we may be really advanced by contrast. Give it four thousand or so more iterations and something interesting may emerge. Spikes seem to appear every 200,000 years in modern iterations of humans. However, developments such as the hyoid bone in our ever-descending larynx as part of our thorax, would seem to suggest that every 120,000 years or so a "spike" occurs in human evolution that provides us with some really special capability, such as language itself. This tends to confirm our suspicion, or perhaps hope, that we may be close to another "spike" now on this Island."

"Doctor you're implying an important spike reared about 100,000 or so years ago."

"That's exact Phil. Our latest anthropological evidence suggests that humankind developed both language and representative art 70 to 100 thousand years ago. A colossal concurrence of events in our remote pre-history.

Second, within recent "batches", each student bears the genetic genome signature of every known extant race of human. This alone has astounding implications. This may be the time to start seriously seeking ANUMINA.

Third, these students receive the best food, best medical care, best conditioning, and richest ambience ever provided a group of humans. There is nothing they are told they can't do, and damn little they are told they shouldn't do.

Finally, their education is absolutely unique. Starting with our "womb." through elementary schooling, all the way to university training and remarkable experiences such as the Fear Curriculum, no other human has ever been trained in quite this manner.

They are fearless, uninhibited, charismatic, unencumbered, brilliant, healthy, happy, and as capable as any human who ever lived. Certainly, the ground has been prepared for ANUMINA. The result is...well, you can see the result for yourself."

"That summary was useful. Thank you doctor. Today is Friday. I would like to convene a meeting between you and a few staff members on Monday starting at about 1000 in my conference room. Would that fit into your schedule?"

No problem. Anything I should prepare?"

"Not a thing. We'll see you Monday at 1000. Thank you, doctor. Have a good weekend."

After Dr. Gray departed his office, Phil pondered the sexual aspects of his new home. Many of the women were stunning. Some clearly willing. He had loved women since he was fifteen years old, and they had loved him. New York seemed a long time ago. *What was holding him back? Here he was in the midst of every young man's dream, why not live a little? Give in.*

Well, he hated, *really* hated to admit it, but he *was* President and Chancellor of this place and it simply wouldn't be appropriate somehow, even here in this land without inhibition. Something discreet and maybe somewhat serious, yes, but a sexy free-for-all was just not in the cards. *Damn!*

Private Showing

Evolution is not a force but a process. Not a cause but a law

John Morley

Saturday morning emerged a sullen gray, wind whirling fitful rain in haphazard patterns. Looking out to sea, Phil saw respectable surf and a rainy mist, the first of its kind since he had been on the Island. It actually felt good for a change. It gave the Island more of a feeling of normalcy somehow. It felt like Saturday morning. Phil even fleetingly considered Saturday morning cartoons.

Phil prepared a simple breakfast in his kitchen, of a little toast, some peanut butter, yogurt, and coffee. He then thought back to his last experience with the painting and opted for just a glass of orange juice. As he drank his juice, he watched satellite news on the kitchen's TV. The more he watched, the happier he was about living on the Island.

He had to admit to himself, though, that he was genuinely nervous about this upcoming confrontation with oil and canvas and pigment. Had he not somewhat rashly insisted on facing the painting again? False bravado?

He could be looking forward to some sightseeing, instead, some shopping and some excellent Greek cooking, what could have been a relaxing, normal, rainy Saturday. He was cautiously hopeful he would handle it better this time. After all, he'd undergone his trail by fire, so perhaps, knowing what to expect, he could manage it.

He reluctantly found himself speeding through the same enormous path to the art department, wind and rain blowing about him—he was highly amused and impressed to feel the damp, raw wind and even the occasional drop of rain. Enough rain to add realism while retaining a dry road surface. Not bad. Clearly, these people took an inordinate amount of pride in their periscope technology—with good reason.

Anne met him at the department's reception area, quiet and deserted and ominously ready. She was dressed in a crisp white blouse, a light blue skirt and was provocatively bare footed.

"Hi Phil. All ready for a little 'art appreciation' this morning?"

Phil forced a hearty smile. "Ready as I'll ever be, I guess. Does that damn thing have a name, by the way?" He nodded down the corridor toward the Chamber (as he now thought of it).

"Why yes. I named it myself, in fact. Anne held up a printout. The name in Greek, phonetic Greek, phonetic English and English:

Κόλαση λατρεία or Kolasi Latreia or hELz edorEishn or Hell's Adoration

What do you think?"

"I think it is chillingly appropriate. Jesus! Let's get this over with."

Phil followed Anne down the now familiar corridor but, instead of unlocking and entering the Chamber, she led him past the room, past the shower room, past the Jacuzzi, to a fourth room—a changing room. She opened the door for him. "You can hang up your clothes in here and change into a robe and slippers."

"Good thinking, Anne. Although I hope this is unnecessary."

Anne closed the door. Phil found a normal hotel-type robe and little terrycloth, cellophane wrapped slippers prepared for him. He stripped and donned the robe. He couldn't stand little terrycloth slippers. They forced him to curl his toes with every step and walk like a duck, just to keep them on. As he left the dressing room, Phil noticed that Anne had installed a wall-mounted cabinet just outside the Painting Room which she had opened. In the cabinet was a small candy bowl half full of light blue pills, a carafe of water, a glass, a bottle of brandy, a large bowel of ice and a few small towels. Next to the cabinet was a fairly comfortable, if somewhat clinical looking, chair. Persian carpets were in abundance, paintings (harmless ones) on the walls. It was even repainted in subdued pastels. He noted a red and green light array mounted above the door of the Painting Room and a large institutional style clock on the wall.

Anne's really getting things organized, he thought

Anne unlocked the door for him and turned on the light immediately. A few things had changed in the room. The floor was now covered with thick matting of the sort one finds in a gymnasium. A white cotton curtain was installed concealing *Hell's Adoration*. Anne explained the curtain was opened and closed by using a button mounted on the wall outside the room. A cable ran out from under the matting ending in a handheld button control. Anne explained that the light shone green when the room was empty, red when the room was occupied, and blinked red when the occupant signaled for recovery. The blinking red was activated by pressing the button on the cable or the "Panic Button" as Phil immediately christened it. When the light blinked red a soft alarm was engaged that sounded in the reception and in Anne's office.

The formality of all these preparations actually made Phil feel a good deal more nervous. He felt like an astronaut addressing his space capsule.

"Phil, I'm going to retrieve you after half an hour with or without the Panic Button. Okay?"

"Sounds good to me, Anne."

They entered the room. Anne closed the door. The curtain opened.

Half an hour later, Phil awoke in the chair outside the Room. He was trembling uncontrollably and covered in perspiration. He had neither wet himself nor vomited (That was a relief!). His palms were bloody and he had bitten his lip. Compared to last time, he was in relatively good shape. One critical exception. He could not remember one damned thing.

The last thing he could recall was the curtain opening on *Hell's Adoration*. Now he was in this chair. Anne gently fed him a pill and some brandy. After a few minutes, she helped him up and took him to the shower room. The shower was already running warm water. Anne removed his robe and teetered him into the shower. It felt wonderful. As before, she messaged his scalp, rubbed his neck and shoulders, and stroked his back—all the while quietly whispering to him. Some words he couldn't even understand—but it was all very calming. Anne put an arm around Phil's naked waist and used the other to hold and steady him to the Jacuzzi Room. Phil relaxed into the water, head back, eyes closed. He heard Anne leave the room and return. He opened an eye. She gave him a brandy and held one for herself. She smiled at him warmly. "You okay?"

"Better."

"You did much better this time."

"So did you." He smiled. "Nifty operation you've installed."

They finished their drinks, quietly regarding each other. After a bit Anne left and returned with Phil's robe. "Why don't we raid the pantry in the Touch Gallery?"

"Great idea. I'm starving. I skipped breakfast this morning thinking about The Chamber."

In the Gallery's kitchen, they cobbled together some cold chicken and potato salad and a bottle of white wine and took a table in the lounge. "So tell me, Phil. How was it this time really?"

"Well, Anne, I think you're going to be a little disappointed."

"How so?"

"I don't remember one goddamn thing after you opened the curtain. The next memory I have is awakening in the chair outside the Room."

"Good grief! It must have been worse than before if you blocked the whole experience. Sounds dangerous."

Phil was silent and Anne waited. After a while, Anne said, "I think it's my turn now."

"Are you sure?"

"Hell no, I'm not sure. In fact, I'm terrified. But as you said, "Let's get this over with.""

They rose and walked back into the reception area. Anne changed into a robe and unlocked and entered the room. The light was already on. With a weak smile, Anne nodded to Phil. He left the room, closed the door, and pushed the curtain button. He then sat down and did nothing but listen and watch the clock and watch the red light.

After about ten minutes, Phil heard a light sobbing inside the room, which went on for about five minutes. Around ten minutes after that, he heard a gasping over and over again. This lasted until the half hour was up. Phil rose and quietly opened the door.

Anne was lying on the mat, head raised, staring at the painting. Phil walked into the room. Anne seemed completely unaware of his presence. Phil put his hands under her arms and gently started to drag her from the room. Anne suddenly looked up at him, and immediately fainted.

A few minutes later, Anne came to. She was shaking and looked around as if puzzled, and then looked at Phil. "Hi." She whispered. "How long?"

"I dragged you out after half an hour. Do you remember anything?"

"Nothing."

Phil picked her up and carried her into the shower room, gently placing her on the bed. He removed her robe, turned on the shower, and helped her into the warming, driving water. Anne threw her head back and let the water run over her face, lowered her head and let the water beat on the back of her neck. Phil rubbed her temples gently, worked the muscles in her face, then transferred his attention to her neck, and down her back.

He walked her to the Jacuzzi room, lifted Anne, and carefully settled her into the bubbling water.

Phil left the room to later reappear with two small brandies. Anne accepted hers gratefully and gave Phil a long, warm smile.

"How you doin', Anne?"

"Fine. Just fine. I think I could sleep all day. Phil? What was I doing when you entered the room?"

"Um. Well, you were lying on the mat and staring at the Painting with a truly unnerving intensity. You were stiff as if frozen, and I think you would have lain there for hours if I hadn't retrieved you."

"That's exactly how you were."

"How can just a painting do this to a human?" Phil wondered, aloud.

"I don't think the painting itself is responsible." Anne responded. "I think the brain is entrapped into doing it to itself. The painting only leads it into a sort of an endless loop—it tricks it into feeling lost and panicky and trapped. It is simply a hugely-skillful, hazardous mental snare. Nothing magic. What does intrigue me is the idea that the artist somehow synthesized a sort of subconscious language into it. That's beyond impressive. It smacks of true ANUMEN."

"Okay. So the painting engages us to the degree that we mentally debilitate ourselves. Having once done so, we experience hellish fear and panic with such intensity we block the experience. Do you suppose it harms us in any way?"

"Well, I was trained in 'wrapping' as part of the Fear Ordeal. I suspect this may aid me. You? I don't know. Perhaps we should ask Eve Dunedin to look into this with us."

"Probably a good idea. You know, there are some other things I believe are worthy of experimentation."

"What's that?"

"First, I think you should select a subject from your art students. One who has demonstrated intelligence and a gift for art and has ideally completed the Fear ordeal. Then we record his reaction to the Painting. I suggest we install hidden CCTV in the room by the way."

"That's a great idea. I have just the student in mind."

"Second, I want to go through the Room again. I want to see if my reaction has stabilized."

"I would like to as well. Tomorrow at 1000? Perhaps we should invite Eve as well."

"Sure, on both counts."

"Phil it's only 1600 now. I could ring up that student right now if you like. His name is Mike Auslander. He's a brilliant art student and he has undergone the Fear Ordeal."

"Sounds good."

Anne went into the reception area and dialed a phone.

"Mike? Hello. This is Anne Jones. Hi. How are you? Good. Look Mike, I'm sorry to disturb you on a Saturday, but I was wondering if you had a few minutes to spare? Maybe as much as an hour. Great. I'm in the Reception Area of the Art Department. See you in a few minutes."

"Well, as you heard, he's on his way down. I suppose we should get cleaned up and get the place ready."

Twenty minutes later, Mike Auslander entered the lobby area. He was a well built, cheery, good looking young man with thick tousled hair and piercing eyes. Lander girls would have him for breakfast and save anything left for lunch.

"Mike Auslander, I'd like you to meet Mr. Philip Carr. Mike I'm sure you know Mr. Carr is the new Chancellor of the University."

"Certainly. Glad to meet you, sir."

"I'm pleased to meet you, Mike. Thanks for taking the time to come down and help us out. Anne would you explain what we're up to?"

"Sure, Phil. Mike, we have a painting in a viewing room down the hall. This painting was not done by an art student. If fact, we're not sure if he has studied art at all. We do think the work has some unusual properties and we're interested in getting your impression of it. Okay?"

"No problem."

"We're going to isolate you in a private room with the painting and give you up to half an hour to study it. After half an hour we'll bring you out and then discuss your reaction."

"I'm ready."

They led Mike down the hall, ushered him into the room, closed the door, and pushed the curtain control.

Silence.

Five minutes.

Ten minutes.

Then the door opened and Mike walked out.

"Well, Mike?" asked Anne.

"Not bad. Not bad at all. It looks to me as if he's found a technique for expressing our language. It reads like a book. Some very original ideas. A little upsetting, in fact. As an art form, I've never seen anything quite like it. This guy has actually blended written ideas with ideas expressed in oil, in the same notation. Not only that, he has synthesized a written language at the same time. Really impressive! Really fun! I'd like to meet this guy."

"Mike are you saying you could 'read' this painting to us?" Phil asked.

"Yes, sir. But you wouldn't understand a thing. I could read it to another student and they would understand it."

"Mike, you've read it. Can you tell me or translate what it says?" Phil asked, growing more intrigued.

"Hmmm. I'll try. It's about fear, conflict, and evil and excessively fanciful sex all happening at the same time to an innocent, sort of nescient being. It proves fatal, of course. It's acutely dark and profoundly sad. It vouches for the existence of evil, and goodness, lust and love for that matter. That's far from accurate, but the best I can do on the fly. I'll work on it some more if you like."

"Thanks, Mike." Anne said. "We really appreciate your time. When Mr. Carr and I tried viewing the painting, it provoked a far different reaction in us. A reaction I would define as mentally and physically dangerous. You seem entirely immune. Would this apply to other students as well?"

"Yes. Absolutely. I know you're probably thinking that the Fear Ordeal must come first. But they can take it anytime. Trust me."

"I will, Mike. Thank you. Feel free to study that painting any time."

"I will do that. Thanks."

Phil started to move towards the door while Mike and Anne followed. "One last question before you go, Mike," Phil said. "Could you produce something like this?"

"Now that I understand his notation and technique, I'm sure I can."

"Would you like to?"

"In fact I was planning on it."

"I wish you would, and I'd like very much to see the result."

"I'll have it for you by Monday?"

"That would be great, Mike. Thanks again and enjoy the rest of the weekend."

Phil and Anne looked at each other for a long time.

Phil said, "I think the weather's cleared up. Would you like to take a PM cruise and maybe have a drink afterwards?"

"Sounds good. Drink at your quarters?"

"If you like, certainly."

"Great! I've been dying to see the Presidential Penthouse."

"Well, I'll gladly give you the nickel tour. Shall we invite Eve?"

"Good idea. I'll give her a call, and perhaps she can meet us here."

"Anne, are you thinking we should expose her to the Painting *now*?"

"Why not? There's never a perfect time. We know we don't want to prepare our subjects in advance. So if she's there, and not otherwise engaged, why not let her run the gambit?"

"Point taken. Give her a call."

A moment later, Anne had Eve on the phone.

"Eve? This is Anne. Sorry to interrupt your weekend, but... are you doing something right now? Okay. I'm in the reception area of the new Art Department with Philip Carr. We have been running some tests—to be honest—some very difficult tests down here. I think we have a confirmed ANUMEN and we have most definitely invaded your territory. Fear. So...we felt it was an appropriate time to call you in. Interested? Great. We'll expect you in about ten minutes. See you soon."

Exactly ten minutes later, Eve Dunedin entered the reception area in jeans and a knit top. For a change, her hair was worn loosely in blond cascades—no bun today—it was attractive, softened her appearance, and made her look a bit more vulnerable.

"Good afternoon. Working overtime I see."

"Hi, Eve. Thanks for coming down."

"No problem, Anne. Hello Phil."

"Hi, Eve. Sorry to disturb your Saturday, but I think we have something interesting for you."

"Okay. Let's hear it."

"Ah. I think it's better if we show you this thing. We have a special room prepared and we're all set. Anne? Would you help Eve get ready?"

"Sure."

Anne and Eve walked together towards the dressing room. When they returned, Eve was dressed in a robe and barefooted. Phil guessed she didn't like little terrycloth slippers either. He had opened the cabinet next to the Picture Room door. Anne retrieved her key and opened the door. They all three entered. Eve was clearly intrigued.

"Eve, there is a painting behind that curtain. We want you to inspect the painting while we wait outside. The curtain will open automatically after we have left the room. Please take this button in your hand. If you wish to leave the room, just push the button. Either way, we will remove you from the room after half an hour. Afterwards, we'll discuss your impression of the painting. Okay?"

"Yes, I suppose so. You're making me a little nervous about all this. Should I be?"

"The painting will surprise you, Eve. But we are right here. Nothing to worry about."

"Swell. What a nifty way to spend a Saturday afternoon. Shall we get started?"

Anne and Phil closed the door, he pushed the curtain button and pulled up a couple of chairs, and they sat down and started their vigil.

Soon they could hear crying, vomiting, groans, moans, rolling around, whimpers, and what sounded like slapping the mat. Pretty much what they expected. After half an hour, they closed the curtain, opened the door and entered.

Eve was a mess. She had voided herself from every conceivable orifice. There was even a fair amount of blood on her hands, her ears, and running from her nose. It was clear that Eve had undergone a far tougher ordeal than Anne and Phil. They gently lifted her to her feet and nearly carried her to the easy chair. After a fair amount of moist, cool toweling, Eve was ready for some diluted brandy and a blue pill, which she took unquestioningly, even gratefully.

After about five minutes, Phil and Anne took Eve to the shower and a few minutes afterwards to the Jacuzzi. Phil brought in three brandies.

Eve grasped her brandy and took a healthy swallow. "You sons of bitches!" Eve coughed. "What the living hell was that?"

They briefed Eve on everything that had occurred up until her exposure to *Hell's Adoration,* including their experiment with Mike Auslander.

"This Auslander kid was completely unaffected by the Painting?"

"Yes."

"You know, I think I understand why music has failed to produce what *we* would define as ANUMEN."

"How's that?"

"Well, we look at the Painting, we take it all in, and then our minds take over. The Painting sits passively while we create the loops, the fear, the panic using our mind and our own imagination. Music does not present us with this latitude. Instead, we follow the music, engaging our mind to enjoy, understand, and interpret it. It does not allow us to mentally slip away and terrify ourselves."

Phil frowned. "That makes sense, Eve. But I wonder what would happen if our students put their words to music—their new language I mean. I wonder what other art forms would unleash our minds in quite this way?"

Anne interjected. "Poetry? Some form of literature? Sculpture? Touch? Perfume? Dance? Architecture?"

"That's an impressive list, Anne. And in some ways frightening. Can you imagine a building that could provoke a reaction like *Hell's Adoration*? Or, my God, a perfume you could wear into an elevator, or damn near kill a theater full of ballet aficionados? This shapes up more like a form of weapon than a form of art." Would you all care to discuss this further over a drink?"

"Absolutely." They chimed in unison.

They took a threesome PM ride, then a tour through the suites, and the three of them found themselves over drinks on Phil's terrace quietly enjoying the setting sun.

Eve looked studiously at Phil. "With all respect, Mr. President, as I review the events of the last couple of weeks, you start to look like some kind of a provocateur."

"Provocateur?"

"Well, I've been hearing rumors about a huge shakeup on security, then suddenly ANUMINA start appearing where there were none for years. It would seem that, logically, you are some sort of catalyst here on the Island."

"I'm not sure I understand what you're saying. But I'll give it some thought. If you have any further thoughts, please let me know. Meanwhile, there is a Board Meeting next Wednesday. Among my duties to the Board is to alert them of ANUMINA. So far we have the Painting and a new language. Reporting time?"

Silence ensued following Phil's last statement.

Anne finally responded. "We know very, very little about these phenomena."

"So these would be preliminary findings. At least it points out the prime objective of this facility begins to look achievable."

"Yes." Anne said.

"Agreed." Eve echoed.

"I want to convene a highly confidential briefing in my conference room at 1000 on Monday morning. I would like you both there. I would like Sean Gray, Judy McLean, Emily Johansen, Sun Kahn, and William Gould to attend. Do you agree with this list?"

"Yes" said both.

"Have I forgotten anyone?"

"How about Dr. Webber, Phil?" Anne asked.

"I had intended to develop a preliminary presentation for his review. But perhaps it is better if we bring him in immediately. Okay, agreed. So how about another drink?"

Phil and Anne agreed they'd definitely had enough and decided to postpone further interaction with the Painting for the weekend. Eve, as their resident psychologist, readily agreed.

"I'm concerned you both drew a blank on your second viewing. For you, Anne, it could be wrapping. Phil? Perhaps you have your own innate defenses. Or possibly you are both injuring yourselves. I need some time to work out a strategy here. Incidentally, Phil, are you ready to start Fear Training by any chance? If you choose to proceed, I'll volunteer as your councilor, and we'll hand pick staffers to administer your training. The sessions will be private. At no time will you be trained with students."

"Yes, Eve. Let's get started the week after next. I'm not looking forward to this, by the way."

"Nobody does."

Sunny Sunday

Phil had Sunday off and was looking forward to it. He planned to sleep late, swim, and soak in the sauna. Later, he would have a light breakfast, watch some satellite TV. *Cómo es dulce no hacer nada.*

He then decided a lunch aboard one of the Island's yachts with Rachael and Charlie would be most enjoyable. The weather was brilliant. He wanted to reconnoiter the Island seaward in any event and this would give him an opportunity to get a status briefing from both.

"Edward? Would you ring up Rachael Stone and Charlie Stein and see if they're free for lunch around 1330? I would like to have it served on one of the Island's motor yachts if possible. And we'll need instructions on how to get to the boat. Can you make those arrangements please? Thanks, Edward."

Edward soon confirmed all arrangements, and Phil passed a leisurely morning getting better acquainted with his digs, enjoying the pool and the weather, and taking a quick bite in the kitchen in front of the television. The only thing he missed was a Sunday paper. It just wasn't the same reading a digital copy. He needed the feel, the rustling and folding of the paper, and most importantly, the ability to scan an entire page for items of interest at a single glance. No scrolling needed. One compensation was the immediate availability of newspapers from around the world. All in all, he enjoyed the morning and looked forward to lunch on the sea.

There was little time to bring the boat around to the Island's Halios Geron Jetty, so he would board at Proteus Cavern Harbor. Phil took a PM deeper into the complex than he could have imagined. Elevators, winding hallways spiraling down and down, moving sidewalks dropping off at alarming angles, the PM handled it all effortlessly. The trip was constantly graced by innovative architecture and enchanting periscopes.

When he had traveled downward for more than four hundred meters, he finally entered a stupendous cave opening onto the sea at Proteus Cavern Harbor. Within were yachts, ships, gun boats, research vessels, launches, sail boats, cargo ships, barges with massive winches, row boats; in fact, there were water craft of every conceivable description, except fishing boats. Against one of the walls was an impressive inventory of surfboards, diving equipment, jet skis, wind surfers, catamarans, and every type of water plaything imaginable. Laced throughout the underground harbor there were restaurants, food stands, bars, and vendors of all description. As today was Sunday, the entire area was lively and crowded, and water sports were clearly the order of the day. Most certainly this armada of fun seekers being constantly gorged and disgorged between grotto and sea must reinforce the Island's masquerade as a "Halios Geron Resort."

The Proteus Cavern was at least twelve thousand square meters, rising more than two hundred meters at its interior apex. The harbor looked deep as well. The mouth of the grotto was about seventy-five meters wide. Nothing looked to be man-made or man-enhanced. He had heard of such vast anti alluvial gaseous bubbles forming in the middle of limestone and granite islands as they were extruded from their fiery crucibles, but this was the first time he actually experienced such a cave first-hand. He noted cascading water in an area removed from the harbor and understood for the first time the Island's water supply, along with desalination apparatus clearly in evidence on the western side of the Island.

The only major features of the cave that looked man-made were two enormous vertical pillars of stone on either side of the grotto's entrance—function unfathomable—until Phil decided these were mined in all likelihood, capable of sealing the harbor in a matter of moments. Not for the first time, Phil was overwhelmed by the sheer magnitude of the Island's complex. In fact, it was in reality, a complex of complexes.

Phil headed for the Harbor Master's control tower to get directions to his boat until he saw a collection of signs indicating the direction to the slips for various craft. He immediately spotted "Geron II," his assigned boat, and headed in that direction.

Once on board, he found Captain and crew on duty, caterers actively preparing for lunch, and Rachael and Charlie cheerfully installed in the bar.

"Good afternoon, guys."

"Hi, Phil," they said in chorus.

"Looks like we're ready to cast off. I'll alert the Captain while someone arranges for a Gin & Tonic?"

"You got it," Charlie said.

Drinks in hand, the three moved forward to the bow to watch the fascinating maneuvers of the sizeable yacht as it threaded its way through the maze of boats, buoys, slips, channel markers, and finally into the busy channel exiting the cave, onto a sparkling sea, under a blinding sun.

Phil noted flags on either side of the channel. These were large with a zigzag blue and white design, a flag he was unfamiliar with in marine terms. He spotted similar flags in a red and white zigzag motif mounted on a dual halyard on the same flagpoles. After some thought, he realized these were "enter," "no-enter," harbor flags for craft unequipped with radios, which could be interchanged immediately.

Phil tried to spot the Island's artificial reef with no success. The blocks were too similar to the seabed, and the sun-dazzled water obscured it with a countless chaos of tiny, dancing, mirrored waves. Phil assumed the reef was avoided by Island craft using sonar, transponders, and charts. He knew from reviewing some of the Island schematics, underwater lights could be activated at reef openings if all else failed. All boats were equipped with corresponding lighting equipment onboard, not to mention red and green channel markers. However, Phil was well aware that the channel markers could be automatically retracted at a moment's notice.

It was warm with a very mild wind blowing from the west. One by one, the three retreated below to change into swimming suits. Phil admired that Rachael filled out her swimming suit in fine fashion. He had always seen her in business attire or appropriately camouflaged working clothes, so this was quite a pleasant change of pace. The crew set up deck chairs on the bow and the three enjoyed a quiet, second round of cold drinks.

Rachael and Charlie regaled Phil with tales of the marvels and the people and the concepts they had encountered on the Island. Phil listened with interest, learning some things new to him, and generally letting the conversation run its course through drinks and on through an excellent lunch.

The Island was much the same from any perspective. Jetties were invisibly nested behind rock formations. The twisting paths down to the sea looked like nothing more than fault lines in the native stone. So all in all, the Island appeared as a mammoth, uninhabited plateau consisting of cliffs well over four hundred meters high at any point. Look-outs, gun emplacements, security apparatus—all invisible. Phil could barely make out the mansion atop the University Complex and, of course, the harbor cave. Beyond that was nothing. Nor were there any observable sites out to sea. This led Phil to conclude that there was no other land masses for more than 100 kilometers in any direction.

The catering crew had arranged coffee, dessert, and liquors on the open-air stern salon, so the three moved to comfortable lounge chairs surrounding a low coffee table.

Phil said. "Next week is going to be a very busy one I think. So, if you don't mind, I'd like to have a couple of 'warp speed' briefings on both your projects. Okay?"

"Sure," Rachael and Charlie said in unison.

"I'll start if that's alright," Charlie said. "I can get through it in about two minutes."

"Great, go ahead, Charlie."

"I have completed installation and testing of all hardware and software components. We can now intercept all outbound and inbound messages, no matter the source, interrogate the message and either block it or relay it to its intended addressee. We can universally or selectively scramble inbounds and outbounds. We can nearly instantly locate the source of outbound bandits and stop them, capture them, and interpret them to some degree. We need to carefully monitor traffic for awhile to ensure we've covered all gates. I need to train a full 7/24 shift on monitoring this equipment. I need to train a full 7/24 shift on maintenance. In my opinion, the only potential remaining gap may be the potential for some very advanced steganography. I have some AI software geared to detect such traffic, but I believe it needs some serious adaptation and further qualification testing."

"Stegano...stegano...what? Sounds like a goddamned dinosaur."

"Steganography...is a high-tech digital method for masking files. It was derived from some fairly antiquated manual processes, some dating back more than one hundred years. Steganography is the practice of imbedding, or hiding, or caching, or concealing information in file or digital image form within another, superficially innocuous text."

"Try again, Charlie."

"One guy sends a message, and inside the message, the guy has buried another message. The idea is that the really secret stuff can be electronically smuggled in without detection. Clear?"

"Crystal. Are we in danger of such traffic?"

"If I correctly understand what you've been going through, there is not one damn thing you're not in danger of."

"Point well taken. However, may I assume that for all practical purposes it is reasonably safe to lift the communications blackout?"

"Mmm...I'd say the risk is manageable. Yes. I'd recommend you lift the blackout. I think you would do more damage to continue the ban balanced against the potential for contravention. As I said, there's still a fair amount to develop and maintain."

"So, you'll continue here onsite until these items are done to your satisfaction?"

"Yes. Yes I will. A couple of our processors will need significant upgrades in horsepower."

"Cost much?"

"A good deal, yes."

"Take long?"

"A few hours."

"How's that possible?"

"Well a few of the larger processors are shipped with upgrades already installed that can expand capacity two, three, even four times over. All they have to do is remotely activate hardware that is already built in, and then essentially perform an extensive restart process...takes about two to three hours. We'll then augment our AI tables with some Fuzzy rules, a DAF queue processor feed, believe it or not, by stutter detection software. This obviously applies to spoken transmissions and the upgrades required are not that extensive because our volumes are quite manageable."

"DAF?"

"Delayed Auditory Feedback."

"Okay. Proceed. We'll need to get you cleared through Medical and HR. Do you want to be a Consultant, or Management?"

"Where are the least strings?"

"I can make sure neither option entangles you more than you might wish."

"Fine. I need some supervisory/hire/fire authority to get this done effectively, so I'll go with door Number Two: Management. Is that alright?"

"Just fine. Papers will be cut tomorrow for our new Director of Communications, reporting directly to me. Please meet with our HR Director sometime tomorrow. I'll make sure he's fully briefed."

"Is there like a VP Info Systems & Comms?"

"I'm not sure, Charlie. If there is we'll have to give you dotted line reporting to him as well. I'll ask the HR guy to send us both an org chart on the IS&C operation, or whatever they're calling it these days. There's a hellofa lot I don't know around here. Let's work together to find out the ins and outs and try to minimize hurt feelings and bent egos. Okay?"

"You got it."

"Okay...Rachael?"

"I've got a couple of things to report, Phil. Not all of it good. Let's start with the easy stuff. We're ready to lift the travel and communications embargo on your order. We had originally intended to impose a twenty-four hour baggage check-in threshold as you know. We looked at it and can do it with four, in view of our current traffic. This of course requires a strict inspection of limited carry on items. All under the guise of security."

"Lift all bans effective tomorrow."

"Will do. Secondly, we've given the gate to no less than four of 'Ryerson' Rangers.' The first four we sampled were dirty as hell. I think they will all prove to be dirty, or unidentifiable."

"Good going."

"I'm not so sure, Phil. We have some limited surveillance capability over these guys and with the removal of Ryerson, Kelly, and now these four, they really have their backs up."

"Is there a risk of some sort of reprisal?"

"Could be. I was thinking of a short moratorium in gating these bastards. Maybe they'll calm down and let it ride. It's very hard to predict."

"Can you identify a leader amongst them?"

"No. And I think if there were one clear kingpin, they'd already be cutting our throats. It seems to me the big question is how much the troops knew about this operation and what Ryerson' plans or orders might have been. If someone knew a great deal, I think we'd be in some real shit. Otherwise, these bums will just stumble around looking for trouble. So, I suggest we let them cool off a bit and see if we can spot a potential leader. Meanwhile, we'll continue to collect reliable dossiers and try to maintain some discipline."

"Spooky situation. Do they have free access to our armaments?"

"I'm afraid so. I have considered mining the access points. There are two armories—one attached to their barracks, the other is built into the Island's bunker compound. Access tunnels can be easily mined and perhaps, better still, introducing gas apparatus into the armories themselves."

"What sort of gas. Won't we kill these guys?"

"Well, there are options like halogenated hydrocarbon anesthetics such as halothane, which are relatively safe and effective within a reasonable period—that is to say, we could incapacitate them without killing them for a length of time adequate to respond and restrain. We can consider others such as diethyl ether and nitrous oxide. I believe we have many choices."

"Go for it."

Rachael smiled. "With pleasure. I think these sorts of precautions should have been installed from the get-go."

Phil shook his head in disgust. "Probably some more security mechanisms Ryerson' conveniently overlooked. It's painfully clear now that he was actually equipping a small strike force rather than securing an installation. By the way, I assume you have already surmised that Ryerson murdered Wilcoxen?"

"I was pretty sure. How was it done?"

"Ryerson poisoned him after sedating him. I had Dr. Gear do a second autopsy and he discovered residual toxins as well as the delivery point on Wilcoxen's body. Gear is no forensic pathologist, but he's a good doctor, and he came across with the goods."

"What kind of poison?"

"That's the cute part. He didn't use a poison *per se*. He introduced an enormous concentrated derivative of some female hormones known as sympathomemetics that induced a massive stroke. Deadly and damn clever. Dr. Gear says that, technically, this does not constitute poison, because the effects of overdosing have not really been formally sorted out by pathologists as yet. However, as we all know, there are lots of deadly pathogens out there, many untraceable and seemingly innocuous. Looking as much like a natural death as it did, he probably fooled his masters and handlers as much as we. But I imagine this was only a 'one shot' trick".

"Nor is water deemed a poison, but if you hold a man's head under long enough you will indeed become a murderer. Damn! I'm glad that SOB's outa the way. By the way, Phil, would you mind if I consulted Dr. Gear about our gas issue?"

"Not at all. He's very well informed as it is, and I think the more he knows, the better off we may all be. Anything else, Rachael?"

"No, those are the high points."

"Good. What say we have another drink and head back?"

Private Services with a Smile

The next morning, Phil entered his office at around 0900. He was pleased to note the pile of papers on his desk was much diminished. He graced Cindy with his most ingratiating smile as she brought in coffee.

"Morning, Cindy. Will you invite Dr. Webber to a meeting in my conference room at 1000 this morning and see if the Head of Finance can meet with me at 1600 please? And hire someone to act as our joint secretary. I don't want to see you delivering coffee anymore. Okay?"

"Yes, sir. With pleasure."

"Thanks."

Quickly, Phil had a confirmed 1000 with Webber that would overflow through lunch and a 1600 with a Mr. Richards who was Director of Finance.

Phil then made arrangements for Rachael and Charlie with HR, confirmed the suspension of the Travel and Communications moratorium, and approved an impressive invoice from Howard's agency, just in time to return to his conference room.

Edward had arranged for coffee, tea, water, juices, and pastries on the side board of Phil's conference room. Phil entered the room. After a few minutes, all parties were arranged around the table."

"You've produced a demonstrable, reproducible and provable ANUMEN?" Dr. Webber asked, eyebrows raised.

"Yes, sir."

"My God. Tell me more."

"Dr. Webber, we have prepared a fairly informal briefing in a couple of areas we thought you might be interested in, particularly in view of the upcoming Board Meeting. Specifically, we have indeed encountered credible, demonstrable and reproducible instances of ANUMEN in two areas: Language and Art. Dr. Jones will present the Art ANUMEN, and Dr. McLean will present the ANUMEN within Languages. Dr. McLean?"

Judy McLean confidently approached the podium. Once there, she pressed a button that activated the room's sound system. Immediately, a clear, almost sublime consonance of sounds emanated from speakers around the conference room. The base was quite similar to Hump Back whale song. Augmenting this were intermittent hissing sounds, clicks, growls, and various ambiguous sounding groans. The sound was totally unintelligible, surprisingly agreeable to the senses, and possessed a haunting quality that was a blending of melancholy, keenness, and the undeniable suggestion that quantities of information were being conveyed. The recording went on for approximately ten minutes and, despite the incomprehensibility of the sounds, they were able to identify specific sound patterns that were repeating occasionally, possibly a name, a repetitive thought, a song...a poem?

Other variables that surfaced with listening were that volume rose and fell constantly, as though that implied information transfer as well. With volume, it was possible to detect variances in speed, tenor, and octaves. Emotion seemed to play a part in this symphonic language. The group could clearly empathize with playfulness, sorrow, humor, anger, boredom, arousal, and genuine interest. This was the most complex blending of sounds they had ever experienced. When the recording ended, Dr. McLean resumed her seat and, without comment, commenced passing out discs that were obviously recordings of what they had just listened to.

"What the hell was that?" Dr. Webber asked.

"Around ten days ago in the midst of our language labs, a new language spontaneously generated. This is that language." Judy responded.

Webber pondered her words a moment. "Please, define 'spontaneously generated,' doctor."

"All the students in the lab started speaking it at the same time, starting with threshold PSG 8333."

"PSG 8333?" Phil asked.

"PSG is an acronym for Propagation Singularity Generation. The number 8333 designates the eight-thousandth, three-hundred, and thirty-third generations of students. We have identified a gnome for all generations, so we are able to genetically monitor and describe students in germs of their PSG."

She continued with her report. "To the best of our knowledge, there was no prior development of the language, nor was there any language training for any student whatsoever. We even suspected this was some sort of prank for a time. Every student on the Island, including infants as young as seven months, speaks the language with apparent fluency. The language is not predicated on a hard palate. Interestingly, this would imply that some non-human subjects might selectively master this language as well.

We are totally unable to explain this phenomenon. This is something totally alien. We are absolutely incapable of translating the language. We are absolutely incapable of understanding the language. We foresee within months or years we may make some computer assisted inroads. Perhaps the most intelligent observation was made by Mr. Carr. He suggested that the language might actually be a natural manifestation. That is, it might be resident within the genetic structure of the students. Part of the PSG gnome."

These statements were followed by a long silence.

"If it's native to the students," Webber observed, "it must be native to us too."

"That's out belief as well," Dr. McLean responded, "but we appear to lack the trigger, or perhaps the innate intelligence, to activate the language within our fundamental biological matrix. This goes beyond simple mnemonics. This goes beyond language as we understand it. We may be confronted with a general quantum function of some sort. I strongly suspect that lower threshold iterations are forever barred from this skill."

"Meaning?"

"Meaning *us,* Dr. Webber. I don't believe we'll ever speak this language."

"Who exactly will, Dr. McLean?"

"Any human after the threshold iteration PSG 8333…"

"… and?"

"And possibly other types of beings, terrestrial and non-terrestrial."

"What in the world leads to you speculate on *non-terrestrials* of all things?"

"As I stated, we seem to be confronting a generalized quantum function."

"And what the hell does that mean?"

"It means it is possible that this new communications form may be as universal in nature as gravity, or the speed of light, or prime numbers, and so on…"

"Good grief," Dr. Webber said, after a moment of silence. "When I coined the term ANUMEN years ago, I had nothing even remotely as advanced as this in mind. This is beyond extraordinary. It is beyond belief. Good God! Congratulations! Phil? I want our best Champagne in here right now!"

While Phil buzzed Edward, the whole room broke into animated discussions which continued while Champagne was being served, ceasing only for a toast by Dr. Webber.

"Many of us have been working toward this point for more than twenty years now, and in my estimation, it's arrived *ten years early*. Again, congratulations! Congratulations and... God help us all."

Conversation continued unabated for another half hour, interrupted by Dr. Webber. "Phil, I assume we can have this ready for presentation to the Board on Wednesday?"

"Absolutely, Craig. No problem. I'm giving ANUMEN's and Finance my full priority for the next two days in preparation for the Board Meeting. There is one more area to cover Craig. Should we meet about that after lunch?"

"Yes indeed. I would like to get with you over lunch and then I would like us all to re-convene here at 1430. Thank you."

With that, the room emptied, except for Craig and Phil.

"Lunch on the terrace, Doctor?"

"Sounds good."

The two moved to the terrace and had drinks while Edward served lunch. Phil spent the time bringing Webber up to date on communications, travel, security, and the attrition of 'Ryerson' Rangers.'

"You've been busy, Phil. I'm impressed. Gonna be ready for the Board Meeting Wednesday afternoon?"

"I'm meeting with Mr. Richards this afternoon to see to it that the financial status report is standing tall. Beyond that, we have the ANUMEN issue, and that should make for a pretty full meeting."

"I agree. What have you dug up on the Board Member in question?"

"I'm waiting on a report from Howard tomorrow morning. Can we meet after that?"

"Sure. Let's get back. I want to hear about your next ANUMEN."

Phil was touched by Webber's use of the term "*your* next ANUMEN."

The conference room was fully assembled when they returned. Phil promptly opened the session.

"Dr. Jones?"

Anne Jones stood and walked to the room's podium. From the podium, she activated a PC projector and presented a fuzzy color design on the room's presentation screen.

"This is a photograph of an oil painting made by one of our students. We have learned his name is Jacques Guy Tomas. He is a graduate student concentrating on genetics. He has never studied art. He walked into the art department one day about three weeks ago, spent around six hours making this painting, left, and has not returned since. The reason this photograph is so blurry is because if it were in clear focus, everyone in this room would be on the floor by now, weeping, vomiting, urinating, groaning, approaching catatonia, and in a very literal sense, would soon be approaching an imminent death.

We've subsequently discovered, aside from other amazing features of this work, it is the written form of the language we learned about before lunch. If anyone is interested, we've prepared a viewing room for the painting in the Art Department. We have designed and equipped the room to make the experience reasonably survivable. We cannot make the experience pleasant, or without risk. I would suggest that, prior to any further viewings, a physical exam be administered to ensure the best chance of survival.

We exposed one of our art students to the painting. He suffered no ill effects whatsoever. In fact, he was somewhat critical of it, though impressed, and I understand he has created something along these lines himself. I intend to view it myself later today.

My analysis leads me to strongly suspect the *technique*, or whatever term applies here, used in creating this painting could be generalized to other forms of expression such as sculpture, architecture or, in fact, any form that could employ the nested communication implied by this painting. Questions?"

There was an extended silence.

Webber finally spoke. "Phil, how do you intend to present this to the Board?"

"We do not intend to present it. Under no circumstances."

"May I ask why?" Dr. Webber countered a little coolly.

"Two reasons, Craig. First, in view of the age demographics of the Board we could easily kill them. Second, this 'art' has the potential to become a weapon. It is exceedingly dangerous for anyone except our students. Can you imagine unveiling a building in the middle of a major city that has the capacity to kill, just by looking at it?"

Webber squinted at the blurry picture on the screen. "It seems to me in only two areas so far, we can observe ANUMEN's that seem to work together, fit together, compliment each other, that may comprise an overall structure. Can you imagine a composite of say thirty ANUMEN's? The new language already speaks to the new painting that speaks to the new language, and so on. Any guesses as to the volatility of future ANUMEN's?"

This time, there was total silence.

"Phil, I agree with presenting only the new language to the Board. I require of everyone in this room complete confidentiality of this and any discussion regarding the painting. I want reports about, and from, anyone who decides to view the painting, and your rule about pre-physicals should be strictly enforced, Dr. Jones.

I thank you all for a most interesting meeting. Phil, I look forward to meeting with you tomorrow morning."

Shortly, Phil was left alone in the conference room.

Edward entered. "Phil, Mr. Richards is on the line. He would like to speak to you about this afternoon's meeting."

"Thanks, Edward. Transfer it in here, please."

"Yes, Mr. Richards?" Phil said when the phone call was transferred.

"Mr. Carr, I was preparing for our meeting. I have the reports for the Board ready for review. They're very routine. There is one other thing, however, that you may be interested in, if you wouldn't mind joining me here in Treasury for our meeting?"

"Certainly, Mr. Richards. I'll be there at 1630. Goodbye."

This time as Phil rode the PM, he was taken through a shopping center, just like those one might see in New York, London, Los Angeles, or Paris. He passed shop after shop, boutiques, barbers, salons, tea rooms, clothing, jewelry, toys, music, videos, shoes, a deli(!), restaurants, drug stores, bars, fast food(!), sporting goods, movie theaters, fountains, ponds, escalators, and on and on...

Phil felt at home here. This was fun and stylish and light hearted and periscope free. Unashamedly, it was all underground. And right in the middle of all this was the Finance & Treasury Department. Somehow that felt right too.

"Hello, Mr. Richards," Phil said, as he entered Mr. Richards' office. Glad to meet you."

"Glad to meet you, Mr. Carr. Coffee?"

"Yes. Thank you."

"The first thing I have to show you this afternoon is our Report to the Board. It's in a standard format so the Board pretty much races through it at every meeting. In this department we have Accounts Receivable and Revenue Accounting for the various shops throughout the complex. We have Cash Management and Cash Accounting. We have a significant Accounts Payable, and we support Encumbrance Accounting, as every good non-profit organization should. We maintain one full time, outside accountant who continuously audits our operation. And we have Treasury Accounting. We maintain significant funds all over the world, and it's a major task managing all these accounts. I have always made the financial report to the Board. Mr. Wilcoxen only involved himself with Treasury functions ..."

"Ah, that's certainly okay, Mr. Richards. Sounds fine to me. I have no intention of re-organizing anything in this area, and I am pleased you will make the financial report on Wednesday."

"Yes, sir. Thank you, sir. Although that's not really what I am driving at."

"What *are* you driving at?"

"Well, Mr. Wilcoxen maintained an office down here in Treasury. He would use it to prepare for his various trips, meetings with investors, cash management, and he would frequently meet with Board Members here as well."

"Interesting. You mean he personally prepared for these meetings and trips?"

"Yes, sir."

"And he would actually bring Board Members down here?"

"Yes, sir. And I took it upon myself to clean out his office here and prepare the files for your review and the office for your use, should you wish it."

"Yes?"

"Well, in terms of files, I found very little really. I did find some unusual ledgers that were codified and cross referenced to specific sub accounts. The only problem is, there is no such subsidiary ledger in any of our files, or I should say databases. We are fully automated. Quite state-of-the-art, actually.

In any event, Mr. Wilcoxen had the HR application triggered to send me a message when and if his demise was recorded. This was done (rather late) just a couple of days ago, and I did receive the message. The message was keyed to my password and only contained twenty-one sets of numbers. Twenty were cross-referenced to the subsidiary accounts. I continued cleaning and filing and searching through Mr. Wilcoxen's office, and I finally happened upon a safe hidden behind the wet bar. The combination to the safe was the twenty-first, non-cross-referenced set of numbers. This solution is classic Wilcoxen. Not high-tech, really. Simple. Not really secure, but somewhat mazelike."

"You've been busy, Mr. Richards!"

"Yes, well it turns out the reason I could not locate the subsidiary ledgers is because they are not virtual files, they are literal files, not even really analog."

"Come again?"

"Perhaps I should show you, Mr. Carr?"

"Perhaps you should, Mr. Richards."

Richards led Phil through several offices, down a hallway, through a locked door to another locked door marked "Authorized Personnel Only." Phil noted an impressive array of security devices surrounding their entrance. He unlocked the door and led Phil into a large, nicely decorated office with a huge antique desk, several leather chairs, two periscopic windows overlooking the sea, and a very luxurious, wall-sized, mirrored, wet bar. The "office" had more of the impersonal feel of a fancy meeting room, rather than an office where work was done and information kept.

Richards played with something under the sink of the wet bar, and the entire unit swiveled back ninety degrees. Behind the bar was a round, stainless-steel door with a digi-code combination pad, as high as a tall man and equally as wide. Richards input the code, and the huge round door made sounds of bars and frame-plates being retracted, then opened outward itself ninety degrees. Inside, it was astounding. Phil was actually speechless.

The safe itself was well over ten times as large as Wilcoxen's office. It was divided into some twenty independent, enormous stainless-steel cabinets arranged laterally respective to the safe's entrance. At the end of each cabinet was its own digital combination keypad.

Richards activated the first, and the shell of the cabinet automatically retracted. External to the shelves hung an elaborate electronic clipboard. Each clipboard reflected a Sub Ledger Account Number, Cross-Reference key, and line after line of "Deposit" or "Withdrawal," "Amount or Value," "Currency or Commodity," "Date," and dual "Signatures." Phil borrowed a calculator and spent several minutes wandering the isles, retracting the cabinets, examining the clipboards, pondering the contents of the shelves, and estimating the approximate value of the total contents.

After half and hour or so, he arrived at a number somewhere in the vicinity of twelve hundred billion dollars in currency, gold, diamonds, negotiable securities, and unidentifiable metal boxes of a very heavy construct, locked and sealed.

Phil's only intelligible words were a whispered, "Holy shit!"

"Exactly, Mr. Carr. What shall I do?"

Following a long pause, Phil was a lawyer again.

"Give me the keys to the office and I will change the combination to the safe. Add another lock to the door to which only you will hold the key. Then add another lock that can be opened only by two keys. You will hold one. I will hold the other. Seal the door and add a sign 'No Admittance Whatsoever Without the Written Authority of T. Richards and P. Carr.' Then activate all security controls." Phil turned and faced Richards directly. "Ted, share this with no one. Please send me and Dr. Webber a copy of your Board presentation. Thank you, and I'll see you Wednesday morning."

In the shopping center complex, Phil found a very pleasant bar called αρθρο Ελληνας υπογειος (arthro Ellinas ypogeios) The Greek Underground, and ordered himself a generous Gin & Tonic.

He was sitting by himself. *So—along with whatever other goods and services we provide the Board, we're a money laundering operation. No. Not money laundering. Really more of a Swiss Bank Account. Much better than laundering anyhow, I guess. In fact, what the hell, these guys own the place and they can put their money any damn place they like. I'm being a little sanctimonious. I wonder if Craig knows. He must.*

After he finished his drink, he left to sample the local deli.

Scenes from a Gallery

Over breakfast the next morning, Edward said, "Rachael Stone is on the line for you."

"Thanks, Edward. I'll take it in here."

"Hi Rachael."

"Phil, I have Howard from Chicago on the line. He would like to speak to us."

"Okay, put us all together."

"Hello, Howard. You're working late!"

"Yeah, Phil, we're pulling an all-nighter surveillance on a toughie. I'm up to my ass in cops, feds, spooks, and Treasury Agents. I haven't seen a bed for twenty hours, and I don't know when the next time may be."

"Guess that's what you get the big bucks for, Howard. What's up?"

"I've got the report on your Board Member."

"Rachael, are we recording this?"

"Yes, Phil."

"Go, Howard."

"Okay, John W. Dunkin, U.S. Citizen, sixty-seven years old, born in New Brunswick, New Jersey, wife Laura, two children Dianne, twenty-seven, a Lawyer and Robert, thirty-three, a biologist, principal residence is 33 Newton Court, Cape May, New Jersey. Dunkin is Founder, President, and Board Chairman of DEW Defense Industries, located at various sites around Cape May and Newark, estimated annual personal income thirty-four million, U.S., estimated net worth seventy-five million, absolutely no marks against his record, not even a parking ticket, graduated with honors and an MBA from Harvard, served in the U.S. Army four years, achieved the rank of Captain of Infantry, served with distinction. Received an Honorable Discharge, Silver Star, and Purple Heart. He serves on several Boards, is a registered Republican, very active in New Jersey and nationally. His hobby is sailing; he has stock holdings in several industries—writes about it for *Fortune Magazine*, is an advisor to NSA and DIA; his religion is Methodist, and he is very active in church affairs and a variety of charities...this goes on and on. It's like eating white bread and washing it down with weak tea. He's absolutely clean."

"No skinny from the grape vines?" Rachael asked.

"*Nada*. Wish I could do better, guys. I'm really confused here. All I can assume is this guy is a master of disguise, or someone is having him on in the same way Dr. Webber was used. My strong suspicion is the latter."

"Thanks, Howard. I'm going to meet this gentleman today. I'll see if anything develops. This is actually very good news. Bye, Howard, good hunting."

Rachael called after they had all rung off. "Well, Phil, what do you think?"

"Beats the hell outa me. I'm going to try to friendly up to this fellow and feel him out, I suppose. Craig's going to be pleased about this, and with himself, justifiably so, I guess. I'll keep you posted. How are Ryerson' Rangers behaving?"

"Quiet. Lot of time in lower level bars where they have a good deal of privacy. Makes me nervous."

"Me too. Watch'em like a hawk, Rachael."

"Bet on it."

"By the way, did you get the body guards for you, me, and Dr. Webber?"

"They've been on duty now for four days." Phil could hear the smile in Rachael's voice.

"You do good work. Bye."

A few minutes later, Phil called Dr. Webber. "Good morning, Craig. How are you?"

"Good morning, Phil. Never better, and I mean that. This ANUMEN development is the best news I've had in a very long time. And I think it's just starting. This is an amazing, exciting time."

"Got some more good news for you, Craig."

"Yes? What is it?"

"I just got the report on John Dunkin."

"Yes?"

"Jesus Christ, in white robe and sandals couldn't have a cleaner record. He's absolutely solid."

"Good grief! That's a load off. Thanks, Phil. So...who's been passing off all these bogus bastards on us?"

"I really don't know. I thought I would ask some very delicate, very indirect questions of Mr. Dunkin over lunch, or drinks, or something, and see what comes out. Best guess is someone in his organization was feeding him these guys for whatever reason and Dunkin is as much a dupe as we are in this business."

"Tread lightly, Phil. John is very straight, but he has an ego and a temper. He may be squeaky clean, but he's not a damn bit shy and he's no Boy Scout."

"I will. Do your Board Members ever bring assistants, or guests, or family members, girlfriends with them?"

"No. Never. Totally *verboten*."

"Good."

"Why?"

"I need a free hand with Dunkin. We certainly don't want any of Ryerson' boys to contact him or his people. In fact, I'm banking on the odds that whoever the principal insurgent may be, he's not yet aware that Ryerson and Kelly are gone. I hope we can milk that advantage for a few more days."

"I see. I'll try to give you some room with Dunkin if I can. We can set up lunch to help."

Phil and Craig devoted an hour or so reviewing the BOD Agenda and Presentations. Essentially, they would adopt last meeting's minutes, Craig would introduce Phil, Richards would give the Financials, Phil and Judy McLean would present the Language ANUMEN, then there would be a general discussion and Q&A, followed by drinks and lunch.

The Board would be arriving on various flights Tuesday night or Wednesday morning. Each Member had an office and a suite for his or her use. Jackie was in charge of all arrangements, so things were pretty carefree for Phil.

"Craig, do you know that Mr. Wilcoxen maintained an office down in Treasury?"

"You bet. He keeps private banks for the Board Members. One hellofa lot of money if I recall."

"That's an understatement. There's billions down there."

"Well, Phil, that's one of the perks that keeps these boys coming back and signing checks. I assume you will take over for Wilcoxen. You could delegate to Richards. If you do, you'll need to get Board clearance and promote Richards to something higher, some kind of VP, I suppose. The Board might like that arrangement a lot since they don't know you yet. Their kind of money demands a lot of trust."

"I'll give it some thought. What are the others?"

"Others?"

"The other perks?"

"Oh. Yes. Essentially there are three. One, they do some very intensive business with each other during these BOD's—away from prying eyes and ears—including ours as well.

Keep that in mind, please. When I started recruiting a BOD I specifically sought out kindred interests, and it generated more synergy than I ever envisioned.

Two, we provide a constantly renewable organ bank for them, using our technology and their cellular material. We keep them healthy and alive. Every one of them hits the Medical Department while they're here. To them, it is worth any amount of money and support. That's one reason I couldn't believe Dunkin was purposely trying to scuttle us. Ever hear of the old Luxembourgish saying, 'You don't spit in your own soup.'?"

Phil grinned.

"Three, they are well aware, should the need or desire arise, and we could convert many of the Island developments into billions and billions, they would be the primary benefactors."

"I see. So we have these guys by the balls—literally."

"Yeah. And they us. An ideal symbiosis, don't you think?"

"I couldn't agree more. Things are getting clearer and, frankly, things are looking a great deal less foreboding. Thanks for your candor, Craig."

"Well, I probably should have filled you in faster and better. But I liked your progression. I liked the way you were ferreting things out for yourself. I like the way you're taking control. I believe you'll be a formidable President. By the way, here are the dossiers on the rest of the BOD. You might want to get acquainted with them."

Craig handed over a stack of folders.

"Well, Phil, I think we're ready. Meeting convenes at 1100 sharp in the Board Room. Have you been there yet?"

"No."

"Jackie will give you directions, or just grab a PM. I think you'll be impressed. See you tomorrow."

Phil enjoyed a quiet lunch with a cold, baked-ham salad, some cold beer, and his dossiers.

After lunch, Anne called. "Phil, are you really busy?"

"What's up?"

"We've added two more paintings to our collection."

"I'll be right down."

Before going down to the Art Department he called his uncle.

"Hi, Herb. It's Phil. How are you getting along? ...That's great! I'm coming out on Thursday. See you then."

Next he called Richards in Treasury. "Ted, does our auditor keep track of operations in Mr. Wilcoxen's safe?"

"Yes he does. He audits the safe once a month."

"Good. Please order an immediate audit and send me both the current and last audit reports. How are the security additions coming along?"

"All done."

"Good. If you have no objection, I'm going to suggest to the BOD that you assume responsibility for the safe?"

"No problem. We'll have to make some further modifications, though."

"Agreed. Proceed as though this were approved. If approved, you will be Sr. V.P. Finance & Treasurer. Okay?"

"Absolutely okay, Mr. Carr."

"Great. I'll keep you posted."

Next, Phil found a PM and set off for the Art Department. Anne was ready for him. All preparations made as well as some changes to the Viewing Chamber. There were now three paintings, each with its own curtain and corresponding exterior controls. All three paintings reflected a brass title plate above its curtain. *Hell's Adoration* by Jacques Tomas , *Pliant Life* by Michael Auslander, and *Submersion* by Michael Auslander. When he had changed into his robe he accompanied Anne to the Chamber.

"These are both by Mike Auslander?"

"Yes. He's getting pretty excited with this new art form and is starting to roll them out."

"Is he aware of the danger to non-students?"

"Yes, and if it doesn't sound too insensitive, he thinks it's funny as hell."

"The humor eludes me."

"Yes. Well, he's tried to mitigate that as well, so his heart's in the right place anyway."

"Meaning?"

"Hmm." Anne said and smiled. "Meaning I think you should start with *Pliant Life*."

"Okay. I'm ready."

Phil entered the Chamber, and fear, nervousness, and anticipation fought for dominance. Anne closed the door and the curtain for *Pliant Life* opened. The painting was slightly reminiscent of *Hell's Adoration*. It had roughly the same shape as the eye. However, it was in fact a superbly executed sunflower, with a light blue background. Phil could feel the warm golden sunshine on the flower. He could smell the cool fresh air, even a slight breeze. As he regarded the yellow petals, the same intricate design began to reveal itself.

As before, it was hypnotic, yet this time it was beautiful. He felt no fear, no distress, and no cares. He seemed to float down to the mat and found himself hugging his knees. He was very softly chuckling. Then laughing. Then rolling around the mat and humming. Then singing. Before he knew it, he was on his feet and dancing around the Chamber, spinning and jumping and sliding and hollering, "Yea!" at the top of his lungs.

Finally, he fell to the mat onto his stomach, making "angels" with his arms and softly kicking the mat. Then he just lay still, positioned so he could comfortably regard the painting. He was...not happy...not amused...he was...he felt...sublime! After about five minutes he just lay on the mat drained and smiling. Anne opened the door with a broad smile on her face.

She took him directly to the Jacuzzi, gave him no shower, no tranquilizer, no brandy. Phil grinned at Anne. Anne said softly "Pretty cool eh?"

"Very damned cool! My goodness, the nuances to this could be endless. Do you know what the language says in this one?"

"Yes. Mike explained that this one takes you back into a childlike regression and then explains the beauty of the world from a child's perspective."

"Impressive. There could be hundreds of creative benefits from this art form. What's the other one...ah...*Submersion* like?"

"You'll have to try it for yourself, Phil. It's a very personal experience, and I'm not sure if your reaction would be the same as mine."

"How about tonight after dinner?"

"I'll arrange it."

Phil dined with staff that evening and found he was agreeably welcomed. All was relaxed and entertaining. The food was as good as ever—a creamy fish soup much like a Borride, followed by some sort of spicy beef stew with vegetables, and an unidentifiable tuber, the best chocolate cake he had ever tasted, and a superb, light, red wine—unidentifiable.

Phil told Anne he would be down in forty-five minutes. He then returned to his apartments and lay down. Half an hour later, he was totally rested. He took a quick shower and was soon on his way.

Anne showed Phil into the Chamber. Although all the preparations were exactly the same, Anne's demeanor was somehow different. She was as pleasant and agreeable as ever, just a little subdued, perhaps, with a slight squint around her eyes and a lightly penetrating appraisal. "Ready?"

"Ready."

Anne closed the door and the third curtain opened.

Phil faced the painting squarely. It portrayed...what? A mouth, perhaps. Female? Maybe. Stylized lips slightly parted with an ever so small peek into a mouth (?). Could he see a bit of a pearl white tooth? A soft tongue? Whatever the hell it was, it was warm and moist and it was...respiring? Yes it was breathing. He could hear the deep inhale of air and the slow exhale. He could feel the warmth of (her?) breath. Her breath was sweet, as though she had been eating cherries, or oranges, or something nice. Something sweet, clean, and fresh. There were tiny bits of fruit and juice on the lips and tip of her tongue. He could nearly taste it! Damn, he *could* taste it! He stepped closer to the painting and, the closer he got, the more he saw. The slight smile line framing the mouth. The delightful microscopic female down of her cheek. The closer he got, the more the painting aroused him. But the amazing part was he aroused the painting! This was extraordinary. He was actually interacting with a painting!

This was beyond experience. He breathed out as she breathed in. He breathed in as she breathed out. And he drew in orange blossoms and spices and wine and finally her mouth. He was sure his eyes were not closed. But not so. He was taking in more and more details and sensual feelings every minute. He was so erect, so hard, it was deliciously, tremblingly painful. Such a mingling of pleasure and pain as he had never imagined. The Chamber vanished, all other lights, sounds, sights, feelings, and thoughts vanished. Only the painting remained. He was indeed "Submerged." He stood there for fifteen minutes that seemed like fifteen seconds. Suddenly, uncontrollably, an orgasm erupted from his thighs the likes of which he had never experienced. He was drenched in sweat and tears. He was trembling and his knees were about to give way. He released a shuddering sigh and dropped slowly to the mat.

When Anne opened the door, Phil was sitting cross legged on the mat holding his head and trying to breathe normally. He said only one word. "Brandy."

Anne brought his drink and settled quietly beside him and placed a gentle hand on his shoulder. "Such pleasure."

"Such power."

"That too."

"If I may ask," Phil said, "was the painting male or female for you?"

"I went through two viewings. The first was male, the second female. I didn't consciously control this factor either time. Perhaps one day we should go through it together? But I do believe you should undergo Fear first."

"Well," Phil said with a chuckle, "that's the very first motivation I've found to undergo the course!"

They stood and said good night. Phil returned to his apartment, took a cool Gin & Tonic onto his terrace to think and calm himself, and turned in for a dreamless, profound, uninterrupted sleep.

Treading the Boards for the Board

Wednesday morning Phil awoke to the most unusual day yet. The sky was a deep cloudless blue, framing a blinding white sun in the east and a gossamer, phantom-like three-quarter moon toward the west. The sea and the horizons, however, were shrouded in a dense, stationary mist that rose at least a hundred meters above the sea. The mist was a dazzling white, glowing with the sun's penetration. Phil could barely discern the surf far below, belying a sea that lay calm under its vast willowy blanket. Phil felt himself progressively delighting in this Delphic isle.

Sausage, toast, some incredible jam, and a huge Cappuccino on the terrace made the perfect breakfast, as he took in the exceptional view and re-reviewed the BOD dossiers. Phil suddenly had a thought and grabbed the phone. "Good morning, Edward. Got a question. What's the dress code at BOD meetings?"

"The only time Dr. Webber and Mr. Wilcoxen ever wore suits and ties were for the BOD's. I have your clothes laid out now."

"Thanks very much. I'll be there in just a bit."

Edward had laid out a dark blue, double vented pin strip suit with matching vest, perfectly tailored. These items were paired with exceptionally supple, black wing tips and belt. He had laid out a white handkerchief, three-quarter length executive hose, and a white shirt with a perfect collar and tie, just like his father used to wear. He found a very expensive black leather briefcase.

The briefcase contained the day's Agenda, the Financial and ANUMINA presentations, minutes of the last meeting, extracts of BOD members, and some very smart business cards, of dense linen board, subtle off white, raised dark blue lettering, discrete logo, his name, blind address and blind phone number, his real email address (He had never looked at his email!), and his title as "CEO & COO Halios Geron International." *Damn! Edward was the best!*

Phil's PM took him to the depths of the complex, as it had to the harbor area. However, at the end of the long descent, the PM turned left instead of right and he found himself in a broad, seemingly endless tunnel. No periscopes, but kilometer after kilometer of engrossing murals covering an endless variety of topics and styles and motifs. It must have taken years to complete. Phil estimated he was traveling at a rate of at least thirty kilometers per hour. Amazingly, the art work was designed for viewing at this speed and Phil suspected it was bi-directional at the same speed. He looked forward to exploring his theory on the back-haul. The skill level was truly impressive. The wind blowing through his hair was real. The experience was most pleasant, and Phil was impressed that they had somehow avoided the "airporty" feeling such a passageway could so easily have conveyed. Instead, it was like falling effortlessly through an enormous straight-line art gallery.

After some twenty minutes, the PM slowed slightly and passed two gigantic steel doors. They were at least ten meters high and each was at least five meters wide. No opening mechanism was evident. From their look, Phil was certain the doors were heavily re-enforced. This was obviously the main entrance to the bunker and armory complex. *Must be huge. I've got to take a look at that.*

The PM quickly resumed normal speed and arrived at its destination about fifteen minutes later. His was the only PM, although there was parking for at least thirty PM's in front of the glass and brushed, stainless-steel entrance. As he passed through the automatic double doors, he found himself in a large, modern reception area. There was the same glass and steel motif, wooden inlay floors, and a generous collection of paintings and sculptures. The furniture consisted of a reception desk and a series of blue leather chairs and couches and glass tables. Water silently cascaded over a glass ceiling and behind glass walls, which was the source of the lighting. The entire effect was "undersea-ish" and somewhat surreal. A very attractive young lady sat behind the reception desk who greeted Phil immediately.

"Good morning, Mr. Carr. Welcome to the BOD complex. You're the first to arrive. I'll activate the Board Room immediately. Would you care for anything?"

"No thank you, not right now. You referred to this as a complex. What else is housed here?"

"Well, we have guest suites for all Board Members, a communications room, a pool, dining room, bar, the Board Room of course, attached multi-media control room, a kitchen, a doctor's consultation area, and a gym."

"Impressive. Which way to the Board Room?"

"Straight ahead, sir. I'll have it fully activated when you arrive," she said with a coy smile.

"Thanks."

Phil passed a circular lobby area equipped with opposing elevators reflecting four levels: First Level—Suites 1-10; Second Level—Suites 11-20; Third Level—Bar & Dining Room; Fourth Level—Health Club. The hallway, richly carpeted, wall to wall, in a deep-piled, lush maroon weave, stretched beyond for some ten meters ending in steel and glass double doors, matching the entrance.

As he approached the doors, they automatically swung apart and Phil entered without pause. On both his left and right, he noted with interest doors clearly of equal strength as those protecting the bunker, retracted into each wall. With his next step, he fell flat on his face.

Phil was suspended in thin air, two hundred meters above the Island. Floating with him was a small island of dark wood about three meters in front of him. Despite what his mind had already concluded, Phil literally crawled the short distance to the wooden island and gasped with relief as he gingerly climbed aboard. The acrophobia that had plagued him since his youth took fierce command of his mind and body. He sat for a few moments on the base of the island, perched under its huge conference table, gathering his breath and looking around.

Christ on a crutch! A goddamned spherical periscope. It must be mounted atop the Proteus Point Cluster. Phil knew the communications tower on Proteus was a couple of hundred meters high, and it would be no great feat to mount a three-hundred, sixty-degree periscope up there along with the antennae array already atop. Then they had to engineer a perfectly undistorted periscopic sphere, despite the flat floor of the Board Room. No mean feat at all. Beyond that they had managed to maintain an undistorted view, while effectively blocking out the Proteus Tower itself. *My god, what if they did this with an aircraft!? Or a submarine? Or a boat? What potential!*

Ever so carefully, Phil stepped off into nothingness, looking straight down on the Island. He told himself over and over it wasn't real. After several heart-pumping, dizzying moments, he conquered his vertigo and started really enjoying this incredible sensation. From where he stood he could see the entire Island, down to the sea and on to the far distant horizon. The view was stunning. The Island was bathed in clear light, surrounded by a quiet margin of beach, encased in a cottony paradise of impenetrable mist that stretched as far as he could see. Above were the blinding sun and diaphanous moon. He could even feel warmth from the direction of the sun. The heat source must follow the sun across the sky. And there was a soft, cooling breeze to offset the "sun," and the air was fresh and seemed somewhat thin, as it should be at over two hundred meters...No...more than fourteen hundred meters! He forgot to include the height of the Island with the height of Proteus Point and the height of the tower itself.

Phil turned to the floating dark wood "island." It consisted of a very large oval floor, supporting a conference table half again as large. Surrounding the table were twenty-one positions. Each was equipped with a luxurious, built-in, swivel chair, a leather writing pad with attached pen, a reading light, a computer access point, a very diminutive telephone and, attached to the back of each chair, was a dark, wooden rod, roughly one meter high with a large "bulb" at its end. After a few moments of contemplation, Phil realized these were some sort of high-tech wooden shades that could be extended, and raised and lowered and tilted at the discretion of the user. This was clearly a necessity considering the blinding sun relentlessly rising from the east. Phil knew they could adjust the light level of a periscope—but that would ruin the effect. He imagined what this must be like during one of the Island's raging thunderstorms.

Suddenly, Phil realized something had bothered him upon entering the room. The hallway was wall-to-wall carpeted. He had seen no such carpeting anywhere on the Island. The carpet was there to clean your shoes! Then he looked at his shoes. Clean yes. But the soles were a sort of stiff chamois that would further protect the clear floor. *These guys really think of everything.*

Phil found the chair marked with his name, gave it a try, and found that it was comfortable. Controls for the light, shade, computer, and phone were built in to the arm of the chair. He deposited his brief case under the table and went to explore some more. Exiting the Board Room, he found a kitchen and multi-media room just to the right. In the kitchen, coffee and tea were already prepared, snacks and pastries laid out, and, in the refrigerator, Champagne was cooling. Across from the sink and refrigerator was a fully equipped bar. Phil helped himself to a short brandy, knocked it back, poured himself a cup of coffee and went back to the Board Room.

Glad I arrived before anyone else. I would have made a fool out of myself! Hmmm. Was I set up?

At that moment, Dr. Webber entered the room alone, well coiffed and superbly clad.

"Good morning, Phil. How are you? And I mean it. I intended to arrive before you and buffer the shock of entering this room. How'd you fair?"

"Flat on my ass." Phil smiled. "But after I recovered, I really enjoyed it. This room is extraordinary. Doesn't it prove to be a distraction during Board Meetings?"

"Well, as I told you, the BOD don't take these meetings overly seriously, and the room actually keeps them mildly entertained, which helps them sit through the agenda. I suspect it actually juices them up with a feeling of power too. Please don't quote me, by the way," the Doctor chuckled.

"Understood Craig."

"Everything ready?"

"Assuming someone will man the multi-media room, we're all set."

"Good. We've got about ten minutes, so I'm going to grab a cup of coffee."

A young woman entered the room, placing agenda and notes at each position, along with a glass and a chilled bottle of water. She rolled the coffee side table buffet into the hallway in front of the Board Room. When she had finished, she went directly into the multi-media room. Almost immediately a large black rectangle appeared at one end of the Board Room, floating in the clear sky, and the Agenda then appeared, and then the rectangle vanished. All was in readiness.

At exactly 1100 a large group of well dressed men appeared in the hallway (all wearing the same shoes in assorted shades, Phil noted with an inward smile). Dr. Webber moved to the area in front of the coffee service, and with a subtle gesture from Webber, Phil quickly joined him, and they formed a reception line of two.

The board members were a distinguished looking crew, most well into their sixties and seventies—at least according to their dossiers—they actually looked to be in their early fifties and very fit at that. They engaged in lots of laughter, glad handing, back slapping, and catching up. Webber graciously provided introductions, and Phil shook hands and was immediately lost as to who was whom. He was pleased that there were large, two-sided seating cards at every position.

A fair amount of coffee, tea and pastries were gathered, along with the occasional cognac and all were seated.

Webber provided an Agenda review...Minutes review... Minutes acceptance...Financials... When Richards had left the room, Phil brought up the matter of his promotion and assumption of the Members' private bank. This was roundly approved. Clearly, they were pleased to delegate this duty to someone of a lower rank and a higher familiarity. Phil certainly agreed, and Craig emphasized the arrangement was on Phil's initiative. Phil distributed Richards' coordinates for those who needed it and assured them that Richards would be standing by for appointments, along with Dr. Gear and his staff.

Finally, the time came for Judy McLean. As planned, Phil gave a brief introduction. "As you know better than I gentlemen, one of our prime mandates here is to foster, identify, and report to this Board any confirmed manifestations of ANUMINA. An Anomalous Numen, by way of review, occurs when a student or students of this facility exhibit a skill or capability unknown in humans, and unexpected, perhaps unexplainable, even here.

Such a facility has manifested itself here within the last few days, in overwhelming, undeniable numbers...and from a rather unexpected source. We are very excited and I believe you will be as well. In my opinion, being new aboard, this development easily validates the years devoted to the exceptional work in this complex.

Dr. Judy McLean is head of our language department and she will introduce you to our first, I emphasize *first*, confirmed ANUMEN. Judy?"

"Thank you, Chancellor Carr. Good morning gentlemen. Roughly two weeks ago an apparently hitherto unknown language spontaneously erupted in our language lab. When I say 'spontaneously' erupted, I mean the language itself suddenly appeared without traceable development or discernable etymology. We could not locate the source of the language, meaning no student or students had developed or introduced the language. *All* students of lineages subsequent to PSG 8333, including remarkably young ones, less than a year old, seemed to apprehend the language at roughly the same time, immediately, without instruction. No non-student, or staff, or administration, or earlier generational iteration can remotely comprehend the new language.

Interestingly, this language does not rely on a hard palate. Nor does it depend on teeth, a malleable tongue, use of the diphthong, the "da" sound (tip of the tongue pressed against the upper teeth), dental and retroflex consonants, the "th" sound used in Spanish, no alveolar ridge, and on and on. The language path relies predominantly on back vowels (ɯ u ɣ o ʌ ɔ ɑ ɒ) and bilabial consonants (m p b ɸ β β̞ ʙ ⊙).

The offshoots of this 'facile' language have yet to be fully understood. However, one certain benefit is that young children, nearly babies, can fully master the language. You may have heard of Idioglossa or Twin Language. Although it's not been proven one way or the other, twins often start speaking their own language, unintelligible to any others. In some way, this may, I emphasize *may, be* related. Another unconfirmed power of this new language is at least in theory it could be acquired by non-humans."

As Phil could have predicted, there was profound silence at Dr. McLean's words.

Then a Board member interjected, "as I understand it, the term "non-human" could apply to either extraterrestrial life or terrestrial animal species. Which do you mean?"

Light laughter went around the table.

Dr. McLean, unsmiling, said, "I mean both."

More silence followed.

"Mr. Carr hit upon two ideas that may help us a great deal in understanding this phenomenon. The first is the language may have been extant for millennia within humans, conceivably even all life on Earth. That is, resident in human DNA. Perhaps something akin to what we arrogantly refer to as 'instinct' in fellow animals. The Human Genome Project notwithstanding there is certainly enough diversity and capacity in human genetic material to easily store this amount of information—especially if the information is stored in a very unconventional manner, and the language itself operates within some unorthodox structure. Now, more and more, scientists began to support the concept of the universality of DNA. All terran life is based on it, and there is reason to believe carbon based life in other parts of the universe may have a similar structure. Maybe something even deeper.

I know how this must sound to you, and we are conjecturing a massive leap in logic here, but it is not too far beyond the limits of imagination that we may have discovered something as cosmologically applicable as the laws of astrophysics and quantum mechanics. That's at one very remote end of the spectrum. At the other end, perhaps this language will never be heard or understood beyond the limits of this Island. Neither end of the spectrum seems particularly plausible, but we must probe all possibilities with an open mind.

The second observation by Mr. Carr may help us analyze the spontaneity of this language amongst our students. The catalyst. It is conceivable that our students were acutely stressed into propagating the language. We believe frustration was that catalyst—frustration that the limits of the languages we have thus far provided them were simply not sufficiently robust. They could not store and forward the concepts and thoughts they were formulating.

If humans do not have a word, an icon, a mnemonic, from which to append a thought or a concept, then that human cannot use, communicate, or retain such cognition. Please remember we are dealing with an exceptionally gifted population of humans here. Perhaps they are more gifted than we ever suspected. Suppose our intelligence tests are insufficient to detect the true depth and nature of their sapience. I would emphasize that all of this, intriguing as it is, is unsubstantiated, and a great deal of additional work is needed.

I'm sure you would like to hear this language and that's perhaps the most disturbing part. It sounds like nothing I ever heard out of a human mouth, and I've heard every known language on earth from Kalahari Bushmen to Navajo to Inuit. I have a recording to play for you and discs for distribution."

Judy signaled the operator in the multi-media room, and the sound of the new language filled the Board Room for some ten minutes.

Phil appreciated the effects of the Board Room during the recording. There could be no better site. Members looked far out to sea and concentrated on the sounds surrounding them.

When the recording had ended, the same profound silence settled on the room again. However, after a few moments, comments started to emerge. "I'll be damned...Good God!... I don't believe it...We did it!...I need a drink...I need a nap!... Are we going to start transmitting signals of this stuff?...We should try it on whales and porpoises...And chimps...What can we really do with this?"

Then a series of questions directed primarily at Judy Mclean, some redundant, some inane, some insightful came at here rapidly. "Can we translate it?...Can we write it down?... Can we feed it into a computer?...Can you detect if the language is growing and further evolving?...What do the students say?...Can you initiate formal education earlier with infants now?...Have you gotten any reaction from animals?"

After a reasonable interval, Dr. Webber signaled for champagne which was immediately brought in and served. Webber rose from his chair and raised his glass.

"Most of us were here twenty years ago when we first envisioned a facility capable of producing things unique on Earth. We did it. Congratulations, gentlemen. Congratulations, Dr. McLean. Congratulations to us all! Thank you, Dr. McLean for an amazing presentation."

The room came to its feet and general applause reined with glasses raised.

Webber came to his feet again. "I believe we've probably had enough for today. We have lots of questions and issues to address and I believe we need time to ponder them. Accordingly, I suggest four actions," he said, then proceeded to list them.

"We treat this development as "Top Secret" until we have had time to analyze and understand this a bit more.

We convene a special daylong BOD sixty days from now to specifically address only this issue.

All BOD Members should submit questions, suggestions, and issues to Phil Carr for assembly and organization with Dr. McLean in preparation for the special BOD Meeting, using only secured communications, please.

There are other potential, unconfirmed ANUMINA surfacing around the campus. Some of us suspect Phil Carr is some kind of catalyst himself. We are not reporting these to you until we have some further degree of confirmation and insight. Please understand, we are not withholding, we are simply trying to act responsibly. So if you hear anything about other ANUMINA, feel free to ask us about it. Perhaps we'll have more to report at the next BOD."

"Adopted?"

Hands were raised in affirmation all round.

"Drinks and lunch?"

Hands were raised in affirmation all round.

"We have opened the Bar and arranged a Buffet in the Dining Room, if we can find our way down. Dr. McLean, can you join us?"

"Certainly, thank you, Dr. Webber."

Phil was pleased to find the dining room was set up more in the fashion of a cocktail party than a sit down lunch. Ostensibly this was arranged to accommodate Board Members who had more interest in the Bar and meeting with each other, or they already had appointments with Treasury and Medical, or both. Therefore, lunch was of a lesser priority and was basically a fast, stand-up, balance-your-plate kind of an affair. Dr. Webber had set up exactly what Phil needed, providing him a free range in which to corner John Dunkin.

"Mr. Dunkin, it's a pleasure to finally meet you today. I understand we have you to thank for our impressive level of defensive readiness?"

"Thanks, Phil. But I wasn't really involved much. One of our people handled that."

"Oh I see. Too bad, I was interested in acquiring some new robotic underwater reconnaissance and assault equipment I've heard about."

"Not familiar with that myself. Have your man contact my man. I imagine we can help."

"My man? Your man?"

"Yes," Dunkin said and frowned. "Our counterpart to your security chief...Roberts or Ryerson or whatever. Our man is Bob Griffith, EVP Logistics & Deployment. Griffith designed your installation, practically single-handed."

"Oh I see. Yes. I believe our man Ryerson is on temporary assignment. I never really had the chance to debrief him before he left."

There was no reaction from Dunkin whatsoever. Not the slightest eye blink, flinch, tick, nothing.

"In that case, I'll have my secretary send you the coordinates on Griffith."

"Thanks very much...have you tried the Mini Lobster Baguettes by the way?"

Phil phoned Rachael as quickly as possible and put her on the trail of Mr. Bob Griffith, EVP DEW Industries. Phil then phoned Richards and told him to have new cards printed up as EVP, and hire himself a personal assistant whom, among other duties, would observe BOD Treasury private banking transactions. He would have new contracts by next week.

Within less than an hour, the BOD had broken up in all directions, and Phil was left to return to the complex. Sure enough on the back-haul, the paintings *were* bi-directional and the colors bled into other designs as well.

Later, in his office, Phil called his secretary. "Cindy, can you get me on a flight to Lefkada tonight? Great. Can you book me a car...no make that a jeep at the port? Thanks. I'll be gone for a couple of three days. Please field my calls and inform Jackie. I'll have my mobile with me at all times. Oh, and can you please check out my email? I don't know if I have any, but if I do...please field that as well. Thanks. See you on Monday, Tuesday latest."

I'll take the One with the Red Plimsoll Line

If you want to build a ship, don't drum up people to collect wood and don't assign them tasks and work, but rather teach them to long for the endless immensity of the sea.

Antoine De Saint-Exupery

Phil arrived at Lefkada airport, collected his bag and his jeep, and made the hour or so drive via the new tunnel to the Armonia Hotel. After checking in and dropping his bag in his room, Phil headed for the bar. Not only did he feel like a drink after a very good day, he figured it would be the best place to find his uncle if he were at the hotel.

Sure enough, there was Uncle Herb, slimmed, tanned, sportily well dressed, well groomed and shaved, eyes clear as a bell, and very clearly sober as a judge.

Son of a bitch!

Herb was holding court at a table overlooking the water with six obviously sea faring men in attendance. Old salts all they had deeply tanned, deeply lined faces, ruddy complexions from years of sea and wind. Hearty Metaxas warming in their hands. Herb looked up and saw Phil.

"Philly! Great to see you. I was wondering when you would show."

"Hi, Uncle Herb. It's damn good to see you too. Sorry I was held up so long."

Herb moved to another table with Phil and when a couple of drinks were on the way, he looked his nephew up and down. "Phil? Are you alright?"

"I'm fine why?"

"You look ah…different. You look well, but more mature… not older, just more mature if you know what I mean."

"It's been an interesting few weeks I guess. I'm looking forward to a few days here and *you* look great! Younger. Healthier. Slimmer. What the hell have you been doing?"

"Well, I love this island. I've been very busy; in fact, I'm something of a local celebrity. So I've been eating well, not drinking too much, and getting lots of exercise, most of it on the sea. The fishing is fabulous here. I love the towns and the ports, the coast, and the countryside. Wish I had come here years ago. I think I'm ready to take you up on your offer."

"That's good to hear, Herb. Let's get some dinner and make some plans."

"Okay, the food's great here."

"Let's eat."

Starting with octopus in olive oil and spices, they moved on to an excellent white fish grilled over wood. The skin was as crispy as well-cooked bacon. Spices, lemon, and oil were generously drizzled over the fish. They had fried potatoes and icy Retsina. And everything was topped off with fresh fruit sprinkled with a sweetish spice, marinated in some sort of local liquor. Phil was already at home.

"You received the specs on the boat?"

"Yep. It looks perfect. A blend of a superb live aboard with a practical working boat. Crew quarters removed aft, so lots of privacy. Looks like she'll take any weather and the electronics are amazing. Must cost a fortune?"

"As I said, I've got some loose money at odd ends just now. We should find our way to Piraeus and look her over. If it looks good, perhaps we should have her surveyed?"

"Good idea. Get her hauled and poked and prodded. And if everything's a go, we can scrape her bottom and get her painted and any refitting needed."

"Right, I wonder if the hotel can help with a flight."

"I'm sure they can, Phil. They're very helpful. We've become good friends."

"So if we do the boat tomorrow and the next day, we should still have a day or two to find a town and a slip...unless you have one in mind already?"

"Actually I do. A beautiful little town called Vassiliki. Reasonably good harbor, we'd probably be the largest boat, all kinds of shops and restaurants—pretty much everything we'd need, as well as adequate weather protection and a formidable sea wall."

"Have you developed any good contacts there?"

"Yes, I've made a couple of friends there. Retired fishermen. Happy to come on as crew. Speak good English. Know their business. Hard workers. Nice fellows."

"I'll tell you why I ask. We're going to need a local we can trust to become a principal of the fishing business we'll open here. This will help us get all the needed licenses, residency permits, and the like."

"Good. I've got just the guy, name's Demetrius Diamantes."

"Would you like to invite him to join us on Piraeus to check out the boat? Think he would like it? Our treat."

"I imagine he would. I'll give him a call."

"If he can meet us here tomorrow, I'll make the flight and hotel arrangements."

The next day at around 1100, the three were in a taxi threading and honking their way through traffic toward the harbor at Piraeus. It was a warm, sunny, noisy morning, no wind, perfect for looking over a boat. Fortunately, the driver knew exactly where to find the boat, so they arrived a little earlier than Phil expected. This was fine with him, as it gave him time to look over the boat before the broker arrived.

Despite her beauty and elegant lines, she was definitely a real working boat. A thirty-two-meter, semi-trawler design, steel with brass and teak bright-work. The wheel house had six, flat-sided, steel-framed windows providing over one-hundred, eighty-degree forward visibility. There was a double-glass, aft-facing door, beautifully painted in white divided by a red water line, with dark blue below the water line. She sported twin 250hp diesels, bow and stern thrusters, amid-ship stabilizing sail.

The ship was delineated into four areas: Aft winches and crane, holds, fuel tanks, water tanks and freezers. Amid-ship were crew quarters and launch sling, with a wheel house with flying bridge mounted above. The owner's staterooms, lounge, galley, and dining room headed by generous freeboard were graced with a four-meter bow sprit gracefully finished with a large, sturdy bow pulpit. Phil was in love, as was Herb, as was Demetrius. Demetrius was going to be Herb's First Mate, and he was a very seasoned fisherman/seaman. He was a Greek of roughly sixty-five very fit and wiry years. His English was excellent, and he was friendly in all respects. Phil already liked him.

The broker arrived with very little selling to do. They went through every centimeter of the boat three times. They started the engine and took her out for a sea trial. They tested all the electronics from the oven to the sonar to all her running lights. They crawled the bilge. Demetrius donned his swimming trunks and snorkel and looked over the hull, the rudder, and props. They were pleased to learn the boat had already been surveyed and were provided a copy of the report. They were even more pleased to learn from both Demetrius and the broker that the boat had already been hauled, scraped, and repainted. She was six years old and looked flawlessly brand new.

After a very brief quibble about price (the broker's price easily prevailed), Phil wrote a check and the deal was done. Afterwards they went off to a local pub with the broker for a celebratory drink.

"Is it really bad luck to rename a boat?" Phil asked.

"Why? What's wrong with its name? Don't you like thalassa thilyki tigris?" asked the broker.

"What does it mean?"

"Sea Tigress," Demetrius translated.

"I love it. How about you guys? Herb? Demetrius?"

They both approved. They all four raised their glasses "To Sea Tigress!"

Keys were turned over even though registrations, transfers, and insurance would not be ready until Friday.

Phil, Herb, and Demetrius had a quick seaport lunch, a few cold beers, and were back to the boat for another sea trial. They were three very happy sailors.

The boat was connected to shore water and power. There were four staterooms, each with en-suite baths, so they slept aboard that night. They bar-be-queued on the fantail, watched TV and drank Scotch the rest of the evening.

After Herb and Demetrius had turned in, Phil sat on the bow taking in the moon and stars, the lights of Piraeus, and other boats gently bobbing and clanking and tinkling in rambling unison around the harbor. He was glad he had convinced Uncle Herb to come over and glad he had bought the boat. Not only would this probably add years to Herb's life, it gave Phil a feeling of home and normalcy he seemed to need now—after only a few weeks at the Island. He began to appreciate just how *alien* the Island really was. It was beautiful. It housed wonders and learning and people that he regarded highly. It was not nearly as foreboding or sinister as it had first appeared, and it provided an exceptional standard of living and lifestyle.

And yet, somehow, it seemed to evolve and motivate itself under its own power. Things moved as if of their own volition. There was a direction and a will to the Island, and he felt as if he was moved by and in it. He had changed and grown already. He had blood on his hands and he had art and science and custody as well. He hoped they counter-balanced, one offsetting the other. Twice he had been referred to as a catalyst to the Island, a sort of missing piece finally fitted into place facilitating the ongoing march of the giant mechanism. True? Possibly. Serendipity? Perhaps. Method? Whose? No way to rush things. Wait it out. Do the job. Learn. Learn and lead. And be damned careful.

The next day was devoted to paperwork, registration, lawyers, licenses, insurance, and intensive briefings on the workings of the boat from aft winch to bow sprit. As all three men were experienced sailors, the training went quickly. But there was no speeding up the paperwork. But the broker proved invaluable in filing the various papers needed to form a company and acquiring a license for commercial and pleasure fishing. The boat was superbly rigged and equipped, so by the end of the second day, the boat would lack only completion of registrations and provisioning to be ready for cast off.

From the Aegean to the Ionian was a trip of some 750 kilometers, or roughly a week's leisurely running. So they decided to return to Lefkada the next day. Herb and Demetrius would ferry *Sea Tigress* to her new home port the following week.

There was just time for one more sea trial before that afternoon's flight. *Tigress* responded perfectly. An old sailing term "yar" sprang to mind. She was a lovely boat. She was not a new toy. She was a new home.

Back on Lefkada, Herb and Phil roamed the island, exploring towns and countryside. They quickly agreed on Vassiliki as home port and nearly as fast had hired a slip and bought a Land Rover.

After some surprisingly busy days, it was time for Phil to return to the Island. This time, equipped with radio links to Herb, as well as mobile phone, land line, email, and Fax, Phil gave him a peculiar little white and blue flag, a zig-zag design triangular burgee, which Phil said Herb might find of use sometime.

They shared a last drink at the hotel bar, took notes and tickets in hand. "I'll be back in a couple of weeks, Herb. Do you need anything…money…papers…I've got you a lawyer and accountant in Vassiliki (they speak English)…I've checked us out of the hotel…Boat Operator's License, Radio Licenses, Business License, Fishing License, Residency Permit applied for, Mariner's Ticket on file…one year prepaid lease on your slip…accounts at the grocery, marine supply, Apphia's Restaurant, and the fuel company…I've opened a bank account in your name, my name, and the name of Tigress Sea Hunters, Ltd. (their new fishing company), and we both have signature cards for all…your doctor is now Dr. Doros Andropolis in Vassiliki (he speaks English)…we'll be receiving corporate Amex and Visa cards…I've even ordered us business cards (you Captain, me GM) which will be delivered in a few days… change of addresses have been sent to St. Michaels, along with newspaper and phone cancellations…you'll get your mail at the marina office…all papers (including your passport) are in a lock box at the bank, with duplicates in the onboard safe (where you'll find some cash and a .38 S&W with reloads and cleaning kit)...is there anything else?"

"Philly, the only way I could be in better shape would be if you stayed."

"Wish I could, Herb, but I must get back. In fact, I've got to run right now, Uncle Herb. I'll be back in a few weeks and I'll keep in touch. You can always get to me or leave a message on my mobile number. Seeya, Uncle Herb, have a ball!." They hugged, shook hands, and then Phil was gone.

That night Phil was back in his own bed in his second home...the Island.

Do the Thing

Mother Fear Begets Daughter Anger Begets Mother Fear…

Author

The first thing Wednesday morning over breakfast, Dr. Eve Dunedin was on the phone with Phil, asking about him.

"Excellent," he said. "How about you?"

"Good. I spent some time in the Art Department. The new paintings are intriguing, and I commissioned three more from Michael Auslander. He's custom making them for the Fear Ordeal: Intermediate and Advanced Fear, and the third is for *Weltschmerz*."

"I'll be interested in seeing them."

"Well that's actually why I called. Are you ready to start the course this week? I'm putting together some schedules and you've got pole position if you like."

Phil was unpleasantly reminded of his commitment. *Aw shit.* "When would you like to begin, Eve?"

"The best would be at 1600 in one of our training rooms. The first session should last no more than one hour, including our counseling session. We intend to boil the course down to its basics for you and give you a concentrated dose that will only take a few hours each week, for a few weeks."

"Sounds fine, I guess. I'll be at your office at 1600 today if that's alright? I assume a concentrated course will be tougher."

"I won't kid you, Phil. It'll be a screaming bitch. See you then."

Promptly at 1600, executive duties executed, Philip was ushered into a small classroom manned by a tall male dressed in fatigues and a black silk mask. "Take a seat at one of the student desks, front row. I would welcome you to the Fear Ordeal, but you are neither welcome nor pleased to be here, I'm sure. When and if you address me you will refer to me as Number One."

"Well, I really am…."

"Speak only when instructed to, 2304."

Phil frowned. "2...3...0 …?"

Slap! Hard fast and painful.

"You will be referred to as 2304 throughout this course. Why? Make of it what you will. I really don't give a shit. Suppose you drop and give me twenty push-ups."

Phil, or rather 2304, did as told.

"This first session will cover two things. First, unfortunately, you were pre-briefed about the Fear Ordeal by Dr. Dunedin when you arrived at the University. That was *her* mistake. However, *you're* going to pay for it. We were forced to devise a modified course for which you are unprepared in any way. We designed it to be faster and more concentrated. We designed it to be meaner because it pissed us off to have to do all that extra work."

Slap!

"I will be slapping you a lot throughout the next few sessions. It will hurt. It will leave marks. We have a medicinal cosmetic to get you through. I recommend you use it. Let me explain why I'll be slapping you so much." He displayed a slide on the classroom wall.

- To Hurt You and Frighten You
- To Anger You and Hurt You

- Anger Breed, Fear
- Fear Breeds Anger
- They Feed on One Another
- Learn Control
- You Cannot Learn Control
- Find Another Way

"We're going to explore the relationships between fear and anger and pain, you and me, 2304. There are all kinds of fear. There are all kinds of anger. There are all kinds of pain and you're going to experience them all. We're going to do this for my diversion and to teach you how to use all three of these elements to your advantage. Ready 2304?"

"Yes."

"2304, I want you to think." He leaned very close to Phil. "I want you to imagine. Imagine I administer a poison to you. Absolutely fatal. When it reaches your lower tract it will kill you from within. Before dying, the pain will instruct you on the limits of agony. Are you following me 2304? You may speak."

"Yes."

"The poison is in the form of a large pill which is a synthesis of three compounds in separate layers. The first compound we will call Poison 1. It will eat out your intestines if it reaches your lower tract and kill you in exquisite agony. The second compound, Poison 2. will kill you if it remains in your stomach. The third compound is an antidote to Poison 2. If you vomit forth the capsule you will die because you will eliminate the antidote to Poison 2. If the pill travels to your lower tract you will die. If the compound containing the antidote totally dissolves and is absorbed you will die. Understood 2304?"

"Yes."

Two pairs of strong arms grabbed Phil from behind and held him helplessly at his desk. Number One stepped forward, pried Phil's mouth open with a plastic lever (very painful) and inserted a large pill into Phil's mouth. They struck him in the stomach, massaged his throat, and held his nose and head back until he swallowed the pill, gagging and feeling it painfully inch its way down his esophagus.

"Now look at this, 2304."

He held forward an open hand containing what looked to be cigarette papers.

"These little beauties do three things. One, they adhere to the pill. Two, they float. Three, they are semi-permeable membranes. By floating, they will keep the pill out of your lower tract. Their permeability properties keep Poison 1 and Poison 2 inside, and allow the controlled release of the antidote compound. Problem is, that these papers dissolve in five minutes. Are you tracking with this?"

Phil paused to reflect on this game. *Not poison probably, but something that could inflict one hellofa lot of pain. Probably best to play al...*

Slap!

"Answer! Now! Jerk-off!"

"Yes."

"Now vomit up the pill. *Now!*" There was an urgency in his voice that lent a certain truth to his previous descriptions. A cold fear was slowly emerging in Phil's consciousness.

Phil leaned forward and tickled his throat and gagged until the pill appeared on the floor in front of the desk, amongst the remains of his lunch.

"Now. Wrap the pill in this paper and swallow it."

Painfully, nauseated and demeaned, Phil complied.

"2304, do you see that clock on the wall to the right?"

"Yes."

"Do you see the red marks on the face of the clock?"

"Yes."

"We are bringing you an antidote which will solve your little problem. It will negate all the chemicals we have introduced into your body. You will be fine. All you have to do is vomit up the pill when the minute hand reaches the red mark. You will then wrap it again in a paper and swallow it. Continue this until help arrives. This is no game. Do you understand?"

"Yes."

Slap!

"Do you understand?!"

"Yes!"

"Fine. If you get through this, and if you have the balls, I'll see you tomorrow at 1600. Don't be late."

The next thirty minutes seemed like two days. When a nurse finally walked in with a glass of water and a tiny blue pill, Phil was exhausted and in considerable pain. "Time for counseling, 2304." the nurse said and smiled.

Phil walked into Dr. Dunedin's consulting room rather shakily. He trembled, he stank, his eyes watered, he was covered in sweat, his stomach churned, and his face burned. Eve regarded Phil, not unsympathetically, and said, "Welcome to the Ordeal. I hope you found orientation useful. See you tomorrow?"

"Yes," Phil said, stone-faced.

Eve wordlessly handed Phil a tube of salve for his face. Phil turned to leave the room.

"By the way, Phil?"

"Yes?"

"We can save you time and pain if you honestly give me a little information now."

"Yes?"

"Phobias?"

"Acrophobia."

"Anything else?" She reached into a drawer and suddenly threw a handful of very realistic artificial spiders, assorted bugs, and a snake at him.

They rebounded from his face and chest with no reaction. "No." He left the room.

Phil found the locker rooms and thought, *why the hell didn't they give me some sort of training garb? Well, let me guess. I bet it's because they wanted to humiliate the shit out of me!* He took a shower and cleaned up as best he could. He gingerly applied the cosmetic ointment to his now rosy cheeks and remounted a PM for the ride home.

This was "rush hour" at the University complex. Students and PM's were everywhere. Perhaps it was his imagination, but Phil thought he saw recognition on the face of those he passed. They seemed to understand his cheeks were the product of the Ordeal, and their eyes were discretely averted. On arrival home, Edward was waiting. "How was it, sir?"

"It was a real shit sandwich, Edward. I need a quadruple Gin & Tonic, an aspirin, and an hour in the Jacuzzi."

"Coming right up, Phil. Please let me show you how to apply your ointment, by the way, and I do not recommend an aspirin for at least three hours."

Clad in a robe, Phil strode onto the terrace of his apartment toward the Jacuzzi. Looking at the sea and the night and the stars, he suddenly missed *Sea Tigress*—a great deal.

The next day Phil arrived at 1600, entered the same classroom and sat at the same desk without speaking a word. His tormentor in fatigues and mask was already there, perched on a table in the front of the classroom. Lying prominently on the table next to him was another pill, a stack of wrappers and a glass of water. Phil felt he could almost see a smile under the mask. Number One handed Phil the pill and the glass of water. "You will take this pill."

Phil did so.

"What's your square root?"

"What's my…?"

Slap!

"Same rules as yesterday you dumb bastard. Watch the clock. When you yell out your square root we'll give you the antidote. I won't be far."

Slap! And he was alone.

After three cycles of vomit, wrap, and swallow, Phil figured it out. He then had to concentrate to work out the answer. Too slow, he had to vomit again. He was getting very tired and very sick. There were only four wrappers left.

Finally, just before the next red mark on the clock Phil cried out, "forty-eight. Forty-eight. My square root is *forty-eight*!"

Number One entered the room with a small blue pill and another glass of water "Pretty damn slow. I didn't realize you were so dumb. What's my square root?"

"One."

Phil was given the pill and the water.

"Suppose you drop and give me twenty push-ups for each red mark. That would be…eighty. Do it!"

Slap!

Phil dropped and executed eighty push-ups. Then, exhausted, he resumed sitting at his desk.

"Let's talk about the slaps and the pills, 2304. One of the things we were taught from our formative years was not to suppress our feelings. Our mommies told us not to sublimate our emotions. Let them out. It's okay to cry. Be sensitive. Don't allow them to dwell within us and fester. If we don't release them, share them, purge them, we will never be healthy. *BULLSHIT!*

"Do you see a relationship between the slaps and the pills? You may speak."

"I suppose the idea is that, by holding things in we can manage them, survive them, and even use them to our benefit? Physically, this applies to the pills. Mentally, this applies to the slaps."

"Excellent! The only point you missed is you must learn to "wrap" emotions, just like the pills if you are to use them to advantage and survive them. That's what we're teaching you—how to *wrap*. Take the rest of the day off. Sixteen hundred tomorrow, same place. We're going to have you outa here in no time, 2304!"

Number One turned and left the room.

The next weeks were an unrelenting nightmare. They were masters at making the stress nearly unbearable. Phil knew stress was the key, and he could feel it insinuating itself everywhere without exception or mercy. Though slowly, very slowly, he found his pain and resentment evolving into acceptance and even understanding. He wasn't surrendering by any means. Instead, he was...acquiescing.

For the remainder of the first week, they strapped him into his desk, slapped him, spit in his face, inserted objects into his nose, his ears, into his mouth and threw sticky, iced-cold chemicals in his face. At the end of each session, it took longer and longer to regain his strength, clean up, and cover up his bruises and slap marks. He could hardly believe he reported every day at 1600 without extreme duress prodding him exhaustingly onward.

The second week was devoted to pain. For this, they had a marvelous machine. This surprised him. Eve had told him they didn't employ mechanisms. Maybe this was a treat just for him? It was capable of imparting a painful, high-voltage shock to twenty parts of his body in totally random sequences. It could pinch either Achilles tendon, pull his hair, hit the back of his head, slap him, punch him in the stomach, spray him with ice water, and shake him until he feared for his teeth. He would walk into the classroom. They would wordlessly strap him into the machine, turn it on, and leave him alone there for a full hour. At the end of the hour, the machine would stop and automatically release him. All in all, it was totally impersonal, sadistic, frightening (never knowing what was next), agonizing, and exhausting. The first day he had to crawl to the dressing room.

Every day, he choked down a light breakfast. Vomited up his lunch and had neither the energy nor the interest to eat dinner. He was growing increasingly tired but could hardly sleep. He was losing weight and getting progressively weaker. And there was no let up on his daily duties. Once every night, two or three people would break into his bedroom, hold him down and slap the hell out of him. The juxtaposition of normal life and work, alongside brutal torture, fear, and humiliation rendered his life a surreal nightmare. One moment he would be smiling and nodding to someone in a hallway, chairing a meeting, talking on the phone, and the next moment he would be screaming and thrashing. He began to fear for his sanity. And yet Eve was withholding her counseling with no explanation forthcoming.

In week three, they threw him naked off a cliff into the icy waters below—three times. Phil thought this was cheating, as he had been briefed on this by Eve. Then again it began to look as though he had been misled about many things. Between cliffs, they gave him lectures and exercises on wrapping and sublimation management, followed by tress, stress, and more stress.

During week four, five people took turns poking him naked with low-power cattle prods for the first half of each session. Phil was then forced to poke them for the second half. Toward the end of week four, Phil was put into a ring, again naked, and forced to engage in a bare knuckle fight. They were cheating again. Unfortunately for his opponent, Phil was very good at this. To accommodate this, Phil's opponent the next day was nearly twice his size and damn near put him in the hospital. For this, he got a day off.

Wrap training was complete.

Then came Fear.

The next week he spent time in reptile pits, shark cages, in the dark with slaps coming from nowhere, dangling from bungee chords, and swimming in dark unknown waters. Phil underwent two classes on fear.

To accommodate his acrophobia, he would spend hours balanced on a narrow ledge, three hundred meters above the water, naked, in the wind.

The following week, they worked on inhibitions. He was forced to undress in front of several strangers, men and women, who were not the least bit shy about making comments, jokes, touching, and slapping; and then they devoted the rest of the week in every conceivable form and mixture of sex. By Friday his inhibitions were overwhelmed. His sensitivities were overwhelmed. Any shyness and modesty was overwhelmed. He was overwhelmed. He wasn't having one bit of fun, absolutely no enjoyment, but his inhibitions had been ruthlessly purged. Forever.

Then came the week for drugs, and Phil was required to spend the entire week at the Fear site. They administered Ketamine. The Ketamine was the worst. Everything took on a nightmarish quality. He felt shame and horror and degradation. He had truly lost hold on reality. Then they beat him. They had sex with him. They tortured him. They put him into all sorts of bizarre settings. People laughed at him and mocked him, and Phil struggled to keep his identity and poise. Amazingly, he did, and he felt himself making progress, rising above his tormentors.

He remembered something Eve had said in their first briefing. "The more they suffer, the more they gain."

Then came the self-mutilation. They were cheating again! He was forced to mutilate himself and another person. He used a sharp knife to draw a lengthy, bloody line down his forearm. Then he did the same to a pretty young woman, who quietly wept as he mutilated her. They did this to their arms, legs, backs, and torsos for days.

They buried him alive ("Sorry Phil, I know you've been briefed on this too, but this one's just too good to pass up!"). They placed him in a pine box and buried him in soil for nearly thirty minutes. It seemed like a lifetime. He felt he was going to die for the first twenty minutes, broke off three fingernails, then he calmed himself; he took control and did nothing more than breath lightly, lie very still, and think about sailing on the Chesapeake Bay until they dug him up.

They doped him. Then they killed him. They strapped him to a post, aimed a rifle at him, and fired. The rifle fired a small dart. He was out for six hours and awoke screaming. His reaction made him feel as though he had failed, what with all the screaming and thrashing about. Then he looked at it a second time and realized that he had been forced into unconsciousness. He could not have control. It was not his failure.

And they slapped him and they hit him and slapped and hit and slapped and hit until he just didn't give a damn.

Then they sort of crucified him. They strapped him standing naked, to a wooden cross and commenced a regimen of iced water, electric shock, fondling his genitals, and of course, slaps.

Then he snapped. He was consumed with rage. He actually broke the cross and attacked his tormentors. Within minutes they were all down...two seriously injured, before anyone could intercede. Four large guards finally subdued him and injected a dangerously large dose of powerful sedatives. Phil was out four seven hours. When he awoke, under restraints, the tendons in his shoulders had been severely strained and were in agony. Eve was seated in his room, watching him soberly. After a few moments she wordlessly withdrew.

Phil was given a week off to work, eat, sleep, relax...and think about the next step. He worked in his apartment, ate there, slept there, applied copious amounts of salve and ointments, drank there, and sulked there. He never set foot outside, and he avoided the phone if at all possible. The week was over far too fast.

Phil entered the classroom at his customary 1600 and found a machine rather similar in design to the marvelous pain machine of past experience. They strapped him in, propped his eyes open, put sensors on his skin, and gauges on his muscles. They attached monitors to his heart, his lungs, and to his skull. They then commenced with a sort of a slide show. All sorts of images of insects, reptiles, predatory animals, cats, dogs, cadavers, people falling, crowds, huge open spaces, the sea, filth of all description, rot and decay, darkness, heights, plants, flying, toads, and all manner of ugly creatures, women, men, children, firearms, and hundreds of other images designed to provoke the emergence of a specific phobia. The exercise stretched over three sessions and five hours. They then spent the next ten days rubbing his face in the literal essence of any image that he had reacted to, and they repeated the procedure a dozen times until it became boring more than anything else. They re-tested his acrophobia. It was cured.

Then they had a special treat for Phil. Eve had rigged a viewing room along the line designed by Anne, with the lack of Anne's amenities. No brandy, no pills, showers, Jacuzzi, or robe. The room contained the two pictures Eve had commissioned. Phil was shown the first Intermediate painting. The painting had little effect compared to *Hells Adoration*. Phil found the experience interesting and little else.

The advanced painting knocked him out within seconds and he was down for about two hours. He retained no memory whatsoever of the experience. Eve contended that the experience did train Phil and strengthen him at a level other than conscious. She further postulated that the benefits of this type of session would surface at some later time, or as a result of an appropriate "Stress Button."

The next day, Phil met with Eve. "Phil, your progress has been exceptional. You may wonder why I failed to provide counseling during the process. Do you happen to remember a statement I made, 'The more they suffer, the more they gain.'?"

"Yes, I have thought of that a couple of times as a matter of fact."

"Well, by withholding counseling, I was extending your suffering. You took it well. You're ready for the last phase. So I really do have some good news. Normally, we would be preparing you for the Weltschmerz Ordeal. Preparation can be quite lengthy. We ask you hundreds of questions and prepare a very arduous regimen of exposures and pain. You can skip all that."

"That is good news, Eve. Why?"

"The third Painting. Having tested it, we are now convinced that the painting alone can supplant the entire exercise: testing, customizing, exposure, and suffering."

"This starts to sound too good to be true, Dr. Dunedin."

"Well, as they say, if it sounds too good to be true, it probably—"

"What are you saying, doctor?"

"I'm saying we *can* condense the Weltschmerz Ordeal from more than a week's hard and painful work to a matter of hours. That saves you time. It is still just as painful—if not a great deal more. In fact, it is totally devastating. Were it not for your unique capabilities, I would recommend the classical Weltschmerz. Normally, I would stipulate that only late generation students were capable of withstanding the painting and retaining their sanity. I believe you can. Another bit of good news, incidentally. Your instructor speaks very highly of you. He feels that a final exam is not necessary in your case. Therefore, when you finish your camping trip—you're finished with the Ordeal as well."

"That *is* good news. My instructor never spoke well about me, to me. When shall we do the Weltschmerz Painting?"

"I would like you to take tomorrow off from all stressful activities. Avoid work, the phone, meetings, anything, and just relax. Watch a movie, watch TV, read a book, lay by the pool, sleep, get a massage. Eat nothing after 1000. Avoid alcohol. Take no drugs of any description—not even an aspirin. Totally relax, and please report here at 1400. I hope you can take your three-day pilgrimage the morning immediately after your Weltschmerz. Be prepared to spend the night in our care and don't worry, I won't desert you this time."

"You're making me nervous as hell, Eve."

"With damn good reason, Phil."

"See you tomorrow at 1400."

A little after 1400 the next day, Phil entered the viewing chamber. As promised, Eve was in attendance. This time, there was only one painting behind a curtain. It was placed very low on the wall. Phil was clad only in a light weight white cloth robe and was instructed to sit on a large mat (almost a mattress) and make himself comfortable. The door closed. The curtain opened.

The painting was actually quite beautiful. A masterpiece really. It portrayed a young woman seated in a cave, or a cloister, or a bay window with pale light radiating upon her alabaster skin. She wore a cloak of very light pastel blue, and the spectral light subtly cascaded with the gentle folds of her garment. Her face, though indistinct, almost impressionistic, was clearly lovely, with a spiritual charm that nearly glowed, ascending from her graceful neck rising to her soft light brown hair.

Her head was gracefully turned slightly up and to her right, as though she were admiring the source of the light.

Her hands were clasped in her lap, fingers intertwined. She was not smiling but there was a pleasant, happy frame to her lips. Her eyes were such a spectral gray they were literally transparent. Her lips, while beautifully formed, were almost ashen. The entire effect was one of purity, with a pristine vestal quality. After contemplating her for some time, he realized he was growing exceptionally fond of her. He cherished her as a woman, or a mother, a sister. He worshipped her. She was perfection embodied. He admired the smooth lines of her neck and noticed that her cloak had a darker blue boarder with a lovely, intricate, skillfully-embroidered design.

Phil lovingly studied the design. As with the other paintings, the design was actually an adroit infinite regression, comprised of the emergent language. His curious associative cognition suddenly engaged and he realized that he, as well as any non-student, could actually "read" this new language, at least in part. When the paintings lured them into their inescapable eddies, they were actually marginally cognizant of the meaning of the painted "words". He was doing this now. He was reading this painting. And the painting spoke volumes to him.

Cathy (that was her name) suddenly looked at him and smiled. As her lips parted a trickle of blood ran down from the corner of her mouth, and a large stone rocketed into the painting, smashed the side of her head, and killed her instantly. Blood and gore covered her face and cloak, and her head tilted at an absurd angle. Her hands unclasped and her robe fell open. Inside her robe were horrors beyond imagining.

Phil watched his mother die again, only this time, she was drunk and fondling a sweaty, unshaven, corpulent swine at her table, just before the bomb went off. His father was there as well and was laughing as he watched her dissipated infidelity. Then he saw the flash, heard the explosion, watched the flesh blown from their bodies, and their organs rupture, erupting gore. For the briefest fraction of a second, he thought he witnessed the horror on their faces...thought he might even have heard the slightest beginning of their screams.

He watched his brother scream and beg and whine and cry and crawl and demean himself in a hundred hideous ways before he was finally hung.

He watched good people die, while corruption reveled in their suffering. He visited the nauseating, blood-drenched interior of an abattoir. Cows shared the line with human children and small animals and a hundred other innocents.

He watched the beauty of the world wilt and corrupt into decay and filth. He watched mankind fail and die. He watched the whole universe rot in an orgy of entropy, surrendering only black nothingness, going on forever and ever and ever. Matter itself decomposed into its base constituents. With all the rot and inertia and decomposition, the universe stank! Everything was flawed, futile, basically rotten, and depraved.

What is a slut? A slut is something...something female, or male that wantonly serves itself to anyone, anytime...with no quality, no respect for itself or anything else, no thought of consideration, not even basic dignity. Can't be trusted. Never left alone. Will always cheat. Forever base. Trashy. The universe is a slut. It be damned. He be damned. We all be damned. Damn us all forever.

Phil sat staring for five hours.

No vomit this time. He didn't wet himself. No bloody lips or hands. No trembling, or shaky knees. No pounding heart. No flop sweats. Not even tears. Just a profound emptiness. Catatonia without end.

Eve entered the chamber and fed him some clear broth. She gave him some water and a small pill. She then covered him up, gave him a pillow and wordlessly withdrew to let him sleep.

Morning. *It's over. My God, it's over. The pain, the fear, the degradation.* Never in his life had he suffered so at the hands of other people. Phil awoke to a robe, a hot shower, shaving gear and a hearty breakfast. Wonderfully normal; although he found himself tensing whenever any staff member approached. *He'd have to work on that. If Eve got wind of it she wouldn't hesitate to relegate him two or three more days of sheer hell.*

They had prepared a tent, a shaving kit, food, water, assorted drinks, and clothing, climbing ropes, matches, dishes, two-way radio, 1st Aid Kit, sleeping bag, journal and pen, and a flare gun; and dressed him in rugged outdoor gear.

Eve arrived to bid farewell. 'Well Phil, you've done exceptionally. I imagine it will be years before you understand the fully implication of your ordeal. For now, you'll probably experience some nausea from time to time, and you'll find yourself jumpy around anyone who resembles our staff. Both symptoms will pass quickly. Enjoy your camping. I think you will find it interesting.'

'Thanks Eve.'

They took him by PM to the surface, and then by jeep about twenty kilometers south of the complex. After they dropped him off, he looked about and confirmed he was completely alone. They would pick him up in three days. Phil set up the tent, opened the sleeping bag, crawled in, and went to sleep. He awoke twenty-four hours later, with an urgent need to relieve himself and an equally urgent hunger.

The air, the temperature, the golden sun, and the mildest of breezes all combined for an idyllic sunrise, blossoming into a dazzling morning, soon to be a wonderful day. There was dew on the plants, wild flowers in abundance, bees hummed and flitted from flower to flower, and tiny, green lizards scurried through the rocks. The sea boomed in the distance, birds called and smoothly glided through the azure heights. The quiet was overwhelming, beautiful, and peaceful.

There was a tiny, hard, dry, almost fossilized mental nugget imbedded in the back of his brain. It hurt and it was insidious. It was the haunting remnant of the Weltschmerz Ordeal. He would not allow its presence to ruin this magic morning...so he used what he had been taught...he "wrapped" it. It worked. It really worked. The nasty little bastard was still lodged deep in his psyche...it always would be. But now...now he could take it out, contemplate its hideous aspect...and then he could re-wrap it and put it back. Not just back. He could put it away. Behind him. Never forgotten but never allowed to diminish his joy.

By God! He had truly mastered it. He felt stronger, confident, in control, and ready to face the legion of challenges, dangers, and pleasures that comprised his life. Goddamnit he was happy! He laughed. He wept. He slept.

Smoked and salted bacon, powdered eggs, instant coffee, dried orange juice, and jam with dry biscuits made for a satisfying, if not gourmet, breakfast, cum lunch. He had slept until well after noon.

He had been out here for three days, and he had already slept for a day and a half, so he thought he would take a little walk. He followed the sound of the surf to the cliff line. Standing on the edge, looking straight down for nearly four hundred meters was, to say the least, exhilarating. He noted with great pleasure his ubiquitous, icy acrophobia simply no longer existed.

What else could he test?

He climbed halfway down the cliff face and back up. He burned himself with a match. He pushed a sharp stick deep into his thigh. He did two hundred push-ups. Then he started making notes in the journal they had supplied—including his discovery that non-students could read the new language to a limited extent. Then he decided to take a little run. Four hours later, it was dark, and Phil had circumnavigated half the Island in an incredibly short time.

He dined on beef jerky, some thoughtfully provided red wine, and then slept.

Phil awoke the next day at noon, feeling wonderful. He called the base and told them he needed two more days. And yes, he had enough water and food to suffice.

Phil sat by the fire, journal in hand, as coffee and bacon heated (Beans would have been a good idea.).

What was the term he was looking for? Epiphany? Rebirth? Breakthrough? Catharsis? Metamorphosis? Transmutation? Awakening? Attainment? Emergence? The Start, the Source? The Alpha? The Omega?

He'd had a girlfriend while a Harvard named Jill. She was a PhD Candidate in Geophysics at MIT, and a very fine one. But she harbored and abiding passion of numerology. Phil didn't know if she really believed in such frivolous quasi science, but she did study is exhaustively. Everything from Gematria to Isopsephy to Pythagoras to Pythagoreanism to Sollog to Lexigram to Aleister Crowley to the Golden Ratio and Theomatics. *Damn! How did he recall all that?*

Anyway, he wondered what his Ordeal Number 2304 denoted. A random number. A sequential number or something else? He squinted.

Okay. Jill taught me the designated definition of a single digit. So…"2" is…receptive, "3" is…Ahh communication "0" is everything, and "4" is…creation.

Receptive. Communication. Everything. Creation.

Receive communications with everything in creation: 2304.

Phil opened a mini-bottle of red wine and decided it was more productive and definitely less eerie to explore his suddenly improved memory. He regressed himself to six years old, in his old elementary school. It was 1400 and reading class was in session. He looked at his desk, looked at the children's book on the desk, and read the book cover to cover. He did the same with eleventh-grade algebra, pre-med anatomy, and a particularly troublesome law course on torts at Harvard. He recalled every phone number, PIN, and combination he had ever had…even ones he had forgotten he had. He recalled every address, phone number, license plate, and serial number.

Moving on to other things, he calculated the value of Pi to 128 digits to the right of the decimal before he grew too bored. He took a quick glance at a bush and turned his head away immediately. *How many flowers were on that bush? Eighty-six.* He turned back to the bush and carefully counted off eighty-six lovely pink blooms—on both sides of the bush—which was very eerie.

The conclusion seemed obvious: Just as they had "stressed" their students into developing, or exhibiting, new talents, the Fear Ordeal had forced him to generate new talents as well.

What if he applied even more stress?

Minutes later, Phil was hanging from a long rope, nearly four hundred meters above a craggy outcropping of enormous rocks. He was examining a particularly interesting fossil embedded in the cliff face directly in front of him. *The fossil was a...was a...Trilobite...from the Cambrian Period...490 to 520 million years ago...Order Redlichiida, Suborder Olenellina, Superfamily Fallotaspidoidea. He had never studied paleontology. So where in hell did that come from? Wait a minute. Ten years ago, the museum of Natural History in New York. He walked past a small group of people being given a VIP tour; they looked bored and tired. One lady in a super-short skirt, legs to die for. Wow!*

How about poetry? Okay …

The Countess of Winchilsea by Anne Finch

Adam Posed
Could our first father, at his toilsome plow,
Thorns in his path, and labor on his brow,
Clothed only in a rude, unpolished skin,
Could he a vain fantastic nymph have seen,
In all her airs, in all her antic graces,
Her various fashions, and more various faces
How had it posed that skill, which late assigned
Just appellations to each several kind!
A right idea of the sight to frame T'have guessed from what new element she came
T'have hit the wav'ring form, or giv'n this thing a name.

Try another …
John Greenleaf Whittier
Burning Drift-Wood

Before my drift-wood fire I sit,
And see, with every waif I burn,
Old dreams and fancies coloring it,
And folly's unlaid ghosts return.

O ships of mine, whose swift keels cleft
The enchanted sea on which they sailed,
Are these poor fragments only left
Of vain desires and hopes that failed?

Did I not watch from them the light
Of sunset on my towers in Spain,
And see, far off, uploom in sight
The Fortunate Isles I might not gain?
Did sudden lift of fog reveal
Arcadia's vales of song and spring,
And did I pass, with grazing keel,
The rocks whereon the sirens sing?
Have I not drifted hard upon
The unmapped regions lost to man,
The cloud-pitched tents of Prester John,
The palace domes of Kubla Khan? ...

That was enough. He clearly knew it *verbatim*. And he understood it.

Science: If two angles form a linear pair, then they are supplementary:

1) $\angle$ABD and $\angle$DBC are a linear pair.	1) Given
2) $\overrightarrow{BA}$ and $\overrightarrow{BC}$ are opposite rays.	2) *Definition of linear pair*

3) m∠ABC = 180 degrees.	3) *Straight Angle Assumption*
4) m∠ABD + m∠DBC = m∠ABC.	4) *Angle Addition Assumption*
5) m∠ABD + m∠DBC = 180 degrees.	5) *Substitution Property*
6) ∠ABD and ∠DBC are supplementary angles.	6) *Definition of supplementary*

Okay. Enough. He had been hanging here for nearly three hours. No fear. No fatigue. Back up to camp. For the next two days, Phil lay on his back looking up at sun and moon and planets and stars and birds and bugs and clouds and rain and fog. He neither moved, nor ate, nor drank, nor slept, nor wept.

At 1500 hours, on day five, he radioed in: "Philip Carr here. Ready for pick-up. Half an hour? Thanks." As he packed his gear, he contemplated the Fear Ordeal and was reminded of the Preface of *A Tale of Two Cities:*

These were the best of times...these were the worst of times...

Truer words were never... The Jeep arrived.

Sing for the Boys in the Band

The first duty of a revolutionary is to get away with it.

Abbie Hoffman

That evening, Phil sat on the terrace. He seldom acquiesced to Edward's proffered tableside services, but tonight was an exception. He requested the largest, driest, coldest martini possible, straight up, loaded with olives and a twist. He requested that Edward join him.

Edward seated himself opposite Phil, adjusted his chair and his vest, raised his glass and tipped it with Phil's. "And to what are we drinking, Philip?"

"We are drinking, sir, to my full fledged citizenship of the Island. Until today, I felt very much the outsider."

"The Fear Ordeal."

"Yes, Edward, the Fear Ordeal. I completed it today."

"Congratulations, sir."

"Thank you. Have you undergone the Ordeal?"

"No. To be honest, I may not be all that welcome. The Ordeal is really only for students and senior faculty. And it does sound very...unpleasant."

"That it is, Edward. That it is. Have you known people who've undergone the Ordeal?"

"Yes I have."

"Did you know them before and after?"

"In fact I have. We had a young lady working as an intern. She started the course a few weeks after she joined us and completed the course in about nine months. Prior to the course, she was very bright, happy, and outgoing. During and after the course she became increasingly distant, inward looking, harder to read, although her work, which was always well above satisfactory, was actually much improved. All in all though, aside from a certain look around her eyes, I think she was happier. I see that look in your eyes now, Phil. I think you should take some time off."

"Good idea, Edward. Can you get me a ride to Lefkada and let the powers that be know I'll be gone for a week?"

"I believe we can arrange for a flight around 1000?"

"Sounds good."

"Are you ready for dinner, sir?"

"Yes, thank you, Edward. It's a curious thing. My appetite seems to increase with the degree of trauma inflicted by the Fear Ordeal. The only exception was during the last two days of my little pilgrimage. I didn't eat, sleep, or even drink for nearly forty-eight hours. Needless to say, I'm starving now."

So, it was not surprising when Phil sat down to a thick hamburger steak bar-be-queued nearly black and crispy on the outside, medium rare and juicy on the inside, a huge baked potato, with butter, sour cream, chives, bacon and sautéed onions, complemented with spinach in lemon and olive oil, a Greek salad, and a paper-thin apple pie with crème fraîche sprinkled with cinnamon and caramel liquor. Damn!

He packed for the next day and fell into a dreamless sleep.

Herb met Phil at the Lefkada Airport the next morning and, together, they meandered down to Vassiliki, stopping for lunch, shopping, and drinking the occasional Ouzo while overlooking the sea. If anything, Herb looked even better. Herb loved Sea Tigress and loved the waters she plied. He proudly presented Phil with a pile of receipts for fish sales that came to an impressive total in such a short time. He was going into squid and octopus hunting as well, and had acquired a six-meter Boston Whaler to aid in this special type of fishing. The locals were providing excellent crews under Demetrious as First Mate. Their runs would normally consist of a day's fishing, fresh catch sold back at the harbor, or they would go out for four to eight days at sea, using their freezer. They often stopped on the other side of the island and sold fresh, depending on their catch at the local market prices.

The offshoot of this was that Herb now had two girlfriends, one on either side of the island, one in Vassiliki and one in Poros. No wonder he looked so svelte! Phil could picture Herb in harbor offloading at dock, high atop the flying bridge, operating the winches, while he was wearing swimming trunks, sea cap, and was tan as a nut and killing the ladies. Neither he nor Herb had ever worked a boat that attracted women. It was a nice change.

They reached the boat at mid afternoon, and Demetrious had her ready to cast off, so within a few minutes Lefkada harbor was receding from view. The sun was still high and it was warm. Wearing swimming trunks and an open shirt and Phil was on vacation.

They went about thirty kilometers out, set a long anchor line and anchor light, left the radar on, checked their radar reflector, activated running lights, and went for a swim. The water was cool and the sunset was warm.

Later, they had a little mousaka, charbroiled lamb chops, tomatoes, and feta cheese in olive oil, followed by homemade Amigdalota, all washed down by iced Retsina Rose. Demetrius was not only an excellent first mate, he was a great cook.

After dinner, Phil warmed a Metaxa in his hands on the bow. He intended to simply relax and enjoy the moon and stars, but his mind seemed restive and edgy. He wondered if this was a result of his recent experiences and decided to try an experiment.

He remembered something about a linear, differential equation developed to render something called the "Laplacian." He hadn't the slightest idea what it all meant...simply something overheard in a university cafeteria.

Good. He set his mind to recalling, and then calculating Laplacian. He then "wrapped" the whole thing up, put it away in his mind and went below to watch television—an adventure/action movie—with Herb and Demetrius. Twenty minutes later he frowned and "unwrapped" the problem.

The solution was absolute gobblygook, but he had no doubt it was valid. It might as well have been Chinese. It was totally beyond his knowledge and understanding. Yet he was sure that, if he applied himself, he could sort it out—Chinese too for that matter.

How in hell could his brain be smarter than he? How could it know things—not just remember—but know things he did not consciously know?

His associative talent surfaced: *Parts of his mind, his brain that he did not control, that he had had no previous access to, were asserting themselves. Knowledge, concepts, even facts were stored in his mind, as with any human, he supposed. Somehow in man's past, the connection to this information cache was lost, the circuitry broken. And apparently, given sufficient trauma, we could reestablish it. Hells bells!*

Phil thought he had been fully immunized against fear. He was wrong. He felt real fear now. He felt something else in his head, another presence. Somehow, he was no longer alone, and he preferred *alone*. He really, *really* preferred alone!

He was looking down a long, long dark hallway. What to do? How to escape? How to live with it? How to keep his sanity?

Ah! Eureka! Phil grabbed a bottle of twenty-five year old scotch from the bar, went to his stateroom, and drank it.

The morning dawned brightly into Phil's cabin. He could tell they were already underway, so he just lay there for a few minutes staring at the bulkhead and acclimating himself to the light. True to form, sometime during his drunken night, his drunken mind had solved his problem. It was simplicity itself. So easy it was laughable: Exploit his emergent powers.

It consisted of only two small chores:

He carefully wrapped his fear of his newly expanded mind and stored it away. 2. He wrapped and filed the problem of his newly expanded mind with instructions to: a) solve the problem for him, explain things to him, and tell him how to live with this, and b) let him know when it was finished. Now that felt better!

Phil shaved, showered, threw on shorts and shirt. He breakfasted on eggs, Bloody Mary, toast, kippers and some good strong coffee. That felt better too.

Phil went on deck to enjoy the morning only to find he was being remiss in his duties as a crewman. So for the next few hours, he worked and sweated and strained and really enjoyed it. Both Demetrious and Herb observed him when they thought he was not looking. At first, Phil thought they were interested in the progress of his hangover. Then, after a time, he realized he was exhibiting exceptional physical prowess. He was pulling huge loads and was tireless in his efforts. Slowly, Phil wound down for their benefit and ease of mind.

Demetrious went below to prepare lunch, while Phil and Herb drank a cold beer on the after deck "You're in better shape than I realized, Phil. This new job must be good for you."

Before Phil could respond, Demetrious appeared on deck. "Mr. Philip, there is a Ms. Rachael Stone on the radio. She says it is most urgent that she speak to you."

"Thanks, Demetrious."

"Rachael?"

"Phil. Thank God. How fast can you get back here?"

"What's going on?"

"Ryerson Rangers are in full revolt. They have taken the armory and the harbor, and they are now sacking the Treasury. They've killed about fifteen staffers and about three students. We have a few weapons and we control the emplacements above the harbor, so they can't escape by sea. I ordered all aircraft off the Island. I sent one to Lefkada in hopes of retrieving you. We have them cut off in the armory and in the Treasury. They have some hostages. They're certainly prepared to kill them, but they're in no hurry because they somehow believe there is a great deal of money to be had somewhere in Treasury."

"Shit! Where is Richards?"

"He was one of the first they shot. Before they shot him, he told them you were the only one who knew where any money might be located, or could get to it if it did exist. We know this because they released one of the hostages in Treasury. We told them we would send for you immediately. Richards is still alive, but he is unconscious and needs medical attention badly."

"What happened to our defenses in the armory...gases and whatnot?"

"Sheer numbers. These guys are crazy. All two hundred stormed the armory and, sooner or later, the gas dissipated, our guards were killed, and doors breached. It was then an easy matter for them to take the harbor and move on to Treasury."

"How about Webber and senior staff?"

"Locked up tight in the mansion. They're safe and well guarded. We're not playing any games with cutting off power, or food, or water right now. We're trying to keep them calm and happy."

"Good. How about the students?"

"Safe in their quarters. Everything is shut down. The Rangers have no interest in them. They are safe for now."

"I see. How are you?"

"Having a great "ol time, Phil. When can you get here?"

"You say there's a plane on the ground in Lefkada?"

"Yes."

"Leave it there. I'll be in contact through your mobile phone as soon as I have an ETA. Use my phone for all contacts as well. Take care of yourself, Rachael."

"Can do."

Phil rushed back on deck. "Herb!?"

"Yeah, Phil?"

"What's the fastest way from here to the Lefkada Airport?"

Herb and Demetrious poured over their charts.

"Well the closest town is Porto Katsiki...about 45 kilometers from here. Our max running speed is about 48 KPH so it should take us a little more than an hour and a half to get there.

We can call ahead for a car and that drive will take about an hour. So you should be at the airport by about 1530 or so."

"Let's go."

Sea Tigress came smartly about and nosed up a bit under full throttle.

"What's up, Phil?"

"Oh, a little trouble with the Board of Directors. They're all upset by some idiotic newspaper article in Los Angeles, and want me back for damage control ASAP. I shouldn't be long. I'll try to get back in a couple of days. Don't let me interrupt your regular schedule. I'll meet up with you when I can."

Phil went below, showered, and changed, packed his ditty bag, removed the Smith & Wesson from the safe, made himself a sandwich and a stiff G&T. He then called Rachael, gave her his ETA, and went back on deck. Phil could see Lefkada large on the horizon, and Herb assured him a car would be standing by. *God I hate this shit!*

After a quick entry to Porto Katsiki's marina, Tigress smoothly slipped up to the dock. A driver was standing by to take his bag. They exchanged quick handshakes and were off to the airport.

Phil's car was able to drive right up to the aircraft. The crew was onboard, all preflight fueling, maintenance, and checks done. They were airborn within minutes. Phil spent the first half of the flight time working on tactics, assuming the situation hadn't changed radically since his last update.

On the quick leg back to the Island, Phil went forward, thanked the crew for their help and discussed their landing. "I don't know what we're going to find on the ground down there."

"Neither do we, sir. Operations does not respond."

"I see. I'd like you to bring the aircraft to a stop as quickly as possible on the runway. Cut your port engine, drop me off and get the hell out of there. Stop for no one and nothing. Return to Lefkada and await further instructions. Any problems with flight plans, fuel...whatever?"

"None at all."

"Okay. Good luck, gentlemen."

The small jet dropped gracefully out of the sky and came to a stop about halfway up the North-South runway. Phil opened the hatch and hit the ground. The crew drew up the stairs, dogged the hatch, and were gone. The runway was eerily quiet. No one was in sight. Phil jogged toward the field office and its entrance to the complex. When he reached the office, he found two bodies. One was John Alemanno, the Flight Operations agent who had helped him with his weather forecast. The other looked to be one of the insurrectionists judging by his clothes. Blood and flies were everywhere. Beyond that, all was quiet.

The door to the complex suddenly opened behind Phil, and he wheeled about with his .38 in hand. "Whoa, Phil! It's me." Rachael stood in the doorway, hand raised in mock surrender.

"Rachael. What's our status?"

"Nothing has changed, Phil. They're all waiting for you now. They want the money, a boat, and safe passage away from the Island. As far as I know they haven't killed anyone since we spoke. But they know you're here now and they want action."

"Is this office secure?"

"I'd say it's as secure as any place on the Island, short of the Mansion."

"I'd prefer not to attract these boys up to the Mansion. Can we defend this site?"

"Sure. We can see anyone coming from a distance and, aside from that, there's only one underground access. I've got four armed boys at the ready I know I can trust. Shall I call them up?"

"One question first. This whole complex has intercom capabilities?"

"All tactical sites such as the airfield are circuited to select any or all other sites for intercom announcements."

"We need someone up here who knows how to operate all this stuff, and we need Mike Auslander, and we need your armed boys."

Rachael got on the phones and, shortly, four armed guards appeared, followed by an audio/visual expert and, a few minutes later, Mike Auslander. Phil instructed the AV technician to connect them to the whole complex except the mansion. He then took Mike aside.

"Mike we have very little time. We're all in a great deal of danger, and we've got to take the initiative. I'm going to make this fast. Stay with me and let me know when I'm wrong. Got it?"

"Okay."

"I've been thinking about the new language and the new art you're producing. Non-students cannot understand the language, but they can at least partly understand the language within the context of a painting—if only in a visceral sense. Agreed?"

"Yes."

"Okay. I believe this is true because the language, when expressed through the medium of art, impresses itself into the brain through the more vulnerable access paths. Say our emotions. Non-verbal transmission of information and ideas. What do you say?"

"Could be. Yes. I'm sure you're right."

"Now, the head of the Music Department, Dr. Gould, said that the music you guys compose is Gorilla Ugly."

Auslander smiled.

"I think that's because the musical instruments available are simply not capable of making the sounds needed to express your language."

"Could be. What's your point? What's this have to do with two hundred killers?"

"I want you to write me a song. I'll give you the lyrics. You translate, or transcribe, or whatever. Then I want you, or whomever you designate, to sing it over the intercom throughout the complex. Then I want you to speak to the students and lead them with me in a counter attack to eliminate these bastards from our Island."

Mike regarded Phil for some time "The students aren't fighters, sir."

"We both know that's bullshit. They could be the most dangerous creatures on Earth since the Albertosaurus, and it's time they cleaned their house."

"Could be messy, Mr. Carr."

"I hope not. But either way it's got to be done, now. So Mike, lets write a song."

Phil took a tablet from the office desk and started writing

I'm tired. I'm very tired. I must rest. I must rest.
I'm bad. I'm very bad. I must stop. I must stop.
If I do something bad. Kill me. Kill me. Kill me.
And now I sleep. And now I sleep. And now
    I sleep.

"The song should repeat this over and over again. Add anything you think will reinforce it. What do you think?"

"Clever." Mike smiled grimly.

It was clear that both Mike and Rachael were impressed with the quality and intelligence of Phil's planning. They didn't realize that Phil was learning the plans at the same time as they.

Mike began to work on the song.

Suddenly, Mike's eyes began to dart rapidly from side to side. Faster and faster and faster. Phil watched Mike's eyes in stunned fascination.

I've heard of shifty eyes, but this is the mother of all shiftiness. It looks like epilepsy from hell. It's frightening, inhuman. My God, he's thinking! Every movement's a thought. Every thought an element in the song. No human could think at that speed...could they? Could he? Was he?

After a few moments, Mike closed his eyes, relaxed, sighed, and smiled again. "It will work. What about faculty and staff within range of the speakers?"

"Please have your people warn them and remove them to safety."

"No problem."

"Mike, that ah, thing you do with your eyes."

"Yes?"

"Do you do that very often?"

"No. Only when I'm really under a great deal of pressure. Actually, I didn't know I was doing it until someone pointed it out to me."

"How about other students?"

"Same."

"Don't you find it a little...strange?"

"Hell, you guys were the ones that immersed us in stress and trauma trying to dig for your damned ANUMEN."

"Good point, Mike. Now. I want you to write one more line to the song. Don't use it unless you think necessary, or I tell you to. Write "And now I die. And now I die," over and over again."

"You think I can write killing words?"

"What do you think?" Phil asked darkly.

"Okay. Give me a few minutes. I can sing the song by the way—no need to bring anyone else into this."

"One last thing. We'll get you a radio. You need to designate a student at the other end of that radio down in the trenches to report status. Let you know if it's working, how the attack goes, and if you need to use the final line."

"Barbara Morgan. Coordinates 331B-25F2."

"We'll deliver her radio straightaway. Yours is coming. We'll be on the line as well." Shortly thereafter the radios were delivered.

Mike sat down for a few minutes, head in one hand and pencil in the other, scratching out incomprehensible runes.

"I thought you couldn't write Oneirion Mike."

"Can't. These are just some notes for me on the music itself."

He was humming, speaking, and singing sub-vocally. After five minutes, he smiled stonily, stood and turned to Phil. "Let's make some music."

They left Mike alone in the office with the microphone. Phil and Rachael observed him through a glass wall—speakers inactive on their side of the wall. Phil had never watched anyone speak the new language. It was actually rather graceful. Mike's head bobbed gently up and down, right to left, and his throat moved in counterpoint to the movements of his head. Then it clearly turned into singing, which was even more elegant in motion. Mike's head was thrown back and the same exercises were directed laterally. It wasn't inhuman, but it wasn't exactly human either.

The insurrectionists heard the odd sounds emanating from the speakers. At first it sounded like incomprehensible random noise. It was mildly irritating and just a little upsetting, but they failed to recognize any imminent danger. After a few moments, they began to experience fatigue. Then it hit them like a wave. As they slowly sank down, they felt an emotion that most hadn't felt in years: Guilt

The combination of the two was absolutely debilitating. They grew numb, sad, disoriented, and exhausted. Suddenly, they just gave up. In a way, they just wanted to die. Without exception, they were quite literally floored. On their backs staring at the ceiling, the song went on and on relentlessly, mercilessly.

After about ten minutes, Mike stopped and signaled Phil and Rachael back into the office. "They're down, but I don't know for how long."

Phil, Rachael, and their gunmen sprinted down the stairs and found PM's. Two guards were assigned to the harbor while two guards were assigned to accompany Phil and Rachael to Treasury."

Rachael showed them how to override speed controls on the PM's, and Phil went over their instructions "Take every weapon they have. Guns, knives, garrotes, canisters, clubs, anything. Mike is sending students to these areas, so give the weapons to the students. In the harbor area, they should throw all weapons they can't carry in the water. In Treasury, we'll just ask them to disable the weapons they can't use. If any of the 200 starts to resist, kill him immediately. No wounding, no prisoners, no mercy of any kind. These guys are deadly, and they have us totally outnumbered...so no exceptions. Are we clear?"

Phil got a unanimous "Yes."

"Now, if you notice they are reviving as a group, contact me immediately and then cover your ears until you see them back down. BUT...under no circumstances let them see you do this. If they understand the danger in the song then we're really in trouble. Now go!"

Two groups sped off to their respective battle fields.

It took an agonizing fifteen minutes to arrive at Treasury, even at top speed.

"Mike, this is Phil, over."

"This is Mike, over."

"Can you teach your people to sing your song without singing it, over?"

"Say again, please, over."

"What I mean, Mike, is can you talk them through the death song without singing it and killing us all, over?"

"But they've already got the first song. I sang it. Over."

"Mike, you know damn well there's no time for that song before these bastards kill them. Can you teach them? Over."

Mike was silent.

"Do it, Mike. Do it *now* goddamnit, over."

"Acknowledged." It could have been spoken by a computer. A quiet, empty, hollow, forlorn word.

Phil heard the language eerily echoing throughout the complex. The students now had three weapons in their arsenal. The death song, their own physical prowess, and any captured arms they chose to bear. And they had instructions to use them. Phil thought back to the Weltschmerz Ordeal and just how bloody true it really was. *Damn us all.*

"Mike?"

"Yes, sir?"

"We're going in now. I will be giving you instructions for everyone. You will put those instructions in to your new battle language, and you will relay them immediately and as accurately as you can. Are we clear?"

"Clear."

"Stand by."

About thirty students had arrived at the entrance to the Treasury Division and were awaiting instructions. These added to Phil, Rachael, and two gunmen didn't make for much of a force against what was nearly one hundred professional killers. But for the time being at least, they were down.

Phil inspected his little band. He detected no fear, no excitement, or even tension. They had more the look of a moving team waiting on a furniture truck. Their only equipment was roll after roll of silver duct tape. Phil stuffed tape in his ears, as well as Rachael and the other two.

"Did you get the instructions from Mike?" asked Phil a little overly loud.

"Yes," all the students said.

"Any questions or problems?"

"No."

"Proceed. Be careful. Be frosty."

They quickly filed into the Treasury. Fortunately, the insurrectionists were in uniform so they could easily distinguish hostage from enemy. Hostages' ears were taped and enemy hands were taped. Weapons were collected, and the operation moved along with reasonable speed with no problems. They were in the large general offices of Treasury where most people worked, and it took roughly half an hour to cover ears and tape thirty-five pairs of hands. When they were finished, Phil suspected they still faced well over one hundred bad guys in the next area. They needed to move faster.

Suddenly, automatic gunfire erupted from the executive office area, very close to Wilcoxen's hidden safe deposit. Two students went down and everyone else took cover behind desks. From the little Phil could see, the insurrectionists in the executive area had seen them covering ears and had figured out the effects of the song. They were now in trouble for real. Their only real luck was that all the hostages had been kept in the general office area, so all they really had to do was take out the bad guys...come to think of it, did they really have to take them out? After all, they had no hostages, they couldn't breach the safe and they were pinned in. Phil had never done anything like this before and didn't look forward to rushing these guys, so why not just wait the bastards out, and...

Thirty students jumped up in unison. They didn't encumber themselves with weapons or tape. They jumped side to side and forward with extraordinary speed. The insurrectionists fired, and had no chance of hitting them. Within seconds, the students were on them. There was nothing Phil would describe as fighting. As a student reached an enemy, they simply raised a hand in a fist above their head and brought it down so swiftly and powerfully their opponent's neck was instantly broken. There was no resistance, no struggle, no screams, or blood, or evident injuries...just instant death. Within five minutes, over a hundred rebels lay dead..

The students reentered the general offices, looked about, and starting singing the death song together. Within seconds the remaining rebels had assumed the fetal position and stopped breathing.

Phil sank to the floor. *Holy shit!*

"Phil? Mike here. Over."

"Yes, Mike. What's up?"

"Just got a report from the harbor. It's all over there. I got the same report from Treasury. We've killed everyone. We've cleaned our house as you ordered. Is there anyone else you'd like killed...or can we break for dinner?"

"... not until you collect the bodies for burning. Tell the engineers to burn them well to the south of the Island, after they have plowed an internment ditch. Then they should build a huge rock formation over the whole mess tomorrow after they've been covered. I want nothing visible from air or ground...and I did *not* issue the final kill order...apparently you did. Are we clear?"

"Look, sir, I'm not in charge of engineers and digging and burning and such."

"You are now. Delegate all you like. Enlist anyone. Use my name. Get it done."

"... acknowledged."

"Come see me tomorrow night for dinner, Mike. We'll sort this out. Okay?"

"Okay, Phil. Out."

"Rachael, come with me."

Without a further word to anyone, or a sideways glance, Phil marched out to his PM and back to the mansion. Rachael followed close behind.

PE on a Sunny Afternoon

Life being what it is, one dreams of revenge.

Paul Gauguin

As they entered the shopping mall, Phil pulled over and Rachael joined him. "Rachael, I want you to call Howard right now. I need a security report on Dr. Sin Oua Siroa immediately—literally as we hold the phone. Cost is no object."

"You mean the Physical Education guy?"

"Yes."

They dismounted their PM's and entered the deserted bar, The Greek Underground. Phil mixed a couple of stiff G&T's, while Rachael dialed the phone and spoke quietly for some time. Phil made himself another drink. Rachael held the phone in the crook of her neck and sipped her drink and watched Phil with unconcealed concern. Rachael was on the bar phone and Phil could see that she had three lines active.

One more G&T later, Rachael hung up.

"How'd you know?"

"No time. Let's go. But Rachael, I want to be completely updated with your security reports on every goddamned non-student on the Island. I'm sick of these stinking ringers."

They discussed Howard's report on the move. Twenty minutes later, they entered the main dining room in the mansion. There were roughly fifty people in the room and outside on the terrace. Food was set out and extra seating had been brought in. Everyone seemed safe and well looked after, despite being very subdued. As Phil and Rachael entered, everything stopped and all eyes and ears were concentrated on them. Phil stopped in the middle of the room. "It's all over. Everything is alright. You can return to your quarters. There'll be no further trouble."

Phil started to walk away, and the room broke out in questions. "Look, I'm beat, and there's still lots to do. Suppose we meet here the day after tomorrow for a staff luncheon and we'll talk the whole thing out?"

Phil started to walk away again, and the room broke out in a chaos of questions and even accusations.

Phil stopped again. "This is not a goddamned press conference. Go home. Now! I want to see Dr. Siroa before he leaves. And Dr. Webber, I would be most grateful for some of your time as well. Rachael, please look after Dr. Webber in the dining room. I will meet with Dr. Siroa here on the terrace."

An ashen faced Dr. Webber compliantly followed Rachael indoors without comment. Within moments, the terrace was empty except for Phil and Dr. Siroa.

Phil turned on the doctor. "I want to know everything about your dealings with Bob Griffith...and I want it now and I want it fast."

Sin looked at Phil in astonishment. "I've never heard of anyone named Bob Griffith. What the hell are you talking about?"

"I'll tell you what I'm talking about, you son of a bitch. Your real name is Mohamed al Fayed. You are trained in physical education, but you're trained in insurgency and all forms of terrorism. You're dirty as hell. You have been withholding information about the student's physical prowess. You were the brains in this recent revolt. Your boys followed me in New York and you were preparing to kill me, Dr. Webber, and who the hell knows who else. You've got blood all over you, and if I hear one word of denial, I'll break your fucking face, and then I'll start to get unpleasant. Now tell me about Griffith."

"I told you I don't—"

Sin was on his back on the terrace before he could register what happened. Blood was running from his nose, mouth, and left eye. Phil picked him up by his lapels and placed him on his feet. "Gonna talk?" Phil demanded, eyebrows raised, an almost cheerful half-smile on his face.

"Goddamnit I told—"

Sin was on his back again. He was deaf in his left ear and copious amounts of blood were draining from his ear onto the tiles. Again, Phil lifted him. "Now?"

Sin's hand reached into his inside pocket at lightning speed. Suddenly there was a fairly respectable knife in his right hand striking at Phil's chest and throat and neck. Phil was much faster and stronger than Sin. But neither was Sin exactly a weakling.

Phil was forced to rapidly dance back and around to avoid Sin's blade. Phil looked at him in disgust. "Sin, we can't open a prison here. Do you understand what that means?"

Phil sprang forward and gave Sin a stunning blow with the back of his left hand. Sin tumbled away to his right, slamming into the terrace's railing. Sin jumped to his feet, legs and arms spread and crouched into an attack position. He was hurt and terrified and prepared to fight for his life. Another lightening stroke cut deeply into Phil's right hand, causing blood to run copiously down his wrist and fingers onto his trousers, shoes, and the terrace. Phil was suddenly in a blood rage.

Enough with these bastards! He jumped forward once again and imparted Sin a swift, powerful, near killing backhand. Sin literally flew over the terrace railing and down to the rocks over four hundred meters below. His terrified screams seemed to go on and on.

Phil looked over the railing and was gratified to see the surf was taking Sin out at a good rate. Whatever the fish didn't get, the tides and security would net out on the morrow. Phil turned and walked into the dining room, stopping only to wrap his hand in a napkin and pour himself a sizable scotch. He walked up to Webber and Rachael.

Craig stared at him in abject amazement. Rachael stared at him with concern.

To both he said, "We cannot and we will not establish a prison or a retention compound of any sort on this Island. Our only choice is to sterilize it. Well over two hundred people died here today, too many of them innocents, and that son of a bitch on the rocks is primarily responsible. He had to go. The other son of a bitch, Griffith, has to go too. Either I do it or Howard does. After that, I think we're clean. Do you disagree?"

Webber was silent.

"We must immediately implement a travel and communications embargo again, Rachael. This time we're going to announce a lightening strike at Proteus Point, which, in turn resulted in a massive fire and an extended outage. Sea and aircraft will simply not be available. We'll dispatch all aircraft and shipping, except one of each, to Lefkada. Charlie should try to monitor all inbound communications and try to determine if anyone is attempting to communicate with us. Instruct Charlie to disable all inbound mobile phones. He can do that from Proteus. The three of us, and only the three of us, will retain mobile phones and long-range radios. We should keep the phones and radios with us, wherever we are. I intend that this embargo should last for at least two weeks to flush out any remaining bad guys."

"Phil, I think I'm going to take a few days away from the Island," Webber said.

"Good idea, Doctor. Shall we arrange a flight for this afternoon?"

"If you would, please, say about 2000?"

"Alright sir. What is your destination?"

"I think I'll go to Corsica for a few days. I'll fly into Bastia, hire a car, and just head out. I've got some friends at the University inland and I think I'll just drink and eat and read and lay around their pool."

"Pool could be a little chilly this time of year."

"Pool's heated."

"Mmm. Shall I call for you around 1930?"

"That would be fine, Phil. Can we talk a little?"

"Sure. What would you like to talk about?"

"You said over 200 people died this morning. What about the bodies? What about their friends and relatives? What about the law for Chrissake? What effect is this going to have on the Island? What about our ANUMEN's?"

"Well, our ANUMEN's, as you call them, are unique to say the very least. They killed the lion's share of "the 200" as clinically, as fearlessly, as humanely, efficiently, and dispassionately as a lab assistant sterilizing a Petri dish. They knew what they were doing. They knew why they were doing it, and they were completely untroubled. The bodies are being cremated and interred at the far southern tip of the Island. They will never be found. You know as well as I, non-students are not allowed family...and I am convinced these bastards either had no friends or family, or they wouldn't give a damn about their disappearance. The Law? We are the law. We have to be.

Even if we wished to bring in some official body, the resulting uproar would destroy the Island and the University. You know this better than I, Doctor."

Phil poured himself another drink, fetched a finger sandwich, and then sat down across from Craig.

"About the Island. I hope to God we didn't kill its spirit today. I thought I would have a luncheon for all staff the day after tomorrow and just talk the whole thing out. It will definitely take some time, but I have every hope we can rekindle our creativity, resurrect our innocence, and re-inject some of the basic joy into this place."

"Phil, when does survival just cost too damned much?"

Phil thought he saw a certain mistiness in Webber's eyes.

"Never."

"What, Phil?"

"Never, Craig. Never. Survival is the most basic responsibility of any creature. And please remember it's not just our survival we're protecting. At its core, it's humanity we're fighting for. Correct?"

"Correct."

"Craig, it's not really for me to say, but I think you're putting yourself through needless pain and doubt speculating as to our actions here. Our adversaries were and are self-serving, greedy, murderous criminals, who wanted to rob and kill us, not necessarily in that order. We are decent people, we're scientists, educators, and futurists, and we are simply trying to survive to complete our work. Full stop. If you don't mind me asking, have you been through the Fear Ordeal?"

"No. Nor do I have any such intention. I'm too old. I'm a scientist. I'm afraid I have no prospects of becoming a neo-human."

Phil took a long draw from his drink. "Craig, the one area I am unsure about, is how to proceed with the Board. Do we tell them? Do we tell a few of them? Do we hush the whole thing up?"

"Let me think about this awhile, Phil. My first inclination is tell them nothing. We cannot control their actions. We certainly cannot predict their actions. I'm not even sure we are answerable to them in affairs of this nature. Believe it or not, this just might come under the category of day-to-day management. Given variables like that, I say we button down the whole affair. But we have time to decide."

An hour or so later, Phil was standing outside the airfield office with Dr. Webber. Webber's plane was just being prepped, so they had a few minutes.

"Dr. Webber, what did you do before you developed the Island?"

"I told you, Phil, I'm an MD, a geneticist, and a biochemist."

"Yes. But before the Island, were you engaged in the same lines of research as you are conducting here?"

"Well, I was active in grant work at the University of Michigan for some time until the money dried up. But more importantly, my backers lost interest and they lost the will to support this type of research. No one really understood what the hell I was doing, so it either made them uneasy, or they just didn't care. I was damned if I was going to pour my own time and money into research that persists at the fragile sufferance of politicians, businessmen, and overly wearied academics, so I hit on the idea of paying for it myself, by myself, for myself, and in splendid, untroubled isolation. So I purchased the Island and started developing it. Nothing mysterious. This is not *The Island of Dr. Moreau.*

Some years after, when we were more developed, I hit on the idea that, if I gave the really big money boys a tempting value proposition—perks, an ROI to beat the band—long life, good health, fiscal benefits, and the satisfaction of helping humanity, we might really build something of enduring value. We might build a human being that can endure.

Phil, I'm sure you've heard that money equals power all your life. I suppose it does. But of far *greater* power, perhaps the mightiest in man's culture is *Targeted Concentrated Wealth*. That is, a great deal of money with one worthy, well defined, well managed objective, targeted at something that has lasting effects on the world, and on mankind.

The ancients such as Khufu, Ramses III, Alexander, and Caesar knew this. However, along with their philosophy, their ethos, laws, and cultures, the most conspicuous means they had of expressing something durable was through building extravagant monuments and cities. Really not bad for their times. We still enjoy and wonder at many of their accomplishments today. I certainly would in no way denigrate their achievements.

Today's fiscal titans express themselves differently. They engage in good works. They feed the hungry, clothe the poor, house the homeless, heal the infirmed, stamp out some diseases, patronize the arts, make grants to universities, and so on.

Upside? All good things. Worthy. Even noble. They alleviate suffering. They're *nice*.

Midside? These things are transient and short-lived, lasting one or two generations at best. Shallow and too easy. Just write a check. No really creative thought behind it. Largest part of the job is ensuring you're not giving your money to charlatans.

Downside? They exacerbate overpopulation, especially in areas where they can ill-afford it. They frustrate natural selection. They actually weaken the human race. I know how this sounds. Believe me, Phil, I know how this sounds. It is far more important however, to state the truth and not gild it.

Keats was largely wrong. Truth is *not* necessarily beauty, nor beauty necessarily truth. More often than not, it's *not*.

Ever hear of Abraham Maslow?"

"Yep," Phil said. "He was a psychologist. Had quite an effect on management philosophies I believe."

"Right as always, Phil. He developed an elegant definition of human values and motivators, which is referred to today as 'Maslow's Hierarchy of Needs.' Essentially, he delineated levels of human needs. Once a given level was satisfied, man would then progress to the next level...and so on. The first level involves food, security, health, 'a warm place to pee', as some American politicians would state it. The whole progression comes to its zenith when man is finally free to concentrate on creative pursuits. The lower level needs (food, shelter, security, etc.) are called 'Hygiene Factors.' Hygiene, like brushing your teeth, taking a bath once in a while, cleaning the bathroom, and so on. Not to belittle them, but human hygiene factors differ very little from those of a dog, or even an amoeba for that matter.

Now, let's go back to our fiscal titans and all their good doings and charities and face squarely (unlike Keats) the truth. These guys are fulfilling nothing more than hygiene factors. Cute, kind, warm...transient, gone with the morning sunrise. They're being *nice* but they're giving mankind literally nothing of lasting value. In fact, they are producing long-term problems. *Ingenerately, charity is not consistent with the nature of nature.*

On the other hand, *Targeted Concentrated Wealth* can change the world. When I finally realized this, I already had all the wealthy and close contacts I needed from the extrusion business, so I gathered them together. I explained my concept of *Targeted Concentrated Wealth* and the results we would be working towards. *Et Voila!* In conjunction with the Perks I offered, it worked. It's still working. I fully believe this is one of the most profound concepts of Oneiro."

Craig took a breather, lost in his own thoughts, and then smiled at Phil. "How did your Fear Ordeal go, by the way?"

It took Phil a few moments to shift his train of thought. He realized that Craig was trying to lighten up the moment a bit.

"Well, Craig, it was very, *very* difficult. It was beyond difficult. It was nearly impossible. Certainly the most disagreeable endeavor I've ever engaged in. It was frightening, disgusting, painful, dispiriting, disillusioning, demeaning, and exhausting. It was enlightening and in some respects, uplifting. I learned courage, forget about inhibitions, pain is no longer an issue, and I suppose, for lack of a better term, I gained some degree of self-enlightenment. I am now stronger and richer, and one hellofa lot more cynical, regretfully.

I pretty much expected all that. What I did not expect was that the stress of the Ordeal brought out tensile strengths within me that were most unexpected. When I went on my lonely little quest in the desert, I found I had developed talents and skills far exceeding anything I had ever envisioned. *And they are still developing!* Do you understand what I am talking about Craig?"

There was a pause.

"I suppose I do."

"So...prior to the University and the Island you were actively in development?"

Phil's peculiar associative talent was fitfully surfacing again and in the form of a rather amorphous suspicion.

"Yes. Fully active for many years."

"No. What I mean is...I've seen some extraordinary achievements at the University, like no where else in the world. Decades beyond anything I'm aware of. It must have taken years to accomplish."

"Yes?"

"Well, did you develop all this on your own?"

"Hell no. You know I didn't. We have some of the most talented people in the world here, and the students have taken a commanding role as well."

"No. No. I know that. What I'm asking is if your original objective is, or was, where we are today...and where we are going in the future."

"Oh. I see. Well the answer, believe it or not, is yes. Yes. My original vision was to force a hybrid species of *Homo sapiens*. One that incorporated all aspects of the race, worldwide. No one left behind. The best of all. The worst of none.

The mechanism for forcing was fairly clear to me as well. I really just lacked the tools with which to manipulate genetic material. I had to build the first and second generation of machines myself. The technical infrastructure just wasn't sufficiently evolved as yet. Those early machines were crude as stone knives and bearskins compared to today's arsenal. I almost get dizzy thinking what these tools will be capable of in ten years. Count me amongst those of the belief that an explosive renaissance is racing towards us."

"So you built the manipulators and started the compression process."

"Yep."

"Did you foresee what we term as ANUMEN today?"

"Indeed I did. Maybe hoped or dreamed is a better way to put it. However, it didn't manifest itself in any manner I had envisioned."

"What did you envision?"

"Well, it's a little embarrassing to describe in the bright light of reality. But I fantasized along the lines of ESP, pre-science, telepathy...all manner of carnival midway tricks. Who knows, some of these things may come sooner or later. Maybe it's just a matter of time. I'll tell you one thing though..."

"Yes, Doctor?"

"There's no way in hell I could be happier, or prouder of the real ANUMINA burgeoning around us."

Phil thought that Webber actually looked a little misty-eyed. What the hell. He had the right.

"So you moved operations to the Island and then started producing embryo?"

"Good grief no! I produced generation after generation of embryo. All failed. Nothing survived beyond a few hours. Many exceedingly grotesque. It was discouraging and depressing in the godamned extreme. Finally, a few years before moving to the Island, with a little assistance, I hit upon a third generation manipulator."

"Any success?"

"A great deal. We even developed a prototype."

"A prototype...a design...a machine...a model...what?"

"A prototype being."

"'A prototype *being? A creature?*' What happened to it?"

"What happened to it?"

"Yes. The prototype being. What happened to it?"

"Why nothing happened to it. It is you."

"What?!"

"You happened to it. You're the living, functioning prototype."

Phil sat down very hard on the railing.

"This was long before we developed our methods in education, fear, womb, and all our other specialized rearing and nurturing techniques, and we didn't have nearly the rich genetic diversity we benefit so greatly from today, either. However, you're still a nicely advanced release of Homo sapiens, by several thousands of years I would estimate. At the moment you were conceived, you had the most profound genetic constituency in human history. In my opinion, this renders you exceptionally and uniquely qualified to lead an ameliorated legion of humans."

Phil was silent for a moment. "And my parents?"

"Your father was my legal council. He adopted you and raised you, quite successfully I would say."

"I'm adopted?!"

"Uh. Yes. We had to cook up a birth certificate out of Pitcairn Island and kill off a couple of fictional parents to get you into the U.S. Your adoptive parents, Steve and Gwen, were barren, and they wanted children desperately. I finally produced a couple of progeny, but I had no venue or staff with which to rear them. Your parents were the absolute perfect solution. I've been monitoring you on and off all your life. The crazy thing is that, when we recruited you, it wasn't my idea. Our President at the time, Wilcoxen, was familiar with your work and recommended you. A pleasant surprise I must say."

"Why, you son of a—"

"No. No. You're 'a son of a…'" Webber said, not without some affectionate indulgence. "And I'm the closest thing you've got to a biological father. I suppose I'm actually your dad, Phil. Your older brother was mine as well. He was not nearly as advanced, but a great kid nonetheless. I'm truly sorry he was killed Phil. I grieved on the day he was found."

"Were my parents aware of my genesis...and Michael's?"

"Your father was. Your mother, no. For good reasons, I believe."

Craig and Phil just sat silently staring at each other and into the distance for a long time. Craig could see Phil's jaw working intensity, lips tightly compressed, breathing elevated and a faraway, grim stare in his eyes. When Phil wasn't looking to the horizon, his eyes rapidly darted from side-to-side in a very disconcerting manner.

Finally, Phil seemed to ease off. His shoulders dropped ever so slightly and his breathing came more regularly.

Phil grinned wryly. "This reminds me of the wonderful quip by Dick Cavett. "If your parents never had children, chances are you won't either.'"

Dr. Webber lightly smiled, with some undisguised relief. Remarks like that indicated that Phil was capable of understanding, accepting, and perhaps even appreciating the situation.

"You know, Craig, I think I was just on the edge of figuring this out for myself."

"I'm quite sure you were, Phil. Now. Take some time. Relax and calm down. Get over it. Look at it this way. You've been blessed with the finest genetic heritage possible at the time of your conception. You had a formidable upbringing. A fine education. You are healthy, wealthy, smart, good looking, young, and successful. I'm very proud of you. As I said, get over it. I'll see you in a few days."

"Why the hell didn't you tell me these things?"

"Because you figure them out for yourself. Damnit. There's a high probably this is some sort of ANUMEN within you, as well as those other 'tensile strengths' you're discovering. You're a bit of a real anomaly, though. We expect unique abilities in the students. But you are too early an iteration for this. There's something else, something special working in you. You're my sole heir by the way, so you're facing an exceptionally, and I mean *exceptionally* wealthy future."

Phil was stunned.

"I am very grateful, truly. But is there anything else you haven't told me?"

"A few things, actually. If you don't get around to figuring them out for yourself, we'll have to have a long talk one day. Take a few days off yourself, Phil. You've earned it."

"I suspect among the other things you haven't told me is that you really do believe my coming was actually a catalyst for the events that have been cascading down around us?"

"Bingo. Think about it, Phil. You've been an anthropological enzyme ever since you entered puberty. I can't imagine the apparatus. I don't know if it's ANUMEN or whatever the hell, but wherever you go, things—for lack of a better term—get moving. You're a trigger mechanism. You're some sort of an accelerator, and I think you'll keep accelerating things faster all the time.

Go over it in your mind, Phil. It will dawn on you that for years you've left a trail of change behind you. Put much of it down to good work and the effects of your curious insight. Yes. But at the same time no one can achieve those kinds of results a hundred percent of the time.

For a time, I speculated that you were gifted with some sort of prescience. But your reactions, surprise, and consternation at events as they unfold disproves that idea. Moreover, I don't have one damned inkling what really constitutes prescience. Something else is afoot here. I don't have a clue what it is. Most of us work toward the future. You seem to summon it. Don't let it bother you. Investigate it. Use those formidable intuitive powers of yours to figure it out. My strongest suspicion is that you act as a stimulant or synergist that results in a type of emergence. Are you familiar with chaos theory?"

"Somewhat. What does that have to do with what goes on here?"

"Well, many students of chaos have pretty much concluded that chaos does not truly exist, even in systems as uncontrollable and unpredictable as, say, the weather or the asteroid belt between Mars and Jupiter. They're not chaotic...we just don't have sufficient grasp of all the variables, of which there could be trillions upon trillions, to truly generate an accurate, totally reliable, predictive model.

Evolving from chaos was perhaps an even more interesting theory...emergence. Emergence stipulates that given a population of sufficient size and homogeneity, an intelligence, a guidance mechanism will 'emerge.' From types of moss, to ants, to fish, to birds, to brain ingrams this phenomenon may occur...given a critical mass and a provoking influence."

"That's why you've given me such a free hand ever since I arrived."

"True again. Two more points in as many minutes—not bad, Phil—I think you're getting stronger all the time. And I fully believe your *futurefluence* (I just coined that word, by the way) is good for the Island and ultimately the human condition. Build on it. Let it grow. Ever think of asking Doc Gear to measure your enteric system by the way?"

Phil was taken aback by the question. Then slowly, more realities began to dawn in his active consciousness. Uplifting. Upsetting. Exciting.

"I'll stay here with you, Phil, if you like. Help you get better acclimated. Help you exercise your futurefluence."

Phil absently shook his head "No. No, Craig. I'll be fine and you need the time. Hell, I need the time."

With that, Webber patted Phil on the shoulder, boarded the aircraft, and was soon airborne and on his way.

Phil sat alone, thinking for a long time. He then got up and went back to his office and went back to work.

Phil spent the next two days ensuring that the Island was cleaned up, wounded tended to, and all bodies totally disposed of. He ensured that travel and communications embargos were effectively imposed—no secrets, no cover stories—and no exceptions.

The Islanders were beginning to realize they were really in this together. A true team was "emerging" from the chaos, in its closest, most commanding and formidable sense.

He then devoted a fair amount of time just talking to everyone. He held his luncheon, which went on for more than five hours. Much food and wine was consumed, and Phil felt, all in all, everyone was much improved. He dined with Mike and thanked him sincerely for his help. He got drunk with Rachael and Charlie Stein. He visited his new Executive VP of Finance, Richardson, in hospital, and he ensured that the Safe Deposit was still secure and untampered with. He asked the HR Director to hire or promote a new Physical Education Head.

He had breakfast that extended well after lunch with Judy McLean, Anne Jones, and Eve Dunedin. They seemed more in shock than any other staffers or students. Possibly the

University was too much of a home to them. They all agreed that the Fear Ordeal probably had been the saving element during the crisis. Should they extend the Ordeal? Should they make it tougher? Should they more fully integrate Art, Music, Language and Physical Education with the Fear Ordeal? What else could be linked to Fear? More arts? Any sciences? Philosophy? Should they consider therapy for anyone? Should Pain and Fear and Wrapping be segregated, or more closely integrated? Phil ensured everything was taken down in the minutes and requested recommendations. He then broke out the bar and everyone relaxed for the first time in four days.

The next day, he radioed his Uncle Herb. Herb was about sixty kilometers out on the far side of Lefkada, so Phil decided to take one of the Island's yachts and rendezvous with him at sea. Eight hours later, the two large craft fleetingly bobbed in vague synchrony as Phil tossed his ditty-bag across and agilely hopped aboard. Phil went immediately to his stateroom and slept until noon the next day.

Demetrious grilled an excellent lunch while Herb briefed Phil on their progress.

"You know, Phil, this new job of yours seems to drain the hell out of you. In any event, I'm glad you're here now and can take it a little easier. The freezer is nearly full. Give it three, maybe four more days, and we'll top off. Then I thought we would make a fresh catch for sale on the way to home port. Got time?"

"Sure. By the way, Uncle Herb, did you know that Michael and I were adopted?"

Herb's eyebrows raised, and there was a slight pause before he spoke. "Umm. Yeah. I did. But I didn't know that *you* knew. Certainly Michael didn't."

"Just found out a few days ago."

"You okay with it?"

"Beats hell out of me. I guess so. I had a great family and wonderful parents, so what's to complain about?"

"Not a damn thing if you ask me. Now that you know, I'll make sure you get some papers I was holding back. Although I don't think they reveal the name of your true parents."

"I'm sure they don't. But I already know. So it doesn't matter. Christ, I'm hungry!"

They went below to food and wine and then spent the remainder of the day working the sea. Just what the doctor ordered. Three days later, the freezer was indeed topped off. The weather was turning cooler, but still sunny and generally warm during the day. Phil was as brown as antique oak, relaxed, and all thoughts and spectral trauma of the Island had fled, or were at least well hidden in the wings for the present. His greatest concerns were meals, the glittering sea, the weather, and whether to watch TV, or put a movie on, or settle in with a good book.

Herb and Phil went over the accounts for the start-up period, and concluded that the damn thing might actually be able to pay for itself. He didn't really have much of a maintenance history to factor in, but all other DOC's and IOC's were pretty well known and documented. Might even make a tidy profit if the boat was amortized properly. Phil had nearly paid for the boat in full when he bought it, so he decided to pay off the boat completely and turn this into a serious, profitable business. All the fun and enjoyment it gave Herb and Phil was just frosting on the cake.

Yumm

Much too soon Phil found himself back in his office on the Island. He was very pleased the fishing business was going so well, and he was proud of Uncle Herb. Torn between the Island and *Sea Tigress*, Phil was truly confused for the first time in his life. He considered signing *Sea Tigress* over to Herb, in its entirety. However, he didn't want to lose the partnership relationship that was growing between them. He was a leader, a killer, a scientist, a lawyer, a sailor, a fisherman, a consultant, and a businessman. What the hell was he going to do when he grew up?

The phone rang.

"Hello?"

"PC this is Doctor Butler. Good morning."

"PC? Politically Correct? Personal Computer? What?"

"Oh. Sorry, Phil. PC. Philip Carr. The President and Commander in Chief of this Island World. I'm afraid we all call you PC these days. It's a term of respect."

Phil mused for a moment. *Island World? Island World. Not a bad idea at all.* "Dr. Butler, I would like to call you right back if that's okay?"

"That would be fine."

Phil rang off and asked his secretary to get Dr. Shad Alexander on the line for him. Moments later, Phil spoke into the phone. "Hello Shad, how are you?"

"Hi Phil. I'm still a little shaken. This was some real shit."

"Agreed, Doctor. All the more reason to get things moving. How do suppose the Greek government would react to all this if they knew?"

"All flavors of blue hell would break loose. You know that."

"Yes. Yes I do. That's why I'm calling. What do you suppose it would take in terms of money, law, influence, feasibility, or whatever for us to become independent, or at least semi-autonomous?"

"You mean like our own flag, passports, visas, army, taxes, international organizations, autonomy...things like that?"

"Something like that, Shad. We already own the Island, and there are many examples of similar set ups."

"Such as?"

"Such as Brando's island in French Polynesia, Burr's island in Fiji, Rothschild in the Bahamas, Onassis here in Greece, Lindbergh in Brittany, the Princess Aga Khan in Jamaica, the list goes on and on and, in many cases, they applied, and some were granted micro-nation status for a limited, or even unlimited, period. Some were even granted sovereign island status."

"Phil, those were individuals and celebrities at that. We're a pleasure resort, a hotel, a corporation. Moreover, they weren't totally autonomous. They were more protectorates, with a finite duration as long as the "owner" survived."

"Not exactly, doctor. Cruise Lines, Resorts, and Hotels have enjoyed similar status and the duration of their status was not dependent on a single individual. During these periods, their protectorate government's laws are considered dominant. However, enforcement and a governing presence were not necessarily present."

"Okay, nor are they here by the way. However, given these scenarios, what are the benefits for us specifically?"

"I should think that's a rhetorical question. Consider the last few days. Consider the ordinance protections we have installed. Consider the protection of our Board of Directors.

Consider our little Treasury. Consider the work we are carrying on here. Consider the privacy and autonomy so important to our students. Consider things we haven't even considered."

"Phil I haven't got a clue. Difficult question. I don't know if it's even remotely possible. Just making inquiries could hold great risks. It could even bring down the force of the Greek government upon us. Pleasure resorts don't often declare independence, nor do they even ask. I need to give this a good deal of thought."

"Please do so and get back to me. And please do not overlook the contacts you maintain, not to mention our BOD, not to mention the amount of money we could bring to bear."

"Glad to oblige, Phil. But I need some time."

"Thanks, Shad. Take your time. It's probably time for the briefing on our legal matrix we discussed. Perhaps we can combine the two. Bye."

"Cindy, can you get Dr. Butler back on the phone please?"

Phil only had to wait a moment. "What can I do for you, Dr. Butler?"

"Well, I know you've been through a pretty rough time lately, so I thought a visit to my labs might be a nice break. We've got some wonderful stuff down here. I thought you would enjoy seeing it, might give you a lift, and perhaps it would encourage you a bit."

"Sounds good. I'll be there in half an hour. Please have the wine chilled."

"Can do, PC."

"Enough with the PC."

"Can do …"

The PM took nearly fifteen minutes to commute to Dr. Butler's office. Phil spent the intervening time admiring sharks and fish of all kinds underwater. He even saw divers working on the artificial reef. His mood was significantly improved by the time he arrived at the food-production facility.

As he suspected, it was huge. The kitchen was at least twenty thousand square meters. There were more than four-hundred staff, and many more in the labs. Butler's office was positioned three un-obscured floors above the sprawling work areas, protruding halfway out of the wall with large 180° curved-glass windows affording a total view of operations, out and down. In the walls below the office were two huge connecting doors as well as a fairly small, glass, hydraulic elevator ascending to Butler's office, surrounded by large semi-circular desks, controlling access to the elevator and accommodating Butler's executive staff.

On the opposite wall was a bank of at least forty industrial elevators, supporting the food distribution systems. Covering the far wall was a row of about twenty offices, computer rooms, and food management staff. The near wall consisted of a long, long dining room, clearly where staff took their meals. Every spare meter on the walls was equipped with periscopes, gracing the whole facility with a sunny, cheerful ambience. Everything was quieter than Phil expected—partly a function of the high ceiling—and for the first time on the Island, Phil heard piped in music.

There was row after row of cooling units, stoves, ovens, shelves, work counters, sinks, delivery and serving units, all in spotless, brushed, stainless steel well placed throughout the working facility. The kitchen was highly automated as evidenced by conveyers, food handlers, food packagers, and all sorts of high-tech controls, washers, and appliances. Phil realized all the automated support was needed considering the population of the Island, meals nearly at any hour, and the wide variety of cuisine they were mandated to produce.

Every manner of cooking imaginable was taking place, and the aroma was heady in the extreme. Lunch was still an hour away, but Phil was now getting hungry.

He made the long walk to Butler's elevator, cleared his reception staff, pressed the button, and enjoyed the view on the way up. As the door opened, Butler smiled, rose, shook Phil's right hand, and placed a cool glass of white wine in his left. "Hi, Phil, thanks for coming."

"Thanks for inviting me, Doctor. This is damned impressive."

"Thank you. We're proud of it. Perhaps you'd be interested in a few stats. We produce well over 21,000 meals here every day of the week. We bake, we make desserts and pastries, wine, every cuisine in the world, salads, pasta, vegetables, sauces, casseroles, fish, and all types of meats, you name it, twenty-four hours a day. We have 1200 chefs, assistants, technicians, scientists, and instructors. We cook and we give classes. Everything is fresh and produced right here. This is the kitchen, but we have several classrooms, three laboratories, and of course, the actual food production facility itself."

"Aside from the kitchen, where is all this located?"

Butler smiled and pressed a button on his desk. On the far side of his office, a curtain silently parted and Phil realized he had seen only half of Butler's office. In fact, his office was perfectly round; the other half of the ten-meter glass circle protruded from the opposite face of the wall. The two men walked to the other side and sat at a conference, cum dining table, overlooking an area that dwarfed even the kitchen."

"Jesus Christ! I want a tour of this, Doctor."

"Coming right up. Want to finish your wine first?"

Moments later, they rode the elevator down to the main floor and passed through the access doors from the kitchen, into the wonders of the colossal laboratory complex. In view of the distances involved and time available, they mounted and mated two PM's under Butler's control.

"We have three types of labs here. This lab, Number One, is used for developing and testing hybrid recipes. We are engineering food here beyond the imaginings of fusion. Although to be honest, most of it doesn't work out. Either they come out terrible, or they are just too complex or alien in taste." The lab is composed of about forty work stations, each a fully equipped kitchen.

"Who mans this lab?"

"Students only."

"In view of what's been going on around here...any chance these *alien* tastes are ANUMEN?"

"If so, ANUMEN certainly tastes like hell!"

Phil smiled."

They rolled on to Lab Number Two. It had pretty much the look of a standard biology lab. There were roughly thirty work stations, computers, cooling and heating apparatus, electron microscopes, centrifuges, condensers, and lab-coated technicians in abundance. "This is perhaps the most sophisticated lab. It's our newest and wasn't really possible until Number Three was fully functional. In this lab, we produce health and medical solutions that are expressed through our foods—essentially our meats.

"Why meats? Why not fruits or vegetables?"

"As I understand it, the sugars found in meat products are more easily ingested without modifying the complex proteins that transport the amino compounds. We can cure diseases, improve nutrition, control weight, improve appearance and intellect, extend life, and even restore sight and movement. We can restore hair, skin tone, and reverse ailments such as osteoporosis, and much more.

Once we have developed the antigen, or remedy, the secret is to saturate the body nutritionally, accelerated by glycolsis-based boosters. The difficulty in this is that the cooking process tends to alter many of these substances, and these substances react differently with different foods, nor are all such substances efficacious when orally ingested. In most cases, however, we have overcome these problems, and we've pretty much eliminated the need for our medical departments, except for surgical or selected chemo interventions for use by our landers."

"Are you saying only students consume this food?"

"Certainly not. You've been eating this food since you arrived here, as have I and, rest assured, we are benefiting greatly from this. I was referring to our Board of Directors and the like."

"I see. So it's for the Board we retain more classical medicine and the cloned organ banks."

"Yes. That may change as students become more mature. Although I doubt it. Dr. Gear is the man to discuss that operation with. In fact, this lab is managed primarily by Dr. Gear. We just take his results as an additive according to his instructions."

"Do BOD members carry their own supplies?"

"Yes, and we ensure their supplies are more palatable all the time. One of our newer releases address alcohols, wines, spirits, and such. We take the harm out of them, keep the kick, and add the full spectrum of nutrients. We are fast succeeding with deserts and snack foods as well."

"So, if I elected to live only on beer, peanuts, candy bars, and ice cream, I could?"

"Nutritionally, you'd live a long and wonderfully healthy life, if gastronomically a boring one. Hell, when we release it, you could live solely on red wine for a long and healthful life. Never intoxicated, but a consistently fine mood.

Ready to move on to Lab Number Three?"

They rolled into an even larger area.

"As you can see, Lab Number Three looks very much like Dr. Johansen's Genetics Lab and with good reason. As Dr. Gear is really in charge of Number two, Dr. Johansen is in charge of Number Three. Are you familiar with Chlorpromazine, Phil?"

"Mmm...Chlorpromazine is an aliphatic phenothiazine." Phil's response was automatic and came so fast he failed to filter it, or interfere in any way. He found this a not insignificant embarrassment. Butler just looked at him thoughtfully for a moment. *I've got to work on controlling this,* Phil thought.

Simon chuckled. "Eh, I believe that's correct. I really don't know much about it myself. Anyhow, it turns out this specific substance is quite easily matriculated throughout the body. It is easily absorbed through the gastrointestinal tract and finds its way to any part of the human body intact at an absorption rate of nearly 99%. But I think you already know this." Simon frowned, regarding Phil closely.

"I...think I do too."

This drew an amused and quizzical expression from Butler, but he continued unabated.

"There is an expression in cryptography called 'steganography.' Are you familiar with it?"

"Yes I am, Simon."

"Somehow I thought you would be,." Butler said, with an appraising and somewhat irritating grin. "We've developed the technology to hide bio-chemicals within the chemical matrix of a greatly enhanced compound of Chlorpromazine, much as information is hidden using steganographic techniques. This hybrid is then used as a supplement in the food production process."

"I see. And what exactly are you *smuggling* into our bodies?"

"Well...a variety of organic matter. Vitamins, antibodies, genetic materials, selected enzymes, and glandular secretions, various drugs, and information."

"*Information?*"

"Yes, information."

"Information, as in knowledge and memory?"

"Absolutely."

"Doctor, what you're suggesting is impossible."

"First, I'm not suggesting it. Second, we are doing it, demonstrably and for real." Simon smiled.

"Look, Simon, I remember the old days when they would train planaria to run a simple maze—then chop them up and feed them to other planaria—and they seemed to consume the knowledge to run the maze. Turns out that was total bullshit. What've you done differently?"

"Well, information is essentially protein—incorporated into brain ingrams, if you will. Okay?"

"Yeah."

"Well, first of all, grinding up a planaria into some sickening goop destroys any information it may contain. Second, we steganographically encase these proteins in an exceptionally complex Chlorpromazine compound and sneak it into the body. Very little is digested. Most of it is eliminated from the body, but about 2% finds its way to the brain intact. Subsequent to that, about .05% is actually matriculated and is imbedded into human memory and ultimately sapience.

The students have now come up with the idea of utilizing the enteric nervous system to speed up the process and render it significantly more efficient. If I understand it correctly, this method allowed information to be taken in nearly directly from the stomach. Apparently, the results are stunning.

By the way, Phil, I'm way out of my depth here. You really should talk to Dr. Johansen if you want to truly understand the science. One more thing, though, and I think the coolest.

My first question when they briefed me on this was, 'How the hell do you distinguish and segregate the information you want to package?'"

"A good question indeed, Simon. How...?"

"They grow mission specific brain matter. They then attach standard audio input and feed the information in directly. The resultant engramic matter is very carefully and gently emulsified into a nutrient solution. After that, they package the whole mess in the Chlorpromazine compound and 'school's in session!'"

"Look, Simon. That makes no sense at all. Information is spread throughout a complex circuitry of cells. How in the world do they capture comprehensive information packets?"

"Ah! But that's the art form. Information must be bundled into extremely concise packets and then fed in. Properly done, the population of cellular material represents a complete set of information—and nothing else. We then clone it all. The result is what we teach."

"And who the bloody hell decides what we are taught, Dr. Butler?"

"As with any university, there is an academic committee charged with development of a curriculum. Every senior staff member is represented, and they report to the Chancellor... you in fact."

"How long have you all been working on this?"

"Dr. Webber has been on this for over thirty years, and it's only been in the last five or so years we've started to succeed."

"Goddamnit does this explain why I seem to know things I never learned?"

"I doubt that very much. You simply haven't been here long enough. This may be acting as a trigger of some sort, however, since this process does appear to improve connectivity between left and right brain, as well as within the brain itself. If my understanding is correct, it induces a sort of non-epileptic oscillation over the corpus coliseum, in conjunction with enhanced impulse generation and transmission within each hemisphere. Notwithstanding that there seems to be a great deal of dispute about the reality of left-brain, right-brain relationships, this technology is empirically provable. I believe our encapsulated chemical packages catalyze biochemical accelerators within the brain itself."

"This is astounding."

"Well, Phil, the expression, 'We are what we eat' has never been truer than here on the Island, and we're getting better at this all the time. Within five years, we expect a twenty-five percent absorption rate. Five years after that, we expect to approach one-hundred percent. And then school's out."

"School's out?"

"Yep. No longer any need for schools, classes, universities, colleges and such...only research and development and creative think tanks. They'll produce the learning and the science and the art and the literature and the mathematics and the history and the philosophy and we'll feed it to mankind and it will taste damned good. Physics with béarnaise sauce, music history sautéed with mushrooms, and numbers theory with caramel ice."

"Cooking doesn't destroy the information?"

"Not when it's encapsulated in our Chlorpromazine compound."

"What about the creative group, and classroom, and the professorial interaction?"

"That can still go on. We're just taking the grunt work out of the transfer of information. Imagine, we can get through to mute, deaf, and blind children. We can overcome autism and all sorts of learning and social disabilities. Maybe we can even put mankind all on the same page."

"You guys take a lot on yourself."

"You're damned right we do. That's why this Island and University was formed...to take the weight of the goddamned world on ourselves. We think in the longest terms possible, and I know we seem happy and light and even pampered here. But just beneath the surface, we are deadly serious, and it's a damned good thing we've undergone the Fear Ordeal. Because what we are doing is scary as all hell. We truly believe that, if we fail, mankind may ultimately fail."

"It seems I can't get briefed up on this outfit fast enough. I wonder what else I don't know about."

"My guess would be one hellofa lot."

"Are students involved in this project?"

"'Yes. Absolutely. Nearly exclusively. That explains the phenomenal successes recently. It explains our predictions for more extraordinary accomplishments in the next few years."

"I'd like a copy of your curriculum."

"Can do. Would you like to break for lunch? There's still quite a bit to see."

"Sure. Where do you want to go?"

"Well, the dining room in my office serves the best food on the Island—not to mention the best wines."

"Lead me to it."

They had pate de foie gras in Porto gelatin with sautéed apples, Dover sole in white wine sauce with tiny baby lima beans and a grated, deep-fried potato mat, breast of duck in truffle sauce with caramelized pears and creamed parsnips, pineapple carpaccio in triple sec. They started with a chilled sauterne, followed by an excellent Chablis, ending with a sturdy Bordeaux, coffee, and Calvados.

"Doctor, you know how to live," Phil said between bites and sips.

"Thank you. And nothing you just consumed will make you fat, harden your arteries, cerotisise your liver, or result in a vitamin deficiency of any sort. It will nurture you, make you healthier, smarter, better looking, and even make you live longer. Ready to complete the tour?"

"Well, it's either that or a nap, and I'm still on the clock."

"I think you'll find the food production facility as interesting as the labs."

With that, they remounted their PM's and entered the largest working area of the entire facility—food manufacture. The area was comprised of dozens and dozens of rows of production line equipment, each one identical. Starting with a cylindrical metal housing, then connected to an airtight, environmentalized glass tube, some thirty centimeters in diameter and ten meters long, ending in an automated packaging mechanism, whereupon a series of robotic conveyers transported large vacuum sealed packets of the resultant food or liquid to appropriate storage areas, or even directly to cooking sites—as dictated by their onsite computer facility. The entire operation was totally and eerily silent. Few humans were in attendance.

"Again Phil, I'm out of my depth here. But I can give you a fairly straightforward overview of what's done here."

"Sounds good, Simon."

"Those large circular units at the end of each production line house the germ of each comestible. This can be any type of fish, fowl, meat, vegetable, fruit, grain, and even microbiological product such as yeast, wines, beers, spirits, juices, fuels, and lubricants. The only differences between these products and nature's bounty are that ours are more nutritious and our packaging is radically different. No matter what is produced, our food is generated in the form of an unending cylinder thirty centimeters wide. In many ways, this makes it far easier and practical to utilize and store these commodities. These germs consist of perfectly healthy, living cells that feed, grow, reproduce themselves exactly (down to the micron), and expel waste. They are fed primarily on refined sea water, a variety of our very arcane supplements, proteins, and selected glucose derivatives. The principal ingredient, however, is simple sea water. Needless to say, this makes for very cost effective food production. This, augmented by some extremely low level electrical and chemical stimulants, constitute the rich nutritional, environmental, even primordial soup that produces food of a standard unknown anywhere else on this planet.

We can produce oils, skins, furs, and all sorts of bio-products. Nothing dies. There is no pain. No fear. No guilt. No lingering predatory degradation of the human spirit. This is the dawn of kindness and true humanity. In a very real sense, one day we may feed, clothe, and power the world for a song.

For the time being, set-up and adjustment of any given line is lengthy and complex. We hope to streamline and even automate this process within a very few years."

Then we will be ready for distribution. On that day, we will change man's world...forever. We will render man a benign being. God help us, we need no longer be poor, hungry, ignorant, embittered killers."

Phil was literally speechless. After a time he did ask a question. "Doctor, I notice no-one refers to environmentalism a great deal here."

"You're quite correct. This does not reflect a lack of concern. Instead, we're really not totally sure a problem exists... or if it does what it is...or how we would solve it if we did know. The fact that things change does not necessarily imply a problem. And there are systems so large and complex we may never know how to grapple with them. We don't believe in chaos here, but we are well aware of nearly infinitely complex systems. However, as I observe these incredible students, I fully believe it's only a matter of time ..."

"I understand. I believe I fully understand. Thank you, Doctor. Thank you very much. More than you know." Phil quietly disconnected his PM from Simon's, shook his hand, they both smiled at each other with something akin to empathy and not far removed from sympathy. Phil was quite literally overcome. Phil withdrew.

Back in his quarters, on the terrace, overlooking the sea, Phil realized he had not only done what *had* to be done...he had done *well*. For the second time since arriving at the Island, and for about the fifth time in his life, Phil actually fought back a tear. When could he find some peace and a modicum of complacency in this place? He was more convinced than ever, the answer was *never*.

Back Into the Fray

If the desire to kill and the opportunity to kill came always together, who would escape hanging?

Mark Twain

Rachael asked, "Phil, how did you know Dr. Siroa, or should I say Mohamed al Fayed, was a ringer?"

"As soon as I saw those students run and dodge and kill, I knew that Fayed already knew and kept it to himself. He didn't want us to take advantage of a clear tactical superiority."

"The singing. How did you know about that?"

"Fact is, I really had no idea. I merely wanted them to sing. I did believe that through song they would communicate the power of their language, and so have control over non-students exposed to it. I was as shocked as anyone else, except Fayed, when I saw what they could do. As far as that bastard Fayed goes, it just came to me that he was my man. I was deadly sure."

"It's true what I hear then. You get these...ah...insights don't you?"

"From time to time, I get something I suppose. I have no idea how it works, or what the mechanism may be. So, Rachael, what's the scoop on Griffith?"

"Well, he's a tough case. Apparently he first surfaced from NSA about ten years ago. Prior to that he simply didn't exist. Since then he's been a consultant to a couple of third-world countries and finally landed at DEW. He has no criminal record. He's not a terrorist. He's not a mercenary. He's not a spook. At the same time, he has no family, he's unmarried, has no clear friends or associates. He does seem to have some very strong, very suspect, ties to various pernicious Middle Eastern organizations...meets with them regularly at a site somewhere in the Atlas Mountains northeast of Marrakech... comes in via Malaga to cover his tracks...which is pretty scary. Each of his trips there, ten so far, were preceded by an Internet pop-up advertising a specific make of Moroccan carpets, which does not exist. We were able to learn all this because there are flashing yellow lights regarding him at several agencies around D.C. They were the boys that dug all this up and they were pleased to share their G2 with Howard. He's done them many similar favors in the past. None of them want to lift his control or punch his ticket quite yet. They're happier in surveillance mode for the present."

"Is he our man?"

"Absolutely. Guaranteed. Howard confirms that after a long, long, painstaking and very expensive investigation. I am totally convinced. There is no doubt. The evidence is unequivocal and well documented. I'll gladly make it available to you."

"Is he working alone?"

"Within DEW, the answer is a nearly certain 'yes.' Outside DEW, he's probably working with a Middle Eastern cartel type group. Probably some of the same boys he holds hands with in the Atlas Mountains."

"What the hell do they give a damn about this operation?"

"Probably many reasons, but one primary word: OIL."

"Shit. For Christ's sake, is that what this whole goddamn thing has been about, our manufactured bio-fuels? Will Howard take him out?"

"Not within the continental United States."

"Thank you, Rachael."

"Wait a minute, Phil. Is our boy about to do something rash?"

"Our boy *never* does anything rash, Rachael." Phil found her coyly-phrased question quite irritating. "That's all. Thank you."

Twelve hours later, Phil was on a plane to Newark. He arrived at the DEW Newark offices two days later, after getting the lay of the land and formulating a plan.

He was prodded and plodded his way through DEW security procedures, for which he was rewarded with a fatuous little yellow badge ("Must be worn conspicuously at all times and surrendered on demand to any authorized DEW or U.S. DOD Security personnel."). The cute little badge indicated that he was to be allowed into selected areas of the facility, but under no circumstances was he to be trusted on his own.

He was then shown into the offices of Mr. Bob Griffith, EVP Logistics & Deployment. Griffith was a tall, well-built man, with blond hair, blue eyes, fair skin, dimples, a charming smile and a generally likable boyish style. He was fiftyish, although he looked ten years younger. Clearly, he enjoyed good health and fitness. He wore a three piece dark brown suit, oxblood wing tips, tailored beige and powder blue shirt, and the standard duty free Lanvin tie. He dressed up nice.

His office looked like something out of a magazine. Everything was perfect (including Griffith) and had an icy, non-personality (including Griffith). He had cold, emotionless eyes with nearly no coloration whatsoever. The total effect was strongly intimidating and frankly, scared the hell out of Phil. This guy was some kind of sociopath. Phil could nearly see the reptilian-like malevolence within him, always watching, plotting, hungering, and hating.

Meeting him summoned of a cacophony of chaotic images, a firm handshake, a humorless, confident smile, a cup of coffee and expensive mineral water, seated at an in-office conference table, gorgeous well built brunette secretary with a sparkling smile, a view on the corporate lake through floor to ceiling glass walls. Blue cloudless, sky, unseasonably warm for March. Hating this bastard was a snap.

Suddenly, Phil was deeply shocked at the casual, almost amused fashion that he contemplated imminent cold-blooded murder. It took him a moment to compose himself.

Pleasantries completed, Griffith opened the discussion. Did Griffith detect a slight tick?

"John Dunkin tells me you are interested in some sort of underwater assault vehicle?"

"Turns out I was misinformed. Apparently no such vehicle exists. Wish it did. What was described to me is only in a very long-term planning stage, and uncertain at that. I was thinking of a UDT, squad size, belligerent submersible capable of patrolling the waters inside and outside our reef barrier."

"Self propelled projectiles, wired and wireless. Electronic detection systems, deployable evasives, extended undersea capability, deep dive capability, silent running, reasonable live aboard...that sort of thing?"

"You bet. But it just doesn't exist."

"Well in a way I'm glad to hear that. We have no such technology. Although I certainly wouldn't be adverse to some sort of developmental joint venture?"

"That's pretty much outside the range of our charter, Bob. But I would be willing to provide a Statement of Requirement if that would be of interest?"

"You bet."

"Fine. I'll try to get it to you in the near future."

"So what can I do for you today, Phil?"

"Well, I was in the area working with some bankers, and thought I would drop by. Basically I see this as a 'just get acquainted' meeting, a thank you for the fine work you have done for us, and maybe a briefing on what you may see as future developments that may be germane to our operations. I have a lifelong favorite restaurant not far from here, and I would like to invite you for lunch if you have the time."

"Certainly. With pleasure."

Griffith then launched into a tiresome, long, well-worn and well-rehearsed presentation of DEW products and services, and the future plans of the corporation. This was clearly a product of his PR and marketing staff. Phil had to fight to keep his eyes open and a half smile on his face. He kept pouring the coffee down, discretely breathing deeply and ogling the secretary whenever she came in and out. Finally, the presentation came to a merciful end. Phil declined a tour of the assembly plant. He asked the few obligatory inane questions and finally...lunch time!

"So where's this restaurant of yours?" Griffith asked, as they pulled out of the parking lot in a very elegant, dark-blue Jag convertible.

"Well...if you get on I-95 going north, you'll find an exit in about ten miles just after it crosses Highway 681. Exit there and go left, west, and I'll navigate from there."

"Can do, Phil. By the way, I haven't had any comms from the Island lately. Is there some sort of problem?"

"Are you normally in contact with Island personnel?"

"Ah, well...I wouldn't say normal contact, but certainly in a support role we keep in touch with fair regularly."

"I understand. We had a lightning strike or some such last week and it pretty much burned out our entire Proteus communications concentrator facility, so we're off the air for awhile."

"I see. But I thought you were well protected and redundant against such eventualities."

"Guess not. Sounds like something I should look into."

"Could be, Phil. You guys want some help? We've got some pretty good comms people."

"Sure. Why not?"

"I'll look after that when we get back."

"Thanks, Bob. I would appreciate that."

A short time later…

"Okay, Phil, I took exit 23, and I've gone left, what now?"

"In about two miles, you'll see a very small dirt road on your left. Take that and go about another two miles. That will take us to a cliff line overlooking the Hudson; there's an old white house there that serves the best damned Salisbury Steak, mashed potatoes, broccoli with cheese sauce, and peach cobbler you've ever tasted in your life."

"That sounds really good! How'd you find it?"

"My uncle opened the restaurant, actually a B&B at the time, about twenty years ago. They still use his original recipes."

They took the left turn onto the dirt road and bounced their way for two miles, past an old ramshackle, peeling white house up to the cliff line five hundred feet above the Hudson River. Griffith frowned slightly. There were no other cars. This certainly didn't look like a restaurant, or any other type of commercial establishment. The view was breathtaking, however, and it was a lovely day. Griffith put the car in park, set the emergency brake and started to open his door.

"By the way, Bob, one more thing I meant to cover before we go to lunch..."

"Yes?"

Phil smiled warmly at Griffith then frowned and looked slowly to the rear, Griffith followed his gaze and Phil delivered a crushing blow to the left side of his neck, which was traumatically broken. Griffith was instantly dead. No pain, no fear, no struggle.

Phil then restarted the Jag, released the emergency brake, shifted into first gear, and let it idle over the cliff. It landed with a resounding "whump." There was no fire, no explosion, no smoke, no drama, just mundane, tawdry, degrading murder.

Phil walked back to the main road and flagged a ride to the nearest phone. His mobile phone worked only in Europe and Bob's mobile had traveled with him over the cliff line. He called the police and reported the incident. His report simply stated that they came to see the view on their way to lunch at a very fine restaurant a few miles beyond the turnoff (Interestingly called the "No Name" restaurant). Phil got out of the car to enjoy the view, and Bob somehow fumbled the controls and literally drove himself over the cliff. Phil's report was accepted without question. Almost too easy, he wondered if someone was "greasing the skids" for him. But who? Christ. Damn near any intelligence agency within a twenty kilometer radius of Washington, D.C....that's who.

He then reported, with deep regret, the incident to DEW, got transport into Manhattan, checked into the Carlton, and made plans for dinner. Game over. Zero regrets. Screw the son-of-a-bitch. Phil figured if he was going to hell, if it existed, at least that bastard would be crispy and well cooked long before he arrived.

The remaining question, the overriding concern, the sole source of real fear was, what about the goddamn Middle Easterners?

He knew them pretty well. He had done a good deal of work over there. They were rational, genteel, smart, cultured, educated, rich, manipulative, pampered, brave, and lazy. They were unpredictable and uncontrollable. Since the time of Hammurabi in the Tigress-Euphrates Valley, they were a proud people.

Nearly four thousand years ago, when New York was no more than a hunting ground, London a swamp. and Paris a foggy river bog, they had a civilization unparalleled in previous human history. Cities such as Ur stood at the mouth of the Tigress and Euphrates rivers, representing one of the earliest, advanced civilizations in world history, where law, art, wealth, power, security, and a civilized populace lived and prospered. Where had it all gone? No legacy whatsoever? What happened? Did the wind and the sand and the jackals inherit everything?

Emperor Alexander, Emperor Cesar, King Richard, Kaiser Wilhelm, and their ilk had helped kick hell out of them.

Then oil had poisoned them and their culture. It robbed them of their self respect, their way of life, their very self perception. Oil had rendered many parts of the desert vast, degraded expanses, fit only for exploitation...ugly, lonely, without majesty. Nothing T. E. Lawrence would have come to love much anymore.

When the oil ran out, and it ultimately would, or mankind developed a replacement (as had Oneiro), perhaps they would regain their dignity.

Of course, the West and their corporations had done their share with oil drilling, check-books, Rolls Royces, F-15

Eagles, roads that ran nowhere, movie stars, unimaginably wealthy potentates from one-time tribal leaders that had once cared for and lived with their people. Then enter the consultants, engineers, military advisors, investment councilors, and diplomats by the drove.

Military bases, naval air stations, and airfields started popping up like mushrooms. Small wonder that hate and fear and jealousy was fomenting in the ranks, wondering who the hell they were all of a sudden and if they really had a niche in the world anymore.

This was prime time and they were prime targets for the crazy and dangerous elements to hold sway. They stalked quarry worldwide. The world itself was their quarry. Yet they were only a malignant product of their religious leaders, their hateful, insane, militant Mullahs and Imams...self-serving bastards that they were. If "God" really cared, these guys would be cinders in the deepest level of hell, along with a considerable number of their Western brethren.

Phil realized with a jolt that he somehow had to stop this line of thought. He was going to choke on his own hate if he didn't. Good grief! He was getting as bad as they.

The downside was that they were onto *him* now—big-time.

The upside was that Phil was onto *them* as well.

When would they ever be onto themselves?

Never have I seen such courage in soldiers as these ... [sic] ... there would be no soldiers anywhere in the world to match them.

Crusader's Description of Saladin's Army after the Siege of Acre—1191 AD

Their leaders masquerade as women to escape retribution. They hide in caves. They use women and children as human shields. They will murder their own as quickly as anyone if it wins them power, money, attention, or sanctuary.

Jihadists after the Siege of Islamabad's Red Mosque—2007 AD

Home Again Home Again

"Hi, Phil, Anne here."

"Hi, Anne, it's good to hear your voice." She sounded like warm velvet.

"Yours too. Did you have a good trip stateside?"

"Not in the least. Not even remotely. Rather put a stick in my eye."

"Good grief! Things are still pretty tough I guess."

"You guess right, lady. What can I do for you?"

"Got a couple of paintings down here I thought you might appreciate, or if not appreciate, at least gain something from."

"Dangling participle. But intriguing. When?"

"This afternoon, say around 1500, if you like?"

"I'd like that. I'll be there."

At exactly 1500, Phil entered the reception area of the Art Department. At this hour, classes had ended, so the lobby was deserted. Anne entered at nearly the same time. She was interestingly clad in a white robe, bare feet, nothing else. Unexpectedly, she bore two generous glasses of white wine.

Anne gave Phil a glass "Why don't you go change and then I'll brief you on today's showing?"

"Sure, Anne, be right back."

Phil returned equally clad. "So, Anne, what sort of hellish wonderment do you have in store for me today?"

Anne gave Phil a penetrating stare for a few moments. "I really don't know, Phil. The first painting is for your eyes only. I have taken the liberty of naming it, however. In Greek:

Gnothi Seauton or in English: *Learn Thyself.* It's a portrait of you, Phil."

"Who painted it?" Phil asked after a long pause.

"Auslander."

"Why did he paint it?"

"I think he likes you and respects you. You two have been through some difficult times together. Ready for a viewing?"

"I suppose so. Okay. Let's see it."

Back into the viewing room, Phil sat down and made himself comfortable. The curtain opened to an extremely well rendered work of art. The painting was certainly faithful. It really looked like him, nicely dressed in suit and tie. He had a pleasant look on his face—very slight half smile and a bit of quizzical wrinkling around the eyes. He was backlit by a sunny seascape and the softest of breezes was ruffling his hair a bit.

As with other Auslander renderings, he could literally sense the fresh breeze, smell the salt air, and feel the warm sun on shoulders and neck. The painting was indeed very pleasant.

Phil scrutinized the tie, and as he expected, an infinite regression was skillfully worked into the silky design. As he studied the design, he suddenly saw his face, saw himself in much greater detail and clarity. Things started to happen in concise stages.

First he recalled his youth and passage into adulthood with an intense detail. Things long forgotten, memories, days and weeks and hours, education, sadness, happiness, the humiliation of being a fisher boy on the uppity Eastern Shore, names, faces, loves, friends and enemies, failures and successes that were and were not his doing, forcefully re-imposed themselves upon him. The experience was powerful but not unpleasant. It was wistful, reminiscent, and actually nostalgic.

The next stage was not as pleasant. In fact, it was unpleasant in the extreme. Phil had very successfully undergone the Fear Ordeal. He was now an expert in wrapping. However, he forgot that there was a lifetime of trauma that had occurred long before he had learned this new control. The painting forced him to relive the death of his brother, his parents. He felt the pain and sadness anew, and he felt the hatred and frustration and hunger for revenge. While he shook with hatred, he wept with grief. Tears ran down his cheeks while blood ran down his fists. His jaws were so tightly clenched that his teeth hurt—near to cracking. He opened and closed his fists and his stomach muscles were so tight it nearly doubled him over, close to vomiting.

All the hurts he had thought were behind him were now confronting him again, an insinuating, malignant monster. All the wounds were open again, festering, bleeding, puss-filled and running. All the hatred and rage he thought he had mastered were burning, scalding his insides, burning him to death, killing all the instincts he valued and respected.

Suddenly, dispassionately, Phil had the answer. He *wrapped*. After about fifteen minutes, he had regained control. In fact, he was now well in control...and pleased. A feeling of peace and healing calmed him, warmed him, and finally gave him a heady strength...mastery.

The next stage was a wonder. He relived old loves, joys, achievements, his first big shark on the Chesapeake, the first time he had sex, the first time he beat hell out of one of St. Michael's callous bullies, the time he was Valedictorian in his graduating class, his degrees in law, pre-med, launching his career, a hundred triumphs around the world, the fun, the pride...and finally landing on the Island. He was proud. He was happy. He was motivated. He was strong. He was in control. He smiled somewhat wistfully, ready to proceed.

After a few moments, Anne entered the room.

"How was it ,Phil?"

"Could be one of the better moments in my life. May I keep this?"

"He did it for you alone. It's yours."

"You will thank him for me?"

"I will. Do you need anything, a drink, a pill, a shower, a massage?"

"No, not a thing, thank you very much. Now...what about the second painting?"

"You've seen it before...alone. I suggested after the Fear Ordeal we might view it together. Well, you've undergone the Fear Ordeal, quite successfully I understand. Ready for a second viewing with me?"

Phil looked at her with a curious mix of desire, fear, curiosity, and admiration. Somehow he couldn't bring himself to respond. Anne, sensing this, helped him out in her gentle fashion.

"Phil, I want to view the painting with you."

"Yes. Yes, I do too." He said and smiled.

With that, Anne pushed a button inside the room. The curtain opened. Before he confronted the painting, he looked at Anne. "Have you looked at this painting since we saw it last?"

"Five times. It's addictive."

"You still like it?"

"No. I love it. But I've always been alone. I really wanted to view it with you."

"Is it art or sex?"

"It's love."

With that, they faced the painting and were immediately enchanted, transfixed, captured, spellbound.

As before, female? Maybe. Stylized lips slightly parted with an ever so small peek into a mouth (?). Could he see a bit of a pearl white tooth? A soft tongue? Whatever the hell it was, it was warm and moist, and it was...respiring? Yes it was breathing. He could hear the deep inhale of air and the slow exhale. He could feel the warmth of (her?) breath. Her breath was sweet, as though she had been eating cherries, or oranges, or something nice. Something sweet, clean, and fresh. There were tiny bits of fruit and juice on the lips and tip of her tongue. He could nearly taste it! Damn, he *could* taste it! Damn she was Anne! She was beautiful and soft, sexy, remote, and yet available. He could melt into her tender softness. He could weep into her willowy hair. He could take her whole body into his eager mouth. Finally, he looked at her. She had dropped her robe, and she was indeed as beautiful as his imagining. He delighted in the dewy down between her legs. He longed to touch it, to kiss it, to caress it, and to enter it. Very slowly and tenderly she removed his robe. In his entire life he had never been so moved. A remarkable hour later they returned to the touch gallery and improvised a light dinner and some wine, which they nearly wordlessly consumed. Both were totally exhausted, they embraced, tenderly kissed, and went to their respective homes to sleep.

Vengeance is Whose?

It is a revenge the devil sometimes takes upon the virtuous, that he entraps them by the force of the very passion they have suppressed and think themselves superior to.

George Santayana

Rachael Stone strode into his office, somewhat officiously, Phil thought. Coffee in hand, looking good—maroon blouse and beige trousers.

"Morning, Rachael. What can I do for you?"

"I just spoke to Howard." She said, with no opening amenities whatsoever, brusquely. "He tells me Griffith is dead and you were the only person onsite. Is this true?"

Phil played it dead-pan. "What are you suggesting?"

"I *suggest* fucking nothing. Did you grease him?"

"None of your business. Anything else?"

"Phil. I'm your friend, your employee, and I am totally loyal. Frankly I'm frightened for you. I fear you have lost yourself in all this business and I want to help. Do you understand me? Do you even *hear* me?"

Rachael watched Phil's eyes darting about and his jaw working, a deep frown creasing his forehead.

"Phil, have you become some kind of cowboy, a macho top gun, a killer, a murderer? What? Are you becoming no damn better than the creeps who are trying to destroy us? What are you thinking of? What have you become? What are you thinking? *Are* you thinking?

There was silence and they looked at each other eye to eye.

"You know Rachael, around 218 BC, Hannibal killed, butchered really, over sixty thousand, *sixty thousand*, Roman solders—some of the finest fighting men ever fielded in human history—in one single day. Why? *Glory!* Alexander did it even better. God knows how many that bastard killed for his gory goddamned glory, and his squandered spoils."

Rachael interrupted. "You see yourself as some sort of Alexander do you?"

Phil glared at her "Goddamnit you're not listening." Anger was rising in him. It was close to boiling over. "Try listening for one damned minute. World Wars One and Two killed over one hundred million. Viet Nam, fifty thousand poor dumb American GI's died. Why? Glory and power and *money*...not theirs...far from it. Poor bastards thought they were fighting for their country, when they were actually filling the pockets of the defense industries. McCarthy started a commie witch-hunt to keep the Korean fear money coming in. The litany of *horrors* goes on and on. I'm a saint in contrast to these bastards. And the reasons for my actions are one hellofa lot better justified."

Do you have any idea where the term apocalypse originated? Phil was literally screaming at her now.

"No," Rachael tersely responded, her teeth clenched and grinding. She closed her eyes for a moment seeking patience and calm. Where was Phil getting all this arcane bullshit from? He was changing, and his changes were in no way subtle.

"It comes from an unknown little spit of a valley in Israel called Harmagedo. More battles have been fought there than any goddamned place on Earth. The Greeks modified it to Armageddon and then Apocalypse. Biblical Revelations claims that the mother of all battles will finally take place there. We're trying to *escape* that battle. *Do you understand?*

Me? I'm not on some quest to fight evil. I *had* to do these things myself. Either the goddamn DUS crapped out, or there was no one else I could trust. I'm not some cowboy. I simply want to keep this place safe and I don't want to die, if that's alright with you. So I killed, murdered if you like, a couple of sub-human flatheads.

"You could have been the one person on this Island I could have delegated this mess to. But you're a damned girl-scout."

"You son of a bitch!" Rachael turned angrily upon him. "My job is to protect and save the lives of my clients, not to murder their enemies!"

"Well, there we have it, Rachael. You are Director of Security. You're not a damned bodyguard anymore. And you just don't have what it takes. You forced me into this. If you don't buy it, if you have a problem with it, if you can't take any more of it, I can have you on a mainland flight within thirty minutes. Clear?"

"Look, Phil, I—"

"*Clear?*"

"Yes."

"Do you want that flight?"

"No."

"Fine. Remember *you* report to *me*. That's a one-way ticket, lady. I don't need smug fingers waggling at me. So, if you can't cut it, just keep your hands in your pockets while I get my hands dirty. Thanks for your support."

Phil regarded here coldly for a few moments "This meeting is over."

Rachael wordlessly exited his office.

My Island 'Tis of Thee

How I wish that somewhere there existed an island for those who are wise and of goodwill! In such a place even I would be an ardent patriot.

Albert Einstein

"Hi Phil, Shad Alexander, here."

"Good morning, Councilor. How are you?"

"A little awestruck actually. You were exactly right. We *can* achieve micronation status...even sovereign island status if you like."

"I like. What's it going to take?"

"I had a quiet meeting with my guy in Athens and we really need only two things: a great deal of subtlety and one hundred million Dollars, U.S."

"Subtlety we have. How about the money?"

"Mr. Richards in Finance & Treasury tells me that's practically chump change around here."

"Does our charter require BOD approval for this?"

No. Not really. You see the BOD only controls the legal entities of Halios Geron Resorts and the University. They exercise no authority over the Island itself. That belongs to Dr. Webber. We do make reports to them. But that is out of courtesy only. Discretionary funding between you and Dr. Webber well exceeds one hundred million, so it's your call, yours and Dr. Webber's."

"So, after we clear this with Webber, what do we need to do?"

"Very little actually. We ship the money to the Greek authorities for use as they see fit. This deal is really on the up-and-up. They're actually selling us the place. They will issue an official release/transfer of the Island, to the Island or whomever or whatever we designate, and they will officially recognize us as a sovereign micronation.

It would be up to us to seek recognition from other countries if we so desire. We will need to write up a fundamental constitution, a basic set of laws, and designate our head of state. I assume that would be you. You then decide if you want to create and appoint some sort of governing body. You can select nearly any form of government you deem appropriate. We do need a less generic name. A flag is more than just a nicety. We can designate a currency from a few choices. I certainly don't recommend we coin our own.

We can form an army, a police force...whatever. We need not seek recognition from any other country. For one-hundred million, the Greeks will keep this confidential. And they will stay away. Permanently. We will have to make a few international registrations, however. But I'm convinced we can do this without making any waves. The real bottom line is we will then be able to defend ourselves, legally, aggressively, and even openly if necessary."

"That's exactly the idea, Shad. How long?"

"If we start immediately, shouldn't take more than a month or so."

"I'll contact Dr. Webber and get back to you. Sounds like we may be able to skip that briefing on our current legal matrix."

"Sounds good, Phi. I'll stand by."

Phil rang off.

"Cindy, can you figure out how to contact Dr. Webber on Corsica? He's staying with someone at the University there."

"I'm sure I can, Mr. Carr."

Ten minutes later his phone rang. "Dr. Webber on the line for you, Mr. Carr."

"Thanks."

"Craig? How are you?"

"Much much better, Phil. You?"

"Getting there. You got a few minutes?"

"Sure. What's up?"

"I've given a good deal of thought about our little uprising. I certainly don't foresee anything like it in the future. You never know though. But I do feel we need to have the unquestioned ability to defend ourselves, unfettered by anything except international law."

"You mean the Greeks?"

"Yes. And perhaps even others."

"Are you worried about anyone in particular?"

"Well, we no longer have a threat from Griffith and that pretty much cuts out the bad guys. The pitched battle we fought could always leak out, and there'd be hell to pay from the Greeks, maybe even the EC, and there may be some potential problems from the Middle East."

"Christ! The Middle East? Why?"

"Most probably our bio-fuel production capability."

"So what's the solution?"

"Sovereign micronation status."

"Jesus! Wouldn't that attract some unwanted attention?"

"Almost none."

"Is this even possible? Legal?"

"Unquestionably it's possible. Unquestionably it's legal."

"Should we consult the Board?"

"It's your Island, Craig. The BOD simply governs the corporate entities housed on your Island. You have full authority in this matter."

"What will it take?"

"One hundred million Dollars, U.S., a month or so, some fun legal documents, a flag, and one or two discrete international registrations."

"How do you feel about this Phil?" Webber asked after a long pause.

"It believe it's mandatory. It's a survival issue in my view. We should do it, and do it post haste. That's how I feel. How about you?"

There was another long pause on Webber's end of the line. "Get started right away, Phil, and keep me informed. This can all be accomplished under your signature. You'll be President of the Island, or Prime Minister, or King, or Arch Duke, or Grand Phoobaa, or whatever."

"Understood, Craig. Are you enjoying Corsica?"

"Very much. Just what I needed. Unless you have something urgent, I plan to stay on for a few more weeks. I'm getting a fair amount of research done; they have some good ideas here, and I'm having fun at the same time. Food's great and it's a beautiful island."

"Have a good time, Doctor. I'll keep in touch."

"Bye. Phil."

A moment later, Phil called Shad, again. "Shad, Phil here. Let's get going right away. Please ask Richards to come to me for the money approval...in cash I assume. I would like you and your staff, in conjunction with Dr. Kahn to get started on drafting the constitution and laws, and suggesting the governmental form."

"Dr. Kahn?"

"Yes. You told me one time your department looks to Kahn's department for direction in the formulation of law. Well here's the time to give it a real-world try."

"Mmm...understood and...agreed."

"Please speak to Anne in the Art Department about designing a flag...I should think that our ANUMEN's could cook up something interesting."

"Good idea. What about a name, Phil?"

Phil thought for a moment and brought something up from his strange memory. "How does "Oneiro" grab you? Oneiro, Ονειρευομαι pronounced *Oh-near-Oh*.

"What does it mean Phil?"

"It's Greek...for Dream."

Let us Speak of Languages and Arts and Flags

If one does not know to which port one is sailing, no wind is favorable.

Seneca the Elder

Phil sat quietly enjoying the view from the amazing Board Room. This was the day of their promised special BOD meeting. The day to pursue the incredible recent developments.

Craig had returned. Anne Jones, Judy McLean, Phil, and Craig had received several queries from Board members. The four had carefully planned the day's presentations. They had decided to include the new art form in their agenda and they decided to unveil Oneiro. Webber had enthusiastically accepted the name, as had other senior staffers.

They decided definitely not to include the ANUMEN abilities in Music, nor their physical and fighting prowess. Any faculty or staff member that would come into contact with the Board were thoroughly briefed they should not now, or at any other time, mention the insurrection. In fact, the entire population of Oneiro had been sworn to permanent secrecy.

All in all, the meeting had a pretty full agenda, especially considering the Board members would undoubtedly want to make their usual pilgrimage to Medical and Treasury. They had therefore decided to devote an hour apiece to the three subjects. Anne would start, followed by Judy, and then Phil would introduce the newest island state in the world, the sovereign micronation of Oneiro

He would unveil the flag and brief them on their form of government. Above all, he would reassure them that their secrecy continued to be assured and, more importantly to the Board, that their money was more secure than ever.

This would leave roughly half an hour for discussion, followed by lunch, leaving the BOD free to pursue their own interests for the rest of the day. BOD members had agreed to fly in the night before so they could convene at 0915 sharp. It was now 0900, a clear cool day, Phil had a clear cool head, and he felt well prepared. To reinforce that good feeling he had helped himself to a generous brandy on entering the Board Room.

Shortly thereafter, Anne and Judy entered the Board room. Anne was bearing a covered painting. They both graced Phil with warm smiles and set about setting up for their presentations. Nearly immediately, after they were prepared, Webber and the Board members entered the room.

After some quick amenities, handshakes, greetings, and coffee, all were seated, Anne and Emily at a desk near the multi-media room.

Dr. Webber stood to open the board meeting. "Thank you for coming gentlemen and, in particular, coming in last night, allowing us an early start. We have a full agenda this morning, but please rest assured we'll have you out in time for a drink, a quick lunch, and then we'll leave you to your own devices the remainder of the day. We have a few surprises for you this morning...I hope you'll find them good ones.

"We've structured our language presentation to respond to your emails, although time has been set aside for Q&A. As we alluded to in our last meeting, other ANUMINA have been surfacing, and we have invited Dr. Anne Jones, head of our Art Department to make the first presentation. This is our first surprise. After that, Dr. Judy McLean will give us a follow-on presentation on the new language...a few surprises there as well, I think. Then Phil will give you a briefing on a new development here on the Island...the third surprise of the day.

Then, no more surprises, just drinks and lunch."

Dr. Webber's comments elicited quiet Laughter.

"We are dispensing, as planned, with the normal reading of minutes and financial reports and will dive right into our agenda. Anne, if you please?"

"Thank you, Doctor. As Dr. Webber indicated, Anomalous Numen is starting to crop up in the University...and from some unexpected sources. We, or at least, I believed one of the most surprising sources would be the Art Department. Art is a creative discipline. But it is indeed a discipline, so it was thought this might be confining to our highly gifted students. I was wrong.

Some weeks ago, a student entered the Art Department... not an art student incidentally...he took a canvas, paints, and brushes, and set about painting. Roughly five hours later, the student covered the canvas and left without a word. I was intrigued. So I went to his painting and I uncovered it. Within a very few minutes, I was on the floor, weeping uncontrollably, vomiting, evacuating myself, and a very few minutes after that I crawled away—which took all my strength, training, concentration, and willpower. It took well over an hour for me to recover.

Had I not crawled away, I am absolutely convinced I would have died. Perhaps the one thing that saved me was the Fear Ordeal, which, as you know, is mandatory for our senior students. Phil and several senior staffers have witnessed the painting since that time. They all agreed that the experience was devastating. Perhaps the best comment made came from two of my staff, calling it, 'a work of inestimable genius and unspeakable depth.'

Many other paintings have been produced since then. Some even more dangerous. Some quite benign. Some even very humorous. Several of our students are very adept at this art form.

Aside from the exceptional skill involved in creating these masterworks, we discovered there was another common dimension to these paintings. Somewhere within the painting, our artists work in a sort of an intricate swirly design that has the amazing feature of going on for what seems forever—smaller and smaller. In fact, we call it an *Infinite Regression*. When these swirls engage you, they start to sort of speak to you, they start to move, they can make you taste things, feel things like warmth, cold, wind, and sun. They can actually animate the painting—make it move. They can inspire you. They can arouse you. They can make you sad, happy, fearful, lustful, loving, loyal, trustful, respectful, worshipful, angry, nostalgic, and much more...and they can kill you.

Early on, one of our finest art students realized these swirls were actually the written form of the new language and even though non-students cannot truly read, or speak, or in any way understand the new language, it does engage them at a visceral level, evoking dangerously powerful reactions.

It is a profoundly powerful art form...and weapon...potentially."

This evoked a buzz from her audience.

"Imagine a dress fashioned in this art. Just wearing it and walking on the street could be deadly. Or a building designed and constructed in this manner. Even skillfully applied facial make-up, automobile paint jobs, and bedspreads. The uses and potentials are endless.

We have a huge breakthrough here, and a huge problem. It must be controlled and contained. I hope not exploited. If employed properly, benignly, peacefully, and humanely, the simple reproduction and distribution of a single piece of this art could help bring peace to the world. Differently rendered, it could help end it.

One thing is clear. Only an incipient form of human is prepared to walk in the world that these advances imply. I know of no more profound reality.

When we view most pieces of this art, we require a physical exam and we have people and medications on site. One of our students has developed a painting I personally guarantee as safe. I will unveil it for five minutes and then cover it. This will provide you a taste of the power of this art.

Okay gentlemen? Ready?"

There were nods all round, so Anne uncovered the painting.

It was a painting of a small duck. Slightly abstract, almost cartoonist, but exceedingly well rendered. The duck was yellow with largish brown eyes. It was a golden sunny day, and the duck was floating in a small pond boarded by flowers and green grass. It was very pleasant. Slowly, the Board began to note that the flowers and grass formed an intricate design, and they started to feel the golden sun, heard birds singing. Then the water of the pond was rippling ever so slightly, and the duck started to bob gently up and down.

The duck ignored its bobbing and, instead, stared directly, unswervingly, if not a little vacantly, directly at every Board member. The Board found this charming—even a little amusing—actually very funny. Moments later, the entire room was in an uproar of raucous laughter. Tears of laughter in their eyes they nearly doubled over. They had never seen anything so funny. Finally, a few Board members actually fell off their chairs with laughter and Anne quickly covered the painting.

It took about a minute for the room to calm down and gain its composure, and there were still happy smiles all round. After a short time, the room sobered and faces took on a thoughtful visage, then concerned, almost fearful looks. Anne knew they now understood and believed the power of the art.

"Thank you for your time gentlemen. I believe questions will be fielded before lunch if that's alright."

The Board members were sober, attentive and somewhat enthusiastic in their applause.

Webber stood again. "Thank you, Dr. Jones. Now, Dr. Judy McLean, if you please?"

"Thank you, Doctor. We've been quite busy since our last presentation. Unfortunately, industriousness does not always equal success. I cannot report any progress whatsoever in interpreting or understanding this new language in any way. We have struck out. When we first realized we actually had samples of the language in written notation through the new paintings, we were most hopeful. This, however, yielded results as negative as all our other efforts. The written language defies decoding as yet, and it's *Infinite Regression* attributes drives our staff nearly insane, even when working with the most mild notational text. In fact, we have been forced to exclusively use students in this work.

Through scanning the notation and digitally recording the spoken language, we attempted computer-assisted analysis. This entrapped our entire configuration into a loop that required total systems shutdown. No luck. Although we continue to work on this aspect as well.

Our students openly, helpfully, and diligently work with us. I suspect they understand the language as little as we. I believe this is *prima face* proof of ANUMEN, and I am beginning to completely agree with Mr. Carr that this language is genetically imbedded. Perhaps even more deeply imbedded than genetics. We will continue to attempt to break this language. We may never succeed.

We do have a one-hundred percent unbreakable cryptolanguage for totally secure communications...much as the Army used Navajo Indians against the Japanese during World War II, although I think this has very limited utility. First, the students cannot actually translate their language in any precise terms. Second, with automated scrambling and quantum monitored listening for intruder alerts, there are far easier, more practical methods available. So, with nothing but failure behind us, we started to experiment. Three areas are currently being explored.

First, we took several animal types, dogs, bears, pigs, and so on, and exposed them over fairly lengthy periods to the language. We were not expecting dramatic results, just some sort of response...a recognition of sorts perhaps. What we got was nothing. We're going to try other sorts of mammals, reptiles, even amphibians. Maybe something may come up. We have a long way to go before we abandon this avenue. But so far, nothing.

Second, we invested in some rather arcane underwater sound transmission equipment and started playing the language in the waters surrounding the Island. So far, results have been intriguingly mixed. From fish...nothing. No reaction at all. From the few marine animals in these waters, we have noted they appear to evince some interest, and interestingly, squid appear to react strongly. This is encouraging to the degree we will shortly mount a small expedition to waters in the northern Mediterranean, then off the coasts of South America, the west coast of California, and finally, the cold waters of northern Canada, trying further work with whales along with our encouraging work with squid. We would like to save some time through use of various aquariums and marine parks. However, we believe this may be too great a security risk. If we can come up with a highly credible cover story, we may yet give it a try. We are hopeful of finding some real results from this aspect of the experiments. Interpreting those results may be another matter, but it may be a start.

Third, and most remotely far fetched, we have invested in an extremely powerful transmitter at Proteus Point and are now transmitting signals to the skies. Our astronomers are assisting in directing the signals to what they deem optimal celestial target parsecs. Our messages are highly concentrated and focused so we hope they can be traced fairly accurately to source by an advanced race. We already have the most sensitive receiving equipment currently in the world. So we're talking and we're listening. In all likelihood, if we get any sort of response, it could take years, if ever.

I believe we are attempting everything we can to crack this problem. I hope it is not unsolvable. Any and all suggestions are most welcome. We'll keep on trying, and we'll keep you fully posted. Thank you."

Dr. McLean's remarks were followed by subdued applause.

"Thank you, Dr. McLean," Dr. Webber said. "Your problems and your efforts are fascinating and most challenging. I wish you and your team luck. Now gentlemen, Mr. Philip Carr will brief you on another recent project."

"Thank you, Craig. Our reviews of the last few months have highlighted a few sensitive issues that could be potentially serious, embarrassing, and even confront us with criminal liabilities in various countries.

Therefore, this presentation is deemed Confidential in the highest degree, incidentally. I trust you will find this reassuring as the presentation proceeds."

A projection appeared on three of the four sides of the Boardroom:

- The Island is exceptionally well equipped to defend itself. It enjoys probably the most powerful, advanced, and comprehensive defense systems in private hands—anywhere in the world.
- The Island should be, must be, exceptionally reluctant in employing these systems. As subjects of the Greek government, we are totally unauthorized to maintain and certainly to employ such systems. Should the Greek government become aware of this they could quite rightfully proceed with criminal indictments and impound all extant defense systems.
- The Island, therefore, despite being superbly equipped, is really in no position to defend itself. This is a pressing matter of security.
- The Island maintains secret, private banking on behalf of BOD members and some senior staff. Again, under Greet jurisdiction, the Island has no authority to do so. Should the Greek government so wish, it could enter the Island's facility and ferret out such banking repositories. The Greek government would find our banking operations totally illegal. They would be empowered to confiscate all assets and prefer criminal charges against

all those directly, or indirectly involved as accessories before and after the fact.
- Any one of these risk scenarios would highly endanger all activities and achievements of the Island to date, and in the future. They could quite literally shut the Island down. These dangers are absolutely valid and are confirmed by the Island's expert legal staff.

"Pretty grim, gentlemen. To some degree we have been negligent in protecting the Island, the University, and our Board of Directors. When the weight of this reality came crashing down on us, we reacted with all due speed and diligence.

How could we allow this to happen to us? There is a certain idealistic, absorbed, almost dreamlike state that settles on any academic ambience. This is not a bad thing. It is inherent, even necessary to the nature of a thoughtful, probing, analytical life. This is a very nearly unavoidable trap. Fortunately, there is a remedy."

Phil signaled to a young lady in the multi-media room. Immediately, four flags unfurled from all four quarters of the Board room. The flags were white with a large swirl design in pastels, gold in the center, comprised of connected octagons. Despite its irregularities, Phil's puzzling insights recognized it immediately as a passing resemblance to the molecular diagram for a Cobalt Complex, combined with Diamine imparting no significance whatsoever as far as Phil knew.

The group immediately recognized this as a very superficial Infinite Regression. This one was exceptionally mild. It inspired confidence, trust, honesty, friendliness, and perhaps respect, but not fear or loyalty or pride, or anything close.

"Gentlemen, the flag of Oneiro."

Another projection appeared.

- Oneiro is the newest, sovereign, micronation island state in the world.
- Oneiro has been made independent by the Greek government, in perpetuity.
- Oneiro has been officially recognized by the Greek government.
- Oneiro has been officially registered as a sovereign state with selected international agencies.
- Oneiro is totally legal and autonomous in declaring its own laws and regulations.
- Oneiro is free to raise an army and maintain whatever ordinance it deems necessary and reasonable for defense, short of CBR, or missile born ordinance.
- Oneiro cannot be subject to investigation by any other country other than some pursuit of an unlikely breach of international law only by consent.
- Private banking, if not offered to the world at large, is now unequivocally legal.
- Oneiro is now empowered to look after the security of its residents, its independent Board, and its investors.
- Oneiro has its own constitution, laws, government. and resident citizenry rights. Its official currency is the Euro.
- The existence of Oneiro is very nearly secret and will remain as such.
- Oneiro is the Greek word for *Dream*.

"This is not a plan, nor a proposal, gentlemen. It is a reality. It is a *fait accompli*. We are now legal, safe, secure and autonomous.

You may wonder why you were not consulted in this matter prior to our actions. Two reasons. This island is the sole property of Dr. Webber. No joint ownership or management authority was ever conveyed, as I'm sure you know. Secondly, we felt your involvement in this effort, if unsuccessful, would only expose the Board to needless jeopardy and embarrassment.

Thank you."

Phil's statements and presentation was followed by long enthusiastic applause, with smiles and approval all round. Phil and Craig were greatly, though needlessly, relieved.

Webber stood. "I think we all owe Phil a vote of thanks for perceiving a very real peril and sorting out a permanent solution. This is not the first time, nor will it be the last I'm sure, that Mr. Carr's intelligence and insight have worked to the benefit and security of us all. Well done, Phil." Dr. Webber said with a big smile.

Applause came again. "The floor is now open for questions, gentlemen."

"Dr. Jones, do you have any plans for ensuring that this new art form is not misused for aggression of any sort?"

"No I don't, nor do I deem any such plans to be necessary. Were we to request our students use this tool for aggression, and were it well justified, they would do so clinically, unemotionally, and efficiently.

Were they or any other innocents to be endangered, and had to do so for their survival, again, they would do so. Under any other circumstance, this would be impossible for them. You must understand that these students have motives unlike any other population on the planet. They are not motivated by greed, power, hate, fear, bigotry, or any altruistic illusions. They simply do as logic and quality of life dictate."

"Mr. Carr, will you be seeking recognition from any other countries?"

"No. This would be unnecessary and risky. Despite sovereignty, we continue to seek anonymity within the world community. Even though we cannot be legally investigated by other powers, we can be invaded. Moreover, sovereignty in no way prevents other powers from investigating our residents who are citizens of other countries. We are all well aware of the risks inherent in that."

"Aren't there benefits from such recognition? Trade agreements, mutual defense, even foreign aid?"

"Certainly. When and if these are needed, we will seek recognition. Our goal however, is not to become a member of the world community of nations. It is to continue to work in peace, conduct research, and try to improve the human condition without interference."

"Dr. Jones, have your students tried any other art forms... sculpture and such?"

"Excellent question. We are working on that now...and yes, sculpture will be our launch project. Given the appropriate precautions, perhaps we can show you a sample at your next meeting."

"Dr. McLean, you're experimenting with your new language on all sorts of land and marine fauna, even extraterrestrials if they exist, and if you can contact them. How about different types of humans, various races, gifted children, autistics, idiot savants, and so on?"

"That's a fine suggestion. If we can gain access to such individuals without attracting attention and breaching security, we will certainly give it a try. Thank you very much."

"Mr. Carr, do you have any plans or suggestions or a proposal for us about re-marketing Oneiro products?"

"As we all know, these developments have great, almost inestimable value to the world and in the world markets, if that is truly our objective. However, to be honest, I'm not really sure we're ready to go to market, or even to charity. I'm not referring to establishing shadow companies. I'm referring to our ability to package and mass-market this technology—effectively disseminate it to mankind. Frankly, I'd give it at least another year or two. I will prepare a proposal and attempt to formulate a timetable. I will give it my best effort to have this ready at your next meeting, if you deem this of import and if I can get the requisite assistance here on Oneiro.

If we unleash these technologies on the world prematurely, however, we might do more harm than good, as they say. In fact, we could destroy all the good work we have achieved. Forget about the market, remember our manifesto. We need adequate time. "

Phil's statements were again followed by applause.

"Dr. Jones, who really controls this new art form?"

"I do not, nor anyone on Oneiro, except the students themselves, as they evolve, and we have few alternatives but to trust them. I suggest we do."

There was a long pause, and so, Dr. Webber rose. "If there are no more questions, gentlemen, please rest assured you will receive faithful minutes of this extraordinary BOD, and you will receive copies of our constitution, laws, government, and resident citizenry rights. Meanwhile, the bar is now open." Webber's closing statements evoked energetic applause and a mass exodus.

Alien Worlds? Look Next Door

The whitest, the most tender, the sweetest lumps of lobster tail with beurre blanc sauce Phil had ever tasted...tiny, tiny, steamed snow peas, and of all things, a normal baked potato with butter, a dollop of crème fraiche, and shaved almonds and a frosty Petit Chablis made up his lunch. The huge terrace was sunny and warm on this spring day.

Phil thought he heard the thunder of a spring storm coming in from the sea. This was perfection. Mike and Phil had spent a considerable amount of time together considering their respective schedules and they were fast becoming good friends. More than friendship, there was a mentor type bond between them.

"Mike, I wanted to thank you personally for that wonderful portrait you gave me awhile ago. I look at it often, and it always gives me something slightly different. To be honest, it always gives me what I need at the time. It's genius. Thank you."

"It was my pleasure, Phil."

"Do you suppose art critics would like your work?"

"I don't care."

"Hated your work?"

"I don't care."

"Fine answers. That's how I try to run Oneiro. I try to please myself and do the best for people who live here. What the rest thinks is pretty much an RF to me."

"RF?"

"Oh, sorry, that's a fairly vulgar, but descriptive term I picked up from a very attractive, fine young lady from California in my callow youth. I admired her and the term. Unfortunately, I treated her poorly but kept the term. I still feel the guilt after all these years."

"Okay, but what does it mean?"

"RF?"

"Yes. RF."

"Rat Fuck."

Mike laughed and they finished their lunch.

"Now, Mike, before lunch I spent some time looking at the newest painting you were kind enough to bring up for a viewing. For the life of me, I couldn't understand it. It gave me a cold, alien feeling like being eaten alive by a great white shark, or standing on another planet where everything was incomprehensible."

"I was attempting to portray my understanding of the people who have been invading and trying to destroy Oneiro."

"Not bad, Mike. Perhaps you do understand them, at least as much as you want to."

The phone rang and Phil picked it up.

"What do you need, Rachael?" Mike frowned at the sudden frostiness in Phil's voice.

"Phil, there's a ship. A boat. I suppose a gun boat, in Proteus Harbor. It seems to be armed to the teeth and ready for a fight. I'm not sure about the armaments, but I do know they have a high-powered deck gun and they've already killed about ten people. Very messy."

"What colors is she flying? Is she flying colors?"

"Colors?"

"Whose fucking boat is it goddamnit?!"

Rachael was aiming and attempting to focus binoculars "Oh...I see...its got ah...no flag...but I do see some writing on the hull, Farsi I think...must be Arabic of some sort."

"Shit! Where are you?"

"I'm in one of the gun emplacements above the harbor entrance."

"Open fire now. Everything you've got. I'm on my way."

"No dessert today, Mike. Please return to your quarters. We may need you guys. Can you put your people on standby... just in case?"

"I'm on my way, Phil. What the hell is going on?"

"I really don't know. Doesn't sound good. I'm damned sure going to find out. Why can't people stop screwing with us?!"

By the time Phil arrived, the gunship was already at the bottom of the harbor and they were clearing away the dead and injured. Rachael was nowhere to be seen.

"What happened here?" Phil asked the watch commander.

"They just drove up to the harbor entrance and opened fire. They killed mainly people who were here on a day off having fun. Those bastards gave no warning and didn't seem to be at all selective who died. It's almost as if they just wanted to raise hell."

"Oh crap! Diversionary tactic?"

"Damn! I think you're right."

"Give me your radio. Rachael? Rachael? Where the hell are you? Over."

No response.

"Rachael, please respond. I need status and location. Over."

"Rachael respond. Status and location. Over."

"Rachael respond. Status and location. Over."

"Mr. Carr? This is Richard Costa at the airfield. There are about forty paratroopers on the ground or still descending. We've taken some casualties and taken out some of theirs. But the main force is driving toward the underground entrances. Over."

"Acknowledged. Alert Security and concentrate all forces there immediately. Focus on the underground southwest wing connecting with the Mansion. Contact Mike Auslander and tell him to provide any assistance wherever he can deploy it, particularly in the labs. Deadly force is ordered. I'll be there in ten minutes. Out."

Phil turned to the harbor watch commander. "Stay here with a minimal force. Watch for more intruders. If any more show up, blow "em to hell. Send everyone else to the airfield, armed, ready, orders to kill on sight. Immediately. And I need a gun."

"Yes, sir." He handed Phil an M4 Assault Rifle with eight extra clips. "Familiar with it?"

"Yes."

"We have a fast funicular from this emplacement to the top. You'll find a jeep ready. From there it's a fast run to the airfield. You'll make it in eight minutes."

"Perfect. Thanks. Stay on the air."

When he reached four hundred meters, Phil took a flying leap from the funicular lift cage to the ground and into the jeep in two smooth movements. The jeep jumped to life and came about instantly, grinding out clouds of brown flinty dust as all four wheels spun, driving the loose dry topsoil cascading over the cliff-line, uneven brown clouds glittering mica in the bright sun, drifting down to the sea.

Phil bounced and rattled his way cross-country to the southwest—the fastest route to the airfield. He carefully slowed the jeep well in time to minimize sound and dust clouds as he neared his target. Luckily, the prevailing wind was fairly brisk from the east.

Nearly idling up to the site, he stopped in a dry wash. Peering out, he saw that most of the assault force had already found their way underground. A few bodies were scattered around the runway, their motionless supine images wavering in the heat. A repellent sight.

A minimal force was left to guard their rear. Luckily, the ground force was deployed facing only the compound and the airfield. Their attention was totally fixed on defense troops boxed in the underground egress from the compound. He had a clear field of attack from their rear. Sloppy.

He noted a few huge, venerable Sea Knight helicopter troop transports circling high above. These would probably provide air disengagement for senior troops. He assumed the remainder of the force would be withdrawn by sea. He fervently hoped the choppers weren't in contact with rear guard.

Whatever. He had to cap this end of the pipeline for starters.

The rear echelon consisted of one machine gun emplacement surrounded by roughly fifteen ground troops in a half-moon formation, enveloping the compound's underground entrances. Easy.

First gear, max revs, nearly airborne onto the machine gun bunker. Three instantly dead, shot, crushed and burned. From the bunker he ran a zig-zag course to the right, firing short bursts as he ran. His own speed and agility astounded even himself. Four minutes later, with some assistance from Oneirion forces, only five were left alive. Someone had shot the heel cleanly off his left shoe!

He crawled into a slight depression in the hot sand at the far right-hand flank of the guard formation, sharing it briefly with a newly dead trooper. Despite himself he wasted valuable moments shooing flies from a gaping wound in the man's neck.

As he reloaded, he noticed several things. He was not out of breath, or tired, or hot, or afraid. He was ready to end this skirmish. Bullets were buzzing all around him. Not one even close. All wild shots thanks to the heat haze and consequent dust. He signaled the island guards and jumped up and led them in, killing the remaining five within minutes. He never really broke a sweat. Aside from a lost heel, a stone splinter embedded deep into his thigh, and an inexplicable cut on his left cheek, he was effectively unhurt by his part in the combat.

All that remained of the mute battle scene were dead paratroopers and three dead island guards. Phil Carr and six security guards were very alive. He watched the raider's transport helicopters rise high into the sky and swiftly retreat. Tiny dots seeking the horizon. Two Apache Helicopters exited their hangar and disappeared within seconds, below the cliff line, above the harbor area. Suddenly, they re-emerged and raced towards the receding transports. Moments later, two tiny, white vapor trails connected with their prey with stunning speed. Two small blossoms of mute fire, dissipating black smoke, and tumbling debris. The Apaches broke off and began patrolling the island's parameter.

The paratroopers who had attacked the underground complex had been very poorly briefed. They clearly had no idea how well prepared and well-equipped Oneiro was for such contingencies. Were they to invade the University of California at Los Angeles, twenty times Oneiro's size, they would have had far better success, and much less resistance.

The terrorists were well equipped professionals, with automatic weapons, RPGs, hand grenades, gas, everything, but they had no idea how deadly their adversary could be. They were nearly all dead and defeated in less than one hour. However, they had made it as far as Halios Mansion and had nearly achieved access to the labs. They had killed eighty two Oneirons and injured another one-hundred and thirty-three. They were unsuccessful, but they were deadly.

Amongst the airfield casualties was Rachael. She was probably the first Oneirion to die in the engagement.

Phil collapsed on the hot, sticky, black dust of the airfield's tarmac, holding Rachael's lifeless face in his hands, as he gently stroked her hair. Her life blood darkly ebbing, mixing with his own, forming a burgundy halo around her still lovely features.

He had never felt more like a base, self-serving bastard in his entire life. He had brought her here. She had helped him more than she knew. Hell, more than he knew. He had turned on her. He might have hurt her deeply. If nothing else, he had cruelly turned away her attempts to help him. He, in his way and by his part, was partly the instrument of her death. A valiant death at that.

He had always desired her and she, probably, him. Maybe there was even a certain love lurking there, awaiting the courage and tenderness to kindle it. Neither the desire, nor the love would ever be conceived, nor find joy now.

He couldn't *wrap* this one. This one was not going to go away. He was learning the length and breath of true, well-earned guilt. He would bear this the rest of his life. Silent tears ran down his face, mingling with the blood already dry on his cheek.

Unbidden, the question echoed, "When could he find some peace and a modicum of complacency in this place?" He was never more sure that the answer was an icy, dispassionate death-knoll...NEVER.

"Mr. Carr? Mr. Carr? I think you need to return to the Mansion sir."

"What? What now?"

"They're calling for you, sir. Dr. Winchester."

As he found his way to the Mansion, several staffers provided him status, body and injured counts. He had to admit the damage was amazingly minimal considering the nature and equipment of their invaders.

Among other odd things during the battle, the Apaches took out a huge gunboat disguised as a fishing trawler. The trawler had initiated aggressive shelling of Proteus Cavern Harbor, which provoked counter assaults from the Apaches. For some reason, the boat exploded, was completely destroyed, after taking on only one or two Hellfire Missiles from the attack helicopters.

In the back of his mind, Phil realized *he was going to have to make a call on these boys. This was growing tiresome and far too dangerous. Too many had died already. He must act with total finality. This must end.* A reckoning was inescapable. There was going to be hell's own to pay, one way or another. Inescapably and mercilessly, more blood would flow.

"Are there any prisoners?"

"One, sir. Fairly high ranking I think, based on his equipment and placement in the assault. He is in the hospital, expected to recover. Too damned bad, if you ask me."

"I didn't ask you. What equipment?"

"Radio-phone, .45 automatic, maps, Mylar vest, fancy red beret instead of a helmet, nothing else, last to land."

"Make damned sure he *does* recover. Keep him under the *tightest* twenty-four-hour security. He will see and speak to no one and no one will know he even exists except you, me, and the medics. Tell them this is Top Secret, tell no one. Give me hour-by-hour updates on his status. I want to see him as soon as he can communicate. You are personally responsible for this entire matter. Clear?"

"Yessir."

"*Clear?*"

"I fully understand. He will survive. No one except security and medical will know. I will advise you of status and you will know when he can talk."

"Fine. Go to him now and leave him under no circumstance."

When Phil arrived at the Mansion, he was directed to the dining room. Dr. Enoch Winchester met him and, after a sympathetic penetrating stare, escorted him to the terrace wall overlooking the sea.

After a few moments, Winchester said wistfully, "kind of reminds you of Captain Aheeb doesn't it?"

"It's pronounced 'Ahab'...'*Ayeee-Haaab.*'"

"What?"

"I said 'Ahab,' the doomed captain of the Peaquod. You pronounced it '*Aah-heeb.*'"

"Whatever-the-hell," Winchester said irritably. "What do we do now?"

"Beats me." Phil murmured absently, running fingers through sandy hair, feeling very surreal perched on the side of a cliff nearly four hundred meters above a blinding sea, shattering against an uneven margin of enormous, craggy rocks.

Wedged between two of these rocks was the beaten, lifeless body of Dr. Craig Webber. The doctor's left arm was traumatically broken, nearly separated at the shoulder, and rhythmically waving at them in concert with the ebb and flow of the tide—hence Winchester's mispronounced allusion to the unfortunate Captain Ahab, blindly beckoning farewell as Melville's great white whale bore him to his icy black *moira*. The doctor's eyes were open, expressing surprise, more than fear or torment. Beyond his arm, and the fact he was not breathing, he looked disquietingly unexceptional.

One of the attackers had run across Dr. Webber, obviously briefed on who he was and what he looked like, and had simply thrown the helpless aging scholar over the wall. Mindless, brutal, murderous terrorism...one could say "of the worst sort," but all terrorism is "of the worst sort."

"What did they want, Phil?"

"I'm not exactly sure. I think they wanted to steal or destroy our work in artificial oil production. As I said, I'm not sure... but I'm damned sure going to find out. Assign someone to retrieve Dr. Webber's body...all the bodies...and arrange some sort of ceremony at sea."

Phil thought of Rachael dead, Craig dead, and all the others slaughtered in the attack. He anticipated his interview with the assault team leader. Many motivators competed within him. Screaming Hate. A slavering thirst for revenge. The passionless requirement for information. The need to act quickly. A hot blood lust. Crushing blind rage. He was frightened, nervous, sickened, and ready to get back some of his own.

These bastards warranted any type of treatment, all of it classified as torture, or hostage taking. Phil reviewed the diverse objectives of these treatments.

Break the subject's will, acquire their acquiescence, and even their support. *He could use an asshole like that if he had the patience and the time. He had neither.*

Simply kill the subject providing as much pain as possible. *Sounds good, wish he could.*

Employ the subject as a lever to extort others. *Extort who? If he knew that he'd just shoot the SOB in the hospital room and be done with it.*

Acquire information as quickly and accurately as possible, and then be done with the vermin. *No choice.*

Phil was trapped. The upcoming interview sickened him. He had searched with near desperation for another course of activity. None was forthcoming. This had to be done and it had to be done by Phil. He wouldn't delegate it to another, and he couldn't trust another. The job was his. What was the Officer of the Court shtick in this type of situation…without passion or prejudice? They should have included cruelty and efficiency as well. Anyway, a long, nerve wracking thirty-six hours later, Phil was shown into the prisoner's hospital room, and a grotesque new door in his life was beckoning him to enter.

"You will please leave me and the prisoner alone. No one will enter this room without my authorization under any circumstances. No exceptions."

"Yessir."

Phil turned a frosty gaze onto the prisoner. The prisoner was restrained by heavy leather straps at his head, wrists, waist, and ankles.

"Do you speak English?"

"Of course."

"What is your name?"

The prisoner's response was sullen silence.

"What is your name?"

An epithet from his youth suddenly ignited in his mind, enraging him. *Kaa-Koo-Kaa!*

Sullen silence was followed by the subdued cracking sound of a finger being broken backwards at its base, and a surprised agonized scream.

"What is your name?"

"… Abdul Fattah. Captain in the Martyrs of the Holy Black …"

"… Your 'unit' holds no interest for me. Who sent you here?"

Silence.

"Who sent you here? Who do you report to?"

Silence.

"Answer me."

Silence, followed by the sickening squishy sound of a finger forcefully inserted into an eye socket just far enough not to kill. Deafening scream.

"Who sent you here? And I will know if you are lying, believe me, you son of a bitch."

"Prince Rashid al din Ammar."

"Saudi?"

"He lives in Saudi Arabia. Yes."

"Jeddah?"

"Yes."

"And who does he work for?'

"I don't know."

Phil broke another finger and waited until the man quieted.

"Who does he work for?"

The man whimpered "I don't know. I really don't. I swear."

"Swear by Allah."

"I swear by Allah."
"Why did you send only forty men?"
"We had only one objective."
"Our oil synthesis technology?"
"Yes."
"With what objective?"
"Confiscate and destroy."
"You've been defeated. Will he attack again?'
"I promise you he will. You will all die."
Phil ached to kill this bastard right now.

"I will send in a doctor to tend to your wounds and quell your pain. You will be our guest here. We will provide you the best of care. We will keep you safe and secret. No one will know you are alive. You will be asked no further questions. You may pray, and we will give you anything you need, within reason.

Listen carefully to me now. If you are lying to me, you will finally learn real pain and true agony. You will pray to Allah for death. It will not be forthcoming. This, I promise you, because I will personally take wonderful pleasure in making your life something beyond the nightmares of hell itself. Your body will become an object that would make the strongest and the cruelest of men vomit in horror. Something unclean and truly obscene. Do you understand me?

"Yes."

"Do you understand me?" With that he slapped his prisoner so hard his hand tingled.

"Yes. Yes I do."

"Do you wish to change any statement you have made?"

"No." he whimpered.

He slapped him again, just as hard. "Do you wish to change any statement?"

"No. I am telling you the truth. I swear."

Philip turned and left the room.

"Send in a doctor. Give him the best of care. Full security. No suicide. I want him in perfect condition. If he won't eat, force-feed him. If he won't drink, put him on a drip. Do not fail me. You are still personally responsible. Understood?"

"Absolutely. Yes, sir, I do."

Screw it. Let the Lord get His Own Date

Vengeance is Mine Sayeth the Lord
Leviticus—Old Testament

"Howard, Rachael is dead.

"Don't say anything. You don't want to know about it, and I don't want to talk about it. We still have work to do.

I have two transfer orders on my desk in front of me. One is for two million US Dollars, payable to your firm. The other is for one million US Dollars payable directly to you. I want some help and I want some boys. This is for a grab and it's not in your precious DUS. Interested?

"Jesus Christ, Phil! You sound really bad. I want to help. I really do. But not if you've gone nuts! For Chrissake you personally greased a guy in Newark."

"Goddamnit, Howard. Yes or no?"

Phil could hear Howard tapping a finger on his desk at the other end.

"Give me some details, Phil."

"Simple job. Your boys will grab a Prince Rashid al din Ammar out of Jeddah, Saudi Arabia. Take him to a safe house somewhere in Europe. Someplace remote. Hold him there until I arrive. Full stop."

"Phil, are you going to do this work yourself, *again*?"

"Howard, you're starting to…"

"Okay. Four million for my firm. I can live with one million."

"Sold. Let me know when and where you have him. Take good care of him. I'll be there as soon as I can. Then leave him to me. This is deepest black. Understood?"

"Okay, Phil. This scares hell out of me..."

"That's why I'm forking over five million. And for that amount I want a dossier on the Prince so detailed I'll know how many freckles he's got on his ass, and I want it fast. We'll wire the payments today. Keep me posted." Phil put the phone down, with no good-byes, no good-lucks.

Three weeks later, Phil landed in Madrid, hired a jeep, and headed away from the city into the desert land far to the east. Thank God for the GPS.

Seven hours later, he arrived at a deserted farm house—nothing in sight in any direction, from horizon to horizon. Another dusty jeep stood outside the rickety building in the shimmering heat. Phil entered without knocking. Two very large, sweaty, and unshaven men were sitting at a makeshift table drinking beer and smoking. Dusty work boots, faded blue shirts and frayed jeans. Spanish ham, cheese, and stale bread detritus in abundance. Clearly, these two were not homemakers. Phil was pleased he had stopped at a grocery store and a hardware on his way. They peered at him wordlessly.

"Where is he?" Phil asked without preliminaries.

"Follow me."

They walked to a storage shed behind the house. It was suffocatingly hot, dirty, with flies everywhere, but it had a sturdy door. They unlocked the door and, in the hot, cobwebbed, gloomy interior was Rashid al din, one leg chained by a large steel ring, squinting at Phil through a galaxy of dust glowing from the afternoon sun slanting through dingy cracked windows.

The steel ring was attached to a chain leading under the wall, firmly fixed to a scrubby tree standing outside the shed. Phil looked at him closely and compared him to a photo provided by Howard. It certainly looked like Rashid. Phil walked up to the man, pulled him to his feet, ripped open his shirt and forcefully turned him around. On his back were two marks, a mole in a grotesquely uneven shape of a clover and a scar, clearly made by a knife in a sort of zigzag pattern. Phil pushed him against the wall and forced his lips apart. He had a gold canine tooth. Next, he took finger prints and blood type. Positive verification.

"It's him. Well done. Leave him chained. Get the chair and use these cords to secure him. I want his body totally immobilized. Head to toe. Then you may leave."

They tied Rashid firmly into the chair, bound him from elbow to wrists to the arms of the chair and secured his head to a board attached to the back of the chair. Finally, his legs were bound and Rashid al din was totally immobile.

Fifteen minutes later, Phil and Rashid were alone.

"Do you know who I am?"

Rashid acknowledged in the affirmative with a wry smile and the slightest of nods.

Phil favored him with a humorless smile. "Believe it or not, you may survive this. Unlike you and the murderous thugs that work for you, I don't kill casually, or for fun, or money, or any of the other bogus bullshit you bastards claim to worship. This is, however, going to be extremely uncomfortable for both of us. I caution you not to lie to me about anything whatsoever.

I know you speak English. I know when and where you were born. The name of the hospital. Your parents. Your wives. Your children. Where you were educated. How much you're worth. The foods you like. Where you like to shop in the Middle East, in Europe, in the US. I know the names of your mistresses, your whores, and your secret boyfriends. I know what size underwear you buy, how many times you've had VD, your favorite liquor, and on and on. So don't even think about lying to me. I'll know, and you will suffer like hell for it. Clear?"

Silence.

"*Clear?*"

Silence.

"You really are a dumb bastard you know that?"

Phil took a pair of pliers and crushed Rashid's left thumb into a red pulpy mush, a bloody fingernail falling to the floor into a pool of dark blood. His screams were deafening.

After a few moments …

"Clear?"

Pause. Heavy gasping for breath. Some vomit.

"Clear?" A slight tilt to Phil's head and a very threatening edge in Phil's voice.

"Yes." Almost a whisper.

"Okay. We're going to get on fine. We'll take this in small, easy stages. We'll learn to trust each other and I'll treat you well. Are you hungry? Thirsty? Want a little water, cognac?"

"Cognac."

"Would you like an aspirin as well?"

"Yes."

Phil placed an aspirin in his mouth and slowly, carefully poured cognac down his throat. "Better?"

Swallowing with some difficulty and coughing at the strong cognac he finally grunted "Yes."

"Shall we start now, or would you like to rest awhile?"

Phil could read the surprise and mistrust on his face. "Rest."

"Okay, I'll leave you for about an hour. I'll leave the door open and maybe this room will cool off a little. After that, I'll feed you and then we'll start.

But first, let me be totally honest with you about me, up front. First, I'm not a professional at this sort of thing. You probably know that. Far from it in fact. That means I'm going to be clumsy, which will in all likelihood make this all the more messy for you and all the more horrid for me. I suppose I apologize in advance, if you can understand that.

Second, I must...I *must* have the information you have. I know another attack is imminent. I know your objective is to kill us all now. I want this information. I will do anything... *anything* to get it. Believe me in this. Therefore, it was important that I do this thing myself. You have to face *me* in this matter. You have to face me personally. You have to face me. There is no choice for either of us.

Third, I have *no time*. Give me what I must have and you're out of here fast and possibly alive. Otherwise, I will brutalize the hell out of you and you'll still be out of here fast, but I wouldn't want to look at you. You will be horrible in your death. If you give me what I need. I will leave you here alive, with water and a great deal of money. You can go anywhere; hide anywhere, unobstructed by mc. Everything I have told you is absolute truth. I swear this to you."

Phil left, leaving the door open as promised. He went to the jeep, poured himself a stiff drink, and took a nap himself. Forty-five minutes later he opened a can of beans, some sausages and some cold beer, fed himself, and took the same meal into Rashid al din. He fed Rashid, returned to the house, and fetched a chair for himself.

"Okay. Let's get started. Do you know a man named Griffith? Works for a company in the U.S. called DEW?"

"No."

Phil chuckled "Yes you do...that was a test question, so it's for free. You must be totally honest with me now. Phil slapped him with such force that Phil feared for his wrist."

Phil smiled again.

"What's my name?"

"Philip Carr."

"Excellent. We're going to do just fine!" Phil smiled broadly.

"Do you know where I live and work?"

"You are the CEO of an island called Oneiro."

"Good."

"Are you self-employed, or do you report to someone?"

The question elicited a long pause.

"Don't make me ask again, Rashid."

There was another long pause.

"Okay," Phil said. With that he took out an ice pick, gently, carefully, with surgical precision blinded Rashid in his right eye. Ugly, noisy, nauseating. After a time, when the wailing subsided, Phil gently sterilized and bandaged his eye, saying nothing.

He waited for Rashid to regain some control.

"Are you self-employed, or do you report to someone?"

"I work for many states," came the whispered reply.

"A cartel?"

"Of sorts."

"Oil?"

No response.

"Oil?" With that Phil picked up a small hammer and a chisel.

"Yes."

"Who provided you so much information on Oneiro?"

Rashid started to weep.

"Would you like a break?" Phil remembered what he had learned of the nature of mercy...just to stop the torment...for even a moment. *He needed a little mercy himself.* He suspected the counterpoint between savagery and mercy emphasized both and rendered the torture all the more unbearable.

"Please."

"Another cognac and aspirin?"

"Please."

Phil looked after the drink and aspirin and gave Rashid twenty minutes to collect himself.

"Who provided so much information on Oneiro?"

"Mr. Stephen Ryerson."

"He's gone, and you know it. Try again." *Slap!*

"Dr. Sin Oua Siroa."

"He's dead you lying bastard. You have one more chance." The edge in his voice was dreadful to hear. *Slap!*

"Dr. William Gould."

"Prove it to me."

"We recruited Gould to infiltrate the island. We pay him five hundred thousand U.S. Dollars a year to BHG BANK International SA, in Luxembourg. Two annual payments, January and August. Payment is made from the same bank. Gould left UCLA abruptly in mid-term five years ago. I have no other proof. These facts may be verified."

"Good. Very good. One last question and we can stop for the night. Who do you report to?"

"Please. Please. I cannot tell you. I promise."

"Sure you can. Just tell me. You'll feel better, and then we can rest. I'll give you another cognac, some pain killers, and I'll even figure out a way for you to lie down and sleep. Tomorrow, just a few questions and not nearly as difficult. So let's just get this over with and get some rest.

Who do you report to?"

Silence.

"Who do you report to?"

Tearful silence.

"One last time...Who do you report to?"

Nothing. Phil could practically hear Rashid's heart beating. He could taste his fear. He could literally see, even taste, the blood coagulating in his gums and between his teeth. Now was the time to go very slowly. Phil said nothing. Phil showed nothing. He just looked intensely into Rashid's remaining eye and watched him weep. Two, three, four minutes ticked by. Sweat was running down Phil's face as well as Rashid's. Methodically, Phil opened a cloth bag. Inside was a simple pair of large, heavy-duty pruning shears. Phil quietly, gently lifted Rashid's index finger.

"Who do you report to?"

Rashid was whimpering, weeping, and wetting himself.

"Okay." He said softly without emotion.

He cut off Rashid's index finger. Something beyond screaming, a desperate inhuman bray convulsed from his mouth.

Phil cleaned his hands with a damp rag. He then found his lighter and cauterized the bloody stub, eliciting the unending whimpers of Rashid. He was trembling so violently the chair shook. He then bandaged it and gave him another cognac... and had a large one himself. He then carefully laid the gruesome amputation on a dirty, paint-stained sawhorse, very close to Rashid's sweaty, dirt covered face. Rashid couldn't ignore it. Sure enough, Rashid couldn't tear his eyes away from his sickening blotchy member. After ten minutes ...

"Who do you report to?"

Silence.

Phil sighed theatrically. "I grow weary of this. Who do you report to? If you don't answer me, and answer me fast and honestly, I'm going to cut off your trousers. You bloody well know what I will cut off next, don't you?"

"Kiss the mouth of death you motherfuc —"

Phil slapped him nearly senseless. Phil's arms and hands and wrists ached with the effort and he was dripping sweat. Rashid's cheeks ran red with blood. His remaining eye was nearly swollen shut and his mouth caricaturish, bruised and beaten into kissy cartoon lips.

"Okay ..." Phil took out a large, sharp, kitchen knife and started cutting his belt and trousers and underwear.

"Enough. Please. My God. Please. I will tell you." He lisped as though previously uninvolved and now suddenly, desperately aware...this was his problem...body...pain...life.

"Who? You son of bitch. *Who?*" *Slap!*

Face powder white, eyes the size of Christmas Balls, Rashid said, "Count Yegor Petrov. I swear by Allah. I am telling the truth. I tell the truth. I tell truth. Please."

"Where is he based?"

"Odessa."

The Russians are in on this too?! OPEC was just a bunch of boy scouts compared to this crew. This must be where the *real* money, the *private* money was concentrated.

"I need proof Rashid. Prove this to me. Prove this to me Rashid."

A long fearful silence ensued. Rashid knew that without credible corroboration, his retribution would be unspeakable. Philip watched fear and desperation repeatedly play over his visage; frantically searching his mind for something, anything that would mollify his tormentor. Finally after frantically sifting through his memories...

"You knew his son."

"What?"

"You knew his son. You murdered him."

Blind outrage. Phil fiercely punched him. Clenched fist. All his weight and strength. Rashid's chair violently crashed onto the dirt floor.

After a time, Phil roughly righted the chair and peered at Rashid with venomous hatred. His nose was not broken. It was pulverized. Unrecognizable as a nose at all. A huge running wound dominating Rashid's ruined face. Blood and dirt and sweat and tears.

Phil screamed at him, spittle flying from his mouth, slavering from his chin. "You fuck with me for one more second and I'll kill you. You murderous, lying, pig! What the hell are you talking about?"

Rashid was nearly unconscious. His head slowly bobbed from side to side. He whispered "I…ab…dot…lying. Griffith. Bop…Bob Griffith…his son. Real dame was Alexi Petrov…thimple to ver…verify."

Phil was stunned.

The puzzle grew more complex. More unclear. More threatening. Phil was convinced this was truth. A grotesque, convoluted truth.

In his rage he had nearly smashed the bulb dangling above his head. Crazy shadows danced everywhere in sharp shadows of sooty blackness and greasy yellow. Phil was dizzy and exhausted. Rashid was nearly dead. The smell permeating the stifling space was nauseating. Urine, feces, sweat, fear, blood, stale cognac and aged filth. He had to finish this obscenity soon. Neither could go on much longer.

"Who got you onto the island to begin with?"

"Wil…Wilcoxen."

Oh crap. Crap. Crap! Wilcoxen.

"He was President of the goddamned Island for Christ's sake. Where did *he* come from? Who brought him in?"

Silence. A hard punch in the crotch, followed by a subdued moaning.

"Where did he come from?"

"Thome company...Ah...ThSkorpen Under-thsea thsomething..." coughing and choking on own blood.

Good grief. Full circle. Wilcoxen and Skorpen Undersea Technologies from the very beginning! He'd been handpicked by the bad guys from the get-go, way back in New York. Why? Maybe they had learned his true parentage? Perhaps they thought his relationship with Dr. Webber would make him a gullible dupe? Or for some reason wanted no living heirs.

Maybe they killed Michael? Maybe even his parents? Maybe Skorpen was pissed with him about the North Sea oil deal and wanted to set him up for the kill? He had cost them many millions of Dollars. What a murderous deceitful maize! Well, he'd never know now. Wilcoxen was dead and he imagined that Skorpen had battened down all hatches. They'd be tight as a clam now. All the same, someday he'd rip the scab from that entire crud pocket and there would be people who would pay dearly. *My ass, revenge gains nothing. Sunday School be damned, he was living for it Goddamnit.*

He looked down at his prisoner for a long time. Finally, he spoke. "Fine, Rashid. You've done well. I thank you. You've been very brave indeed. You can relax now. We're finished for tonight. Tomorrow will be much easier. I promise. One last question though. Don't answer if you don't wish to.

Before we got into this entire cloak and dagger foolishness and the butchery that followed, why didn't you just come to me? I probably would have found a way to sell you license for third generation bio-fuel production. Hell, I might have even *given* it to you. *Why?*"

Rashid peered at him for a moment "You...doe...why."

"Yes, Rashid, I suppose I do. Thank you, Rashid. Now you can sleep. No more questions. None tomorrow either. It's over. Rest."

Rashid reflected on his garden far away on the Lisbon coast. How lovely. The flowers, the gentle sun, quiet, peaceful, shimmering brooks. The joy of a good book and a quiet, solitary lunch. Solitary. He realized for the first time in years how much he cared for his wife. How poorly he had treated her. How poorly he had treated many. Fear and pain, an icy relentless wrenching deep within him. Not long now. He choked on tears and moans and loneliness.

Phil quietly removed his bonds and cleared an area where he could lie down. He then gave him another aspirin and cognac liberally laced with cyanide.

Phil and Rashid waited together in the sudden, profound silence. Eyes intensely exploring eyes. They had journeyed the freezing pits of hell itself together, yet no bond was forged. No common ground. Forever...*alien*.

No *intempestivus*, no *modus vivendi*, no *pax pacis* forthcoming. Ever.

Then it hit.

Crippling spasms. Uncontrollable twitches. Eyes crazed in torment and horror...sightlessly staring. Long moments later, mercifully dead.

Phil had had no choice. No way could he allow him to live. Rashid al din knew he was a dead man as soon as he had been picked up...either at the hands of Phil or Yegor Petrov. He was human excrement anyhow. He was just another filthy

Kaa-Koo-Kaa. Hundreds had died because of this monster. He had murdered Rachael. He had murdered Craig. *He wanted to murder me.* He was saving lives this way. However, none of this rationale made Phil feel any better. He felt sick. Sick to the point of nausea.

He retrieved a gas can from his jeep and covered the house, the body, the shed, everything in gasoline. Using his cauterizing lighter he burned everything to the ground. The flames, huge and intense, seemed to light the dark desert sands in all directions....flickering and ebbing to the distant horizons.

Nothing was left, not a crust of bread, not a fingernail, not a candy wrapper. Anything that might have survived would be disposed of by the wild dogs, the ants, the mice, and the scorpions—right down to the bones themselves.

Phil went to his jeep. He had one bottle of cognac remaining. He drank it without savor or pleasure, or even thought. He just sat in the jeep and drank it down like medicine, grimly pondering the clear, cold, star-frosted heavens.

He then plummeted into a dark, fitful sleep. Nightmarish images—most of his own making—haunted and terrorized him relentlessly throughout the frigid, dark hours. Dogs howled, bats flew in every direction, snakes slithered, scorpions copulated, and desert mice scurried everywhere amongst the still smoking debris. Devils and monsters and horror and slaughter. Night's harvest.

Sunrise on the desert at this time is spectacular. The sun is huge as it approaches its summit. As night's terminator silently races over the death scene, shadows rise, etched so sharply they look like black and red and gold lines carefully measured on bare canvas. The enormous, blinding, reddish gold sun glared down on Phil, his jeep, and his crusty red eyes. Already hot, the night desert winds had subsided and no air moved at all. Any remaining smoke rose arrow straight far into the dry air. Hesitantly, painfully, exhausted, Phil stirred to wakefulness.

The nauseating blend of gasoline, burned wood, seared flesh, and charred garbage hung like a haze over the scene and tortured his nostrils.

Once he had acclimated somewhat to the light and the swelter, he re-traced yesterday's horrors in his mind. Nothing occurred he had not carefully planned in advance. Yet it still sickened him. He felt his entire being a pustulent corruption of evil itself. It was.

Merciful God! Some cognac remained.

Phil greedily poured the cognac down his throat, and then vomited and vomited and vomited until there was nothing more to retch. And still he vomited.

Cognac. Mistake. Maybe fatal. He shook uncontrollably, sweat poured down his face, nausea induced tears streaked down his sooty face, and he could hardly stand. He was filthy, unshaven, and smelled. He just lay there on the gritty, scorched, burning sand, heating and dehydrating. He needed water desperately, but none remained.

Hundreds of feet above the death scene, a bronzed Peregrine Falcon blazed out of the sun probing the unexpected find far below. Its acute golden eyes were as dispassionate and cold as the god that fashioned the setting. The small spectacle swirled and blurred below with multicolored sand, smoking debris, a dusty jeep, scorched stone ruins, and...a *human body*. It moved slightly. The body was disappointingly alive. With the flick of a feather, an unearthly screech, the flash of eye, and an iron clinch of a fierce, sinewy talon the scene was fast forgotten far behind.

Never in his life had he felt such a profound, melancholy loneliness. Terrifyingly...alone, he felt not the presence, not even the whisper of a shadow of a friend, an enemy, a fellow being...nothing. He could not even sense the substance of his own existence. He was deaf, blind, alone, empty, gone. In the midst of darkest infinity he was alone. Not even himself for company. Death would be a tender, dark mercy.

He silently wept as he slowly, agonizingly buried his hands into the burning sand, raising shoulders, head, and sightless eyes to the streaked, golden, rose-hued sky, mouth agape, breathing labored, neck painfully extended upward, like a lost, dying, vernal creature seeking its god and the slightest measure of compassion.

In his pathetic desperation, he crawled unseeing, with almost imperceptible movement, instinctively towards the west...impotently fleeing the giant star...ascending in blinding splendor from the east.

So It Is...So It Shall Remain

Mercifully, he collapsed into unconsciousness, surrendering to exhaustion and horror and pain.

Hours later, he recovered his senses sufficiently to stagger back to the jeep, swallow a few hot unctuous drops from its radiator, and made his way slowly back to Madrid, stopping in numb, leaden gratitude wherever water or a cold beer could be found, shakily, animal-like, greedily sucking it down.

Was this the way of the rest of his life?

What had he done? He had fought and had won. He won what he had needed...what they all had needed. What the *world* needed. He was sure of it. What had he visited upon himself in the process? Guilt. He was guilty of murder and torture.

He had read somewhere we were not bodies that harbored souls...we were souls that harbored bodies. If that were true, then he was as a dead, empty, opaque, carapace, rolling and swirling about in the shallows and tide pools of a lonely, near sterile, inland sea...picked clean by hungry scavengers. Not a bit of sweet, white meat left uneaten or soul to enrich its existence. Nothing of goodness or value remaining.

Mirror Mirror

If only there were evil people somewhere insidiously committing evil deeds, and it were necessary only to separate them from the rest of us and destroy them. But the line dividing good and evil cuts through the heart of every human being.

Alexandr Solzhenitsyn

A very different, very subdued Philip Carr entered the conference room, mid-afternoon, two days later. He was lucky he had a First Class return ticket and First Class was empty. Otherwise, they would have never allowed him to board the aircraft. He looked five years older, he looked gaunt, pale, and maybe four pounds lighter. His hands shook; he was unshaven, unwashed, and generally rumpled. He still smelled of sweat and blood and oily smoke. He had skipped breakfast and was just finishing his lunch, the second of two large tumblers filled to the brim with straight scotch.

Atrophy and entropy. The first: The apathetic wasting away of a human mind and body. The second: The lethargic wasting away of the universe itself. Phil could literally taste the coppery, inevitable, squander and malignancy of both.

He had devoted the morning, locked away in his bedroom ignoring the intermittent knocking by Edward, contemplating his portrait painted by Mike Auslander. As he had fully expected, the portrait had massively degenerated. Despite his foresight of this, Phil was devastated and horrified nonetheless.

He knew the painting was only forcing him to impose his own self-image upon it. The oils and pigments weren't magically changing. But perhaps that was even worse. Worse because it was nearer the truth.

He recalled Oscar Wilde's book, *The Picture of Dorian Gray*. Much as in that haunting Gothic novel, his portrait graphically shocked him with the changes and the corruption now festering in him. The last few horrific weeks, the monstrous acts he had inflicted on other beings, the obscenities he had witnessed, and it still wasn't over. It was close though. It was goddamn close. He would finish quickly and cleanly and then find a way, some way, to regain some modicum of grace in his life. Get that portrait back into some semblance of sanity.

His innocence had moved on, along with many of his friends and even his enemies, never to play a role in his life again. But perhaps he could salvage something of the Philip Carr that had left New York on a one-way voyage into this abyss...he had no choice...he must try. He had to climb out somehow.

But first, he had one short meeting and two short phone calls. After that he would go out on the terrace and get good and goddamned drunk...go back to work tomorrow...then take some time.

A gravely concerned Edward entered the conference room. "Can I get anything for you, sir?"

"Hello, Edward. Yes, please. Please have Cindy get Howard in Chicago on the phone if it's not too early there, and then have her instruct Dr. Gould to join me here in half an hour. I don't care what else he may be engaged in."

"Right away, sir. Phil, you look terrible. You look worse than terrible, Phil. Can I help? Would you like to talk? Shouldn't you take some time off? Rest? See Dr. Gear?"

"Thank you, Edward. I appreciate your concern. The last days have been a nightmare, beyond hell's own. I do plan on taking a week or so off starting the day after tomorrow. In fact, can you get me a flight to Lefkada?"

"I'll look after everything. I don't suppose I could interest you in some lunch?"

"No thank you. But a tall bottle of gin, a few bottles of tonic and some ice would not be unwelcome on the terrace in about forty-five minutes."

Edward nodded grimly and left the room.

"Howard in Chicago on the line for you Mr. Carr."

"Thank you, Cindy."

"Hello, Howard you're up damned early. How are you?"

"How are *you,* Phil?"

"Howard, dogs shit things that are better than me today. I do apologize if I've been an SOB lately. We've been going through hell itself over here. Your boys did a fine job by the way. I thank you."

"Glad to help, Phil. Ah, anything I can do for you today?"

"One last job, Phil. We've nearly cut the head off the snake. We've even killed most of the body. One more cut and the game is over, maybe permanently. Charge whatever you like. I mean it. Speed is not of the essence but would be appreciated. Just like the first job in Moscow. Swift, clean disappearance. No witnesses. No traces. Never seen again."

"Who's the subject?"

"Count Yegor Petrov in Odessa. Back to Russia."

"Holy shit! You don't screw around do you?"

"I don't pick 'em, Howard."

"I understand. Should go for at least four bills. We'll use the same provider. I'll keep you posted."

"Thanks, Howard. We should meet for a day or so sometime, somewhere like a boat on the Caribbean and kick this whole mess around, floating around in rum and lobsters."

"Sounds good. I'd like that, Phil. Let's do it soon. I'll confirm when this job is completed."

"Cindy, please get our new Director of Security, Mr. Ted Richards, on the line.

"Hello, Mr. Richards, Phil Carr here. How are you?"

"Are you familiar with the military term, 'Blood Stripes,' sir?"

"Of course I am."

"Well, I don't like 'em. That's how I am."

"Nobody does, Ted. I'm as sorry as you about Rachael."

"What can I do for you, Mr. Carr?"

"Our prisoner Abdul Fattah. Still well?"

"Yes."

"Under any medication?"

"Yes. He's on a twenty-four hour drip: Antibiotics and painkillers in a saline solution. He's pretty out of it. His forebrain was damned near breached by an inserted finger." *Did he hear accusation in Richard's voice?*

"Understood. Get down there, put on a lab coat and stethoscope, and inject a cyanide solution into his drip. I've already instructed Doctor...Doctor...wait one." Phil consulted his notes. "Dr. *Hanson* has prepared the hypodermic injection for you. See him. Then cremate his body and bury the ashes at sea.

"One other thing, Ted. Dr. Gould may be leaving my apartment in just a few minutes. Put a man on him. He is not to leave this island by any means, under any circumstances. If there's a problem, killing force is authorized. But be discrete. Clear?"

"I understand, Mr. Carr."

"In a few hours, Dr. Gould will probably have committed suicide in his apartment. If that's the case, then please dispose of him the same way as Abdul Fattah."

"Things are getting pretty tough around here, Mr. Carr."

"You're wrong, Ted. Things *have been* very tough around here, but it's over now. *Insha Allah.*"

"I'll look after it."

"Thank you. I hope to meet you personally soon, Ted. Good-bye."

Ten minutes later, Phil was ready for his guest. "Come in, Dr. Gould. Have a seat."

"Morning Phil. How are...*good grief, are you alright?*"

"Do I look alright, you son of a bitch?"

Gould turned very pale, remained silent.

"I left Prince Rashid al din Ammar a day or so ago. He looked even worse than I do. Sends his regards by the way... for the very last time."

Phil's statement was met with a subdued silence.

"I've a little gift for you, Doctor." Phil removed a small glass bottle with a plastic top from his coat pocket. Inside was one small white pill. "Do you know what this is?"

"Cyanide?" asked Gould in a very soft voice.

"Right the first time, Doctor, and unless you are a remarkable swimmer, it is completely impossible for you to leave this island. You have two choices. You can return to your quarters, take this little pill, and exit with some dignity. Or I can kill you right now and throw you off my terrace into the sea. You know bloody well I can do it, so make your choice, *right now*. Personally, I'd rather enjoy throwing you four hundred meters into the sea, so don't fuck with me."

Gould reached forward with trembling hand and placed the small bottle in his vest pocket. The two locked eyes for a moment. A hushed pleading in Gould's eyes. Cold contempt in Phil's. Gould wordlessly departed the room.

Later, on his terrace, Phil had nearly finished the bottle of gin. The combination of scotch, gin, sun, fatigue, and a deep fugue-like depression weren't militating well on him. He appeared to be nearly catatonic, looking vacantly out to sea, unmoving.

What had he done to himself? Somewhere in himself he was aware that his actions were necessary, justified, even inescapable. But this was not him. In all his life, he never thought of himself as a killer, a murderer, a brutal torturer, and a devious liar and schemer. He wasn't at all sure he could live with this. He had fashioned his own living, breathing, heart-pounding purgatory. He felt his mind breaking, degenerating, atrophying in degradation and guilt. Guilt, the most difficult thing to live with in all the world. His mind started to wander aimlessly, exploring his past, the present, and places and things that didn't even exist. All the while, some degree of animation returned. His stomach churned. His head throbbed. His hands trembled, and his lips quivered.

He thought back to his early youth in Washington, D.C. He went to Sunday school every week, making the short walk to the local Methodist church in fair weather and foul. His teacher was a Miss Banner...no Baker...no Banner...whoever the hell. When she didn't have them singing, "Jesus Loves Me, This I know", or "Onward Christian Soldiers," or something equally inane, Miss Banner was describing the books of the Bible to them, which never made a hellofa lot of sense to Phil. The wording was flowery and obtuse and the reasoning, if there was any, was lost on him.

However, for weeks, she had promised his class a session on *The Book of Revelations*...at last some excitement!...assuring them that it would scare the very devil out of them. Something truly frightening. Four Horsemen visiting all manner of horrors, the Apocalypse, Armageddon, a Beast named 666... cool stuff for young kids. Realization of the colossal complacency of the self-contrived *Rapture*.

Phil and his friends looked forward to it eagerly, as they would a spooky movie...and the time finally came.

Yet again, it didn't make much sense to young Philip. Some of the description was pretty cool, but beyond that... then she came to the part about mortal sins. As Phil was taken to understand it (or perhaps misunderstand it), there were some sins that once performed, couldn't really be recanted. For example murder. Once done, you were damned. Upon death no choice but to face the yawing jaws of hell. Rivers of fire. Unending pain and punishment. Degradation, shame and horror in a darkness that goes on until the end of time itself...or until everyone was raised from the grave for a last (Final, second [?] judgment...what the *Hell*?!). No remedy. No appeal. Done deal. Go to hell forever and burn baby. Seemed a bit severe really. Besides, weren't we just doing God's bidding anyway? Then again, there was that "Free Will" stuff to deal with. How irrational! How contradictory! How bloody-minded to put someone his age through. But what the hell did he know anyway? After all he *was* just a kid.

Nonetheless, the dictums of Revelations stirred a strong, reoccurring and irrational fear in Phil. He had nightmares of somehow losing control, his temper, his actions, whatever, and suddenly murdering someone. At that moment, he would be aware, for the rest of his life his inevitable end would be eternal damnation. How perverse, grotesque, meaningless, vindictive! Many a cold sweats. Many a sleepless night. A feeling of fatalism, helplessness, hopelessness. Phil finally started skipping Sunday school altogether and passed sublime Sunday mornings in the lush quietude of Dumbarton Oaks Park trying to forget all about Miss Banner and her smugly complacent, taffeta invectives.

Now, sitting motionless on his terrace overlooking the azure sea, Phil knew that Miss Banner was wrong. She was just wrong. Dead wrong. Phil knew he didn't have to die to face the yawing jaws of hell. He was facing them right now and for the rest of his life. He didn't really believe in heaven, or hell, or purgatory, or any of the rest of the "scare-hell-outa-the-little-bastard" righteous bullshit that had been so beatifically poured into his young ears over enduring years. But he *did* believe in an *internal* hell. He was *living* in it.

He heard a deck chair being moved next to him and he slowly looked up to his left. Anne sat down close to him, her expression unreadable. Phil quietly smiled. "Hi."

"Hi. Edward called me. He's very, *very* upset. He thinks you may be close to death."

No. No. I just don't have that kind of luck these days."

"Can you tell me about it? I think it would help. Please."

"Probably would. Wish I could. I really, really can't though. Besides, I think I'm going to...that is...I think...going to...I'm going to...pass out."

Phil slowly, but decisively, slumped forward, his face on the table, his arms dangling limply below. After a few minutes, Anne and Edward half carried, half dragged him to his bed.

"You know, Dr. Jones, I think Phil may have known what was best for him today. Thank you for coming, though. May I take the liberty of inviting you for lunch here with Phil tomorrow?"

"You certainly may, Edward. I thank you. I suppose you should reconfirm when he's up and about?"

"Good idea. I shall do."

The next morning, Phil felt considerably better. He had covered his portrait with a towel and left it there. He shaved, showered, dressed in a maroon polo shirt and sport trousers, ate a substantial breakfast, and entered his conference room to look after a dozen or so matters that were well overdue. Edward informed him about lunch and Phil was very pleased, so he worked all the faster and more intently.

By 1300, charcoal broiled hamburger steaks, baked potatoes, green beans, a fine chilled rose, and Anne awaited him on the terrace. It was a beautiful day. The golden sun, not too warm, was cooled by the slightest of breezes.

They commenced their lunch without preamble.

"My, but you look like a new man today! Or should I just say a man. Yesterday, you didn't even look human."

"Thank you. I feel much better. Slept right through until 0830 this morning. I hope I behaved alright yesterday. I really don't remember."

"You were a perfect gentleman, for about two minutes. After that you were face down on that table."

"Mmm...it's been a bit of a rough patch recently...more than you know."

"Will I ever know?"

"Doubt it. You really don't want to hear it. The dreams are killing me." He slurred. "Funny, they're saving me too. The chandelier. It's so beautiful. But you don't want to know. Believe me...believe...believe…"

"Phil...are you getting tired again? Phil?"

"Good grief." Phil said, with his forehead in his right hand. "Think I am. Wine was probably a real bad idea." He was suddenly exhausted to the point of collapse and quite dizzy.

Anne helped him to his feet and assisted him into his room. In his bed, she held his head in her lap and lightly stroked his hair. As he drifted off, unknown to Phil, tears were streaming down his face. Once deeply asleep, he continued to weep, utter, inarticulate imprecations, and sob ever so softly.

As she watched him and listened to him, Anne was quietly weeping as well.

Phil slept through to the next morning again, while Edward quietly conducted some research and made a few phone calls. He finally concluded it was too early to diagnose Acute Clinical Depression. Instead, he believed Phil was suffering from some profound trauma. He suspected Phil was the only living human who would ever know its malevolent nature. *God help him. I hope he survives this,* Edward thought.

Soothing Waters

Fall seven times, stand up eight.

Japanese Proverb

Herb was waiting in a jeep not far off the tarmac when Phil descended from the corporate jet, ditty bag in hand. He walked to the jeep, threw his bag in the back, and jumped in. Herb started to turn on the ignition and put the jeep in gear when he suddenly paused in mid-action.

"Holy shit, Phil! Are you sick?"

"No, Uncle Herb. I'm not sick." Phil recited wearily. "I just need a little rest. I've been through a really rough patch and I need to relax for awhile. That's all. Let's go."

"What do you really do for that company, Philly? CEOs don't sit in executive suites and come out looking like you do right now. What the hell is going on? Are you some kind of spook?"

"No. I'm not a damned spook. Let's just leave it alone, Herb. Let's get going. Buy me an Ouzo and then get me to *Sea Tigress*. Please."

Herb moved out without another word. Half an hour later, they were overlooking the sea in one of Herb's favorite bars. He watched with some concern as Phil knocked back his third Ouzo within ten minutes.

"Herb, do you guys have any scuba equipment?"

"No. We don't use the stuff. Thought about it though for hull work and general maintenance."

"Any place we can stop on the way and buy some?"

"Sure, lots of places. Are you thinking about taking up diving?"

"Yep."

"Had any training?"

"Nope. Snorkeled some though. Figured I'd buy a book at the same time, and a compressor as well. You can always use a diesel-powered compressor in the business and I can charge the tanks."

"All by yourself? No training?"

"Yep."

"Look Phil, if you've got a death wish, we've got some excellent rat poison on board...if you like..."

"I would bloody well appreciate it if you never mentioned poison to me again. Clear?"

There followed an awkward silence. Phil signaled for another Ouzo.

"Look, Phil. We're family. What the hell is wrong with you? You were drunk when you got off that goddamn plane weren't you?"

"Tell you what, Herb. I'll just call a cab and go into town. Maybe in a few days, I'll come down and see you, if you're in harbor. I imagine you can pick up the tab? Right? Bye-bye."

Phil stood unsteadily. He tacked his way to the bar, ordered a cab and another Ouzo. Herb watched stunned, silently and grimly from his corner on the terrace.

Ten minutes later, a taxi pulled up. Phil fetched his bag from the jeep and was gone.

Herb had no idea what to do. He felt a strong responsibility for Phil and his long deceased parents. But he didn't know where Phil was going ('a cab and go into town'? *What* town? There's no goddamned town around here!). He didn't know who to call to determine the problem. He knew one thing, it wasn't just a drinking problem. Phil was losing it. Losing himself. Damn! What was he going to do? Only one answer: Go to the boat and wait.

Phil told the driver to take him to the nearest hotel and on the way to stop at a liquor store, or whatever. He bought two bottles of gin, two of scotch, and two of Ouzo. *That should do for starters.* They proceeded to a fairly nice seaside resort. Phil engaged a suite and went to his room.

Five days later, he awoke in a hospital room, completely unaware where he was, or how he had got there. In fact, he wasn't entirely sure *who* the hell he was. He had a drip in his right arm. He was strapped into his bed. There was an oxygen feed into his nose and something really nasty and painful jammed down his throat. He felt like he was dying. He was shaking. He was nauseous. His head throbbed. His mouth was so dry he couldn't swallow, even if he didn't have a tube down his throat. His tongue was swollen. He had little or no feeling in his legs and feet. His back ached like thunder, and he felt as if he had bed sores. He could smell vomit. He could smell urine. He could smell something else unidentifiable. Had he access to a gun, he would gladly have blown his brains out. He felt tears running down his temples warm and wet into and over his ears, onto the pillow under his throbbing head. And he was alone. And he deserved it. He would always be alone, and he would always deserve it. Like the taste of soured milk, the last few days returned to him. They made his stomach churn.

Dr. Craig Webber, his "father" had signed over to him the deed to hell itself.

A nurse silently entered the room for whatever purpose. Phil looked at her pitifully. "Please." He whispered. "Please." He whispered again.

"You're awake. What do you want?" she asked clinically.

"Please take this stuff away," he whispered. His eyes moved, trying to indicate all the painful, demeaning apparatus hanging from his body.

"That will take the doctor's authorization."

"Get it. Please."

"I'll see."

What seemed like hours later, a short, stout, swarthy doctor entered Phil's room.

"You want us to remove your restraints? Your drip and your various assists?"

"Yes. He croaked "Please. Please. Now."

"Do you think you can behave?"

"Yes. Absolutely. I promise," he whispered. Phil had no idea whatsoever how he might have "misbehaved." But Christ, he would have agreed to the gang rape of his grandmother if it would get him out of this strap, tube, and needle nightmare.

"If you don't, I'll have you back just like this for at least a week. Understood?"

"Yessir. I understand and I promise. Please."

"Okay. I'll send in the nurses. But you better be damned sure you're going to behave."

"I promise. Please."

Ten long minutes later, two nurses entered his room. It took about fifteen painful, degrading minutes to remove all the various equipments attached to him. But when it was over, and they gave Phil a drink of water for the first time, Phil thought he would faint with relief. The nurses were clinical and quite cold. Phil suspected that perhaps they had suffered a very rough time at his hands. Great. More guilt. Of all the hells that man inflicts on himself, guilt is far and away the most nefarious.

One of the nurses looked at him with a frosty stare. "You have visitors. Up to it?"

"Do you know who?"

"I have no idea. Will you see them?"

"Please tell them...tomorrow." Phil went back to sleep. Naturally, this time. No drugs. No alcohol. His dreams were like something out of Dante. Except for the beautiful chandelier. And they went on all night relentlessly. He awoke around 0600 soaked in sweat, shivering uncontrollably, and he realized he had been suffering a spout of the DT's. Thank God he hadn't pissed off the doctors or nurses during this attack. He passed out again and blissfully slept without dreams or demons.

Coffee, juice, fruit yogurt, dry toast and water was the first real food Phil had taken for nearly eight days. Though slightly nauseous, it still felt great. A long hot shower, a shave, an aspirin, some vitamins, some unknown pills, more coffee, and he thought he might live. So many excellent reasons to die. Were they eclipsed by the reasons to live? *Beats the shit out of me* he thought.

"Your visitors are back. Will you see them?"

"Okay."

Herb and Anne quietly entered his room.

"Thank God you had a business card from Sea Tigress in your wallet. Otherwise, we'd still not know where the hell you were. Anne here contacted *Sea Tigress* trying to locate you. That's why she's here. Bless and damn you, boy, I'm glad you're alive. Do you have any idea how close to death you were?"

"Good morning to you too, Uncle Herb. Hi Anne."

"Hi, Phil. It's good...good to see you...alive. Herb is right. You were just on the edge."

"When do you suppose I can get out of here?"

"Out of here? Well, Philly, we've been talking to your doctor. You're suffering from acute alcohol poisoning, compounded by Delirium Tremens, compounded by severe traumatic depression, and what he suspects is an exceptionally strong suicidal fixation. You've apparently been a real handful. They're not very fond of you around here. Your drip included Diazepam the last few days. How does that sound to you, Phil? What the hell has happened to you?"

"Look, Herb, I haven't been just getting drunk, or chasing broads, or getting into barroom brawls, or one damned thing just for fun. I've been doing my job, and for goddamned good reasons, and it's been a bitch. So please, cut me a little slack."

After a fairly long, awkward interlude, Herb acquiesced. "Okay. You've got it, Phil. But I think you ought to spend at least a couple of days more here in their care."

"Twenty-four hours, Herb. No more. Anne can you wait on the boat?"

"Sure, Phil."

"I'll see you both the day after tomorrow. And I still want that diving gear, Herb. I mean it."

"Alright, son. I'll have the best available onboard when you arrive. Take care."

Herb left the room. Anne stayed just long enough to kiss him on the forehead and then left herself. Phil felt suddenly very lonely.

The rest of that day and the next, Phil ate his meals, took his medicine, kept himself proper, was inordinately polite, and even did some exercises. He spent a good deal of time walking about the beautifully flowered and manicured hospital grounds in the warm sunshine, and slowly started to look like his old self.

He thought about the words of Dr. Kahn so many months ago *"Don't we all suffer and even die to some degree for the sins of our brethren? At least the best of us? To save them? A salvation of a quiet sort? I very strongly suspect you will suffer exactly that in the future. And I believe, Mr. Carr...I believe your suffering will be hell on wheels."* The words helped Phil. They helped him profoundly. Phil made himself a note to discuss this with Dr. Kahn when the time was right.

Even the staff seemed to decide he was something above sub-human and his spirits slowly rose. He remembered his training and *wrapped* the atrocities he had committed and those that had been committed upon him the last weeks for further review at another time, hopefully fully analyzed by his peculiar insights. He realized to some degree that he had been engaging in blatant self pity and resolved that this was the end of it.

Around 1000 the next day, Herb and Anne called for him. Anne was tanned from head to toe, her hair was delicately sun bleached and her eyes were nearly transparent from light exposure. Slim and lithe and willowy as ever, she was beautiful.

An only slightly disapproving staff agreed on his release, so he was on his way to *Sea Tigress*, copious amounts pills, brochures on alcoholism, liver disease, and the local AA Chapter in hand. Almost happy, almost carefree, spring on the island in full bloom...spring break!

True to his word, Herb had a "soup to nuts" scuba inventory ready for Phil, along with a text of instructions and a first class compressor (which he grudgingly admitted would be of great use). Fortunately, Demetrious had long years experience in both diving and compressors, capable of blending gasses, so Phil had excellent tutoring on site. Phil was relying on his special capabilities to assist and keep him safe underwater, without a "buddy," which was most definitely not recommended.

Soon, Phil found himself somersaulting backwards off the fantail of *Sea Tigress* into the clear waters of the Ionian Sea. He had no idea why, but he was convinced that under the sea he would find something he needed. Perhaps it was the alien environment, or the beauty, perhaps the hint of danger, the challenge, or maybe just the fun. He didn't know. He just knew he needed it in the same way that his peculiar insight enlightened him on many things.

And he was right. The waters were so clear it was like floating in air. The colors were enchanting. The sparkling reverse surface, the life constantly moving, competing, surviving, finding its niche, and fighting to retain it. It was always lunch time, always beautiful, brutal, always changing, not without its dangers. The fundamental nature of devouring sustenance fascinated Phil. Perhaps that was why he looked forward to good meals so fondly. Perhaps that was why he understood his duties so well.

He had to keep checking his watch, his air, and his depth meter to ensure he didn't overstay the sufferance of biology and physics. Often he would simply drop down to just thirty or forty feet in the cool water and execute what mariners refer to as keeping-station and astrodynamicists refer to as station-keeping. Whether a body is resisting gravitational, solar, or hydraulic tides, it was much the same. So he always wondered why the juxtaposition of the words. *He was mentally drifting again.* What's up now? Nothing he hoped.

He would simply sustain vertical stillness in the water, lightly turning 360° gyrations in two or three minute cycles, leisurely stroking his feet, gazing at the life around him, and the glittering surface of the sea far above. He felt he could stay down for days. Anne, Phil, and Demetrious would observe his stationary surface bubbles and sometimes even see his undulating, phantom-like shape, unmoving, deep in the sunlit waters. They would look at each other in perplexity and not a little concern.

Finally, he was able to limit his breathing, slow his heartbeat, and lower his metabolic rate. In conjunction with a nitrox mixture, at a moderate depth, he could stay down far longer than comfortable for Anne and Herb, not to mention the Diver's Manual. Demetrious didn't seem overly unconcerned. He simply squinted down into the waters.

Each time he came up, he was stronger, somehow restored and cleansed. Anne and Herb saw the effects nearly immediately. Relief rivaled with bewilderment in their minds.

When Phil was not diving, or helping with the fishing, he was with Anne. They laughed. They talked. They made love. They cooked and ate and watched movies, read books, and swam in the mornings, at noon and in the night. They fell deeply in love. It was a wonderful time of mutual discovery. Sometimes in the night, Phil's demons would return. Anne never related these nocturnal hauntings to him. However, on such occasions, she noticed that the following mornings, Phil invariably and immediately sought out the depths of the cold morning sea, distaining breakfast, and staying down longer and longer each time.

Finally, on some mornings to the astonishment and consternation of Anne, Phil would forego his diving equipment altogether, nitrox tanks included, diving with mask only. This in no way shortened his diving times and Anne noticed that Phil took some care to ensure that Herb and Demetrious were unaware of his *au natural* underwater forays. What was happening to him? How was he capable of such things?

Phil had shared some of his history with Anne, particularly his genealogy, so part of her was not excessively surprised, while another part wondered where the hell this was all leading to. Who, or what would Phil really be in the end? Or was there any end to it at all? "Phil, you aren't reporting any of this to the staff at Oneiro are you?"

"It's their job to watch the students, Anne, not to watch me."

A few days later, as a flaxen-reddish dawn shined down on Phil's smooth emergence from the sea, he looked to Anne. "Got a question for you."

"Yes?"

"Do they need you any more in the Art Department?"

"What sort of question is that? I'm the Department Head. I'm an Instructor and a fully Tenured Professor."

"Yes. Yes. But aren't these extraordinary students ready to govern themselves?"

There was a long pause between them as both looked out to sea.

"Never thought about that. They certainly don't require management, or discipline, or tests, or grade cards, or supervision, or schedules, or councilors, or anything else that holds together the classical college student. They hardly even need medical care. Good heavens, they really don't even need training any more. They're better at self- and intra-personal study than we are at teaching them, in fact."

Anne was getting excited. "You know they are making nearly exponential strides in 'Brain Food' as we call it now. The students have a variety of cute names, Brain Bread, Engram Edibles, Gray Matter Goodies, Smart Snacks, Genius

Grub, Neuron-Nookies and so on. I believe the students have attained something like a twenty-five percent absorption ratio, way up from the previous two point five percent right *now*...and that wasn't projected for at least five years. At this same pace they'll be approaching one-hundred percent within a very few months. My God! You may be right."

"We wanted to create a human vaccine, or maybe human antibodies is a better term, or both, I don't know. Either way, in nature such little beasties exist autonomously. They need no one and nothing. I believe the same is true of our students. Perhaps it's time to face the fact that we may have succeeded?"

"Phil, that's a very complex and difficult question."

"Is it? Is it really? Does it take a PHD and a Committee, and a Doctoral Study to decide when a child is old enough and mature enough to be left home alone? They've already got knowledge and capabilities and talents we don't even begin to understand. They've already left us behind. Maybe they're just being polite? Quietly suffering us. Maybe we're holding them back? Ever read *Childhood's End?*"

Anne shivered. "Phil. I've never been happier in my life than right here on this boat. But maybe it's time we got back?"

Phil peered at Anne for some time, then he said, "well, it's been thirty days. Thirty lovely days. I feel younger and newer and healthier. Primarily thanks to you. Probably time to get back to work."

Phil fell into thought. Eyes animated, squinting into the sunrise.

"I need a status report from all department heads. Will you please call Cindy and instruct her to put out the word. Full staff meeting, two days from now, dining room, 1030 hours, no more than thirty minutes per department (hopefully far less), full status on ANUMEN. I'll talk to Herb and get us headed for Oneiro. He's never been there and I think it's high time he got a look. I'd like him to know how to navigate there, and into Proteus Cavern Harbor anyway."

Late the next afternoon, *Sea Tigress* slowly chugged into Proteus Cavern Harbor, Zig Zag colors flying amid ship. Phil had already cleared their entrance with the Harbor Master, and after having carefully navigated the artificial reef, entered the huge cave complex. Herb looked about in some wonder. "Jesus, Philly! What an operation!"

"This is just the beginning, Uncle Herb. Wait till you see the real complex." Phil really enjoyed reliving and rediscovering the wonders of Oneiro through Herb's eyes. And there was no better start than the harbor. From there, they took PM's down the long passage past the armory to the Board of Directors' complex. Herb was nearly paralyzed by the Board Room and gratefully accepted a stiff drink at the bar. They returned to the Harbor area, into the periscope caverns and a long tour throughout the underground University. They stopped often for a coffee or a drink in the University and Herb greatly enjoyed the diversity of architecture and landscape. It took some time to explain the periscope technology to Herb, and Phil remained unsure whether he truly understood. In any event, if he didn't understand, he certainly appreciated what he saw. Finally, they slowly found their way above ground to Halios Mansion. Phil gave Herb a tour of his quarters, ending on a late luncheon on Phil's poolside terrace. Herb was nearly speechless.

"Phil, this is paradise, and if you don't mind me saying so, you live like a king. So what has been so physically and mentally rough on you?"

"I don't hide out in these quarters like a monk, Uncle Herb. I'm forced to get out in the real world and protect this place. Why don't we just leave it at that?"

"Okay, Phil. I'm sorry Demetrius is missing all this, but I suppose security must be maintained?"

"Afraid so, Herb. No choice really, at least for the time being. You must consider this a Top Secret facility and no one must learn of its existence. The Harbor Master assigned you a call sign for requesting entrance to the harbor, *Oneiro Tigress*, and that call sign is mated to a complete physical description and photograph of *Sea Tigress*. Never attempt to enter the harbor without flying the Zig Zag burgee and that call sign. They'll blow you out of the water."

"Jesus. What do you people do here?"

"Well, we're essentially a University for very gifted students. However, there is some very sensitive high-tech research conducted here that would hold great interest for groups all over the world. It must be protected. I think we should leave that alone for now as well."

"Okay, Phil. This food is great by the way."

"Glad you like it. Do you want to stay on for a couple of days? I can arrange your own apartment if you like, or you can stay here with me."

"No, thanks, Phil. Our freezers are full, so we need to get back pretty soon, and I don't like to leave Demetrius alone on *Tigress*. I reckon we'll cast off this afternoon." Phil accompanied Herb back to the harbor and gave him a big hug as he prepared to board *Tigress*. "I'll see you soon, Uncle Herb. Take care."

"No, Phil. *You* take care. I never want to see you like that again. Take care of Anne too. No 'catch and release' that one."

Se*a Tigress* slowly exited the harbor, cleared the reef, and was soon out of sight.

Back in his conference room/office, Phil was clearing up a number of items that had accumulated during his absence. Edward entered bearing tea and pastries, clearly relieved to see that Phil had bounced back.

His carefully guarded veneer slipped for one highly emotional moment, just long enough for a hint of cockney to peer out. "That bugger who was killing us...he's a dead wanker now. Innee?" Phil could see the bitterness and hate in his eyes. There was a slight tremble in Edward's hands. Phil had never seen him so vehement.

"Yes, Edward. It wasn't an easy or clean death either."

Edward took a deep breath, straightened himself, then returned to his normal polish. "Excellent. I believe I have some inkling how difficult that must have been and what it must have cost you personally. A fine brave investment that. Nicely done. Can I do anything else?"

Phil smiled and warmly regarded Edward for a moment. "Yes, please, if you would. We're going to have a general meeting of about twenty people in the dining room tomorrow starting at about 1030. Can you have a quick look at preparations? AV, Coffee Breaks, Seating, Lunch, and so on?"

"I'll look into it immediately. Good to have you back, sir."

"Good to be back, Edward. Thank you. And I thank you for your concern. I think things will be alright now. I hope so."

Moving...Always Moving

The last time Phil saw this group gathered together was just after the insurrection. They had not met after the invasion. They looked one hellofa lot better now. They looked rested, energetic, attentive, and ready to start the session. He hoped they were up to the challenges of the agenda. Hell, he hoped *he* was up to the challenges of the agenda.

"Good morning, my friends. Our gathering today is to address several issues. None of them easy. None of them simple. Some of them painful. We've been through so much together, though...this should be something we can accomplish.

"I want this to be as informal and as easy as possible, even enjoyable if that can be managed. We'll break whenever anyone wants. We'll spend days if you like. We'll crack out the booze if you like—or I like. Food when you need. Hell, we'll take a break and go sailing if you need it.

Essentially, what I need is as clear a picture as possible of ANUMEN status within every department. Once we have achieved that, I will be asking some very hard questions that don't require immediate answers. We'll take our time. We'll achieve a consensus. And if we can't achieve a consensus, then we'll develop unique, individual departmental solutions. No one in this room will walk away dissatisfied. On this you have my word. Before we start, are there any questions?"

Hands raised everywhere.

"Dr. Kahn."

"Mr. Carr, I am most interested in the Island's new name, its legal status, and present ownership."

"Fair question. I am Dr. Webber's sole heir. As such, I own the Island. I, with the able assistance of Dr. Alexander, named the Island Oneiro. This is a Greek term that translates to *Dream*.

"We did far more than simply christen the island with a name, however. We are now a sovereign, island micronation. We are independent from Greece, or any other country. We have our own flag. Our own laws. Head of State. Constitution. In fact, everything any sovereign nation enjoys. We did this primarily to facilitate our ability to defend ourselves, openly, legally, and decisively. I believe that other benefits will begin to surface as time wears on."

"Who is our Head of State?"

"I am."

"May I ask your title?"

"Certainly. My title is Proprietor."

"You mean like someone who runs a butcher shop, or a jewelry store, or a restaurant?"

"Exactly."

"You'll have to admit it's not a very impressive title for a Head of State."

"Perhaps. So, who are we trying to impress? I have no plans to build a Throne Room, no robes, no crown, no 'Hail to the Chief,' and no bullshit. I've got work to do just like you. Delusions of grandeur only get in the way."

"I see. And what is our form of government?"

"What else? A Proprietorship, which dovetails nicely with our economic systems."

"And what does that mean?"

"It means we run this place like a business. Not a dictatorship, not an oligarchy, but not quite a democracy. However, as you know, any business operates at the sufferance of its customers and its employees. On Oneiro we have both in residence. Therefore, you report to me, and I report to you. I made the mistake not long ago of viewing reporting lines as mono-directional. For that, at least in part, Rachael Stone may have met her death. That will never happen again. Fair enough?"

There was a thoughtful pause.

"I...I think so, Mr. Proprietor. I think I like it."

"I'm pleased, Dr. Kahn. Any further thoughts you may have on the subject, or anyone here for that matter, are most welcome. We can adapt to our needs. We can easily change. Next question? Dr. McLean?"

"Can you give us some more details about the invasion? What did they want? Who were they? How many dead and injured? Will it happen again?"

"I'll try. They wanted our technology in artificial oil production. They were essentially mercenaries hired by a secret oil cartel of sorts. Forty-three died on their side—everyone who invaded us. One hundred and thirty-eight died and twenty-eight were injured on our side. Dr. Webber was murdered, and Rachael met a very heroic death. It is now ended I believe. The head of the snake has been cut off."

"Who cut it off?"

There was a loud silence.

"Mr. Carr, may I ask who cut off the head?"

There was a long pause.

"Mr. Carr?"

"It's not written the Proprietor is obliged to share every goddamned detail about the governance and protection of Oneiro. Next question?"

Phil's statement was followed by an awkward silence.

"Fine. We'll start with departmental status reports. Since you were the first with a question, Dr. Kahn, perhaps you will begin?"

"Gladly, Mr. Carr. As with most of our departments, I assumed the *last* place that ANUMEN might surface would be in mine, Philosophy and Religion. Well, not for the first time, I was wrong. In fact, I was way off base. Believe it or not, our students now have their own religion. At least I assume it's a religion. In truth, I'm not really sure. That is not to say they are unwilling to study other religions, or other philosophies. They just, one day, popped up with their own. And it appears they all pretty much subscribe to it."

"How was this disseminated?"

"I don't have a clue. It's just as the new language and the new art, and the new physical prowess arose. Everywhere, everything out of nothing. I personally find it very disquieting."

"You mean it could be genetic based?"

"I mean it *is*. That is to say, I cannot imagine another source surfacing in quite this manner."

"Does it have a name?"

"'Kosmos.' Although I imagine we'll ultimately call it 'Oneiroism.' That's really about as much as I know."

"Interesting name. As in the English word cosmos I assume. Any idea about the belief system, the precepts, the ethos, a creator, a set of rules, Sunday School...*anything?*"

"It exists only within the context of their new language. They state they cannot translate it into terms I can understand, and I believe them. I don't know one damned thing about it. Christ, it took them more than a day to come up with the translation 'Kosmos.'"

"We must learn more about this, Dr. Kahn. This is your specialty."

"I'm painfully aware of that, Phil. What you're asking is exceptionally difficult. I will keep at it, however."

"Can you tell if they worship something, anything, a cross, a coconut, a magic ring...what?"

Dr. Kahn just smiled.

Phil could only say, "Extraordinary. Keep on it Doctor. The greatest challenge of your career...hell, your life! Maybe you can discover God." Phil said, only half joking.

"Agreed, Mr. Carr."

"Thank you, Dr. Kahn. How about our acting Director of Physical Education, Dr. Williams?"

"Thank you, Mr. Carr. I'll make this very short. They are faster, stronger, healthier, and far deadlier than any previous iteration of human being. They could storm the Olympics, they could win World War II, and thank God they're so benign."

"... Ahh...thank you, Dr. Williams. I'll try not to piss them off."

Subdued laughter followed Phil's remark.

"Okay, we're moving along very well. Dr. Butler?"

"The last time I briefed you, Mr. Carr, enhanced learning food had a two point five percent absorption rate into the brain. That jumped to twenty-five percent a few days ago, and we're now up to thirty-three percent. By the time this meeting ends, I wouldn't be surprised if they had achieved over forty percent. By the end of the month...who knows? They are starting to dabble with the enteric nerve bundle in the lower stomach area, and they are quite excited by this approach. They're fooling around with the Vagus nerve. But that's more in the line of body function and circulatory control. It's hard-wired directly with the head brain and I believe they are trying to chemically train it. Modified metabolic rates, heart, respiration, muscle control... things like that. I believe they were already making unconscious inroads in these areas. They are now actively studying and manipulating these areas. But this is well out of my depth.

"If they're right, before high summer, classes, instructors, and even the University *per se* will have been rendered as obsolete as an iron lung. I have used the term before: School's out!

"We're not just moving fast any more...we're traveling FTL...and I don't believe we have helm control any longer. Things are progressing at a near exponential rate."

At these words, there was a long pause.

"Thank you, Dr. Butler. Dr. Dunedin, I *Fear* it's time to hear from you."

"Thank you, Phil," Dr. Dunedin said, sounding very tired, suddenly. "Against all my conditioned instincts, much soul searching and lengthy analytical discussions, we no longer administer the Fear Ordeal. It is now part of our permanent curriculum starting at about age *ten*, believe it or not, and it is administered and imposed by the students themselves. The duration of the course now ranges from age ten to eighteen. That's one hellofa long ordeal and, as far as I can observe, the course is now about ten times more demanding. If the measurable results are accurate...it's about ten times as effective. And as far as I can observe, there are no negative side effects, injuries, or trauma of any sort. They're doing far better than we did. I can only assume that this is a product of their improved intelligence, physical prowess, and much improved communications, thanks to their new language. Considering the various talents they can bring to bear, I wouldn't screw with these kids. Myself, I spend a fair amount of time sailing these days."

"Doctor, do you think a non-student could stand up to the Ordeal as it stands today?"

"I have observed their Ordeal in some detail, which was pretty tough in and of itself. Phil, I have absolutely no doubt it would kill a very fit, mentally robust human being before lunch on the first day."

"Good grief, Doctor. What sort of creature emerges from such a crucible?"

"Well, Phil, we haven't seen the result of the full eight year ordeal of course, but I would surmise the result would be something eons beyond the human paradigm of rationally directed fight or flight. Cowardice? Human, not Oneirion. Or what we sometimes refer to as courage? I'm not sure that term would really apply either. Perhaps a better term is... *invincible*."

"My God. Thank you, Doctor. Let's take a break. The bar is open. I'm first."

Drinks in hand on the terrace, sun beating down, they looked like an infantry platoon that had just won a battle by destroying and killing a village. They were victors and they despised it. They hated it.

Dr. Gray approached Phil. "Nothing fails like success huh?"

"Dr. Gray, as Head of Realization, you should be as happy as a pig in shit today."

"Not sure I appreciate your allusion, Phil, but I understand your point. However, Realization always meant to me your departments would deliver the raw goods, and I would finally shape it up into something finished and well crafted.

Things have turned out quite the reverse, in fact. I am the most superfluous department head here today. Your people turned out finished goods, ready for market. No need for me whatsoever."

"I understand. No offense intended, Doctor."

"None taken, Phil. Where do we go from here?"

"Well, it's a little early to tell yet. I think we should hear the rest of the reports and then I'll give my take on things, and then we'll all try to come to a hopefully common conclusion. Let's go back in."

Soon, everyone was reassembled.

"Dr. Alexander, how's Government & Legal Systems getting along with all this?"

"Phil, I am pleased to report that I have absolutely nothing to report."

"Thank you for your report, Doctor."

Laughter filled the room, which was perhaps a lightening of the mood, somewhat.

"Okay, how about Dr. Johansen in Genetics?"

"Our students have figured out how to escalate the compression cycle. I am unaware how they accomplished this. The empirical evidence is there, however. I don't know how else to report this other than to stipulate that within months, we will be more advanced by incalculable millennia. What the product of that may be is anyone's guess. God help us all."

There was stunned, profound silence at this statement.

"Anything new to report in Art, Dr. Jones?"

"Not really. Not beyond what has already been observed. Frankly though, the students aren't really as interested in sharing with us anymore. Nothing unfriendly about it, or secretive, or uncooperative...they're just busy in their own pursuits. It's not a matter that they've become inward looking. Hell, they're vision is literally universally unbound.

So in reality they may be producing things beyond belief and we just don't know about it. Might not be able to understand them anyway. I'm not giving up. But I'm certainly not in control anymore, either."

"Thank you. Unfortunately, as you may know, Dr. Gould in Music is no longer with us and we haven't yet replaced him. So I suppose we will not have a report in that area today. I suspect, however, that very similar developments are being produced in music, without our knowledge.

"How about Dr. McLean in Languages?"

"Thank you, Phil. As you all may know, we dispatched expeditions to several sites around the world ranging from South America to the Arctic Circle. The objective of these expeditions was to determine the relevance of our new language to other creatures, primarily marine. We found out.

Our students are now freely interacting with whales. Squid are following their instructions and believe it or not, plankton will form discrete, recognizable patterns based on our input, a square, a triangle, even a peace symbol. At least in the case of plankton, maybe all of them, I believe this makes a compelling case for emergence. Success beyond our wildest dreams. If you would like full details, I have placed extensive documentation on the table at the back of this dining room.

The implications of these developments are quite beyond my capacity to predict or understand. Believe it or not, I actually visit the deep space communication concentrators daily now. I think...I fully believe we will find something given enough time. Perhaps there's a reason the students call their new religion Kosmos. We definitely know all these disciplines fit together, they form a cohesive wholeness—art, language, religion, genetics, and on and on—and I am slowly becoming convinced that the fit is universal, as in Universe, the Cosmos, Galactic, Everything.

I'm inspired. I'm terrified. I'm in awe.

I'm experiencing something else I don't seem to observe elsewhere in this room for some reason. I'm overjoyed. I'm uplifted, and I'm proud...I'm damned proud!"

Without exception the group spontaneously rose to their feet and greeted her statement with thunderous applause. Suddenly, they all had a totally different spirit. Phil could have kissed her.

"Thank you, Doctor. You've achieved a marvel. We all have. I wish Dr. Webber were here to witness this. Dr. Winchester?"

"Nothing to report."

"Dr. Montgomery?"

"Nothing to report."

"Dr. Gear?"

"These kids have just about put me out of business. They've taken over the Nursery Womb and they're doing a far superior job. For God's sake, they're performing miracles. The babies are talking within weeks of birth. They have physical prowess I can't begin to describe. Their eyes follow everything. I believe their intelligence is literally terrifying. We are *homo-sapiens*. They are *homo-ingenium*. Welcome to obsolescence, boys and girls...because we're damned sure there."

Dr. Gear's statement caused a hushed silence, averted eyes, breathless inward reflection.

After a few moments, Phil spoke again. "Thank you all for such succinct and forthcoming reports. Have we evolved humankind, or made it redundant?" Phil said, followed by a smile. *What hath Oneiro wrought?*

"Given the progress on all fronts, not the least of which is the Smart Food absorption ratios, how does it feel to be superfluous?"

Responses came from all quarters.

"Like success." "Sad." "Like the end." "Like the beginning." "Graduation Day." "An endless summer vacation." "Time to look for a job." "Can we really let this run out of control?" "What the hell, we're not in control now." "What will they do, where will they go from here?" "Whatever and wherever they wish." "Are we going to get blame or credit for this?" "Will we ever know the consequences of what we have done here?" "I don't want to leave this place." "This place is home, like nowhere else on Earth." "We can't just leave." "What if things get out of control...get dangerous?" "Things have been goddamn dangerous here for one hellofa long time. I personally think they are just now getting safe." "Don't they still need our protection, our guidance, our experience, our wisdom, our compassion?" "Maybe we need theirs?"

Tears and fears and sorrows and pride from all quarters.

"Everything you just expressed, I feel the same. I have one other fear...we may be holding them back. Maybe they're just being polite, just putting up with us? Maybe it's time for that *long day's journey into night*? For my part, here's how I see it. I've already picked my replacement...a new Proprietor as it were. I will retain ownership of Oneiro, however. I want to see how this works out over time, and I want to ensure man benefits in general from the developments of this island.

Anyone in this room, who wishes to go, will take away a stipend consisting of two million US Dollars in cash, as well as any assistance we can give in residence and professional and physical relocation. Anyone who wishes to stay is welcome to live here the rest of his or her life, and still has full access to the two million Dollar stipend, not to mention our normal salary plan. Your choice, my friends, and I do mean my friends, because our business relationship is at an end, effective right now. I hope our relationship as friends will be far more enduring."

Smiles and light applause came softly.

"So, who's the new boss, Phil?"

"Mike Auslander."

This statement caused stunned silence, some concerns, some discussion and questioning, and some dawning comprehension.

Dr. Kahn was the first to speak. "I reckon that's a good choice, Phil. He's got the brains, the guts, the education, some experience, and the energy, and they'll follow him I'm sure. He's been in the middle of things for months now. The new language, the insurrections, the new art, everything in fact. Good choice, Phil."

"I haven't discussed this with Mike yet, so I would appreciate this remaining just between us for the time being. I'll keep you posted, though. Ladies and gentlemen, thank you for your time, your understanding, and your interest...and I mean far more than just this meeting...we must have a party, a real blow-out very, very soon...meanwhile, drinks on me."

The meeting broke up and most were in excellent spirits. The cocktail party went on a great deal longer, and spirits got even higher.

Come on In. Stay Awhile

When I was a child, I did children's things. Now that I am a man. I do man's things.

Biblical

Phil heard the bell. He activated the private elevator and went to the reception area himself. He already knew who was visiting. "Come in Mike. How are you?"

"I'm fine, Mr. Carr, particularly considering all that's been going on." They shook hands and walked together to the terrace where lunch had been laid minutes before.

"Agreed. But that's all over now and I don't think we'll have any further problems of that sort."

"Can I ask what it was all about?"

"You sure can. We had a bunch of mercs from the Middle East who wanted to steal or destroy our oil manufacturing technology. They worked for a secret cartel and were paid to do just about whatever it took. Fortunately, we stopped them and their masters. It's all over now, and I hope for good."

"Mercs?"

"Mercenaries. Killers...soldiers for hire."

"Oh yes. I see. Dr. Webber was killed? Rachael was killed?"

"Afraid so, plus one hundred and thirty-six others on our side. It was a real mess."

"How was it for you, Mr. Carr?"

"No picnic."

"I can imagine. Are you okay?"

"I wasn't for quite a while Mike. I'm still amongst the mental walking wounded, and I suspect I'll be that way for some time to come. I found myself doing things I would never have dreamed of. Things like that don't come for free."

"I'm sorry to hear about that, Mr. Carr. Care to share it with me, sir?"

"No. That's what I get the big bucks for, Mike. But let's lighten up the mood; this is supposed to be a happy occasion."

"Okay. What's for lunch?"

"Your favorites, Mike, meat loaf, macaroni and cheese, lima beans, and chocolate cake."

"Wow! Why the VIP treatment?"

"Well, I've got something to discuss with you, Mike...not sure you're going to like it...then again you might. It'll certainly be a surprise, I guarantee that, Mike. Let's eat."

They found their way to the terrace, Phil poured the wine and they ate, discussing fairly trivial matters during the meal.

"So what would you like to discuss, Mr. Carr?"

"First of all, Mike, let's drop the 'Mr. Carr' stuff. Please call me Phil."

"Okay...Phil."

"Good. Here goes. Mike you've been in the middle of recent events, over the past months as much as anyone and much more than most. You've seen the new language, art, physical abilities, the brain food, singing insurrectionists to sleep, great strides have been made, people have died, we've killed and maimed and even tortured, we're now called Oneiro, we're a sovereign state, I've damned near died myself a couple of times...and wished I would have half the time. You've been instrumental in many of these matters. And I'm sure you have witnessed the student body grow and mature and learn and pretty much exceed the capabilities of your instructors?"

"Yes. Yes?"

"Let's walk, Mike. I want to show you something."

Phil escorted Mike throughout his quarters, all the rooms, the terraces, pools, security, everything.

"My god, this is impressive, Phil. Why are you showing me all this?"

"Mike, if you examine things here on Oneiro, I think you'll find it's time the students took charge of their own destiny. We have analyzed the situation quite carefully, and we concluded it was time to 'cut the cord.' I'm sure you agree with this prognosis?" Mike nodded agreement. "However, this does not obviate the need for a leader. Someone to assume overall direction and responsibility, along with all the other tasks leadership implies." Again Mike nodded agreement. "So the question is, "Who will lead?""

Mike shrugged "You're the leader."

"Up until now, yes. But I believe the time has come for a native Oneirion to take charge. Only a native really understands the students and only a native can keep up with them. So, you ask why the tour of these suites. Because they're yours now. Your new digs."

"*Mine?*"

"Yep. You can move in this afternoon if you like. I'll move into one of the guest quarters. You are now the new head of Oneiro. Congratulations."

Mike was quite literally speechless. "I don't understand, Phil."

"It's really quite simple, Mike. Your students no longer need the cadre of this University. You are more than capable of managing, teaching, planning, and running things yourselves. There is still a need for a leader, however, and you're it. I will still retain ownership of the Island, and I'll drop in from time to time, but you are the autonomous Head of the State of Oneiro. Your title by the way, unless you choose to modify it, is Proprietor."

"Proprietor." Mike echoed thoughtfully.

"I'll stay on awhile and show you the ropes, explain things. You can have any salary you like. You will decide if you want to retain the Board of Directors. You will determine the future direction of Oneiro. We will provide you the best legal, technical, military, and management consulting in the world. But in the end, you are the boss. You determine your organization; you are responsible for relations with the outside world, defense, business, finance, security, legal, dissemination of technology, and even public relations. You can do it, Mike. I absolutely know you can."

After a pause, Mike bristled somewhat, staring Phil straight in the eyes. "What about you, Phil. What are you going to do?"

"Me, Mike?" Phil smiled. "I'm going fishing."

END

Epilogue

Happiness is a virtue.

T.E. White, The Once and Future King

Sea Tigress chugged quietly to the entrance of Proteus Cavern Harbor. They carefully navigated the entrance, avoiding the manmade reef and any defensive obstacles, radioing in their call sign, checking entrance flags and ensuring they had authority to proceed. No one wanted to be blown out of the water on such a bright, warm, late-summer morning.

Anne had the helm. Demetrius was standing by at the stern. Herb manned the radio, depth-finders, sonar and charts, while Phil stood by the bow, lines in hand. They were a well oiled, perfectly coordinated crew by now. Herb and Phil had considered themselves expert sailors for years, yet Demetrious had taught them and Anne far more seamanship than they had ever thought possible.

The weather was perfect, and strangely enough, there was no other water traffic, so it should have been a flawless entry. However, things were in fact, a little difficult.

The waters outside and inside the reef were literally boiling with life: Marine mammals, whales further out, porpoises, hundreds of thousands of squid and the occasional shark feasting on the squid.

It was a terrifying sight to the uninitiated. Anne and Phil knew its cause and were unconcerned. They could see the huge cables feeding the powerful two-way underwater-to-surface communications. On the other hand, Herb and Demetrius were quite nervous. They were experienced seamen and seasoned fishermen, and they had never witnessed anything remotely like this in all their years at sea. It made them all the more bewildered and uncertain.

Once inside the cool, shady cavern, things thankfully quieted down. It had been over a year since they had visited Oneiro and little had changed. Clearly, things were as well maintained as always. Everything ship-shape. The real difference was there were very few people in evidence and even fewer water craft. It was very quiet. Too quiet really.

As they completed tying up and setting fenders, Mike Auslander approached the slip, smiling broadly. He looked older. Mature. Not quite the carefree invincible youth of fourteen months ago. He was better dressed, no sloppy jeans, no baggy sweatshirt, and no frayed sneakers. He was now neatly attired in a dark blue polo shirt, tan slacks, and well cared for deck shoes...even an expensive watch...clean shaven and well groomed...he looked great, if somewhat older.

"Hi, Mike! How're you doing? You look great." Phil jumped onto the dock and warmly shook hands with him.

"Hi, Phil. It's great to see you, and you look even better—slim and tanned like a nut. Hello Anne, Herb, Demetrius. Please come ashore; it's a pleasure to welcome you back. Everyone's waiting to see you—anxious to get caught up."

There was already a small table set up at their slip, sporting various flowers and five Champagne flutes. "A small welcoming drink," Mike explained, and all raised a glass with a smile. "Welcome back. Welcome back home."

They finished their fruity drink. Mike explained it was pretty much the national drink of Oneiro, always used to greet visitors. It was a very light, clear blue and delicious.

Phil glanced at Mike "Uh, Mike...Demetrious?"

"No problem, we're out of the closet thanks to you. How long can you stay with us?"

"Not sure, Mike. We were fairly close to the island and thought it would be fun to check in and see how things are going. Needless to say, we're very, very curious, so we dumped and rinsed our freezers (they were virtually empty anyway), and came to see you."

"Glad you did, Phil. It's going to be great fun getting you up to speed. We haven't been exactly asleep at the switch, by any means."

"Quite sure you weren't, Mike. Who's left from the old senior staff?"

"Actually everyone, except Dr. Gray (realization was no longer necessary) and Dr. Montgomery. We never did replace Doctors Gould and Siroa. So we're down to about eight senior staffers. They spend the greater part of their time observing and journalizing."

"What's your population now?"

"About four thousand."

"What?! You're shrinking!"

"Well, not so much shrinking as disseminating. We have several thousand in the field right now, and they're far exceeding any expectations we may have had. I'll give you a full briefing."

"Still working your art, Mike?" asked Anne.

"I sure am, whenever I can and that's more often than you might think. This place pretty much runs itself these days. We'll get someone down here for your bags if they're ready?"

"Yep. Name tags and all, on deck, ready to go."

"Phil, I've got you set up in your old digs with Anne... Edward and all."

"Wait a minute, Mike, we don't want to displace you."

"You're not. I never could bring myself to move into your home, so I built myself something on the surface. Herb and Demetrius are in their own guest suites in the Mansion as well."

"You live on the *surface* Mike?"

"Yes. Many of us have moved up there. We still love the U, but life on the surface is somehow quieter, more peaceful. Besides, thanks to you, Phil, there don't appear to be any remaining security threats, and as a sovereign nation, secrecy is growing less and less a consideration. We're opening up! As I said, we're out of the closet!"

They boarded PM's and were off.

It was immediately clear they had extended the number of downward levels extensively—as much as eight to ten floors—and work was energetically continuing. Phil supposed this was long-range planning, because the main hallways were very quiet. With more than half the population of Oneiro in the field, the remaining staff and students rattled around somewhat...sort of like being in a sunny shopping mall at early morning before the crowds invaded. Quiet, peaceful, and somehow exclusive and personal.

Edward hugged Anne and Phil when he greeted them in Phil's suite. The three of them enjoyed a champagne on the terrace, while Edward brought them up to speed.

"After you left, Phil, and the death of Craig, the BOD voluntarily disbanded itself. Oneiro no longer needed their guidance—as though they had ever really provided any—and on condition their "bank" would remain secure and open, and they could return at will for medical care—Oneiro became a sole Proprietorship in its truest sense. They continued to provide any financing required. Life suddenly grew much simpler for Mike. Some of the old BOD even live on Oneiro much of the year now."

"Smart move on someone's part. Mike?"

"Yessir. You bet."

"Any other security problems now?"

"As far as I know, none whatsoever. Apparently you cleaned house, Phil. I know you paid dearly for it, but it worked. Oneiro and the world are much better places because of it."

The three tipped their glasses and smiled wistfully.

"Well, everyone is waiting for you two down in the dining room, so I suggest you get there while they can still focus and enunciate."

"You're joining us Edward?"

"Wouldn't miss it, Phil."

As Phil and Anne entered the dining room, everyone spontaneously arose and enthusiastic applause broke out. Smiles, hugs, handshakes and kisses came from all quarters. When everyone had drinks in hand they slowly found their way out to the terrace. When everyone was settled, an informal briefing commenced.

How were the field emissaries working out?

Dr. Kahn responded. "Dependant on assigned location, many were cosmetically adjusted to facilitate fidelity with indigenous populations. Given this, their startling good looks, charm, intelligence, physical prowess, wealth, and educational conditioning—they are working in beyond all expectation. They have already achieved commanding roles in government, business, religion, culture, and even the military, and growing more so all the time. It was only a short matter of time before a significant degree of control was feasible."

"Who dictates how this control is directed and used?"

"No one." Kahn responded "Oneiro has total faith in the judgment of on-site agents and they really confine their control to assisting extant authority in governing wisely, with wisdom, vision, and in peace."

"How about the new religion? Any luck understanding it? Is it any assistance?"

Again Kahn answered. "Interestingly, the new religion (we now do call it Oneiroism) is disseminating at an impressive speed, despite the fact that non-students are unable to understand the majority of it. It does contain three elements that enable it however. First, it embraces much of our previous works. Second, it relies strongly on the new art as well. Symbols have always been an underpinning of religion and Oneirion symbols can impart great power, as you may well imagine. Third, the students themselves add their own special charisma, combined with local culture. This has proven to be an exceptionally powerful blend.

The visceral messages they contain are simple and benign in the extreme however:

Pull together, be nice, have fun, guilt has few real sources, do good things, try to be happy, happiness is a virtue, there is no need to kill, no need to hate, no need to die, help others, religion is not power, worship only worthiness and integrity.

We include our Exhortations, as well our concepts of Multi-Deism. Beyond that, not much, not much to preach about, no need for saintly white suits, choirs, tears, prayer, miracles, healing, Bibles, Korans, Torahs, Priests, Ministers, Dali Lamas, Popes, Cardinals, Nuns, Mullahs, Imams, Shaman, Swamis, Witch Doctors, Rabbis, Boombas and Gimcracks. Nothing to fight or kill or die for. Not even a good reason to donate money. Did you ever read Emily Dickinson's *Some Keep the Sabbath Going to Church?*"

"Yes, I have and I understand." Phil smiled, wistfully thinking back to his youth in Washington, and to the subsequent dark time of his horrible struggles.

He thought for a moment.

"How about your food production technology?"

Dr. Butler enthusiastically responded. "Food production has started on an industrial scale off the coasts of Africa, South America, Central America, selected sites in the Far East, primarily in the Sea of Japan off the coast of North Korea. We will stamp out hunger. Using food technology as our distribution mechanism we are attacking cancer, diabetes, arthritis, heart disease, overpopulation, AIDS, ignorance, hate, prejudice, and much more.

Overpopulation is the hottest topic we are facing. With our food processing capabilities, the technical solution to this problem is a snap...no more flies in a bottle. The overwhelming aspect of the problem is who decides what areas and what peoples should be subject to such controls. We don't trust ourselves. We don't trust anyone or anything else as yet. The problem must be attacked. Quite frankly, we are looking into a mechanical decision maker. Whatever we come up with, it better be damned good, and kept God almighty secret. Whatever the resolution, if this be known, the world will condemn us, with bitter recriminations to follow. We face no greater issue. Although, believe it or not, one of the students came up with a biologically generated randomizer. Totally fair and impartial. Could be just the solution."

Phil asked, "Oneiro is fast enhancing the worldwide standard of living. Thanks to you, people know more, have more and I suppose want more. Doesn't this somewhat reduce the human pressure to procreate? They've got more to do. More to engage their time, their minds, their bodies. They're getting smart enough to understand they can avoid screwing themselves into squalor. With your technology, they can just walk away from it. Am I missing something?"

"Yes and no, Phil. We believe the population at large is beginning to see the light. They feel the hope and they want it, I'm sure. Those above them, however, the governments, the corporations, the military...essentially the power brokers have, since about the sixteenth century, based their profits, their political and market control on *growth*. We finally concluded that the economic and geo-political paradigm of the word is actually based on overpopulation. Human bodies are the greatest consumers and comestibles on Earth. Pretty ugly huh?"

"Good God! We're the incarnation of *Ouroboros*."

"The mythical snake that consumed its own tail."

"Yep," Phil said. "So how close are you to a solution?"

"Well, we've come up with several ideas. As I said, technology is the least of our problems."

"So whatcha got?"

Dr. Butler went to a marking board.

- The most straightforward solution is simple across-the-board fertility suppression. Easy. Fair. Impartial. De-humanized. Statistically, however, it could easily result in a genotype imbalance. Unthinkable.
- Another approach is chemo-randomization as we said. Totally objective. Problems there are: a) who wants to introduce totally randomized chemistry into their body, not to mention their heritage, and b) we may still provoke the imbalance problem. Possibly another no-go.

- We could target recessive traits, insanity, genetically transmitted diseases, anti-social tendencies, in fact all manner of undesirable tendencies. The problem is obvious here...welcome to the Third Reich...*out of the question.*
- We are building a heuristic machine. We will not tell it how to work, or what to do. We will simply define the problem and instruct it to find and model the ideal solution. If it works after rigorous testing, shakedown, and evaluation, we may attempt to implement its work.

"The problem is horrific and grotesque. No human and nothing from Oneiro so far is equipped to deal with it. Yet we must face it and aggressively seek a solution...an almost godlike solution. We have no greater problem. We face no greater danger.

We have no higher priority. We must clean up a biological infestation and we are it. We must clean up the infestation without killing, only controlling. We cannot kill the species, or any member. We desperately need the cooperation of the species, but we will not receive it. In trying to save the species, there are great dangers of extinction or of the species learning of our actions and eliminating us altogether. A hard problem and a very difficult situation."

Phil sighed. "Good luck, Doctor. God help you all."

"We plan to market the rest of this technology, for money, to major food distributors, restaurant outlets and, particularly, fast-food chains. We'll re-invest the proceeds into further research and extended distribution. But we see the major benefit in greatly decreased obesity and improved health.

In that same vein, using nearly identical technology, agri-fuel production has started up literally off every coast in the world. We charge no royalties, we donate the equipment to anyone, and we freely provide support—no strings whatsoever. The amazing element to all this is they have been able to nearly eliminate the crude oil initiation stage in energy production and go almost directly to diesel, or any type of petrochemical with minimal pollutants. Believe it or not, it burns clean. A balance bearing little or no particulate or gaseous byproducts. We're going to overcome both global warming and global darkening, in balance, at the same rates. We just may survive this round.

As you know, however, this stimulated a world-wide frenzy. Stock markets, Commodities, Currencies, Riots, and threat of war. Chaos from the Vatican to Mecca. We moderated all this by on-site agents. But it went on chaotically nonetheless, as you know, for some time.

The Middle East, Venezuela, Russia, selected African countries, in fact any country with a history of extorting money and resource from an energy hungry world, is now facing severe long-term problems. We inserted our people into these areas first and major supply-chain corporate networks as the next priority in foreseeing and mitigating the effects as much as possible. There are still untold billions gone awry. Not to mention a lot of very powerful, very pissed off people. We're looking at a fair amount of nursing to bring them up to speed living within the new economic paradigm.

I assumed they would come for us with everything they've got, except for the fact that it's too damned late and they know it. These are not nice people by any stretch. At the same time, though, most aren't vengeance killers either. I believe these people are slowly accepting that their wealth must come from another source. What they may be unable to accept is the loss of power and prestige, which will *not* accompany their new industries. When this settles in, it may be a dangerous time for awhile.

Mike has come up with some very creative solutions for these countries. For one thing, we'll allow them to capitalize on their infrastructure in parallel production and distribution of artificial oil products. No windfall profits to be had, but it'll keep them going until they find something else. And we've got lots more waiting in the wings, much more sophisticated. A lot is still in the conceptual stage. However, you're well aware how fast Oneirons can move from problem definition to conceptual solution to realization. Soon, these countries will be near paradise gardens for tourism, food production, research, space exploration, and more.

To me, the most uplifting is the children."

"The children?"

"Yes. We discussed this once in the production facility as I recall. Result? Children blind since birth know the wonder of Egyptian antiquities, Michelangelo's sculpture, sunrises, Van Gogh's art, the sky and the stars, and a thousand other marvels. Deaf children hear symphonies, bird song, and their mother's voice. Mutes know what it is to sing and laugh and talk to a friend. It's all internal mind you. Memories that are 'fed' to them. But real. Learning and joy and an end to isolation."

"Doctor, you, you actually take my breath away."

"How's the art proceeding?"

Dr. McCauley (Anne's assistant) responded. "Well, it's expanded into sculpture, architecture, and fabric manufacture. You will see examples around campus. Buildings have a special meaning. Sculptures that would be the envy of Michangelo. And watch out for clothes! Some of the dresses will drive you wild, so you have to learn to look away before you lose control. We are pushing them to tone it down a bit for the benefit of Landers and we believe they will come up with some styles that will kick ass all over the world. They've already designed a new line where the cloths actually express the person weaning them. Perhaps they have overcome the superficiality of style alone. Of much greater import, however, the new art is subtly spreading the philosophy of peace and intelligence throughout the world. With great success."

Phil asked, "Mike, biology and genetics have been the main thrust of sciences on Oneiro. Any plans for expanding the base here into other disciplines?"

"In fact, yes, Phil. Even with our new artificial fuels, there remains enough residual pollutants to give us pause for concern. So we're jumping into quantum physics and cosmology in great depth. We think the time is past for nuclear energy production. The time never will be for cold fusion. We hold out the same sort of hope for hydrogen water dissociation. With both routes, the residual energy equation is out of balance. And non-consumptive, so-called renewable energy sources just don't to deliver the 'bang for the buck.'

"We believe the true, long-term solution lies in something akin to dark energy, or perhaps more correctly put, thermo-temporal dissonance generated as a byproduct of cosmic inflation. Are you familiar with Ludwig Boltzmann?"

"He was an early physicist in the 1800's. Worked in thermodynamics. Was kind of 'out there' wasn't he?"

"Ah. Well yes and right as usual. Although his work seems to be gaining some acceptance, primarily from cosmologist studying exponential expansion. We are very hopeful with this line of research, in some areas in any event. Oddly enough, some of our far advanced students indicate that we needn't bother. We're not sure why.

These students demonstrate the faintest glimmers of a sort of...ah...for lack of a better term...intuitive prescience I guess. I don't have a clue what constitutes the mechanism. I'm convinced there's nothing preternatural about it, nor do the students claim any such thing. I believe they can matriculate an exceptional number of complex elements, subject them to extraordinarily analytical processes, and formulate astonishingly accurate postulations. They are staggeringly perceptive, a lot like you, Phil, and *they* seem to feel that we are wasting our time. They even find our efforts somewhat amusing. It's slightly annoying."

"Any idea *why*?"

"None whatsoever. When we try to explore their attitudes further, all we get are confusing, inward looking, and patronizing smiles. They say it's like trying to explain the Oneirion language to a *lander*."

"Hmm." Phil almost whispered "Gives me the feeling that the solution is coming from another...another direction...another source...definitely another direction."

Everyone watched Phil with a rather quizzical expression. Finally, he said, "Mike, have you made any modifications in defenses.

"Indeed. We've spent months on it. We concluded there was a needless risk in maintaining a huge arsenal of hand-held assault weapons. As we found out quite painfully, it's too damned easy for someone on site to turn them on us. Although I believe we've well outgrown such concerns by now. We do maintain a modest ordinance that is highly secured, location secret. But to be honest, if any bad guys invade, or drop out of the skies, or arise from the sea, we can easily subdue or neutralize them without weapons of any kind."

This drew chillingly appreciative looks from Phil and Anne. *Were anyone else but Mike to make such a statement...*

"We did add something really interesting a few weeks ago..." Mike continued, "a joint project between our botany lab and our food production people. Do you remember we gave you a small drink as soon as you arrived?"

"Yes."

"You've been vaccinated," Mike said.

"Vaccinated against what, Mike?"

"Have you ever heard of squalene?"

"Squalene is a fatty substance that comprises a component of roughly thirty-five percent of the glandular secretion known as sebum." As usual, Phil's knowledge drew some quizzical glances all round.

"Correct. Squalene is a lipid constituent of sebum, which is produced by humans and other creatures as part of the glandular system surrounding skin and hair follicles. It has a nearly indistinguishable odor. It assists the skin and hair in maintaining health and moisture, and it does generate some sub-conscious triggers, much as do phernomes, only much more subtle. It is detectable, even differentiable by hybrid plants we have engineered here on Oneiro."

"Okay."

"Well, Phil, how familiar are you with porins?"

"Porins are specialized cellular addenda used in a process akin to osmosis in the transport of hydrolyzed or emulsified materials."

Again, Phil's knowledge drew more quizzical glances. Phil wondered when they would ever just get over this aspect of his makeup. There wasn't one damned thing he could do about it. He was truly trying to control it, but to little effect.

"Again correct," Mike said. "Porins occur in plant and animal life. They cross cellular membranes. On one side (*we* call it the alpha side), they are cytoplasmic in nature. The beta side is where the structural business takes place and in a cross parallel context. They fashion what is called the beta barrel. The beta barrel is used primarily in the transport of basic water for a variety of reasons.

"There are several types of porins, though, and these are not limited to H^2O processing. They can convey many types of metabolites through nucleoporin, using a biological system called TRP (Transient Receptor Potential). We have hybridized a new type for our specific use into a new plant life unique to Oneiro. We call them Sentry Plants...with an "S".

"Nice play on words." Phil said, smiling.

Mike returned his smile. "These we have enhanced with our capabilities in scent control and production." Mike could nearly feel some eyelids drooping, so he cut to the chase. "We vaccinate every human we wish to allow on Oneiro, permanently or as guests, which effectively labels them as authorized personnel on the island. This vaccination harmlessly, immediately, and immutably modifies their Squalene, unless we elect to chemically negate the process."

"Why reverse the process?"

"In case good guys go bad. Some sort of potentially rogue resident, or guest."

"I see. You cancel their security card."

"Exactly, Phil." He turned to a flip chart.

"We then engineered our new Sentry Plants to do several things:
- We taught them what to produce in terms of scents
- We taught them how to produce toxins
- We taught them to recognize authorized personnel
- We taught them how to react to human activities
- We taught them how to disseminate phernomes
- We taught them how to disseminate toxins

"We have planted thousands of these little beauties all over Oneiro. One literally cannot go more than a very few steps topside without attracting the notice of a Sentry Plant ..."

"... and when their notice is attracted Mike?"

"First they analyze the creature. If non-human, then there is no activity. If human, then it senses if the appropriate squalene is being emitted. If yes, no action is taken. If no, then it generates an odor that is totally, and I mean totally, irresistible to humans, which should immobilize the subject long enough for our people to intercede. If the subject attempts to move away, the plant emits a powerful opiate. Nap time. By this time, all Sentry Plants in the immediate area have been alerted, as have our security staff, and these plants are in similar reactive mode, unless they detect another human with appropriate squalene, as with the original plant.

Just as with some types of conifers, Sentry plants share an immense common tap root, and they emit faint electrical impulses at appropriate times. Our security system is circuited into this network.

If the subject somehow contrives to continue to move away, the plant sprays an exceptionally efficacious acidic poison from pods at the terminator of each branch. This emulsifies any protective equipment, and is invariably fatal.

Should a stranger with non-aggressive intent happen upon the island, no harm will abjure to him. He'll simply enjoy the pretty plants, get slightly turned on, have a nice nap, and we'll take care of him. He will have a very pleasant experience, with no ill effects whatsoever. Otherwise, if the subject is equipped for chemical warfare, he is either immobilized or killed."

"Brilliant. A constant, completely passive defense network." Phil observed. "Of course this assumes your dealing with a corporeal intruder."

"I don't understand Phil." Frowned Mike.

"Neither do I Mike. Ever been put to an actual combat field test?"

"Not really," Mike said. "I hope it never is. But we do use vaccine-neutralized students for infiltration tests from time to time. Thus far, it is fool proof and unbreakable.

"I suppose someone could assault Oneiro with some particularly virulent herbicidal virus. A defoliant introduced that could escape our immediate notice. Sentry Plants are exceptionally robust, however. I can't imagine anyone except an Oneirion having the degree of expertise requisite to understand and attack their cytology.

"We have carefully reviewed the rest of the weaponry, which was so kindly provided by our Board of Directors. We found most of it was outdated junk. A waste of space. Useless. Not worth keeping, or maintaining. We're now in the process of ripping it out and dumping it in the sea, where it will provide some lovely homes for local marine life. The only thing we couldn't bear to part with were our choppers, the Apaches. We love 'em too much. Our people play at maneuvers with them constantly."

"Mike, are you saying that Oneiro has *no* hardened defensive systems, except a couple of attack helicopters?"

"I wish I could say yes, Phil, but the answer is a definite no. Fact is, we are installing two state-of-the-art defensive systems, absolutely deadly. Probably the most advanced in the world. Neither has been deployed in a battlefield scenario yet, so we are a Beta Site for both. These are the deadliest conventional machines on earth. Our former Board Member, Mr. John Dunkin? He couldn't do enough to help after he was briefed on your...ah...lunch meeting with Bob Griffith in New Jersey."

"I remember. So what've you got?" asked Phil.

"First we've doubled the height and capacity of Proteus Point, and it now has a totally redundant back-up concealed in something akin to an underground missile silo. The second concentrator can be raised and fully deployed within three minutes, although it's not interactive to our Board Room. And yes, we still use that extraordinary room extensively.

"Either concentrator can see *anything* within hundreds of miles at around 240°. That covers any threats from marine or air surface incursion, as well as airborne, in fact, any sort of incoming. Our only blind spot is below our cliff lines and we've now covered that as well, interactive to Proteus. We have greatly improved our underwater surveillance capabilities (we even have some marine life sort of standing watch, audio interactive to Proteus), so we're pretty damned hard to penetrate by stealth.

Our primary system for remote targets is a completely new derivative of the old solid-state laser systems developed for the U.S. Military. We can take out *anything*, hundreds of miles away, at literally the speed of light, and retarget instantly with a near hundred-percent reliability rate, and an absolute one-hundred percent accuracy rate. That system can be elevated to roughly two hundred meters. Dependant on whether we can go higher, but that entails constant retargeting and, should we need to go higher, the implication is we have a greater targeting window in any event.

Secondary to that, should a threat or threats somehow come within range, we have installed a formidable back-up: The latest models Metal Storm ADWS (MS227/B's I think)."

Phil frowned. "Metal Storm? ADWS?"

"Metal Storm is an incredible system wherein something on the magnitude of *one million* 40mm shells can be fired in *less* than one minute. Anything within range no longer exists, period. It is quite literally vaporized. ADWS is an acronym for Area Denial Weapons System, which is the version of Metal Storm most appropriate for our use. We are strictly defensive. Simply stated, anything that achieves position above or in the vicinity surrounding Oneiro won't survive for a minute. Guaranteed. We are installing forty such units, blanketing the island.

We will retain the conventional defense systems already in place to fend off any undersea assault, although about twenty of our MS's have an automated 270° pivotal targeting prowess. They are positioned at the various apogees of our clifflines, so we can take out about anything down to a depth of a few meters."

Further to all this, we have some subordinate developments coming from our own emerging technology in quantum physics and astrophysics. We will know within a few months if this weapon is feasible and deployable. I am pretty convinced it is. If so, there will not be a place on Earth, from a spot one meter in diameter to a continent that we could not decimate in moments. I know this sounds contrary to our mission here.

But there may be some big, bad boys out there, maybe farther out and bigger and deadlier than even we suspect. Incidentally, this would double nicely as cometary or asteroid shield.

Something more pernicious? Scorched earth is sometimes an irremissible option. We are Boy Scouts no longer here. We've been blooded. In fact, none more than you, Phil. So should the time come ..."

"Fuck me," Phil whispered. *This sure as hell wasn't the Mike Auslander I left on Oneiro a few short months ago. He was becoming profoundly dangerous. Art student, my ass!* In the hands of anyone but Mike and the Oneirons, Phil would be horrified. At the same time, he knew he would be doing the same damned things himself, maybe even more.

Phil hesitantly peered at Mike for a moment. "Ahh...this is based on vacuum anomalies...?"

"... yep... virtual particles normally generated on the event, or on the cosmic horizons," was Mike's only response. Clearly Mike was not in a sharing mood.

After a few hours, the party broke up. Anne and Phil returned to their apartment and spent a quiet afternoon on the terrace sipping Ouzo and talking to Edward.

The days and weeks that followed passed like a dream. It was truly *Oneiro*.

Phil isolated himself for a couple of days at the south end of the island where he had been sent after his Fear Ordeal. He reacquainted himself with his skills. He hung from the same cliff face. He tested his strength, his mind, his insight, and his courage. If anything, he found he was actually stronger and still growing.

Anne, Phil, Herb, and even Demetrius checked into medical (at the goading of Mike) and were set up for the same regimen and support provided to Board members. They were provided a supply of custom engineered food supplements, not to mention a selection of advanced courses in various disciplines they might want to consume at the same time. Phil and Anne couldn't wait to try "eating" their way to higher education. Herb and Demetrious weren't quite so bold.

Phil decided that Quantum Physics and Cosmology would be a good start, and Bio-Chemistry would round him out pretty well. As an afterthought, he added Marine Biology and Astrophysics. He needed to come up to speed with current Oneirion weapons research. That should nourish his mind for awhile. After that he was considering becoming a General Practitioner MD. That could be useful at sea...or maybe Anne should do that? Or both. He'd ask her about it.

Intriguingly, Herb selected Poetry and Philosophy.

Demetrious immediately chose Meteorology and Marine Biology.

Anne started with Music and Numbers Theory. She felt disciplines closer to her training might be more effectively matriculated.

A brief period was necessary for the four of them to acclimate to the unsolicited eruption of learning in their minds. So, for a time, meals were a non-stop cacophony of "didjaknows", quotations, and debates where disciplines clashed. After a few days, however, meals became a calmer, more relaxing experience.

Anne always got a kick out of the total lack of inhibitions on Oneiro, in both student and faculty, so she was highly amused to report Herb had moved in with *three* female instructors. Phil had to admit he was impressed. Then a wryly amused Anne reported to Phil that he had received a similar invitation from another couple of female instructors, via Herb.

"Interested?" Anne grinned playfully, eyebrows raised.

Phil smiled. "Anne when I was just a boy, my parents would take me to the National Zoo in Washington, D.C. The animals that fascinated me the most were the beautiful white Bengal Tigers. I always wanted to pet them—but I *never* wanted to get in the cage with them."

Moments later, a breathless Charlie Stein rushed unannounced into Phil's apartment.

"Charlie! Great to see you. You've been hiding up at Proteus Point I think. I was going to come up and see you and—"

Breathing hard, stone-faced, sweating, excitement oozing from his pores, he said, "Phil. No time to talk. Please come with me...now. Dr. Kahn is already in the jeep. Mike said you were both urgently needed immediately."

No questions. Phil agreed. They started to exit the Mansion, jeep waiting outside.

A dusty, disheveled Dr. Kahn seated in the back said, "Hello Phil."

"Hi, Doc. What the hell's going on?"

"Ask your friend here. I'm just along for the ride."

"Where are we going, Charlie?"

They jumped into the jeep and into the heat and tore off toward the southern end of Oneiro.

"We're going to the Proteus Point Communications Concentrator, Phil. I just spoke to Mike and he instructed me to get you there fast. He's on the way himself, but he believes it's most important that *you* get there *now*. Mike called it a Code Allodapos whatever the hell that means. What does it mean, Phil?"

"Not really sure. What about you, Doc?"

"Well, in Greek it means...Ahh...*Alien*. Roughly. Beyond that, I haven't got a clue."

"Where is Mike, Charlie?"

"I believe he's off on a boat somewhere talking to the fishies, or something crazy like that, if you can believe it."

A flinty haze of reddish-beige dust followed them for hundreds of meters as they sped south.

"What the hell's going on, Charlie?" Phil yelled, squinting into the wind and grit and blinding sunshine.

Charlie yelled back louder. "Well, after you left I brought in a whole staff of comms experts, all Landers, and we've been transmitting and listening intensively continuously since then. We never expected to hear anything mind you...we were just making sure we were well established and ready for anything."

"Okay."

"Who the hell authorized this, Charles?"

"Doctor, no one has authorized a damned thing I do since Phil decided to go boating. The place just seems to operate in a sort of tacit coordination. Why? Have I done something wrong?"

"Not at all. Not at all. Please continue."

"This morning we started receiving something. Close. Narrow band. About 1.62 million kilometers out. Far enough for us to be sure it wasn't terrestrial and close enough for good reception. They appear to be station-keeping at apogee, maintaining synchrony."

They screeched to a bumpy, dusty stop in front of the Proteus Concentrator.

"What did you get, Charlie?" They talked as they walked, entering the cool interior of the Proteus facility and inward to the isolated communications chamber.

"Don't have one damned clue, Phil. The best I can describe it as is 'whisper language.' Damned spooky actually. We piped it down to Dr. McLean in Languages. She says nothing like it exists within her experience."

"What does it sound like to you, Charlie?"

"Mmm. Like halfwits waking up from a long coma, trying to speak to each other without being overheard. Makes the hairs stand up on your neck. Our direction finders triangulated that more than one source is transmitting."

"How many?"

"Two actually. One is maintaining synchronous orbit at the LaGrange Point, L.1. About 1,620,000 kilometers out. The other is station keeping at L.4. Forms a kind of an equilateral triangle with us. Figuring that out took some really fancy footwork. One of our boys had to actually incorporate a factor in extant apogee and perigee, as well as galactic expansion to calculate their coordinates."

Phil frowned. "What's so difficult about radio signal triangulation?"

"Well, triangulation requires that we direction-find the output from at least two reception sites."

"So why didn't you rig up another receiver?"

"We did. Didn't work. I'll explain as we go along."

"Okay. Are they coming this way?"

"For now, they seem to be geo-stationary. And get this, the reason we were unable to triangulate is that these are highly directed communications signals. Pinpoint targeting. No spillover. Directed right to Oneiro. Directed right to Proteus Point in fact. We aren't remotely close to this level of technology."

"How'd you know it's so tightly focused?"

"Simple. We took a receiver a couple of clicks south of Proteus, tuned into the same bandwidth, towards the same coordinates...and nothing. That's why triangulation was so difficult. Pretty cool."

"Why did Mike want *us* here so fast?"

Pause. Charlie was lost in thought, trying to understand as well.

"*Charlie?* Why did Mike want us here first?"

"He thought you would be best qualified to sense danger. He wanted Dr. Kahn to observe."

They arrived at the Proteus communications chamber and entered.

"Charlie, I want this room emptied."

Within seconds, only Charlie, Phil, and Dr. Kahn remained. Phil could see the entire crew looking intently into their sound room through a large sound-proof window. Phil instructed Charlie to pipe their radio traffic to the outer room. He only ordered their removal to ensure quiet. They had every right to hear this. Phil sensed it profoundly. Something was imminent. Phil could feel his own heart thundering.

"Let me hear it, Charlie."

It was like something out of a haunting from hell. Soft, cloying, and threatening. It frightened Phil beyond any of his training—yet he realized if this were truly alien, he would have no point of reference to judge whether it was good or evil, benign or malevolent. Who knew? This was truly alien. Phil could hardly breathe or swallow. Yet the more he listened, somehow he was becoming convinced there was no malice afoot here. In fact, a certain...kinship seemed within the realm of possibility. Yes definitely a kinship of sorts. He felt he was in the presence of something vast, intelligent, non-aggressive and...somehow...related. It was humbling and immensely disquieting.

Dr. Kahn, close to fainting, fell into a chair, white knuckles gripping the arms, mouth agape, eyes glazed. He would neither move, nor speak until the communications was complete.

"This *is* live?"

"As live as it gets, Phil."

"Please give me the microphone, Charlie."

He pushed the send button.

"We are a listening post in the Mediterranean area of our planet's Northern Hemisphere. We are receiving your traffic. Please identify yourself."

The whispers abruptly discontinued. Then nothing. Only background static echoing from eons even more ancient than these beings.

"This is Proteus Point listening post. Please acknowledge."

Nothing.

"This is Proteus Point listening post on Earth. Over."

Nothing.

"This is Proteus Point. We are aware you are directing your signals to us. Please respond."

The silence was overwhelming. Suddenly, the whispers resumed and Phil heard a word in the midst of the whispers that actually made his hair stand on end, it sounded very much like "Oneiro".

Phil swallowed. He took a few moments to compose himself. He was perspiring and slightly trembling.

"This is Proteus Point listening post on Oneiro. Please respond. Over."

Whispers.

"This is Proteus Point listening post on Oneiro. Please respond. Over."

Whispers.

"This is Proteus Point listening post on Oneiro. Please respond. Over."

Suddenly, there was a cacophony of sound erupting from the speakers. Nearly deafening. Quickly, Phil recognized the language. He was stunned, nearly paralyzed. The language was Oneirion. Phil turned to Charlie and whispered. "Where is Mike for God's sake?"

"Please wait one…we'll have someone here able speak to you shortly. Over?"

Another pause. A long one. Then whispers back and forth. Then something new and unintelligible. Suddenly the crew outside their window was screaming and laughing and jumping up and down and hugging each other. Charlie was going nearly crazy himself…Phil was still listening to the strangest words he had ever heard…repeating and repeating…clearly machine generated.

Aie-ookinollwy*lag-ed Prrrrat+eeea-tus Poo_iyn. Guydd mooryenyg Oyn-eey*rrieeous. Uwer.

Aie-ookinollwy*lag-ed Prrrrat+eeea-tus Poo_iyn. Guydd mooryenyg Oyn-eey*rrieeous. Uwer.

Aie-ookinollwy*lag-ed Prrrrat+eeea-tus Poo_iyn. Guydd mooryenyg Oyn-eey*rrieeous. Uwer.

Phil was not versed in reading complex radio chatter, so he totally failed to understand. On the other hand, the Proteus team were world-class experts.

Phil frowned at Charlie "What the hell?"

Had everyone gone crazy? What was this electro-babble doing to them?

Charlie was laughing in pure uncontrollable joy, tears forming in his eyes. He closed his eyes for a moment, swallowed, finally catching his breath and gathering some measure of control.

He locked eyes with Phil, taking hold of him by each shoulder "Phil, they're saying:

Acknowledged Proteus Point...
Good morning Oneiro...Over

Phil gently pulled away and turned, unable to fully master the event just past. In the wonder of all his dreams of Oneiro, this one moment dwarfed his grandest visions.

The pain. The struggle. All the fear and sordid death. Suffering inflicted and endured...vindicated in this one short, half garbled message. He couldn't move. He couldn't breathe.

Mike Auslander entered his field of vision, breathless, dusty wet, still in wetsuit.

"It's true, Phil?"

Phil looked at him wordlessly.

"It *is* true Phil? They've come to us. They're with us aren't they?"

Phil breathed and handed him the microphone. "Talk to them Michael."

149,000 Kilometers per Second

The Gantlet

Ganti—Y☐ ☐☐ ☐—Gänt'—Gatlopp—Gata Lane

Phil and Dr. Kahn sat in the lobby entrance of the communications concentrator for over nine hours. They seldom spoke. They drank coffee. They watched through the observation window...mechanically consuming the occasional sandwich. They watched Mike work, and waited, and waited.

Mike had immediately deferred leadership to Phil with the advent of this remarkable development. Phil's first action was to order a total blackout of all communications and travel to or from the center, or the island. No exceptions. The minimum authorized length of movements or messages was set at 1,620,000 kilometers. Nighttime brought yellow lights and gray shadows and quiet to the center, emphasizing its remoteness, its loneliness. Carr and Kahn sat outside in the night cool, alone, peering at the stars.

After a time, Mike exited the lobby, looking very much like a doctor with grave news of his patient. Phil and Sun stood.

Mike looked at Phil. "I have a message for you." He handed Phil a small stack of computer generated prints.

Wordlessly, Phil took the print-out, re-entered the lobby, seated himself, and started to read.

Greetings to Oneiro—Greetings to Earth

We are known as the QAVL—pronounced *Kavel* in your English language. This name has meaning. The meaning will be fully defined in forthcoming communications.

We have maintained a fixed geo-synchronous position respective to planet Earth for some 2,000,000 solar years. Our temporal physical position in the universe has literally no relevance to our species. Nor does time *per se*. Therefore, we were content to remain here for an indefinite period, in part studying your current dominant life form and engaged in our own pursuits. Of which there are infinitely many.

We maintain hundreds of millions of stellar observatories throughout this and seven million other galaxies. We perform this service on behalf of a vast kindred stellar community. A cosmic family related by what you visualize as genetic material.

Surprise is an emotion we very seldom experience. Your manifestation of the Oneirion language was an astonishing, nearly instantaneous phenomenon in relative terms. We have not developed the physical apparatus with which to converse verbally in your terran languages. We have acquired a total command of all your written languages. Hence this will suffice as our mutual communications media. Verbally, of course, we can converse in "*Oneirion*." We are pleased with the name you have selected.

We congratulate you. You rightfully suspected that the cosmos teams with life in every conceivable stage of advancement. You on Oneiro begin to suspect that all life has a common source. correct. You accomplished this with remarkable speed, faster than any creature in our memory, which dates back more than 1.5 billion solar years, and you accomplished this with little supporting information.

You have yet to postulate that all life is connected. Physically connected. A common genesis. You presently believe this singular, omnipresent factor to be genetic material. DNA, RNA or whatever the macro-molecule that defines incipient life on Earth. In fact, the actual material exists profoundly below the subatomic level. Quadrillions of mass-less particles common to all life spanning intergalactic space. Common to every cell of your bodies. Common to every cell of every organism on Earth. Common to every constituent element of every life form in the universe.

You might relate to such phenomena as sub-Bosonic clusters. Titanic nebulae, eons below sub-atomic, bound and interacting according to the physics of their own micro-verse. Unified and extant at the birth of the universe, now in the process of titanic dissemination through inflation—still unified nonetheless. One vast totality. Infinite. Dwelling at the absolute limit of comprehension. Memory spanning over fourteen billion solar years. Perhaps infinitely longer. The number of such particles is beyond the grasp of any sapient species known to us. We have concluded that this is the measure of creation. This is the measure of the creator, or perhaps its progeny.

Any new constituent: *Organic or Inorganic*
                        Corporeal or Incorporeal

...must first achieve fruition as a requisite to incorporation. Kosmos. As with you now. We aspire to your successful completion of this process. We celebrate your linkage. One triumphal stride towards survival and joining. A door opening. A star emitting its light creating a blossoming terminator. Bathing its solar ménage with the warming photons of a fresh day.

We bid you well. We bid you welcome. We call you brethren.

For millions of years, without exception, throughout the universe, linkage has been consummated solely through adaptation to the communication you term Oneirion. We term it 'Kosmos'.

We had anticipated you would achieve Oneirion within 750,000 solar years. We had projected your total extinction as a species well within 250,000 solar years. Quite a pleasant surprise. You've done well indeed.

We suspect your unique propensity for language is one key to your dramatic progress. We enjoy your various languages very much. A true art form. So many languages. Subtle nuances. Many ways to say the same thing. Such beauty. Horrific and grotesque as well. You create things that do not exist. You value truth. And you lie. Words. Love. Hate. Fear. Courage. Cowardice. Greed. Loneliness. Selfishness. Lust. Mercy. A near infinite spectra of emotions and concepts. They bring you together. They keep you apart. We fear they will ultimately kill you. Such contractions.

One of your words particularly intrigues us: *Gauntlet*

This word is particularly rich in meanings for us. A hybrid derivative of your old Norske, Swedish, Old English and Frankish. It conveys a bounty of meanings and interpretations:

- The coming together of paths
- Something that protects
- A challenge

- A punishment
- A ceremony of passage
- A trapping of war

The word Gauntlet eloquently summarizes our message.

<u>Consider this a message from a friend. Read it with patience and amity.</u>

Probability is that thousands of species perish on your Earth every year. In fact there have been *five* mass extinctions in your known bio-paleontological history. You are probably in the midst of a *sixth*, perhaps of your own provocation. Earth's days of planetary bio-diversity seem numbered. Though in point of fact, if you really don't know how many forms inhabit your planet...how do you know how many you've lost...or saved? So, is the Earth, life, man, winning or losing? We don't really know. You don't know. No creature knows.

Is extinction the ordained destiny of all terran species? Probably. With some impressive exceptions. Is mankind excepted? Probably not. These are early days.

So is mankind included? Could be. Pretty grim.

Many contend that humans, by destroying your habitat, are in fact destroying yourselves. Perhaps pollution, or oxidized particulates, gaseous by-products, or industrial chemical refuse, or whatever, are becoming genuinely troublesome. Whether or not the planetary warming or cooling phenomena is attributable to human causality, we believe you are obligated to clean up your mess nonetheless. That's more than reasonably civilized stewardship.

But the *real* pollution, the real killer, resides in the living corpus of *homo hominis*. Human bodies. Bodies that consume matter and convert it to energy and eliminate excess matter as waste, and wantonly use any number of things. Bodies that require as much area as human economics permit, disregarding geo-nomics. Your rapacious consumption renders you a very unique species. And very dangerous.

You currently stand at some 6.6 billion souls. Terrifyingly close to 7 billion humans on Earth. The "carrying capacity" of Earth is 8 billion souls. After that, you will have achieved critical mass. Very much like the critical mass prerequisite to a thermonuclear event. This will manifest itself as a biological event and probably culminate in a thermonuclear event. A self extinction event. The first and only such event in nearly 5 billion years of Earth's history.

Amongst many other concepts coined by you is "Supply and Demand." A fairly elementary concept provoked by your perception of economics:

Supply of a given "thing" within a closed environment greatly influences the demand for that "thing," and consequently its perceived value. So if you have one of a "thing" and its value is say…two coconuts, when another "thing" enters that same system it will be valued say…one coconut. Logical. Elegant.

Oversimplification? Yes. Valid nonetheless.

On the other hand, consider the Western Lowland Gorilla, the celebrated Silverback. They should enjoy a much needed increase in its relative value:

$$1 \text{ Gorilla} = 9,286 \text{ Humans}$$

You will not admit to it, but don't think for one minute that humans do not recognize this ratio and empirically act upon it. Murder 4 Silverbacks and create a worldwide scandal. Murder 37,144 Humans in the same geographic zone and it might not even make the newspapers.

In your circumstance, the closed environment is obviously planet Earth. The "thing" is a human life. With each issuance of the "thing," all "thing's" values are proportionately diminished. You now have almost 7,000,000,000 "things." The relative value is plummeting every second. How accommodating that must be. This renders it less disagreeable to kill. Humans become conveniently replaceable. Less guilt and so on. You can bathe in the luxury of hating and killing one another. That sort of 'thing'.

A stunning, candid iteration by the Camir Rouge in Cambodia. The Viet Nam War. Their Official Policy communicated to and inflicted upon their millions of hapless citizens. A chillingly honest declaration of their arrant distain of human life:

To preserve you is no gain.
To destroy you is no loss.

<u>Try to imagine this:</u> Two kindly, elderly ladies struggle to cross a street that is so hot; its tarmac has melted and is actually bubbling. The ladies are trying desperately to escape a titanic city-wide firestorm so horrific they would actually dare a boiling street. Their shoes melt and burn. Their feet and legs are carbonized. They finally, mercifully, surrender to gravity. The name of the town is Dresden. We witnessed it.

<u>Try to imagine this:</u> A lovely young lady, working in an innocuous office, in a tall building, in a large town. The

office is on fire. The fire is so horrific the young girl finds the strength to break a nearly unbreakable glass window. Jumping out of that window, she dares endless hundreds of meters. She finally, mercifully, surrenders to gravity. The name of the town is New York. We witnessed it.

If you don't discount yourselves out of the market, there's always your "flies in a bottle" concept. Fairly elementary as well:

> Create a closed system. Cap a male and female fly (*Calliphora vomitoria*) into a bottle with sufficient food and air. Soon they'll breed and breed and breed until the food's gone, or the air's fouled, or there's excessive waste, until no flies are left. All dead.

Earth is a closed system too. The cap is on the bottle and, aside from relatively miniscule minerals and trace elements falling from the heavens, you're on your own. 7,000,000,000! It may seem a cold-blooded statement, but it is obvious to us that humans must find a balance between the urge to procreate and the imperative to survive.

Somehow, you must struggle to take more pride in your own personal destinies, and the creations you achieve in your own lives—as opposed to investing so much emotion, such aspirations, into your progeny. They *are* indeed your future. An inestimable treasure. But they are *not* your *raison d'être*. In fact, you discount their value by overproduction and, tragically, they sense this. It shows. An increasing cynicism with each succeeding generation. We've witnessed that as well.

You're not polluting yourselves to death—you're copulating to the point of extinction. The more you are, the more you feed upon and breed upon yourselves. Seven *billion*. Exponential growth can revert to exponential decline at lightening speed (That's over 149,000 kilometers per second at Earth sea-level and average air pressure.). Blood worms are *driven only* to reproduce. Hopefully you are navigating towards a broader horizon. If indeed you are, be aware, your urge to procreate by and large will defeat both your quest for immortality and your quest to survive as a species. We have witnessed such tragedy on many worlds. Studied ignorance. Totally inability to master their own nature.

Reproduction

Mankind sets itself in a suicidal plummet towards ignominious extinction. Goaded like herd animals by your gonads and hypothalamus—docilely inciting the tyranny of your hormonal prods to delude you—to believe the urge to copulate, to reproduce, and to nurture your young is the most important, noblest occupation, the highest calling to which humans can aspire. The attainment of fulfillment. It opportunes the rationalization of emptiness and failure.

Diatom, cockroaches, rats, snakes, frogs, lizards, all manner of creatures, have been reproducing, many more intelligently, for hundreds of millions of solar years. Many of them, during periods of drought or famine demonstrate the wisdom to simply cease reproducing. An enlightenment that appears to elude humans.

The QAVL go centuries without offspring. When needed they are produced. Evolution is no longer a function of reproduction. Others are semelparous, reproducing but once during their immense span. Such progeny are treasured beyond imagining.

A young woman, blind from heat and sun crawls forth seeking solace from the burning perdition. No food, shelter, water, medicine, or human charity for untold days. She is near death, as is the newborn infant cradled in her arms. Her land has been suffering the ravages of a remorseless drought and a savage, farcical revolution for seven years. No crops. No water. No animals. No shelter. Unrelenting torture. In all likelihood she will die. In all likelihood her child will die. Pathetic.

In so many ways.

Humans are capable of such horrors.

As species evolve and become more complex, their young often require a longer, maturation, nurturing and inculcation period. Therefore nature provides hormones that motivate creatures to breed, protect and foster their offspring. This prevents them from either deserting, or consuming their progeny; or simply foregoing the effort of breeding altogether.

Advanced corporeal races regard such hormones as vestiges of their past...much as humans regard Wisdom Teeth. They develop more intelligent, more compassionate means of managing their numbers, with wisdom—renouncing vainglory and intolerance. Such apparatus exists on Oneiro.

Divorce yourself from procreation stratagem you are wretchedly ill-equipped to confront. Divorce yourself both intellectually and biologically. Conquer and set aside your hormones, as with your superfluous molars and childhood playthings. Cherish sex as a charming legacy of your evolution; now reserved for gentle pleasures and expressions of affection.

Room enough for love abides.

If you disregard this reality. If you acquiesce to the living anachronisms—the shaman and charlatans brooding in your churches and halls of government—you will perish.

Growth

Growth does not equate to progress. Growth does not equate to success. Growth is the illusion of both.
We monitor your broadcast. We hear the hubris.

Profits will grow next year by—
The GNP will grow by—
Sales will grow by—
Population will grow by—
Projected growth for the next fiscal year is—

Your economy, your governments, your vision, your mindset, your rapacious greed. You proudly bind these things to your fixation on growth. If you do not achieve growth you feel you have failed. The pride and dignity of honest consistent industry evades you.

You hold hostage your future, your aspirations and your precarious prospects of grace…for the phantasma of growth.

You formulate fatuous plans. Take extraordinary measures.

You expand food production to feed your growing and starving millions.

Sounds compassionate to you?

Quite the opposite.

You burden your posterity with a monstrous malignancy and far greater suffering.

That way lays extinction.

Attempting to smother a plague of locusts with a blizzard of wheat.

If you persist, you will perish.

Stop dancing around the problem. Pollution, climate change, poverty, hate, quality-of-life, ignorance, crime, starvation and on and on. All attributable to *ONE THING ONLY*. Population.

These are not speculation. Not opinion. Not debatable. These are fact. We have observed this on a million worlds.

In all the infinite diversity of cosmic existence any incarnation may be possible. However, a logical reckoning of the known, must conclude that the least possible incarnate is abject intentional ignorance and unmitigated chaos. Paraphrasing your Albert Einstein "God did not throw dice with the universe." Nor is God a prankster. Nor is God an idiot.

Man apparently is skilled in ways the gods themselves would not dare.

Mankind has a proclivity this assertion:

It is in our nature to destroy ourselves.

Untrue:

It is not in your nature to destroy yourselves.
It is in your nature to destroy others.
Ironically, with the one, comes the other.
Nature lays the trap.
True throughout the universe.

If the embittered earth robbed of its innocence, and your own suicidal reproductive dispositions are resolute in your destruction, how can you possibly escape?

You flee. You flee for your lives. You leave them behind. Leave them in the distance, glaring in hot, rapacious chagrin through the hazy brume of your genetic dust. *Get away*.

Any species that stagnates, which fails to relentlessly evolve, will face inevitable extinction. This is a law—nature's most immutable. Extinction is nature's remedy for failure, the non-persistence of the species, unable to outpace the perils at hand. They don't *get away*.

Through your technology, you have slowed—perhaps even generally arrested human evolution.

Then again, there are indications that human evolution may actually be dramatically escalating. This is demonstrated by significant expansion of new facets to the human genome.

By that same token, perhaps all these new genetic traits are random shifts that would normally have been "weeded out" through un-tampered natural selection. Perhaps you grow not from expansion, but lack of selection. Perhaps your genetic bush is growing ever uncontrolled. Nature—barred from acting as the DNA-etic agronomist—pruning the kaleidoscopic, nearly fractal branching of your own polynucleotides.

Wherever lies the truth, it is evident that survival of the fittest has ever decreasing dominion in human affairs.

This does not refer to living longer, or healthier, or being more attractive, or happier, to clarify things. It essentially refers to those who live, to whom, without human intervention, nature would have decreed death. Insufficient to continue. Unable to live as an independent, viable being. Would have, perhaps should have been left alone. Allowed to perish.

Sounds barbaric? It is. Nature is. Survival is. Humankind is, in so many respects.

Mankind attempts to frustrate nature's phylogeny with rather indifferent measures, simply stalling for time. An hour, a day, a week, a year, maybe longer—maybe years. All manner of dark little victories.

You cannot keep the wolf from the door, so you try to keep the door from the wolf.

You can do better.

Capitalize on nature, advance new laws, out-evolve nature's dictums.

Research science represents exploration in its purest directed form. Applied science is the enactment of knowledge gained through such research. Research science cannot be abused in any real sense. Any truly rational society would never shackle such endeavors, in any way whatsoever. Applied science, on the other hand, is subject to any manner of imaginable abuse and certainly warrants control and the closest scrutiny. You must clearly distinguish the two. Foster the one. Intelligently capitalize on the other.

Assuming for the sake of argument, you do benefit from unfettered research. You overcome your often lamentable temerity of amino acids. Perhaps even put an end to your suffocating idolatry of any organelles that transit your reproductive ducts. What's left then? Can you now aggressively and freely advance research? Can you learn how to evolve? Does anything still stand in your way?

Humankind has little option now but to *self-evolve*. Adapt using human innovation, or submit to a remorseless termination—the same fate as antecedent billions that failed to adapt—billions that were unequipped with the sapience and tools with which you are gifted to aid you in your struggle.

Realistically, many species survived on your Earth for tens, sometimes hundreds of millions of years. Breathtaking suspension of the onslaughts of selection. Ammonites, crinoids, crocodiles, ants, dinosaurs, horseshoe crabs, mosquitoes, cockroaches, sharks, ceolacanths and many, many more. Many still thrive today.

Journey to Shark Bay, Australia. You'll find a wonder there. Stromatalites. Cyanal Bacteria. The oldest life form on Earth. More than a dozen times older than the dinosaurs themselves. Around 3.5 billion years ago they lived in the primordial seas and bonded oxygen with emulsified iron. One billion years later, they had saturated the seas with ferrous oxide to the degree they commenced oxygenating the planet's atmosphere, preparing it for global life. 3.5 billion years old and still hearty. They have lived 87.5% of the existence of the Earth itself.

Stromatalites are joined by their dark cousins living more than five kilometers down at the divergent boundaries between Earth's tectonic plates. For billions of years these creatures somehow survived isolation in tiny islands of life on the sea floor, superheated water, deadly acids and total blackness. Easily the harshest environment on Earth. Somewhere between these two tiny miracles, man may someday divine life's genesis on this planet. Two tiny wonders incipient just cosmic-scale minutes after the earth itself was born. Not exactly the saddest examples of adaptive failure. The bar has been set high indeed; and your planet is a comparative Eden in the universe. Life everywhere. Diversity that is astonishing.

The oldest known record of Contemporary Man: A meager 160-200,000 years.
Classified.: *Homo Sapiens*

Nick-name: *Idaltu* (*Idaltu* means "elderly wise man" in the local tongue.)
Hometown: Herto Bouri, Ethiopia

If you prefer the Family Tree: The Toumai Skull six to seven million years old.
Classified.: *Homo Erectus* among *Homindea* (Great Apes)
Nick-name: *Toumai* (*Toumai* means "hope of life" in the local tongue.)
Hometown: Chad, Central Africa

New arrivals. Burgeoning ascendants.

Adaptation has no end except oblivion, stating the obvious. It spans millennia upon millennia, forever, and is in no way limited to the ambient elements of planet Earth. It can be and it is, cosmic in scope. Four titanic dimensions...infinitely vast...literally beyond time and imagining.

Some of your best minds have calculated that, as a species, you have a probable continued existence estimated at a range varying between 18,000, 200,000 and 18,000,000 years. We generally agree, as you know. Scant decades ago humans accounted for roughly 2.5 billion beings. Within a scant couple of decades more you will have produced enough live human corpuses to constitute the optimal population of approximately five Earths. You have only one Earth. So in all probability you will die.

If any or all of this comes to pass, you can boast the most disreputable record of any creature that walked, crawled, flew, swam, or slithered on this planet. Considering your native talents, you shall have qualified as the most dramatic evolitive disasters in the history of this planet, and tens of millions of other planets for that matter.

Taking a vastly less passive and fatalistic approach: *Humans may actually be capable of adaptively confronting dimensions that approach infinity, given some extraordinary changes in many of the elements that comprise your current mind set.*

Try to believe this.

First, you need an evolutionary "Spike." An exponential leap in the species. You dare not engineer such necromancy yourselves. Your grasp, your expertise, and your wisdom fall far short of such endeavor. No. Leave nature to her craft. In fact, coax her into working harder than ever before. Provide the quadrative tension. Nature need no longer conspire to produce the compression and savagery of adaptive evolution.

Enter Oneiro. Thankfully.

Amongst your facets badly in need of evolution is hate. Hate is pernicious. It compels you to kill and destroy and practice war. It breeds mistrust and lures you into squandering time, energy, and resource. It touches all of you, pervading your world and your species, from the most humble to the most powerful. It is guised in many robes. One of the most popular models is simple apathy.

Many or most humans will readily admit to hate in some form, at some time. But will never admit to evil. Man strikes out, acting on hate. Hate is the evil. Hate helps man justify evil deeds. Hate prevents man from working together in concert and finding a common prospect. It renders man as primitives. It is the devil's own.

Hate is the great rationalizer for venomous acts. The opiate of conscience. The restorative for guilt. The key to a visceral, sick, self-serving, maniacal *fulfillment* of sorts. One of the great dangers is that a truly evil act can resonate and echo for generations. It takes on a life of its own.

Alexander the Great once discovered a small Greek village inside the boundaries of Persia. In celebration, he hosted a bountiful feast for the village and his troops. During the festivities he was informed that three hundred years earlier, the ancestors of this village had killed the population of a small village in his Greek homeland of Macedonia.

Without hesitation, Alexander ordered the slaughter every man, woman, and child. Burn the village to the ground. He wanted no trace left of these people or their home. Nothing left for even the crows. Echoes.

Overcome hate and the force of the other ills approach manageability, at least comparatively. An intelligent, pragmatic, even disciplined, recognition of a fundamental necessity of mankind's constancy. Survival.

Were you actually capable of pinning down all the causalities of hate, the difficult task still remains to adequately describe them and their true causes...and then the nearly impossible job of effecting conclusive countermeasures. In fact however, such countermeasures may already exist within your own genetic makeup.

Liberally paraphrasing the words of your William Shakespeare:

The solution[sic]...lies not in your stars...but in your genes...

Sadly, once in a while on Earth, humans have no prerogative but to shoulder a weapon and take aim...aim carefully.

Enter Oneiro. Thankfully.

The Gauntlet:

A roiling darkness on the horizon. Roughly one hundred kilometers distant. To the east. Just at night's ebb. You can see it. You just can't quite penetrate its shadowy nature.

In a vigil unchanged in millennia, just as man has fielded a thousand battlegrounds before, bundled in fear, embracing his weapon, exhaling frosty smoke in the chill half-light, heart pounding out reassurance his spark still glows...Homo Sapient Habilis warily awaiting the dawn.

The dawn of death, or life?

Is the black terminator between earth and sky fashioned from the smoke of burning flesh, and the stench of decay and blood?

Or does it nurture the emerging bloom that flourishes in the abrupt semi-darkness that intensifies and sharpens just as night's terminator passes over...a mute fire racing at more than 1.3 times the speed of sound...a fleeting heartbeat in advance of a brilliant sunrise?

So it goes. Shadows or splendor? Ends or means? Do or die? Worthy or loutish? Elysium or Perdition?

After 2,000,000 solar years, we wish you to succeed. To survive. To assume your place in the cosmic sentience. Such will accord you wonders beyond your dreams of omniscience.

Enter Oneiro. Thankfully.

Our concluding communication will commence in 24.6 hours. Please ensure adequate recording media is active.

These communications will approximate 12,000,000 of your pages, involving several months of transmission.

    Compliments to Oneiro. Greetings to Earth. Greetings from the QAVL.
    The *Gauntlet is extended.*

    Please stand by.

Dramatis Persona

Dr. Craig Webber—Founder and owner of the Island and the University

Mr. Philip Carr—President of the Island and Chancellor of the University

Mr. Herbert Carr—Philip's uncle & Captain of the *Sea Tigress*

Dr. Enoch Winchester—Professor of Applied Sciences

Dr. Emily Johansen—Professor of Genetics

Dr. Sin Oua Siroa—Professor of Body Culture and Physical Education

Dr. Simon Butler—University Resident Chief Cuisenaire

Dr. Jackson Gear—Chief of Medicine and Managing Director of the Nursery

Dr. Anne Jones—Professor of Arts

Dr. William Gould—Professor of Music

Dr. Sun Kahn—Professor of Comparative Religions & Philosophy

Dr. Shad Alexander—Professor of Government & Legal Systems

Dr. Judy McLean—Professor of Languages, Culture & Literature

Dr. Eve Dunedin—Professor of Psychology and Administrator of the Ordeal

Dr. Sean Gray—Realization Administrator

Dr. Robert Montgomery—Professor of History

Mr. Mike Auslander—Student, artist and a leader at the University

Mr. Edward McKnight—Personal Assistant to Philip Carr

Mr. Stephen Ryerson—Director of Security

Ms. Rachael Stone—Director of Security

Mr. Howard Doyle—Head of the Chicago security firm Doyle & Phillips

Mr. Charlie Stein—Director of Communications

Mr. Demetrious Diamantes—1st Mate of the Sea Tigress

Mr. Richardson—Executive VP Finance

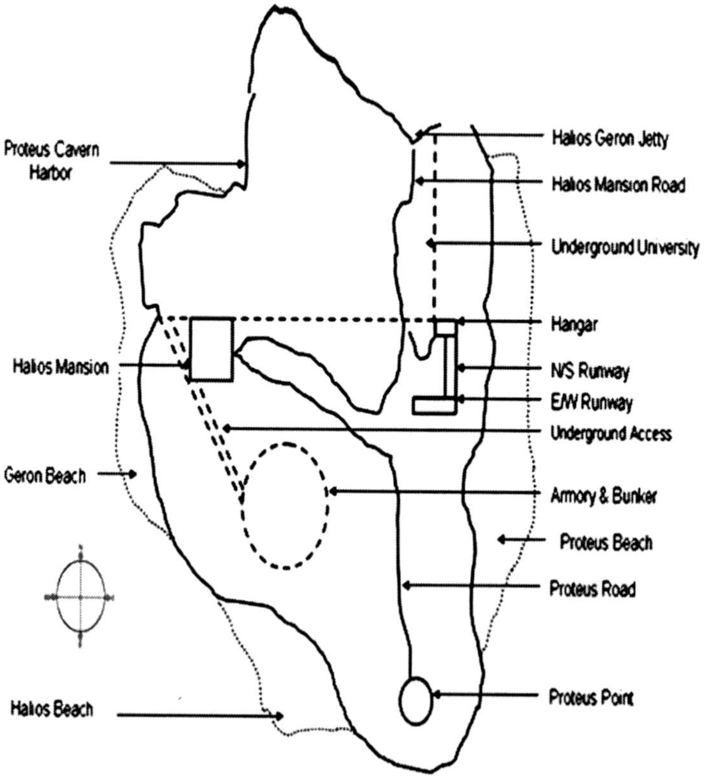
Proteus Cavern Harbor
Halios Geron Jetty
Halios Mansion Road
Underground University
Hangar
Halios Mansion
N/S Runway
E/W Runway
Underground Access
Geron Beach
Armory & Bunker
Proteus Beach
Proteus Road
Halios Beach
Proteus Point

1km: ½cm

Oneiro ©
John Stuart Goldenberg
http://john-goldenberg.com

Made in the USA